ROSIE'S REVENGE

BY

SUZANNE FLOYD

December 2012

www.SuzanneFloyd.com
Cover by Bella Media Management

This book is dedicated to my husband Paul and our daughters, Camala and Shannon, and families. Thanks for all your love, support, and encouragement.

CHAPTER ONE

Dear Miss Evans,

I am writing to inform you that your great-aunt, Rosie Shepard, has passed away. You are the heir to her estate in Whitehaven, Iowa. Please let me know when you will be arriving to take ownership.
Sincerely,
Arthur Meyers
Esquire

Rereading the letter for the third time, I still didn't understand it. As a paralegal for a large law firm in Phoenix I understood the words all right, just not why a distant relative had made me her sole heir. There was only one person to ask.

"Hi, Mom, are you busy? Can I come over? There's something I need to show you. Is Dad home?" My questions were running together, but I couldn't stop myself.

"Of course you can come over, Honey. You don't have to ask. Your dad is at the boys' game tonight. Do you need me to call him? Is something wrong?"

"No, nothing's wrong. I just have something to show you. I'll be there in a few minutes." Before she could ask any more questions, I said good-bye and hung up. Technically, Ben Evans is my step-father; he married Mom after my real dad died when I was four.

"What's going on, Honey? You sounded so mysterious on the phone." We were sitting at the table in her bright kitchen. This was the room everyone gravitated to, always warm, friendly and inviting.

Mom read the letter, and chuckled softly. "Well, well, she really fixed them." She smiled at me. "What are you waiting for, Honey? Pack your bags, and go collect your inheritance."

"I don't understand. Why would a great-aunt I never met leave me everything she had?"

4

"You met her once, but you were young so you don't remember."

"That had to be more than twenty years ago. She has brothers, and probably other nieces and nephews. Some of them must still live in Whitehaven. Why would she leave everything to a virtual stranger?"

"Aunt Rosie always was a law unto herself. She never let anyone tell her what to do. Once her mind was made up, nobody could change it."

"Not very different from her brother," I muttered. We hadn't spoken my grandfather's name in more than twenty years. "Do you know how much of the family is still alive?"

Mom shook her head. "They are as dead to me as I am to them." Stubborn pride ran in the family.

Before we could say more, Jason and Justin, my twin half-brothers, burst through the door from the garage, Dad trailing behind. "Hey Parker, when are you coming to one of our games?" Both boys gave me a squeeze before making way for Dad to envelop me in a bear hug.

"Soon, I promise. I just stopped over to show Mom something."

"Everything okay, Honey?" Even when I was little, Dad could tell when something was troubling me. "Boys, homework," He nodded his head towards the stairs.

"Can't we stay and see Parker? We haven't seen her in a long time."

"Two days is a long time?" I laughed at their feeble attempt to avoid hitting the books.

"Boys." Dad raised one eyebrow, nodding to the stairs again. As usual that was all that was necessary.

"Yes, Dad," both boys chimed in unison as they so often do. "Don't go without saying good-bye, Parker," Justin yelled as they pounded up the stairs.

"I got this registered letter today." I waited while he read it. "Okay." Putting the paper back on the table, he chuckled. "I take it this Rosie had a large estate?" I hadn't even thought about that. We both turned to Mom.

"Unless Rosie somehow lost everything, including her

5

mind, I would say yes. It's very sizable. She inherited the original farm, and managed to make it grow over the years."

"Why leave it to Parker?"

Mom shrugged. "There's no explaining Rosie. She butted heads with everyone in the family as far back as I can remember. Stories swirled around about how she cheated all of her brothers out of land and/or money. I'm sure they expected to get back what they considered theirs when she died. If she thought she could cheat them one last time, that's exactly what she'd do."

Dad shook his head, unable to understand the greed demonstrated by some people. "So what do you suggest Parker do?"

"That's her choice." She looked at me. "If you go back, there will be a battle with my father and brothers. They want the money as much as anyone else."

I could feel my own stubbornness taking hold as she spoke. All these years I've wondered about the family I didn't know. Why did they hate my real dad? Why had my grandfather turned on his own daughter? What kind of people did I come from? "I think I'll go see what's what. It could prove interesting."

"That isn't the word I'd use," Mom said. "Just be alert at all times. Walter Shepard is a manipulative son of a gun." That was a harsh condemnation coming from my mother.

CHAPTER TWO

"What do you mean I have to live here for a year? Why didn't you tell me in the letter?"

"You have to live in the *house* for a year," the attorney, Mr. Meyers emphasized. "That was the one stipulation Rosie gave. She also instructed me not to tell you until you arrived. She wanted you to come here. If you decide not to stay after the year is up, she made no further restrictions on your inheritance. If you don't stay for the year, the estate goes to her secondary heirs." Mr. Meyers is anywhere between fifty and sixty, with thinning, gray hair and gray-green eyes. He's nearly six feet tall, and about as big around as a bean pole.

"And who might that be?" I could guess, but I wanted to make sure.

He looked like he wouldn't answer me for a minute, but finally heaved a sigh. "I guess there's no harm in telling you. Rosie left a sealed envelope with further instructions in case you decide not to stay. Since there is no one else to inherit, I can only surmise it would go to your other family members here."

"Let's get one thing straight, Mr. Meyers," I stated firmly. "I have NO family here. My mother was disowned before I was born. We've had no contact with anyone here in more than twenty years." He looked decidedly uncomfortable, but didn't comment. For several minutes the silence stretched out, and I let him stew before I continued. "I have a job and an apartment in Phoenix. What am I supposed to do about those? How am I supposed to live until the inheritance goes into effect?"

"You can go back to Arizona for one week to make arrangements about your apartment and such. If you're gone longer than that, the other heirs inherit. Once you are back here, you'll receive an allowance, and all your expenses will be paid by the estate." His speech pattern was as stiff and stilted as he appeared.

My mouth dropped open at the figure he gave as my "allowance". It was more than I made as a paralegal, and I had to pay all my own bills. This got more surreal all the time.

"You can turn in the rental car when you return to Phoenix for your things," he went on. "There's a car here for you when you come back. I'll accompany you to the farm, and show you around before it gets too dark."

The large house took my breath away. It sat at the end of a long gravel lane off the country road. Painted white with gray shutters it was three stories tall. A wide porch wrapped around the sides. Rich green fields spread out almost as far as the eye could see. I couldn't believe one person had lived in that house alone for years. How had she taken care of it by herself? Why had Rosie left it to me?

Mr. Meyers removed a padlock, and held the kitchen door open for me, then followed me inside. "Wait here while I light the lamp." He turned to an old kerosene lamp, and struck a match. The shadowed interior brightened only marginally.

"Was the electricity turned off after Rosie passed away?" I asked.

"There is no electricity or running water." He didn't look at me when he spoke.

"You've got to be kidding me!"

"No. The only modernization done to the house is the hand pump." He nodded to the kitchen sink where there was an old-fashioned pump, the likes of which I'd never seen before. "Other than that, it remains just as it was when it was built in the eighteen hundreds."

"Is this some kind of joke? Did she expect me to live here for a year with no modern conveniences?" I snapped. I was ready to go home, and forget this fiasco.

"Rosie's instructions were that you could do anything to the house you wanted except tear it down as long as you live here for the year. All remodeling will be paid for out of the estate."

"And I have to live in the house while this is going on with no electricity, without a bathroom?" Temper made my voice rise with each word.

He smiled coolly. "I can certainly tell you're related to Rosie. You have her red hair, and the temper that goes with it, as well as her flair for the dramatic."

"I'm glad you find this so amusing. And I'm not being dramatic. I'm being realistic. I have never been on a farm before or lived this primitively. I don't know the first thing about lighting one of those lamps or cooking without electricity or gas. How do I even keep warm in the winter? I'm from Arizona. I've never lived in snow country."

"It's only May; you won't have to worry about keeping warm for months. A great deal of the work will be finished before it gets cold. The contractor can begin immediately following your return from Arizona."

"Contractor? One has already been selected?" His Adam's apple bobbed in his skinny throat at my display of temper, but I didn't relent.

"Rosie expressed a desire that you use Shep Baker. He's done restorations on many of the historic homes in the area."

"Expressed a desire. Is that another way of saying I must use him? Are there any more 'desires' I should be aware of?" I have always been good at reading people, and Mr. Meyers was no challenge. "Okay, what else aren't you telling me?"

He heaved a put-upon sigh. "Shep Baker will be over to see you at nine-thirty in the morning. I made the appointment after you let me know when you'd be arriving."

"Did she have a design in mind?" I asked sarcastically.

"No, of course not." He sounded so incredulous I couldn't help but laugh.

"No, of course she wouldn't do something like that," I mocked. "She wouldn't try to manipulate me." He had the grace to blush and the smarts to keep silent.

After a quick tour and instructions on how to use the kerosene lamps, he was out of there, leaving me alone and fuming. And wondering exactly what was going on. Why had Rosie left me the house with so many strings attached? It's hard for me to imagine anyone in this day and age living in a house with no electricity or running water. This is the twenty-first century! Who lives like that? Me I guess if I decided to stick it out for a year.

~~~

Before leaving town, Mr. Meyers had insisted we have something to eat. Now I understood why. There was no way I could fix something for myself tonight. This was beyond primitive. I'd only been camping once as a kid so cooking on a wood stove was out of the question.

The fields adjoining Rosie's house were all green with what looked like corn about a foot high. As far as I could see, green crops shimmered in the waning light. Mr. Meyers said Rosie owned four hundred acres scattered around the county and two hundred acres right here at the original homestead. He hadn't said who was farming it now. I supposed her brothers and nephews took care of it. I'd have to remember to ask the next time I talked to him. I wasn't comfortable with any of the Shepards being involved with anything to do with me.

After several minutes of feeling sorry for myself, I called Mom. At least my cell phone was fully charged. "What do you mean you have to live there for a year?" She echoed my question to Mr. Meyers, her voice was almost hysterical. "Why would Aunt Rosie do something like that? You aren't going to stay there, are you? Just come home, and forget about this. There's no amount of money worth staying in that vipers nest."

"It's not about the money. Rosie had an agenda, a reason, for all this. I want to know what it was." Until I said it, I wasn't aware I was contemplating going through with this ridiculous scheme, "Can you send me some clothes?" I asked. "I'll also need to take a leave of absence from work." It was something I hadn't thought of until right then. I had no idea how my boss would react.

"But how are you going to live in that old house?" she asked. "Unless Aunt Rosie did some serious modernizing, it doesn't even have electricity."

I laughed, "You're right there, no electricity, no water, no bathroom. Did you grow up in a house like this?" The one time we went camping with Dad and the boys, Mom had freaked out about using the bathroom at the camp site.

"No, my folks had a modern house, but the old family house was never updated. Rosie had a fit whenever anyone suggested bringing the house into the twentieth century. Even my grandfather was afraid of going against her when she was in one of her moods. She could really throw a temper tantrum."

"Am I anything like Rosie?" I asked, remembering what Mr. Meyers had said.

Mom was quiet for so long I thought we'd lost the connection, but she finally spoke. "No, Honey, you aren't anything like her. Maybe there is some resemblance because of the red hair. But you're a kind, loving, warm young lady. Those are words never used to describe Rosie. She was as demanding, conniving and pig-headed as her brothers. She was allowed to rule the family, and no one dared question her. If you're determined to stay, at least for a little while, be very careful. I don't know what her brothers would be willing to do to get their hands on all Rosie had."

Chills crept up my spine, but I tried to sound positive. "I'll be careful. I just want to find out what's going on." A few minutes later we hung up. I needed to save the battery on my phone until I figured out how to keep it charged. I had no idea how long it would take to get electricity in the house. I promised to call often, and she promised to send clothes.

A large grandfather clock stood in the entryway. Before going to bed, I pulled the weights, and set the pendulum in motion. The rich ticking and chimes would keep me company all night, alleviating the total silence of the old house. Having lived my entire life in a busy, noisy city, I wasn't used to the silence of the country.

~~~

That was the strangest night of my life, I thought as I walked down the stairs at five-thirty the next morning. A strange house, no lights, and only a chamber pot in case I needed to go to the bathroom in the night. Something I managed to avoid. Now though, I *really* needed to go, that meant a trip to the outhouse. "Oh, joy," I mumbled. I wasn't looking forward to that.

One thing for sure, plumbing and electricity were going to be the first things the contractor did to the house, and that couldn't happen soon enough. Even if I decided not to stay here for the full year, letting the estate go to Rosie's other heirs, plumbing and electricity would enhance the value of the house.

Leaving the outhouse a few minutes later, I wanted to wash my hands, I wanted a shower, but the only water available was the well in the back yard, or the hand pump in the kitchen. That water came directly from the well. No doubt it was going to be very cold. It's nice for drinking, but a little hard for washing up. *How did people keep clean without running water and showers?* I asked myself.

The twins would love this. Maybe when school is out I can convince Mom and Dad to let them come here for the summer. I couldn't believe I was actually considering staying that long. How had I gotten caught up in this? Why hadn't I just told Mr. Meyers to forget it and gone home? A long-forgotten memory moved through my mind; a grandmother who hugged me when I walked in with Mom, and stayed in a corner crying when her husband told us to leave. I realized I was resolute about staying until I got to know her. In that case, I told myself, I was going to have to figure out how to shower.

Growing up I'd watched reruns of "Little House on the Prairie." They took baths in tin tubs with water heated on the wood stove. That didn't sound like much fun, but until I got running water I had few options. I also had to figure out how to keep my cell phone and laptop charged. They were my only connection to the outside world. I laughed at myself. I never realized how dependent I'd become on technology, and other modern conveniences.

Maybe there's a gym in town with shower facilities, I

thought. That would take care of one of my problems. If all else failed, I could charge my phone and laptop in the car. Right now I had more important matters to take care of, like my job in Phoenix and returning the rental car. Mr. Meyers said there was a car here for me. I needed to find out about that.

~~~

After a cold sponge bath, I headed to the rental car. There were several small towns close to Whitehaven where I could get some breakfast. I wasn't ready to go into Whitehaven, and face any of the locals, especially my relatives. Besides, the longer drive would give my phone and laptop time to recharge. I was grateful the rental had someplace I could plug both in at the same time. I wondered if the car here had the same conveniences.

When I pulled into the short lane two hours later, an old pickup was sitting beside the house. No one seemed to be around though. Parking beside the kitchen steps I could see the wooden door was standing open. Mr. Meyers had removed the padlock, but I'd locked the door when I left. Maybe people in the country didn't lock their doors, but I'm still a city girl and everything gets locked up tight when I'm not around.

The only person I knew in Whitehaven was Mr. Meyers, and I couldn't see him letting himself in when I wasn't here. I thought briefly about calling nine-one-one, but I wasn't even sure there was such a thing in rural Iowa.

Quietly I got out of the car, climbing the three steps to the door. An older man was standing in the kitchen watching me. My stomach churned, and my heart rate kicked up a notch. I immediately knew who it was but didn't let on. "Who are you and what are you doing in my house?" I asked, with more bravado than I felt.

For several long moments he stared at me like he was seeing a ghost. I don't look that much like Mom so he couldn't be imagining I was her. Finally he spoke, his voice gravelly, like he hadn't spoken in a long time. "I'm your grandfather, and this isn't your house. It's mine."

"I don't have a grandfather in Iowa, and this *is* my house. How did you get in here?"

"This is my house," he stated again. "I have a key" We stared at each other across the large room like two adversaries in a boxing ring.

Before either of us could say anything more, another truck pulled up beside Walter Shepard's. This one was fairly new with a sign on the door panel advertising Shep Baker Construction. A tall, lanky cowboy stepped out, a big Stetson on his head. "Howdy Ma'am, I'm Shep Baker. Mr. Meyers said you might be wantin' to talk about the changes you need done around here. How you doin' today, Mr. Shepard?" He spoke with a lazy Southern drawl, sending delicious shivers up my spine. There was something about a drawl that tickled my fancy.

While I'd been watching Shep Baker, Walter Shepard had walked up behind me. I quickly moved away from him. I didn't want to give him a chance to touch me, unsure of what he'd do.

"Baker, what are you doing here?" Mr. Shepard barked, ignoring me.

"Miss Rosie contracted with me to work for her great-niece after her own passing." He didn't seem fazed by the older man's animosity.

"Well, that's not going to happen!" he snapped. "If there are any changes to be made, I'll take care of them. This is still my family home, and I'm the one to say what goes on here."

With a shrill whistle I drew their attention back to me. "Mr. Shepard, maybe you didn't get a copy of your sister's will, but I did," I lied. "Rosie left this house and everything in it to me, not you. In the eyes of the law that makes it mine. You have nothing to say about what I do with it. I can even tear it down, and you can't stop me." That last part was pure bluff, but he didn't need to know it. His face turned so red I thought he might stroke out right here. I doubt anyone had ever spoken to him like that, especially a woman. "Now I have business with Mr. Baker, so I'll tell you the same thing you told my mother twenty years ago. GET OUT!" My hands fisted on my hips, and my feet were braced apart waiting to see what he was going to do. My heart was pounding so loudly I hoped he couldn't hear it.

"You're going to be sorry for this, Missy," he growled. "This isn't over." He threw himself into his truck, gravel shot from beneath his tires as he sped down the lane to the road.

"He your grandpaw?" Shep Baker drawled.

"Only by blood." My answer was cryptic enough to draw more questions, but he kept silent. I turned back to the house. "The first thing that needs done is new locks on all the doors. How long will that take?"

"Let's talk about the renovations you want done around here first, then I'll go to the hardware store to get some new locks. They won't take long to install."

At five feet five inches and one hundred ten pounds, I've never felt small, but Shep towered over me. I could feel him watching me as we walked from room to room, examining what needed to be done.

"You're a lot like Miss Rosie," he finally commented. "I feel like I already know you, and what you want done. She was very proud of you. She talked about you a lot."

I stared at him dumbfounded. "What are you talking about? She didn't know me."

He raised his broad shoulders in an expressive shrug. "She knew you. She showed me pictures of you several times."

I rubbed my arms where goose bumps prickled. This was beyond spooky, but for now I let it drop. Maybe later I'd pursue the subject. Possibly Mom had sent pictures to her aunt. For now, I wanted to finish going through the house.

Through his eyes, I could see all the elegant architecture instead of just an old house that needed a lot of work. Each room had high ceilings with molded wainscoting and hardwood floors polished to a high shine. Antique paneling graced most of the walls. The six bedrooms were all large enough that even adding a bathroom and closet to each would still leave plenty of room for the antique furniture.

"If you want to sell this furniture," Shep said, "it'll fetch a pretty penny at any auction or antique store. The quality is top notch, and your great aunt took very good care of everything."

"Except she didn't modernize the house," I stated the obvious. "Why did she live here without any modern conveniences? She obviously had enough money to do it years ago."

He shook his head, "She did have ideas of what she'd like to see done, but said it was up to you."

"How did you meet her?" If I could learn more about her, maybe I could figure out why she'd left everything to me.

Shep laughed again. "I was in town a month or so, and just gettin' my business up and runnin'. When I stopped here, she just stared at me. She got the biggest grin on her face after she saw my name on my card. She thought it was a real kick that my first name was the same as her last name. She showed me around the place, the whole time askin' me questions. She wanted to know about my family; where they lived, what they did. It was weird, but I kept answerin', hopin' she'd hire me. She never got tired of hearin' me talk about my family. I think she was lonely. People steered clear of her because she could be real crusty. I did a lot of little jobs for her, but she never wanted to have the big things done, said that was going to be up to you some day."

I could listen to him talk all day with that sexy Texas drawl. Maybe Rosie had enjoyed that as well. He was easy to talk to; not hard on the eyes either. His hair was almost blue-black, and he had the bluest eyes I've ever seen. "Where are you from originally?"

"Why ma'am," he drawled teasingly, "You don't think I'm from around these parts?"

"Can't say that I do," I laughed with him, "maybe southern Iowa, *really* southern."

He had a good laugh, and his smile lit up his handsome face. "I'm from east Texas, a small town not much different from Whitehaven. I lived there all my life, but my granddaddy was born somewhere in these parts. He was adopted, and never knew anything about his birth parents. It didn't bother any of the family, but I've got a bit of a curious bone. Mom says I'm just plumb nosy. When I got out of the army I decided to see what I could find. All we knew about granddaddy's family was they were from farm country. When I landed here, it just felt like this was where I was supposed to settle down for now. Miss Rosie always treated me good right from that first day."

"That doesn't sound like the Rosie I've heard about. Like you said, she was kind of crusty. She was going to do things her own way, especially if the rest of her family was against it."

"Yep," he chuckled, "I saw some mighty heated discussions between her and her brothers."

By now we were sitting on the wide front porch enjoying the warm breeze. *Warm, not hot*, I thought. So different from Arizona where this time of year, this time of day, most people were inside air conditioned houses or offices. "Did you ever find out about your granddaddy's family?" I didn't want this pleasant time to end.

He shook his head. "I've sort of given up that quest. I learned the hard way questions from strangers never get answered. If I'm supposed to find anything out, it'll happen without me pursuin' it."

Glancing at my watch, I was surprised that it was after noon. He stood up. "I'd better head to the hardware store. You goin' to be here for a while?"

"I'm not going anywhere as long as other people have keys." I didn't want Mr. Shepard, or anyone else, having access to the house now that I was living here.

"It shouldn't take me long to get the locks. I'll bring Miss Rosie's plans with me when I come back. She was one smart lady."

Within forty-five minutes he was back installing shiny new dead bolts on all the doors. "You're gonna need to leave these old locks. They're antiques, and don't do much to keep people out, but they add to the history of the house. I also picked up some window locks."

I hadn't even thought about the windows, but was glad he

had. If Mr. Shepard wanted in, he probably wouldn't let a new lock stop him if the window was available.

While he worked, I studied Rosie's plans. Most of what she suggested was very practical, and what I wanted done. Of course, there were a lot of things on her list I hadn't thought of just because she knew the place and I didn't. "She had good plans for the house," I told Shep. "I don't understand why she wanted to wait."

He shook his head, "I tried to talk her into doin' some of the things, but she wouldn't hear to it. She said she'd lived in this house the way it was all these years, and she was too old to change. There was no convincin' her otherwise."

"Central heating and bathrooms would have made this place much more comfortable in the winter. That wood burning stove couldn't have kept the entire house warm."

"That would've meant gettin' electricity here, and that was up to you." He shook his head again. "She just kept sayin' 'that's up to Parker' whenever I wanted to do some of the big work."

Rosie was proving to be an enigma. "Plumbing is the first thing I want done. We can work on lights, and all the rest later. I just can't do the outhouse thing." I shuddered at the thought of the little building out back. "How long do you think all this will take?"

I gasped at the estimated time he gave. When he added how much it would cost, my head spun so bad I had to sit down. Did Mr. Meyers know how much this was going to cost? Was there even enough money in Rosie's estate to cover it? He hadn't gone into detail on how large her estate was.

"I can't live here that long without bathrooms or lights," I stated when I could finally breathe again. "What was wrong with that woman? She had to be demented."

Shep let me rant for several minutes, a lopsided grin playing around his sexy mouth. "I can have some rooms wired and plumbed before that," he told me, when I finally wound down, slumping in the wicker rocker. "It's goin' to take time and will get messy. You might want to pick out a few rooms to live in while the work's bein' done in the rest of the house. I can put in one bathroom and some of the electrical work so you don't have to wade through the mess everywhere."

"No wonder she didn't want to do this herself. She didn't want to put up with the mess. She must have hated me to put this on me."

"No," he insisted. "She was right proud of you."

For the next hour we went over plans, discussing where bathrooms would be, and what I wanted done in the kitchen. "I enjoy cooking," I told him. "The room is big enough I can have all the modern appliances, and still have plenty of cupboards and counter space."

"You'll need to leave the wood stove. The house is on the historical register, so we'll have to be careful with the changes."

I groaned. "Does this mean I have to contend with a hysterical historical society?"

"No," he laughed. "Miss Rosie took care of that. All these changes and any others you want to make have been approved."

"But she's gone," I protested. "Anything she initiated is null and void now."

"Not really. Miss Rosie carried a lot of weight around these parts. She still does. She told me there wouldn't be any opposition from anyone."

"Why would people still do what she wanted them to do?"

He raised his broad shoulders in that expressive shrug I was beginning to expect. "I asked her that once. She gave a wicked little grin, and said no one wanted her to haunt them after she was gone, so they'd do exactly what she wanted."

"Was she serious?"

"Oh, yeah! I've seen it in action." I frowned, and a slight blush crept up his neck. "After she passed on," he finally said, "I thought some people would start using the other contractor in town but they didn't." I guess he thought that explained things, but my confused expression told him otherwise. His blush deepened. "Somehow Miss Rosie convinced, or coerced, them that I was the only contractor to do any remodelin' on these homes. I still get all their business."

One more question mark in this already confusing situation, I thought.

Turning our attention back to the restorations, Shep sketched out the different rooms, making them come alive. Without ruining the historical value of the house he could turn this into a very modern and livable home. "There's one more thing," I said as he was getting ready to leave. "How do I keep food here? I can't eat out every meal until you get electricity in here."

He pointed to a small refrigerator-like appliance. I knew it wasn't a refrigerator though, I'd already checked. Besides, there is no electricity. "That's an ice box," he told me, "a *real* ice box. You can't freeze things, but you can keep them cold as long as there's ice. You'll have to get that in town because they don't deliver it anymore."

I nodded understanding. It wasn't exactly what I wanted, but for now it would do. "Rosie was eighty or close to it, Mr. Shepard is even older. Electricity was around when they were born. The house my mom grew up in had electricity and indoor plumbing. Why didn't this house?"

"This was her grandparents' house; her mother was born here, so was she and all her brothers. When electric lines made it out this far, whoever was runnin' the family decided not to put it in the house. Miss Rosie saw no reason to change that for herself, but she wanted you to do it."

"Why me?" It always came down to that question.

"She wanted you to have what was hers."

We decided the mud room, kitchen, and one bedroom would be the first areas to be worked on. The mud room was off the kitchen, and large enough that one end could be turned into a small bathroom with a shower. The other end would hold a modern washer and dryer. That still left plenty of room for pantry shelves. The big farm kitchen could hold all the appliances, and still have plenty of room for the large table. The current cupboards were glass fronted, and only needed to be refinished.

A narrow stairway just inside the kitchen door led to the bedrooms on the second floor, and then to the attic. I decided to take the bedroom closest to those stairs for now. When the bathroom was finished, it would be convenient in the middle of the night. The rest of the house would be sealed off when they started working inside, to keep the dust down to a minimum. Even with that, Shep warned, it was going to get messy. I heaved a heavy sigh. What had Rosie gotten me into?

Shep left me with his sketches, and what he called Rosie's idea book. She might not have had any modern conveniences, but she knew what she'd like done. Her ideas and suggestions were all modern, up to date and very practical.

When my stomach began to rumble, I realized it was after two in the afternoon, and there still wasn't food in the house. Until I got electricity, I'd have to shop every day, but at least I wouldn't have to eat out all the time. Cooking on the wood stove would be a real challenge. Shep had shown me how to light it, keeping it going long enough to heat up soup or anything simple. I wouldn't be able to make an elaborate meal though.

I still had to call my boss in Phoenix, and request a leave of absence. If I stayed in Iowa for the full year, I would be a wealthy woman. Even if I did decide to go back to Phoenix then, I wouldn't have to work unless I wanted to. If I didn't stay for the full year, I wouldn't get any money, and I'd need my job. Food first, I decided when my stomach rumbled again. Then I'll call my boss.

CHAPTER THREE

Whitehaven is a small town built around the court house square much like Prescott, Arizona. Stores lined the streets facing the square. There are no big box stores, no supermarkets. Just small mom and pop stores owned by locals. It's quite a culture shock for someone born and raised in a city of over a million people. How long would I enjoy the quaint atmosphere without any of the conveniences, I wondered.

Mr. Meyers said there was a car I could drive but I hadn't seen one around the farm. I hadn't really looked either. Something else to put on my "to do list", I told myself.

Lost in thought, I wasn't paying attention to where I was going, nearly walking into a man standing in the middle of the sidewalk. "Oh! I'm sorry!" I side stepped at the last minute to avoid a collision, looking up into his hard face. He was close to eighty; his snowy hair was thick and full. A fierce scowl drew thick eyebrows together over frosty blue eyes.

"You need to watch where you're going, Missy," he growled, his anger nearly a physical thing. He brushed past without another word.

"Not a very friendly town," I mumbled. "Do I want answers bad enough to put up with this kind of behavior?" I'd have to think about that.

Before getting lunch and groceries, I decided to do a little exploring. The stares my presence generated were down right creepy. Curiosity from the younger people was understandable; after all I was the new girl in town. The older people though, people old enough to be my grandparents, stared at me with shock, even fear, in their eyes; much like Mr. Meyers had when I came into his office. Some stepped off the sidewalk to avoid me. What was that all about? This town was just plain bizarre.

By now it was after three in the afternoon. I hadn't eaten

anything since breakfast. If I had a big lunch now, I wouldn't have to fix something tonight. I could have cheese and crackers with my glass of wine later in the evening to tide me over till morning. I made a mental note to add cheese, crackers, and wine to my grocery list.

Eventually I would have to learn how to operate the big wood stove in the kitchen. I couldn't live on cheese and crackers and cold cereal until Shep got electricity into the house. For now though I'd make do with something simple.

The small cafe was nearly empty when I entered. The name, A Cup-A-Joe, made me smile. A woman, probably Mom's age, sat behind the counter thumbing through a magazine. I could see the cook through the opening into the kitchen. He was starting to clean up after the lunch rush, if there was such a thing in this small town. Both looked up when the bell above the door jangled as I walked in. The woman gave me a big smile while the man nodded, and went back to his cleaning.

"Hi there, Sweetie. How ya doing today? I'm Mary Lou, just have a seat anywhere."

This was more like it. Small towns were supposed to be friendly, but so far I hadn't encountered much of that except from Shep. "Hi, I'm Parker Evans." I returned her smile as I sat down across from her at the counter.

"Oh, everybody in town knows who you are," she laughed. "We've all been dying to meet you."

Not everyone, I thought to myself.

"Now don't go scaring the girl off first thing," the man in the kitchen barked. "Don't want her thinking we're all a bunch of small town busy bodies."

Mary Lou let loose a belly laugh, "Oh, go on, Billy, that's exactly what most of us are." She turned back to me. "Don't pay him no never mind, his bark is worse than his bite. What can I get you to drink while you look over the menu?" She placed a laminated folder in front of me.

"Coffee and ice water would be great." I'd been up since five-thirty; my energy was beginning to wane. She turned away, and was back before I could do anything more than

23

glance at the menu.

"Coffee's fresh. I just made a new pot. Don't have many customers this time of day, but I needed the pick-me-up to get me through the rest of it. We close at seven, and open again at seven in the morning."

"That's a long day. Are you here the whole time?"

"Sure thing. Me and Billy own the place. Our kids help out, but they're getting old enough they don't want to spend time with old mom and dad. Besides, they're busy with school and sports even in the summer."

I could relate to that. The twins always have three things going at once.

"Tell me all about your mama," she said after I gave my lunch order. "What's she doing now? I was real sorry to hear about your daddy. He was a nice man. Did your mama get married again?"

"If you'd stop asking so many questions, maybe she could answer a few," Billy called from the kitchen. He was obviously listening to our conversation.

"You knew my mom?" My heart rate kicked up a notch.

"Sure did. Went all through school with her. I was sorry when she moved out west, but your granddaddy had plans for his only girl, and it wasn't marrying a local farm hand. He wanted her to marry Ed Bodeen's boy. But I guess you already know all this ancient history."

I shook my head. "I was only four when my dad died. Mom rarely talked about her family."

Billy hollered from the kitchen again. "See what you did. You shouldn't go spreading gossip."

"It's not gossip when it's God's honest truth," she shot back, giving my hand a pat. "Your mama was a good person, but just as strong willed as her daddy. That's why they always bumped heads. She loved your daddy, not young Ed. She wasn't about to marry someone she didn't love. Can't say as I blame her either. Money isn't any reason to get married."

Mary Lou was going to be a great source of information. I was too little when Daddy died to ask questions. By the time I

24

was old enough to want answers, Mom and Ben were married, and he was my dad. It didn't seem right to ask questions then.

People were beginning to come into the café. Mary Lou greeted each one by name, reminding me this was indeed a small town. When Billy set my lunch in the pass-through window, she left me to eat in peace, and went to check on the others. After a few minutes, I could feel people watching me. I wondered what they expected me to do, sprout wings, and fly around the room.

Mary Lou leaned across the counter, "You're good for business," she chuckled. "We usually don't have many customers this time of day."

"Glad I could help," I answered, with more cheer than I felt. I didn't like feeling as though I was a specimen under a microscope. Finishing my meal as quickly as possible, I headed to the grocery store.

No one confronted me; in fact no one even spoke to me. But everyone stopped to stare. I grabbed a few items that would keep overnight, and a big bag of ice, heading to the liquor department.

"Did you find everything you need?" the young checker asked. Her voice was tight with the tension floating around the store. She didn't know what the cause was, but she knew it centered on me.

"Yes, thank you." I couldn't think of any small talk to break the tension, so I didn't try. Just let me out of here before I run screaming from the store. That would certainly give the locals something to talk about. A smile touched my lips at the thought.

It was after four when I reached the farm. Before going in, I walked around the house, checking all the doors and windows. Maybe it was big city paranoia, but I needed to be sure. Everything seemed locked up tight. I was grateful Shep had installed the locks this morning.

It was an uneventful evening. Without television or lights, I read by flashlight for a while, then was in bed by nine. I don't remember the last time I went to sleep that early.

Shep showed up bright and early the next morning with a

crew to start working. "I wasn't sure if you drank coffee but..." He held out a hot take-out cup from A Cup-A-Joe.

"Oh, I could kiss you!" I exclaimed, gratefully reaching for the cup.

"Okay," he smiled at me.

Heat rushed up my face. He acted like he was waiting. Well, what was I supposed to do? I rose up on tip toe, placing my hands on his shoulders and kissed his cheek. "I guess that'll have to do for now." His smile turned my insides to jelly, and my mind to mush. I didn't know what to say next.

After a few awkward moments, I cleared my throat, and took a sip of coffee. The whole while he was watching me, a smile tilting his lips, lips I now wanted to kiss. I cleared my throat again, swirling the coffee in the cup. "I guess I'm going to have to experiment with that stove sometime, or I'll starve before you're through with the kitchen."

"I'll be glad to show you again. Cowboy coffee shouldn't be too hard. You'll be makin' the basics in no time at all."

"Cowboy coffee?" I frowned, unsure what that was.

"Coffee made over a camp fire, or an old wood stove."

"I just might take you up on that." My mind was already racing ahead. Maybe I could get a couple of steaks, and he could show me how to fix them. It probably isn't much different from barbequing, I reasoned as I returned to the house, letting him start work.

I was going to do a little work this morning myself. I had no idea what was in all the rooms. There was also a large attic to explore. This house was like a giant treasure trove; there was no telling what I might find.

The house was so quiet I jumped when my cell phone rang causing me to bang my head on the lid of the trunk I'd just opened. I didn't recognize the number and almost ignored it. At the last minute I decided to answer.

"Good morning, Miss Evans," the clipped, no nonsense tone left little doubt who I was talking to.

"Good morning, Mr. Meyers. How are you today?"

"Ah...Ah" he stuttered, clearly not expecting my cordial

greeting. I hadn't been very gracious when we spoke two days ago. "I'm fine. I was wondering if you'd decided when you'd be going to Arizona for your things. Or if you decided to go home for good." He sounded almost hopeful.

"Oh, I'll be staying," I assured him. My words seemed to stun him, and he was silent for so long I thought we'd lost the connection. To test the airways, I continued. "By the way, I forgot to ask if the other heirs were aware of the conditions of the will."

"Um... yes, Rosie's brothers all know you are the sole heir unless you decide not to remain in the house for one year."

I groaned inwardly. "Maybe it wasn't such a wise decision to tell them," I said. "Now they have reason to try to scare me off."

"Whatever do you mean?" His voice was more stilted than usual. "What are you suggesting?"

"You know exactly what I'm suggesting. If I leave, everything is theirs. I get nothing. That's a big incentive to make sure I leave for whatever reason, by whatever means." From the beginning of time money has been a great motivator. That hadn't changed in thousands of years.

"No one would do something illegal!" He was so indignant, I laughed at his naiveté. People do illegal things all the time; why else would there be police and jails? "What I meant is Miss Rosie's brothers wouldn't do something illegal," he said, guessing my thoughts. In my opinion he was still being very naive. Some of the very people he was defending would do anything for money.

"My mom is sending my things," I ignored his comment, answering his original question. "I can take care of the rest by phone. I'll return the car later this week. Where is the car you said I could use?"

"It's in the barn," he said. "I made sure there was gas in it before you arrived. You're certain you don't want to go back to Arizona to finalize things?"

Why was he so eager for me to leave, even for a few days? I wondered. Had one of the Shepards gotten to him? Was he really working for them? I hated to disappoint him, but I was staying. I don't scare easily. "My mom can send anything I need." It wouldn't be quite as simple as that. I still had to call my boss. I pushed the thought aside. I had plenty to think about for the time being.

"By the way, exactly how much are we talking about in Rosie's estate?" I figured that was something I needed to know before Shep started running up construction bills. The figure he gave was staggering, and I sat down with a thump. "Oh, my!" And he thought that man and his brothers wouldn't fight to get that for themselves? He was too naive for words.

After saying good bye I sat for several minutes trying to come to grips with the reality of what I was inheriting. I doubt Mom was aware Rosie had been so wealthy. It wouldn't have made any difference to her though. Money isn't that important to her and Dad.

Finally, gathering my thoughts, I headed to the barn. I wanted to see the car Mr. Meyers said was there. No telling what was there besides a car. Seeing the flimsy latch holding the big double doors closed, I decided Shep would have to put new locks here also. Swinging open the wide doors, I stared into the gloomy interior. Boxes and old steamer trunks were stacked two and three high. Didn't Rosie throw anything away? I wondered. Some of it might have even belonged to her parents.

Walking down the row of horse stalls, I couldn't believe the amount of stuff stored here. It would take all summer just to go through all of this, not to mention the attic in the house. I hadn't been up there yet either. That thought brought my attention up to the loft. From what I could see in the dim interior there were more boxes stored up there. I sighed. It was going to take me all year to go through everything Rosie had stored around the farm, not just the summer.

When I stopped in front of the last stall, my jaw dropped open. I'd found the car Mr. Meyers had alluded to. I didn't have any idea what year it was, but it had been well taken care of. The antique car gleamed in the faint light coming from the open door at the far end of the barn. Dad would go nuts over this. I couldn't wait to tell him.

I ran my hand lovingly over the smooth black fender. There didn't seem to be anything around the farm that was even remotely modern, but this was magnificent! Even if I brought my own Jeep Wrangler here from Arizona, I would still drive this wonderful car around town. More and more I accepted that I'd be staying in Iowa for the specified year. After that, we'd see. My mind wandered to the big cowboy working on the house. He certainly was strong incentive to stay.

I hadn't talked to Mom since the day I arrived. She was probably worrying herself sick, imagining the Shepards had done something awful to me. Outside again, I walked around while I called Mom at work. "Are you all right, Honey? I've been so worried." Her voice shook. "They haven't tried anything, have they?"

"No, nothing has happened. This is only the second day I've been here." I didn't count being stared at as something happening. "Do you remember a car Rosie had?" I changed the subject.

"Of course I do, an old Model T. Why?"

I laughed. "It's now at my disposal. I guess it will be mine at the end of the year if I stay that long. Dad would love that car."

"You don't need to stay so your dad can have the car." She sounded panicked.

"That's not why I'm staying here." While we talked, I watched Shep. The muscles in his arms rippled as he lifted heavy equipment. I didn't know what he was doing, but watching him was interesting. "I just thought Dad would go nuts over this car."

"I'm sure he would, Honey. Are you really going to stay the full year? I know the money doesn't matter that much to you."

"No, it doesn't. I can't explain why I'm even thinking about staying." My gaze returned to Shep. Well, maybe I could, but I kept that thought to myself. "Something just seems so mysterious here. I want to know why she left this to me." When I told her the size of the estate, she gasped, much the same way I had. "Shep said she knew all about me, but how could that be?"

"Shep? Are you talking to 'that man'? Honey, stay away from him! You don't know what he'd do to get his hands on Rosie's money and farm."

For a minute I was confused. Then it clicked. "Oh, no, I've only seen him once. I'm talking about the contractor. His first name is Shepard, he's from Texas." I explained how Rosie was fascinated with their names matching. "He's not from around here," I reemphasized. We talked for a few more minutes. By the time we hung up, she was no longer worried, at least not as much.

She had no explanation for how Rosie knew about me. "Maybe she had talked to your grandma while she was still writing to us," she'd suggested. Shep seemed to think Rosie knew everything about me, but I let it go for now. It was one more question mark, I thought. Too late I realized I hadn't told Mom I'd met Mary Lou. I'd save that for another conversation.

Watching Shep was fascinating. He'd taken his shirt off; his chest glistened with sweat as he worked alongside his crew. The feel and taste of his skin seemed imprinted on my lips and mind since kissing him this morning. Giving myself a mental shake, I headed back to the house. I wouldn't get anything done if I stayed out here watching him.

I walked around to the front of the house checking the flower beds as I went. Rosie had been a great gardener. There were flowers and bushes everywhere. The lilac bushes were just starting to bloom, and I buried my face in the fragrant flowers. This was certainly different from the Arizona desert. Even though most people had grass, at least in part of their yards, the lush green of the lawn and fields here was eye popping.

In the two days I'd been here, the quiet of the farm had seeped into my being. The constant sound of traffic was as alien here as the quiet would be in Phoenix. But now the country lane in front of the house had as much traffic as the street I grew up on. I watched the cars for a few minutes then walked around back again. "Is there always this much traffic?" I stopped beside Shep, my attention riveted on the number of cars passing by.

"Only when there's somethin' worth seein'," Shep answered with a chuckle.

I frowned. "What do you mea...Oh, you mean they're all hoping to get a glimpse of me. Didn't they get a good enough look in town? Maybe I should stand at the edge of the road, waving as they go by. What do you think? I could practice my 'princess wave'." I lifted my hand in an exaggerated imitation of how royalty waves to the crowd of onlookers.

He laughed again, his eyes crinkling at the corners. "I'm not sure that would stop them. It just might bring more people out."

"How many more people could there be? Probably every person in Whitehaven has driven by here at least once this morning."

"Don't think so," he said seriously. "I haven't seen Mary Lou and Billy's big red truck yet, and there's that old clunker from the other side of town; I haven't seen that."

"Okay, I get your point. I'll just ignore them. They'll get tired of gawking at me someday." For the rest of the day, I worked inside trying to forget about the cars. There were portraits of Rosie's family hanging in the wide hall upstairs. Her father looked stern and foreboding. He didn't look like he was much fun to be around. Her brothers were as stern as their father. I stared at the one of Mr. S. He hadn't changed much since he was a young man, still unsmiling and foreboding like his father. One spot on the wall was empty, the wallpaper brighter than that around it, like something had been hanging there not long ago. I wondered if this was where Rosie's portrait belonged and if so, where was it? There were no large portraits in any of the rooms I'd been in. Who would have taken it down and why?

CHAPTER FOUR

Sunday morning proved to be somewhat of a problem. I wanted to go to church, but I didn't want to be a distraction. Every time I went into town, people stared at me; some still stepped aside to avoid me, some just glared. I didn't want that to happen at church. Finally I decided to try it. I would arrive just before the service started, and sit in the last row. That way I could sneak out before anyone saw me.

I hadn't found a gym yet so I was becoming pretty good at taking sponge baths. At least I was clean when I walked in to church. I'll really be glad when Shep has running water installed in the house.

Several audible gasps could be heard as I made my way to the last row of pews. So much for stealth, I thought. Nearly everyone turned to see what the commotion was, causing even more gasps throughout the sanctuary. I'm not going to run and hide, I told myself. I've done nothing wrong by coming to church.

Few people paid attention to the message; they were all looking over their shoulder at me. Maybe I should have sat in the front row. At least then they would be facing forward.

"You have a lot of nerve coming here." Before I could even leave the pew after the last prayer, a small, very angry elderly woman stopped in front of me. "You don't belong here."

"I thought everyone was welcome in God's house." I countered. I wasn't going to be intimidated.

"Certainly not demons." The hatred and fear pouring out of her made me step back.

"Now Miss Effie, that's no way to talk." The pastor gently rebuked her, resting his hand on her stooped shoulder. "All God's children are welcome here."

"You haven't been here long enough, Pastor Jim. You

don't understand what she is." Her voice was a hoarse whisper, still loud enough for most everyone in the small sanctuary to hear. I wanted to hide, but I wouldn't give her the satisfaction. "You can explain it to me this afternoon. I'll come over to see you. How does three o'clock sound?" He didn't give her a chance to refuse.

Looking slightly chastised, and without arguing, the small woman escaped out the door, leaving me so shaken I had to sit down.

"The show's over, folks." Pastor Jim made sure everyone moved on out of the church without another incident.

"Are you okay?" Shep sat down beside me putting his arm around me.

"I'm real sorry about that, Miss," Pastor Jim knelt down beside me. "Are you all right?" He looked to be in his mid-thirties, with dark blond hair and a kind face. "I don't know what came over Miss Effie. She's usually such a sweet woman. I'll find out this afternoon."

"I'm fine," I answered both men. "Thank you for stepping in, Pastor." Miss Effie might be small and old, but the hate radiating from her was more than enough to overcome both.

"I hope you won't judge the entire town by what happened here today," Pastor Jim continued. "Normally we're a very friendly place." I'd have to take his word for that.

Shep followed me outside a few minutes later. Gratefully, most of the people had already gone home. I was angry, but also shaken by the woman's vehemence. This wasn't a very auspicious beginning to a day I'd been looking forward to. Shep had offered to follow me to the airport, so I could return the rental car. I was looking forward to spending time with him on the drive back. I didn't want this to ruin the afternoon.

"You going to be okay to drive?" he raised one eyebrow questioningly. "We can have lunch first."

"I'm fine. I'd rather have lunch later." I didn't want another encounter with someone ready to take my head off. I ran the episode over and over in my mind as I drove, but nothing made sense.

~~~

"How did your parents come up with your name? Shepard is unusual for a first name." We were sitting in a small diner outside of Des Moines. I was eager to learn more about him. He was someone I could get serious about.

"My mom loves to read," he said with a chuckle. "There was a character named Shepard in one of the books she was reading while she was pregnant with me. I got tagged with that name. My three brothers and sister are also named after characters from her books. My brothers are Tate, Cameron and Jordan and my sister is Bailey. Mom always went for the odd names. No Jim, Joe or Johnny for her."

"She sounds like a fun lady. I'll bet you miss them." I was feeling a little home sick myself.

"My older brother, Tate, is in the Air Force. Says he's goin' for twenty. Right now he's stationed in Japan. Cameron is finishin' up law school, he'll be takin' the bar exam this summer. Jordan and Bailey are still in high school, junior and senior years. Bailey is the baby and spoiled rotten."

"And I'll bet you loved spoiling her," I laughed, remembering how much fun it was having two baby brothers.

"After four boys, we all spoiled her. Mom said it was about time she had someone on her side."

The afternoon was ideal, and I hated to see it end. Evenings were the hardest, with nothing to occupy my time. Reading by flashlight was hard on the eyes after a while. I've watched a few television shows on my laptop, but that runs the battery down quickly. Now that I've returned the rental car, it will be more difficult keeping my cell phone and laptop charged.

Maybe I needed a dog to keep me company. I chuckled. A big one might discourage unwanted visitors.

~~~

The wood stove wasn't a mystery any longer, and I could even make a decent pot of coffee and some toast. Who knew toast was originally made by putting a slice of bread on a long handled fork, and holding it over a fire. It didn't taste too bad if I didn't burn it.

I enjoyed the early mornings sitting on the wide porch with my toast and coffee. Rosie had beautiful wicker rockers that I was putting to good use. I'd finally called my boss. He'd been very understanding. "Anytime you're ready to come back, just give me a call," he'd said. "You're always welcome here." But his final warning left me unsettled. "Be careful, Parker. Money is a big motivator. If someone thinks you've cheated them out of what's rightfully theirs, they could be dangerous."

While I was considering his words, a strange car pulled into the lane. My heart skittered in my chest before Pastor Jim stepped out of the car. I hadn't expected to see him so soon after the scene at church yesterday. Someone else was with him, but the glare on the windshield prevented me from seeing who it was. "Good morning, Miss Evans," he called. "I hope this isn't too early to visit."

"Of course not. It's nice to see you." When he helped Miss Effie out, my heart sank. Why had he brought her? She didn't look as demented as she had yesterday, in fact she looked embarrassed.

He helped her up the four steps to the porch, guiding her to one of the rockers. "Miss Effie, I think you have something to say," he prompted.

With a trembling hand, she reached out, giving my hand a poke. "Miss Effie," Pastor Jim gently cautioned.

"I had to make sure," she whispered to him. "She looks so much like her." She turned to me. "I'd known Rosie all my life; we were best friends when we were girls. But she changed into a tyrant. We never knew why. To get her own way she would tell people she would haunt them when she died if they didn't do as she wanted. I thought she was haunting me when I saw you."

"Why would you think that?" I was confused.

"You look exactly like her when she was your age." She opened her purse taking out an old picture of two young girls, maybe fifteen years old. If I didn't know better, I would think one of them was me.

So I look like a distant relative, I thought. There's nothing odd about that. We do share some of the same genes. Was that why she left everything to me? But how had she known I looked like her? More questions without answers. "I hope you know I'm not her ghost." I turned my attention back to Miss Effie. "I'm not haunting anyone."

She looked at Pastor Jim, then back at me when he nodded encouragingly. "I know that now. I never believed in ghosts until I saw you. Pastor Jim said only God knows where Rosie's soul is, and you aren't a ghost, you're a real person." As if testing that theory, she reached out her hand giving mine a gentle pat.

Pastor Jim cleared his throat, and Miss Effie released a heavy sigh. "He says I have to ask your forgiveness for the way I acted yesterday. Can you ever forgive me? I was plain awful." Her eyes were downcast, but I could see tears sparkling in the corners.

It was my turn to reach out to her. "I forgive you, and I'm sorry I gave you such a scare." I patted her hand. "I didn't know I looked like her." This explained why so many people stared at me every time I went to town. Maybe she isn't the only one thinking I'm a ghost.

Turns out Miss Effie is a sweet, gentle lady, and I enjoyed visiting with her and Pastor Jim. "Do you know my grandmother?" If she was friends with Rosie, they were around the same age.

"Milly and I are good friends. She'll be delighted to know you aren't...You know, a ghost." She whispered the last as if afraid of bringing forth just such an apparition.

"Will she visit me?"

She shook her head. "I'm not sure she can."

My heart sank. "Is she sick?" I held my breath, waiting for the answer.

"Oh, no. But I'm sure Walter won't let her visit. He's a bit ah..." She searched for the right word to describe the man.

"Overbearing?" I suggested. "Intimidating, a bit of a tyrant himself?"

She gave a tittering laugh. "All of the above. I guess you've met him."

"Only once and that was enough. I would like to see my grandmother though, but I don't want to get her in trouble with Mr. S." My boss's warning resonated in my mind. Mr. S. felt what was left to me was rightfully his. How far would he go to claim it for himself and his brothers?

"Mr. S." She gave another tittering laugh. "Sort of fits him. I've known him all my life, but he's never been the friendly sort. He hasn't improved with age."

"Maybe I can help," Pastor Jim spoke for the first time except to prod Miss Effie. "Miss Milly comes to the first service on Sunday. Says she needs to be home in time to fix Sunday dinner at noon. If you come to the early service, you can see her."

"But won't Mr. S. find out? I don't want anything bad to happen to her because of me."

He shook his head. "You can meet with her in my office. No one needs to know." It was horrible that she had to sneak around just to see me, but I agreed it was probably for the best.

"I can help too," Miss Effie said. "Milly and I belong to the same garden club. We meet every Tuesday at my house. You can come see your grandma there." She patted my hand again, seeming to enjoy touching me now that she knows I'm not a ghost. "We won't let on to the others that you were there," she whispered as though someone might be listening. She was enjoying the intrigue. Pastor Jim's big car pulled out of the lane a few minutes later. I felt more lighthearted than I had since coming to Iowa.

If I looked like Rosie, I wanted to see other pictures of her. There weren't any in her room. I'd gone through all the drawers in the big dresser and chest. The attic was my next destination.

For the next six hours I emptied boxes and trunks in one part of the attic. The only things I found were ancient clothes, old dishes, and old furniture. There was nothing personal belonging to Rosie though. Her things had to be somewhere else. I don't think Rosie or her family threw anything away. Dust had collected over the years on everything in this part of the attic, and after I was finished, most of that dust was on me.

Another part of the attic was amazingly clean. An old buffet held an entire set of dishes looking ready to use, ladies clothes were hung in the wardrobe or folded in drawers. Even a bed was made up ready for someone to sleep in. Had someone been living up here? But that's impossible, I told myself. Rosie had lived alone since her parents died years ago.

My muscles were beginning to ache from all the lifting and my stomach growled loudly, reminding me I hadn't eaten since the toast and coffee before Miss Effie and Pastor Jim stopped by. I didn't feel up to attempting anything on the wood stove, and I hadn't gone to town for my daily supply of food. Probably the ice was melted too.

Glad I'd put an old bandanna around my hair before exploring the attic, all I needed to wash was the rest of me. The attic had been stuffy, and the cold water from the hand pump felt good as I washed the dirt away. Feeling reasonably clean, I headed to Mary Lou and Billy's cafe. They were open until seven, so I had several hours. I could pick up some groceries after I got something to eat.

Shep had shown me how to start the old car, hand crank and all. I'd just driven it up and down the lane between the barn and the road. It wasn't any different to drive than a modern car. Just before I got to town, a pickup truck ran off the road into the ditch when the driver stared at the Model T with his mouth hanging open. I thought Rosie had driven the car, and people would be accustomed to seeing it, but maybe not. Parking in front of the cafe, a delicious smell wafted out the screen door. As if on cue, my stomach growled again.

"Hi there, Sweetie," Mary Lou called out as I entered. "How are things out at the farm?" People sat at four of the tables in the small room, and two men sat at the counter. Everyone turned as one to see who Mary Lou was talking to. Whispers started immediately.

38

I sat down at the end of the counter, far away from the staring, prying eyes and smiled at her. "Work's coming right along. I don't know what all it takes to get water and electricity installed in a house that's never had it, but Shep knows what he's doing."

She waved her hand in front of her face. "Now there's one good looking boy."

"Hey, watch it, Mary Lou," Billy called from the kitchen. "I'm right here, and I can hear every word you say. You don't want to hurt my feelings."

"Why, Honey, you weren't listening close enough. I said he was a good looking boy. You're all man. Besides, Shep's sweet on Parker here."

Heat flooded my face. "What makes you say that?"

"You're all that boy talks about every time he's in here, and he's here every morning for breakfast, and some evenings just before closing. Guess he doesn't much care for his own cooking." Billy put an order up, and she hurried off after putting a menu in front of me. I must have gotten there just before rush hour. Within minutes every table and stool was filled. There wasn't going to be any chit chat tonight. I thought farm families ate at home, but maybe the town folk didn't. There were certainly plenty of people eating out tonight.

As I got ready to leave, Mary Lou bustled up, mopping her brow. "Monday night special is always popular," she said in way of explaining the crowd. "Everyone loves Billy's cooking." I had to agree; even the simple sandwich I'd ordered was exceptionally good.

"Is there a fitness center around here?" Until now she'd been so busy I couldn't ask. "I know there isn't one in Whitehaven, but how about some of the other towns?"

"Sure thing. There's one in Buena Vista. That's about thirty miles away. Our kids go there all the time, can even go swimming in the winter. Imagine that!"

"That's just what I'm looking for. Now I just need to find somewhere I can plug in my cell phone and laptop. I sure will be glad when Shep gets electricity and water out there. I don't know which I'm more anxious for." I leaned closer. "I really hate that outhouse," I whispered.

She let out a big laugh. "Can't say as I blame you. That was the one thing I hated about visiting my grandma and grandpa. They had electricity, but didn't have bathrooms." She shuddered. "Any time you're in town, you just come in here, and use ours. I know that won't help during the night, but Shep is working as fast as he can."

Picking up another bag of ice, and a few things to get me through tomorrow, I headed back out to the farm. The evening was warm. I could hear crickets chirp as I drove down the country road. The old Model T didn't have air conditioning so the side windows were down.

A pickup was parked in front of the house as I pulled into the lane. Three men were standing around examining Shep's work. So much for getting the ice in the house before it melts. I thought inspectors would come during the day, not in the evening. And why were there three of them?

One of the men stalked toward the car before I could get out. "What the hell is going on around here? Why are you driving that car?" He was in his fifties, several inches taller than me with broad shoulders, and a beer belly hanging over his belt. The other two men were younger, and similarly built, but without the beer belly.

"I live here. Who's asking?" I tried not to show any fear. That would give them the real advantage. He got a closer look at me when I got out of the car, and took an involuntary step back, his face turning gray. The other two men had started forward but stopped now. Color drained from their faces as well. "I asked who you are." My voice held more force now. I knew they weren't building inspectors.

"I'm Charlie. Don't you recognize me?" the youngest of the three spoke.

"Shut up, Charlie. Course she don't recognize you." The first man seemed to be the ring leader.

"But Hank, she's known..."

Hank turned a furious face to Charlie effectively cutting off any more words.

"I asked what you're doing here," he growled at me. "You'd better answer straight out, or I'm calling my old man."

I laughed at that. I couldn't believe a grown man was threatening to call his daddy if he didn't get his way. "You go right ahead and call him. I'll call my attorney." I didn't let on that I knew who they were, but I had no doubt these were my mom's brothers.

Calling his bluff made him back down. He probably wasn't used to anyone standing up to him anymore than Mr. S. was. "You'd better stop what you're doing here." He pointed to the digging Shep's crew had done. "We have an attorney, too." Now he sounded petulant.

"Fine, I'll have Mr. Meyers here in the morning if you'd like to come by and see him."

"Mr. Meyers?" the third man spoke for the first time. "I thought he was our lawyer, Hank."

"Shut up, Clyde. Let's get over to Daddy's." They got in the truck, spinning tires in the gravel as they sped out of the lane. They probably hadn't had an independent thought between them their entire lives.

As quickly as I could, I got my ice and groceries into the house, and put the car back in the barn. I wanted to be behind locked doors in case Mr. S. came back with his three Neanderthal sons. Well, maybe two Neanderthals and a marshmallow. Charlie seemed like he wanted to make friends with the "ghost" standing in front of him. It didn't take a rocket scientist to know what their first thoughts had been when they got a good look at me. If Miss Effie thought I was Rosie's ghost, these men who had known her all their lives had to believe that as well.

CHAPTER FIVE

"Hurry up!" "Get over here and help me." "Will you two shut up? You don't want her to hear us, do you?" In the country, sounds travel and intensify, especially at night. The voices brought me out of a sound sleep, my heart racing in my chest. I lay still waiting to hear more voices. Just as I began to relax, telling myself it had been a dream, a loud bang in the front yard brought me out of bed. I wish I had gotten that guard dog.

Very little light filtered into the room from outside as I made my way to the window. Easing the curtain aside I could see three men in the yard where Shep's crew had been working. It didn't take much imagination to figure out who was down there. Figuring out what they were up to took a little more time, but not much. They were messing with the work Shep had already done.

"Oh, for a shotgun full of rock salt," I groused. I didn't know if calling the police would do any good. In a small town the locals would be protected over a newcomer, a usurper at that. Or a ghost. These thoughts moved through my mind with the speed of lightning while the men jostled each other to see who could get into their truck first. After making all that noise, they couldn't get away fast enough. It was like watching an episode of the Three Stooges tripping over each other in their haste.

For the rest of the night, I slept fitfully, waking to the sound of Shep's truck pulling into the lane. At least I hoped it was Shep. I hurried to the window to check, and relaxed when he stepped out of the truck. He was standing with his fists on his narrow hips staring at the mess made during the night, when I got downstairs.

"Looks like you had some visitors." A frown creased his brow as I came up to him. He took off his big Stetson, slapping his leg in agitation.

"Three men were here when I came back from town last evening." I explained about my earlier encounter, and their return trip in the middle of the night. "They were probably Mr. Shepard's sons."

Shep shook his head, causing a lock of dark hair to fall into his eyes. My fingers itched to push it back in place, but I kept my distance. This man was dangerous in a far different way than Mr. S. and his sons.

"Why didn't you call me? I could have been here in ten minutes."

"At the first loud noise, they were out of here so fast you couldn't have caught them."

The damage wasn't as bad as I feared, some of the trenches were filled in, tools and equipment moved around and knocked over. That must have been the bang that scared them away. Cowards were afraid of being caught, and these men were certainly cowards.

Back in the house, I made cowboy coffee the way Shep had shown me, and finished washing up at the sink. I was getting used to the cold, very cold water, but I was certainly looking forward to having a hot shower. I was looking forward to going to the fitness center. That would be my second stop today. First, I was going to see my grandma!

Miss Effie had given me directions to her house, and said to be there at ten. She'd have Milly come early to help her set up. She wouldn't tell her I was coming, and I'd be gone before the others arrived. All this clandestine activity was necessary so Mr. S. didn't find out.

"Here's my cell phone number," Shep told me when I went out to get in Rosie's car. "Put it on your speed dial so you can call me if they come back. I don't want anything happenin' to you." A shot of electricity pulsed through me, his rough, calloused fingers warm and comforting when I reached for the card. That man could light up a house, I thought as I drove off, butterflies still fluttering in my stomach.

Miss Effie lived on a farm nearby. As at Rosie's, the fields were green with crops. Someone was riding a tractor in a field being readied for more planting. I didn't know if she had children, or if she had ever been married. Calling her "Miss Effie" was an old-fashioned courtesy, not a designation stating she was unmarried.

So much had happened since Pastor Jim brought her over it seemed like a week instead of just yesterday. I had a ton of questions and no answers. Maybe I would get a few of them today. Miss Effie had told me to drive around to the back of the house, and park the car by the barn. The old Model T was very distinctive; anyone seeing it would know it belonged to Rosie.

Miss Effie was waiting for me on the back porch, so excited she could barely stand still. "I'm so glad you let me help you meet your grandma. She'll be so happy to see you." She gave me a little hug, the top of her head coming to my chin. Nerves attacked my stomach. I hoped we could keep this secret. I wasn't sure what Mr. S. would do if he found out Milly was sneaking behind his back to meet me.

A plaque by the back door announced this house was on the historical registry like Rosie's. So no electricity, I thought. Would there be water? I looked at the yard behind me. Sure enough, there was the little building with a crescent moon cut into the door. I groaned. Hopefully I wouldn't have to use the bathroom while I was here. It was bad enough using the one at Rosie's, but using one here...I didn't even want to contemplate it.

Stepping into the large farm house kitchen, I was pleasantly surprised. Lights gleamed over a sink with modern faucets; modern appliances filled the room. "You have a lovely kitchen." It gave me hope that Rosie's house could be modernized.

"It wasn't always like this." She gave her twittering laugh. "When my Earl and I got married, we didn't have electricity or running water. Kind of like yours is now."

Mine? Well, for now, I thought. Even if I stay here for the year, what then? Did I want to move to Iowa? The thought of leaving my parents and the twins broke my heart. Shep's handsome face floated through my mind. Chemistry was definitely brewing between us. A shiver traveled up my spine just thinking about him.

A soft knock on the wooden screen door in the front room broke into my thoughts. Before Miss Effie could answer, the heavy door opened and Milly came in. "Yoo hoo, Effie," she called. "I'm here."

Miss Effie beamed at me, "Come on," she whispered. "She's going to be so surprised."

I followed her into a big room, probably called a parlor. Milly hadn't changed much from my memory of her. She is a tiny woman with snow white hair pulled back in a neat bun. Her crisp calico dress was freshly pressed. Seeing me she gasped, covering her mouth with her hand, her eyes sparkling with unshed tears.

"She's not Rosie's ghost, dear. She's real." Miss Effie patted her hand.

"Of course, she's not Rosie's ghost. Why ever would I think that?" She recovered quickly. "She's my granddaughter!" She beamed at me. For a long moment we stared at each other. I wasn't sure what I was supposed to do. Calling her Grandma seemed a little awkward, but calling her Milly seemed disrespectful. "You're beautiful. Just like I knew you'd be. You were such a pretty child." In three steps, she was across the room, giving me a great big grandma hug. Tears threatened to spill over.

Miss Effie clapped her hands, doing a little jig. Even she had tears in her eyes. "This is so wonderful. I don't know what I'd do if I hadn't been able to watch my granddaughters grow up."

We sat on the comfortable couch while Miss Effie went to get lemonade. Milly kept patting my hand as though reassuring herself I was real. "Do you think you could call me Grandma?" she asked as if reading my mind. "I have four big strapping grandsons, but no granddaughters. You're my only one, and I've missed so much of your life." Sad tears flowed down her slightly wrinkled cheeks.

The three of us visited for the next hour. It wasn't hard

calling her Grandma after all. She wanted to know all about Mom and our life in Arizona. She knew Mom remarried, but hadn't known about the twins. "They're seventeen?! Do you think Laura will come visit us? I want to see her again, and the twins. What's her husband like?"

I couldn't promise anything. I know how Mom feels about Mr. S., but how do I tell her that? "Dad's wonderful." I told her. "He's a clinical psychologist." There was so much to tell, I didn't know where to begin. How do you cover twenty years in just a few hours?

The time for the other ladies to arrive for the garden club came too fast. I had to leave so they wouldn't find out I'd been here. I hadn't been able to ask any of my questions. There's always next time, I reminded myself. This wouldn't be the only time I saw her.

"I want to see you again. Will he let you come over to the house?" We all knew who I was talking about.

She patted my hand. "Of course, I'll see you again, child. He doesn't keep me under lock and key." Why did we have to keep this meeting a secret if it wasn't because of Mr. S? I thought. She'd find out soon enough how I felt about the man and their three sons.

When she walked me out, she started laughing as she stared at the old car.

"What's so funny?" I looked at her, then the car and back at her.

"I've heard whispers about a "ghost mobile," but I didn't understand what all the fuss was about." She pointed at the car. "There's the car, and you're the ghost." She laughed again.

"Didn't you know I was here?" I hadn't thought to ask earlier. I'd been in Whitehaven for over a week and assumed she knew.

"My sister is very sick. I've been staying with her in Buena Vista. She's feeling a little better so I came home for the garden club."

"He let you go?" I was so astonished I forgot to keep my doubts to myself. It didn't sound like something Mr. S. would allow. The man ruled with an iron fist.

"Of course he let me go. She's my sister, and Buena Vista isn't that far away. I told you, dear, he doesn't keep me under lock and key." I didn't argue but I didn't believe it either. She couldn't look at me when she said it.

"Will you come over tomorrow? I have so many questions. How did Rosie know about me? Why did she leave me everything?"

"Rosie was a law unto herself. I'll come over as soon as I can. I've been gone a week. Now I need to take care of my own house." This wasn't the answer I wanted, but I let it go. I needed to leave before the others arrived.

I headed for Buena Vista. I was going to join the fitness center and take a shower. I'd packed a gym bag before I left the house. Maybe I could even charge my phone and laptop while I was there. Both were running out of power. I should have asked Miss Effie if I could plug them in at her house, but hadn't thought of it until now. If there isn't anywhere to plug them in at the fitness center, I'd go to A Cup-A-Joe tonight. Mary Lou would let me stay until they were charged.

~~~

Three hours later I left the gym feeling squeaky clean for the first time in over a week. My muscles were pleasantly sore. I had one more stop before going back to the farm. A hardware store was just down the block. As long as I was here, I wanted a high-powered flashlight and some different lanterns. I could also pick up some groceries. Then I wouldn't have to go into Whitehaven. Mr. Meyers made arrangements with all the merchants in town to send him receipts for anything I bought, but I could give him the receipts for these purchases later.

I was disappointed when Shep wasn't there when I pulled into the lane a short time later. "He can't be here all the time," I chided myself. "You aren't his only client." I still couldn't stop the disappointment. His crew, Wayne, Mike and Jim, were just finishing up for the day. They were making progress connecting the yard to the sewer alongside the road. They'd start working in the house next. Bathrooms were my number one priority.

"Shep said he'd drop by about six to see you," Wayne called before climbing into his truck. The other men chuckled, waving as they drove off. Even being the subject of gossip didn't bother me. I felt more lighthearted than I had just minutes ago.

While waiting for Shep, I replayed the morning over in my mind. Miss Effie had gone to a great deal of trouble setting up this meeting and keeping it secret. Even Pastor Jim hinted that Milly wouldn't want people to know she'd met with me at church. Yet Milly said Mr. S. didn't keep her "under lock and key." Actions and words contradicted each other. "More questions," I sighed. "Am I ever going to get any answers?"

Not only do I talk to myself, I answer as well. I laughed. Being this alone was completely alien to me. I'm used to having people to bounce ideas off of. Maybe a dog is a good idea after all, I thought, one that would guard as well as be friendly. It couldn't talk back, but at least I wouldn't feel so alone.

Checking my watch I still had an hour before Shep would stop by. Maybe I could talk him into staying for dinner. I'd bought steaks and baking potatoes in Buena Vista with that thought in mind. That was about as elaborate as I could get on the wood stove. So far I'd stuck with simple meals. Shopping everyday was a pain when I had to make a special trip into town. How did people survive a hundred years ago? They didn't even have grocery stores back then. "I can just see myself foraging for food every day. I'd starve to death." I laughed at myself.

Carrying the plans Shep had given me out to the porch, I sank down into the wicker rocker with a groan. My muscles were beginning to protest the exercise. After taking more than a week off from the gym, I was paying for it today. I'd discovered the big tub Rosie's family had used for bathing. Maybe I'd heat some water on the stove, and soak my sore body. Then again maybe not, I decided. By the time I got the tub full, the water would be too cool to be any help.

To take my mind off Shep and my sore muscles, I spread out the plans. Rosie hadn't been explicit in what was to be done. According to Shep, she left the details to me. Bringing the house out of the nineteenth century had been her main goal. Adding bathrooms and new appliances in the kitchen would go a long way to that end. "The old cupboards won't have to be replaced," I mumbled. "Granite counter tops will look great." I lost track of time as I sketched out how and where I'd have appliances installed.

The sound of tires in the lane brought my head up, my heart racing. I wasn't prepared for any of Mr. S.'s shenanigans. I released the breath I'd been holding on a sigh. It was Shep's truck, not the old one Mr. S. drove. Now my heart raced for a different reason. Gingerly easing my way down the steps, I barely managed to stifle a groan. I'd been sitting in one place too long; my already sore muscles were protesting new movement.

"You all right?" Shep frowned with concern when he met me at the bottom of the porch steps. "Did something happen today?" He took my hands, looking for any signs of violence.

"No, just too much exercise." I gave him a detailed account of my day. Very detailed, I realized when I didn't stop talking for fifteen minutes. "Sorry about that." A blush crept up my neck. "I don't know when to shut up if I don't have constant human contact."

"I don't mind," he drawled. "It's kinda cute." He tapped my nose with his finger. I could feel my blush deepen. "To offer you some human contact, how about goin' to get somethin' to eat with me?" he chuckled.

I wanted to shout "Yes," but I tried for some decorum. "Sounds good to me. Mary Lou said you go there for dinner sometimes."

He lifted one dark brow. "You been askin' about me?"

"Ah...I...ah...no." I stammered. "I was there the other day and she told me..." I stopped before blurting out that she'd said he talked about me. What is wrong with me? I'm acting like a teenager with my first crush.

"I thought you might like to try somewhere else for a change. There's a great little place in Bentonville." Maybe he didn't want to add any more fodder to the gossip mill either. Like me, maybe he figured Mary Lou was playing matchmaker and didn't want to encourage her.

CHAPTER SIX

It was dark when we pulled into the lane leading to the house. The flash of headlights showed that my nocturnal visitors had been here again. Shep's crew had been taking their hand tools home with them. The larger equipment was stored in the barn. Nothing was left behind to be stolen, but the ditches and pipes could be covered and broken. Shep was going to have to redo a lot of the work again. "Okay, I've had enough of this!" I slammed out of the truck. "He's going to pay for this. I'm calling the police."

"You need to call the police," Shep agreed, "but you can't accuse anyone."

"You know as well as I do Mr. S. sent his three goons over to harass me."

"But you can't prove it," he stressed. "Make a report so the sheriff is aware of what's goin' on but you can't accuse anyone," he repeated. "Without proof, the sheriff's hands are tied."

His argument was frustrating, but I knew he was right. The police would take a report, that's all they'd do.

~~~

The deputy looked no older than the twins. "He probably isn't even shaving yet," I muttered. He certainly wasn't concerned since nothing was stolen. "What do you want me to do?" he asked Shep, ignoring me. The fact that I was the owner of the property didn't matter to him.

"Well," Shep drawled lazily, "I guess I'd like you to do your job and take the report. Just 'cuz nothin' was stolen shouldn't stop you from doin' that." Color crept up the deputy's smooth face. "Miss Evans lives here alone. Wouldn't want the men who did this to come back when she's here alone, would you?" He kept his voice mild, but the deputy got the message.

By the time he left, I was near the boiling point. "Did I get transported through a time warp when I flew here? I wasn't aware women were supposed to be seen and not heard. This *is* still the twenty-first century, isn't it?"

"Small, rural town," Shep said with a chuckle, "not much different from other small, rural towns."

"Well, I'm not from a small, rural town," I stomped my foot in frustration. "And that teenager better file the report." Shep's acceptance of the deputy's attitude was as frustrating as the deputy himself. "I'm getting a dog," I muttered more to myself than him. "A big one!" I stormed inside ready to slam the door, but Shep was right on my heels.

"Okay." he said.

I whirled around, glaring up at him. Was he mocking me? He raised his hands, palms out in a placating gesture. "Whoa there! I was agreein' with you."

I drew a deep breath, releasing it slowly, trying to calm down. "Sorry. I didn't mean to take it out on you. This town's attitude is getting to me. I should just tell Mr. Meyers to forget it and go home."

"I wish you wouldn't." His soft words washed over me, sending shivers down my spine. The look in his deep blue eyes melted my anger and frustration, replacing them with something quite different.

"Okay." I don't know what I was agreeing to, but it was all my befuddled brain could muster up at the moment.

He gathered me in his arms, kissing my forehead, my eyes, before finally settling on my lips to leave me weak and breathless. When he lifted his head again, I was grateful his arms were still around me. I wasn't sure I'd be able to stand on my own. I rested my cheek against his chest listening to his rapid heartbeat.

"I'll stay here tonight," he finally said, holding me away to look at me so I wouldn't misinterpret his intentions. "I'll sleep on the couch. But I don't think you should be out here alone in case they come back."

"What do you think your small, rural town would think of you spending the night?" I almost laughed at the image. "I doubt the small minds would approve."

"That goes on in small towns same as it does in the big city. The difference is people pretend it isn't goin' on unless you're an outsider."

"Oh, goody, small minds and a double standard. It just keeps getting better." I paced away from him, conflicting emotions warring in me. I wanted to stay in Iowa for many reasons, Shep quickly becoming number one. But how do I put up with the small town prejudices, and the long family feud?

My spine stiffened. They chased my mom away, twice. Was I going to let them do the same thing to me? NO, I thought. Not just no, but hell no. That man and his sons would have to work a lot harder than some vandalism before I'd run away. "You don't need to stay. I'll be fine."

Shep raised an eyebrow when I detailed what I bought earlier in the day. "I have the largest battery operated spotlight available. It's also motion activated. If anyone drives down the lane after dark, they will be hit right in the face with a blinding light"

"Is it assembled?"

"Not yet," I reluctantly admitted. "I'll do that in the morning. For now I have a flashlight big enough to light up the yard. I doubt they'll come back tonight. As fast as news travels around here, they have to know we called the sheriff. I'm also getting that dog I mentioned."

It took some convincing, but Shep finally left after assuring himself every door and window in the house was locked tight, even the door to the root cellar. I hadn't been aware there was a root cellar until he pointed it out. Another place to explore, I thought, but only in broad daylight. My mind conjured up a dark, spooky place with cobwebs streaming from the ceiling. A shiver shook me at the thought.

~~~

I spent an uneventful night, and was up bright and early the next morning. I had a lot to accomplish before I could continue exploring the house, the barn, and now the root cellar.

I hadn't even thought about the basement. Hopefully I'll find the answers to my many questions in the house. First and foremost I wanted to know how Rosie had known so much about me when Mom had no contact with her family in nearly twenty years

While I was still assembling my new equipment, Mr. S.'s old truck pulled into the lane. "Great," I muttered. "What does he want now?"

Slamming the truck door, he stalked to the bottom of the porch step. "Did you tell the sheriff my boys wrecked some things around here?" His voice was a low growl.

"No." Technically that wasn't a lie, I'd told his teenaged deputy.

"You didn't?" He didn't know whether to believe me, and I couldn't help but smile.

"No, I didn't." He visibly relaxed before I finished my statement. "I told a deputy someone had been messing with things around here, and suggested he have a talk with your sons."

"You...you said..." he sputtered.

"You asked if I told the sheriff, and I didn't. I told his deputy. There's a difference."

"My boys would..."

"Your "boys" are grown men who follow your orders," I interrupted. "This wasn't the first time they were here, but you'd better keep them on a tight leash from now on. It's on record that I'm being harassed even if the sheriff doesn't believe it's your "boys" doing the harassing. If it continues, I will press charges."

"You have no right being here. This farm belongs to me and my boys and my brother."

"Only if I don't stay here for a year," I said. "But don't hold your breath waiting for me to leave. You just might turn blue. People say I'm a lot like Rosie, and I don't think she'd back down from your threats. Neither will I."

Without uttering another word, he stormed back to his truck, spewing gravel under his tires as he pealed out of the lane. I hoped there weren't any cars coming when he pulled out. I sank down on the top step of the porch. Had I just issued him a challenge? I wondered.

Shep pulled into the lane as Mr. S.'s truck disappeared. He jumped out almost before his truck came to a complete stop. "Are you all right? What did he do? Why didn't you call me?" His rapid fire questions didn't leave me time to respond. He pulled me off the step, looking me over for any injuries.

"I'm fine. He didn't touch me. He was mad because I called the sheriff last night."

"Did he threaten you?"

"He's still trying to intimidate me, but that isn't going to work. I'm not going anywhere." Stubbornness runs in the family.

His crew pulled in, preventing any further discussion. "Damn, Shep," Wayne called. "More trouble?" The men examined the damage done last night. "We've never had this kind of trouble at other jobs before. What's going on?"

"Just kids out for some mischief. Nothing we can't fix in a few minutes." He turned back to me. "You can't stay out here alone. If he gets mad enough, there's no tellin' what he'll try."

Without paying attention to the three men watching us with crazy little grins, I touched his cheek. "I won't be alone. I'll have a big dog for company." While I was in Buena Vista the day before, I'd made arrangements to meet the owners of a kennel. They trained guard dogs who are also good companions.

Snickers from the crew brought us both back to the present, and I dropped my hand. He stepped back, but didn't seem overly concerned about what his men might think. If it didn't bother him, I wasn't going to let it bother me.

~~~

The sun was just setting when I returned to the farm. I'd accomplished a lot, and was feeling pretty good. I left the Model T sitting at the bottom of the porch steps instead of driving around back to the barn. Holding the leash tight, I let Gus out. A well-trained Mastiff, he weighed almost as much as me. We'd spent the day working together, getting acquainted. I'd learned how to handle him, how to let him know where his territory was, who were friends, and who weren't. I still had a lot to learn, but we'd made a good start. "Take him with you anytime you might feel threatened," Dave Brewer, the breeder and trainer, instructed. "He won't let anyone get close to you unless you give the okay. He'll only follow your commands unless you tell him otherwise."

We walked to the end of the lane and around the house. If anyone came around tonight, they'd get to meet Gus up close and personal. I posted warning signs along the road letting anyone who came on the property know there was a guard dog on duty. I didn't want to get sued because they were attacked while doing their mischief.

When I was leaving the breeder's I called Shep; he'd be here shortly with dinner. When my stomach growled I realized I'd skipped lunch, again. Getting caught up in something, and forgetting to eat was becoming a habit. His timing was perfect. Minutes after I arrived, his truck pulled into the lane. Would I be able to convince Gus that Shep was a friend? I know how Dave Brewer said it worked, I just wasn't sure I could accomplish it.

Carefully watching Shep, the hair on Gus's back stood up, a low growl coming from deep in his throat. "Friend, Gus. Friend." I put my hand on his head as Mr. Brewer had instructed, hoping that was all that was necessary to restrain him when Shep stepped out of the truck.

"Did you get a trained bear disguised as a guard dog?" He stayed by the truck for a moment deciding if it was safe.

"Friend, Gus." I repeated the command. The dog had stopped growling, but he was still in guard mode. "It's okay for you to come here." As Shep approached the steps, I met him half way, placing my hand on his chest and looking at Gus. "Friend, Gus. Shep this is Gustav, Gus for short. Gus this is Shep, my friend." To emphasize that fact, I stood on tip toe and kissed him. Shep's arms closed around my waist, deepening a kiss that had started out light. For several seconds,

I allowed myself to relax, enjoying the feel of his lips on mine. When Gus gave a small woof, I pulled away unsure what Gus was trying to convey. Maybe he just thought it had gone on long enough.

"Maybe he'll like me better when I get the food out of the truck," Shep laughed. "There's enough for him too."

"No people food. The breeder said it isn't good for him."

"Let him tell this monster he's not getting our food," he laughed. "If he wants to risk life and limb, that's his business. For me, if this big boy is hungry, I'm feedin' him."

Gus was very well mannered. He didn't beg, but he did keep careful watch for anything to drop on the ground. "How bad can barbeque pork be for him?" Shep asked. "It doesn't hurt people. I feel terrible eatin' in front of him."

"Oh, all right but just one small piece," I laughed. "I don't want my new dog to get sick the very first day I have him." Before I could even finish talking Shep tossed a hunk of meat. Gus caught it in the air, and it disappeared in one swallow.

"Wow, have you fed him today? What kind of dog is he, half bear?"

"He's pure Mastiff. No one is going to argue if Gus takes exception to them being here. He's only eighteen months old, but very well trained. I can let him run loose on the property, and he won't run off. I think he's going to be just fine around here." While I cleaned up the leftover food, Shep made friends with Gus. Later he helped set up the spotlight I'd put together this morning. I wasn't sure if Mr. S's three stooges would make a return appearance, but I wanted to be ready.

The next morning I was a little disappointed. There'd been no commotion in the yard overnight. There's always tonight, I told myself. I let Gus out to run, and headed to the outhouse. Those bathrooms couldn't be installed fast enough. I really hated that outhouse.

After coffee and toast on the porch, I headed upstairs to continue sorting through Rosie's life. There had to be some clue as to how she knew all about me, and why she had left everything to me. I'd already gone through her room, and found nothing helpful. With a cursory glance at the five other bedrooms, they held more of the same; old newspapers, clothes and linens.

This is going to take time, I reminded myself. The ground floor had the kitchen, dining room, great room or parlor, a sitting room and the mud room off the kitchen. All the rooms were bigger than any in modern homes. The attic covered the entire house, and I'd only scratched the surface up there. Figuring that was the best place to look, I headed upstairs.

I found an old wooden jewelry box with intricately carved designs. Lifting the lid, I sucked in my breath. It held beautiful old pieces that glimmered even in the dim light. I assumed it had belonged to Rosie or her mother. If the stones were real, they'd be worth a fortune. It didn't answer any questions for me though. Setting it aside, I continued looking through the trunk where I'd found the jewelry box. There had to be letters, papers, and diaries, something that would give me a little insight into this family.

I hadn't seen or heard from Milly since I left her at Miss Effie's. I'd hoped she'd come over, but so far she was a no-show. I'd take Pastor Jim up on his offer to come to church early and see her there. So much for Mr. S. not keeping her under lock and key, I thought.

I needed to pick up my daily supply of food, and decided to have lunch at A Cup-A-Joe. Gus had to stay home though. He looked like he was pouting with his big head resting on the window sill as I pulled out of the barn. I'd given him orders to "Guard," but that didn't satisfy him. We'd bonded quickly, and he took his protection duties seriously.

I parked the old car in the only place left near A Cup-A-Joe which meant I had to walk a block. No problem unless there is a very large man standing in the middle of the sidewalk blocking my way. "Well, hello there, Missy. I've been waiting to catch you in town to introduce myself. I was supposed to be your daddy, but your mama up and ran away with some other guy. I understand he didn't last too long. Maybe I'm the lucky one." His chuckle was mean and evil.

"She didn't run away; she was told to leave." My back was

ridged, and my hands were curled into fists. "The reason 'he didn't last too long' as you so crudely put it was because someone drove him off the road. Maybe I'm the lucky one. Now if you'll excuse me." I stepped past him heading to A Cup-A-Joe.

My hands were shaking as I pushed open the door of the small cafe. The room was nearly full; people stared at me until I wanted to scream, "I'm not Rosie's ghost, and I'm not haunting you." Instead I ignored everyone except Mary Lou as I sat down at the counter. Without asking, she placed a coffee cup and a glass of ice water in front of me. "You okay, Sweetie? You look ready to spit nails."

"I just met another of your upstanding citizens. He informed me he was supposed to be my daddy." I wasn't making any attempt to keep the sarcasm out of my voice or to keep quiet. I didn't care if the entire town heard me. That man was detestable.

"That was Young Ed Bodeen. I saw him walk by. He's a little hard to take at the best of times. He thinks he's more important than he is. Even as a boy he was a bully. He hasn't improved with age."

By the time I left A Cup-A-Joe the place was empty. I stayed longer than I expected, but once the lunch crowd cleared out I stayed to visit with Mary Lou. I told her Mom said hi. Talking about Mom, Dad and the twins made me even more homesick. I wanted to go home, but I wanted to stay to find out what was really going on here. I knew deep inside there was more than met the eye.

Back at the farm I decided to take Gus for a run. Mastiff's, like all large breeds, are working dogs, Mr. Brewer had explained. They need exercise every day. A quick change into my workout clothes and we headed out. Gus was thrilled, wanting to outrun me, but duty came first. He stayed by my side most of the time, gaining on me only to slow his pace until I could catch up then take off again. "Okay, boy, you go ahead, and play your games if it makes you happy," I called out to him. There was no way I could keep pace with him, but I knew he wouldn't leave me entirely alone.

The country lane was mostly empty with only the occasional car or truck slowly passing by. No one was in a major hurry. One woman slowed to ask if my dog was running away, did I need help catching him? For the first time, I felt the friendliness small towns were supposed to be known for.

As my muscles were loosened up, I stretched out my stride. When I heard the rumble of a large truck coming up behind me, I couldn't believe a semi would be on the narrow road. Glancing over my shoulder, it wasn't an eighteen-wheeler, just a large diesel pickup about a hundred yards back. I moved off the pavement, expecting the driver to pass. There was no other traffic to prevent him from pulling to the center of the road to go around me. "Here, Gus," I patted my leg, to call him back. I didn't want him to get in front of the truck.

Instead of passing me, the truck got closer, the rumble got louder. I moved further off the road, but it didn't make a difference. When he was too close for comfort, he jammed his foot on the gas. The engine roared, and I could feel the heat from his engine looming down on me. Before I could react, something hit my shoulder, sending me tumbling into a small ditch.

Gus was beside me in an instant, barking at the truck as it quickly disappeared. For several minutes I just lay there taking a mental inventory. My shoulder hurt like the dickens, I had scrapes on both hands and knees, but I didn't think anything was broken. Thank you, God. Was he trying to run me over? I wondered. Or just scare me? *Why would someone do that?* I could think of only one person who had a motive to get me out of his way. Mr. S. But it wasn't his truck, or the one I'd seen his sons driving. But they could have another truck. I wasn't sure I could identify this particular one. All I could say was it was big, blue, and there might have been a decal on the side door. Maybe the side mirror got broken when it hit me. That would help identify the truck, but who would believe me? That teenaged deputy certainly wouldn't.

"I'm all right, boy." Gus licked my face, whimpering. He knew I was hurt, and didn't know what to do about it. If the driver had stopped, I had no doubt Gus would have taken him down. I patted his head, struggling to stand up, only to sink back down. "Ah crap!" My ankle was already beginning to swell. I didn't think it was all that far to the farm, but I wasn't sure my ankle would support me.

The Oakridge Boys song "Elivra" started playing in my pocket. Shep and Mr. Meyers were the only ones in Iowa who had my cell phone number. "Please let it be one of them," I whispered. That prayer didn't get answered though. "Hi Mom," I forced a cheerful note into my voice. "How is everyone?" I couldn't tell her about what had just happened. She was already worried about me staying here.

"Is everything all right? You sound... funny."

"Everything's fine, I'm out for a run." She seemed to accept that excuse. "I got that dog I told you about. He needed some exercise. He's really big and very protective. He's not going to let anything happen to me." Sensing I was talking about him, Gus whined, leaning into me. "See. He isn't sure who I'm talking to and he's worried." I forced myself to laugh.

Her laugh was just as forced. Changing the subject, I told her about having lunch at Mary Lou's. She enjoyed hearing what her long ago friend had to say. "How about that young man," she said "Tell me more about him." She hadn't questioned me about the men I dated in a long time.

I failed to mention the sparks that flew whenever we were together, but I think she knew I was playing it down. We talked for several more minutes. By the time I closed my phone, I was feeling better. My shoulder still felt like I'd been run over by a Mack truck and my ankle was swollen, but the throbbing in both had subsided. Using Gus as a prop, I managed to stand up. He's big enough I could lean on him and walk. It'd be slow going, but we'd make it back to the farm. I hoped the driver didn't return for another shot at me.

Limping up the lane, I was glad Shep's men were already gone for the day. I was going to down play my injuries as best I could. There was nothing anyone could do since I couldn't identify the truck or the driver. First I had to get cleaned up, and see exactly what the damages were.

For the first time, I was grateful for the cold water coming out of the hand pump. It felt good on my numerous cuts and scrapes. My shoulder and ankle had gotten the worst of it. Nothing was broken, but I'd have some colorful bruises for a week or two. Whoever the driver was had made a gigantic mistake if he thought this would scare me away. Now I had another reason to stick around. I was going to find out who did this. The "why" was easy to answer if Mr. S. had anything to do with it. He wanted me gone so he could claim Rosie's money for himself and his sons.

Checking my watch, I didn't have much time before Shep would be here if he kept to his schedule of the past few nights. He'd made a habit of either bringing dinner, or taking me somewhere, usually into Bentonville. Tonight I hoped he was bringing dinner.

Within minutes of sitting down in the wicker rocker resting my sore foot on the porch railing, Shep pulled into the lane. Gus growled and stood up, his hackles standing up. I didn't know if he associated Shep's truck with the one that hit me, or if he still wasn't familiar with Shep. "Friend, Gus." I patted his head.

Shep stepped out of his truck, slowly walking towards us. He wasn't taking any chances. "Hi, there." His greeting was for me, but he didn't take his eyes off Gus. He was holding a big bag of food, and another one from the pet store. "I brought your bodyguard something. Thought it might help..." His eyes shifted to me and he stopped short. "What happened? Who did this?" He was up the steps in one leap, Gus's possible threat forgotten. His big hands gently went over the visible scrapes.

"Nobody did anything, I fell."

He wasn't buying that. "Where? What were you doin'?"

"I took Gus for a run and I fell. I landed in a ditch."

He was still skeptical, but couldn't come up with any argument. "You're sure you're all right? No one did this?"

"I'm fine. I twisted my ankle when I fell. I must have hit my shoulder on a rock because that hurts too. I'll be fine."

He brushed my hair aside and moved the neck of my shirt

to examine the bruise there. His low curse was all I needed to know it was already turning purple. "And you're sure no one helped you fall?"

He'd make a good interrogator, or I'm not a good liar because he stood up, his hands on his narrow hips. "What really happened? Who did this?" His harsh tone alerted Gus who stepped between us, his hackles raised again, a warning growl rumbling low in his chest.

"Friend, Gus, friend." I tried to reassure the dog and divert Shep's attention. Only Gus got the message. He sat down again, but he remained between Shep and me. He wasn't going to take any chances.

"Now that you've got your bodyguard all shook up, are you ready to tell me what really happened?" His tone was mild, but the scowl drawing his dark brows together conveyed something else entirely.

With no choice but explain, I sighed. "We really were running. A truck passed by, coming a little too close. The side mirror must stick out farther than he expected. I fell into the ditch when it hit my shoulder." Explaining it that way, maybe it was an accident.

"Who was driving? Did they take you to the hospital?"

"I don't know who was driving. I didn't go to the hospital. It's not that bad."

"Someone hit you and didn't stop. Did you call the sheriff?" He was getting mad again, but his tone remained mild. Gus kept looking between us trying to decide if there was any danger.

"What could I tell them? I didn't see who it was. That deputy won't do any more than he did the other night. He'd say I was making it up to avoid looking like a klutz."

Shep sat down heavily on the top step, resting his elbows on his raised knees. "You're probably right. That kid wasn't impressed when he was here." He released a heavy sigh. "No more running on the road, okay? Next time you might not be so lucky."

If this was lucky, I didn't want to find out what unlucky was. "I can run here on the farm," I agreed. "There's enough empty space to give Gus a good workout."

He brought out the food and showed Gus the big rawhide bone he'd brought for him. Gus didn't move, but his skin rippled with excitement looking at me for the go-ahead. "It's all right, Gus." I waved my hand the way the trainer had instructed. This was the only way Gus would take something from anyone but me.

CHAPTER SEVEN

I was stiff and sore the next morning, but in better shape than I expected. A purple bruise covered my left shoulder but I could move it without much discomfort. If I kept my ankle wrapped, I could walk as long as I wasn't on it for an extended period of time. I would go to the gym just to swim and shower for the next few days. They'd been nice enough to let me charge my phone, and laptop each time I came in.

I still had the rest of the attic, the basement, and the barn to sort through. That would take the rest of the summer. Somewhere there had to be a clue to tell me how Rosie knew so much about me, and why she left all this to me.

By noon I was exhausted, and I'd only gone through four trunks. The separate room was still a puzzle. If I could see Milly again, would she have any answers? She still hadn't come to see me, and I hadn't seen her in town either.

There were boxes and boxes of pictures. The few I'd looked through were a disappointment. There were pictures of Rosie's brothers and her parents, but none of her. Maybe they were in the other boxes. I still hadn't found a big portrait that would fit in the empty place in the hall. Someone had taken it down, and hidden it. Who did it and why was anybody's guess.

Favoring my ankle, I limped down the stairs, putting as little pressure on it as possible. Three steps from the bottom, it gave out. Stumbling, I grabbed at the banister to keep from falling. My hand grabbed the ball at the top of the newel post. It wobbled, but didn't come off." I wiggled the ball, trying to make it fit back in place. This time it came off. "Oh crap! Now you've done it," I muttered. I examined the wooden piece. Nothing was broken. Maybe it just came loose over the years. A lot of people had probably grabbed it, working it loose. When Rosie and her brothers were little they might have slid down the banister, using the ball as a stop to keep from falling off.

Fitting the piece back in the hole where it came from, it wouldn't go down all the way. I pulled it out again, looking in the hole to see what was blocking it. With the strong sunlight shining in the wrap-around windows, I could see something pushed down inside. The hole was too small to get my fingers inside to grip whatever was there. "Tweezers! I need tweezers to pull it out." The quiet house was beginning to bring out the "nut case" in me. Even with Gus here, most of my one sided conversations were to me, not the dog.

I looked down, purposefully speaking to him. "I'm going to have to include you in my conversations. I wouldn't want anyone to think I've gone around the bend." I laughed, limping back up to my room where I kept my make-up case.

Within minutes I was spreading out a small piece of paper, pressing the creases out on the dining room table. The writing wasn't faded but the paper looked old. How long had it been in there? I wondered. Who would have put it there? The bold script was still legible.

My Dearest, Meet me by the barn tonight at midnight. We can be married before anyone even knows we're gone. All my love, Barnard

Who was Barnard? And who was dearest? An easy guess would be Rosie, and Barnard was her admirer. When my grandparents were teenagers, girls were a lot less bold than they are today. But this was signed by a man.

So, the note was meant for Rosie. Had she met him, or had she ignored his plea? I didn't know if Rosie had ever been married. I pulled my cell phone out of my pocket, pressing the speed dial for Mom. Forgetting the time difference, all I got was the machine. Disappointed, I left a message for her to call when she got home. This intriguing find gave me the incentive to keep looking. It didn't have anything to do with why Rosie left her estate to me. But it was interesting, nonetheless. There had to be other clues as to what went on here sixty or seventy years ago, something that would answer my questions.

After a quick lunch of cheese and crackers, washed down with cold water from the hand pump, I returned to my search upstairs. It was like searching for a needle in a haystack. There were so many boxes and trunks, and no way to know what they held without going through each one. Whoever packed them wasn't very organized. Each box held a mishmash of items, outer clothes, undergarments, books.

By the end of the day I was exhausted, and even sorer than I'd been this morning. I could use a shower, but I didn't feel like driving the thirty miles to Buena Vista. Even without all my scrapes and bruises, I wouldn't feel up to swimming. A head to toe sponge bath was the best I could do.

I pulled the curtains, shut the mud room door, and stripped out of my dirty, sweaty clothes. I'd just started pumping water into a basin when *Elvira* sounded from my phone. Mom! I scrambled to get it out of my shorts pocket. Hopefully she could shed a little light on the note I'd found.

"Hi, Mom. How was work?" I didn't want to jump right in with my questions without a little chit chat first.

"Same old same old. What's going on there, Honey?" Mom got right down to business. She kept her voice light, but I knew she wanted to ask if I'd had any run-ins with Mr. S. or the others.

"Did you ever hear any talk of Rosie having a boyfriend or gentleman caller?"

She was quiet for a minute, thinking back to people she'd worked very hard to forget. "I can't recall anyone ever saying anything like that. Why?"

I read the note to her and asked, "Was it meant for Rosie or someone else? Did anyone else ever live here besides Mr. S.'s family?"

"The farm has always belonged to the family, but I can't imagine Rosie ever having a boyfriend. She was in her twenties by the time I was born, and a full blown tyrant. Even her father had been afraid to cross her. I don't recall anyone named Barnard living in town, or on one of the surrounding farms." She was quiet for a moment. "Maybe you could ask ..." She hesitated before finishing her sentence. "Ask Milly." She paused. "Have you seen her again?" Her voice had grown quiet.

"No. Her sister in Buena Vista was sick, so maybe she had to go take care of her again. I haven't been going to town much the last few days either. Maybe I just missed seeing her." We both knew that was a weak excuse. The most likely scenario was Mr. S. wouldn't let her come near me. I really don't know what he expected to accomplish, but it was typical bullying tactics.

I forgot I was sitting in the kitchen in my all-together when I heard a truck pull up to the house. "Oh, my gosh. I have to go. Shep just got here, and I'm not dressed." I limped to the stairs.

"If he's worth anything, Honey, he'll wait until you finish dressing."

"No, you don't understand. I don't have *any* clothes on. I just started to get washed up when you called."

She chuckled at that. I thought she'd be horrified at the thought of a man walking in when I'm stark naked. "Okay, I'll let you go. Call later."

Gus stayed downstairs while I hobbled up the stairs. I could hear him barking when Shep knocked on the door. Grabbing my robe off the bed, I headed back down. If he got worried enough when I didn't answer the door, I didn't want him to break in. He'd made friends with Gus, but I wasn't certain Gus would remain friendly.

"Gus, find Parker. Find Parker." Shep called through the heavy door, worry made his voice hoarse.

Gus didn't move. He'd stopped barking when he recognized Shep's voice, but he was still standing guard. No one would get past him unless I gave the all clear.

"Good boy," I patted him on the head and opened the heavy door. "Rest, Gus." Immediately his stance changed, his tail thumping on the wood floor. "Sorry about that," I told Shep. "I lost track of time when I was talking to my mom. Go in and have a seat. I've got to get cleaned up." There were dirt smudges on my face, and the rest of me was dirty and smelly.

"No hurry," he drawled, trying to keep his gaze from traveling down my body. He wasn't entirely successful, and I could feel heat rushing up my face. "I... ah...I," he cleared his throat before continuing. "I didn't figure you would want to go out to eat yet so..." He held up a large bag with delicious smells coming from it. "Put this in the oven to keep it warm. I'll take Gus outside and let him run." Maybe Shep needed the fresh air? The thought gave me a small thrill. "Will he go out with me?" he asked.

"I'm not sure." I opened the door wider. "Go with Shep, Gus. Run." He's a smart dog, but I'm never sure how much he understands when I talk to him. He cocked his head, watching me. "Go with Shep," I repeated. "It's okay." As though he understood, he stepped onto the porch, looking back at me for the go-ahead again.

"Do I need to take this out of the bag before putting it in the oven?" I still wasn't comfortable with having a fire going all the time in the heavy cast iron stove. I never knew how much heat the low burning embers produced.

"No, it'll be fine. Take your time. We'll be back in a little bit." He followed Gus out. For a minute I thought the dog wouldn't go any further than the porch without me. Slowly he followed Shep down the steps.

~~~

At home, entertaining centers around the television or some form of recreation; hiking, sporting events, movies or such. On a farm with no electricity in the middle of small town America, there wasn't much to do. Somehow the hours slipped pleasantly by. Sitting on the porch swing, snuggled up to Shep's side, we talked about everything and nothing. I don't recall ever spending such an enjoyable evening just talking. Well, the kisses in between talking adding to the enjoyment.

"Are you wantin' to go to church on Sunday? You might be able to see your grandmaw." We were standing at the door where we'd been for the last fifteen minutes saying goodnight. Neither of us was eager for him leave.

With all that's been going on, I forgot the next day was Saturday. Shep and his men wouldn't be working. Now I really didn't want him to leave. I could spend the day exploring more boxes in the attic, but he wouldn't be over for dinner. I drew my mind back to his question. "Yes, I'd like to go. Milly goes to the early service. I'll go then. She seemed so glad to see me when we were at Miss Effie's, but I haven't heard from her since. She has to know I have a ton of questions."

"Are you going to show her the note you found?"

I shrugged my uncertainty. "I told Mom, but she didn't know anyone named Barnard. He could have moved away long before she was born though. I'll ask Mary Lou. She'd know more about the people than Mom."

"How about I pick you up for breakfast tomorrow? We'll go to A Cup-A-Joe. Mary Lou has been grumblin' about not seein' you much this week, complainin' that I'm keepin' you away." His Texas drawl still sent ripples of pleasure through me.

After agreeing to be ready at seven, and a few final kisses, he left. We'd been sitting on the porch the entire evening. There'd been the usual trickle of traffic on the country road in front of the house. The lanterns I'd picked up at the hardware store in Buena Vista when I got my spotlight gave off more light than the old kerosene lamps Rosie had. Anyone passing by would have seen us. Hopefully, if any of the passing vehicles had been Mr. S. or his sons, they decided not to try anything tonight. I was tired of their pranks. I wasn't convinced one of them wasn't behind the wheel of the truck that tried to run me off the road.

Alone on the porch, I felt a little vulnerable. The country wasn't like the city where there was any number of prying eyes to watch an unsuspecting woman, but I still felt exposed. Picking up the lantern, I quickly went inside, sliding the dead bolt in place. I kept the heavy curtains closed at night even though the nearest neighbor was two miles away.

CHAPTER EIGHT

For seven-thirty on a Saturday morning, Main Street was bustling. A Cup-A-Joe was already crowded. I'd always assumed farmers were busy early in the morning with farm stuff, whatever that is. Someone had been working in the fields every day at the farm. Today was no exception. I still wasn't certain who it was, but I was confident it wasn't Mr. S. or his sons. They would have been harassing me if they'd been that close. Someday I'd remember to ask Mr. Meyers. For today I was going to enjoy being with Shep.

"Well, hi there, Sweetie. I was afraid you'd gone back to Arizona without saying good-bye." She came around the counter and gave me a hug. I winced when she accidentally touched my still tender shoulder. "Now, what did you do to yourself? You shouldn't be working so hard out there that you get all sore."

My t-shirt and jeans covered the worst of the cuts and bruises, and I was no longer limping, but a few bruises were visible on my arms. With a raised eyebrow she waited for an answer. Boy, she must be one tough mom, I thought. "I'll bet your kids can't get away with anything."

She laughed, "Not a thing. So what happened? You been trying to help Shep and the boys with their work? That won't get you a bathroom any faster."

Before I could answer, Ed Bodeen ambled across the room, a sneer contorting his face. "Hello again, little lady. How you doing this fine morning? Didn't expect to see you in here for a while. I hope you told your mama I said hi." His tone mocked me. I didn't understand his cryptic remark, but I didn't get a chance to ask what he meant.

Shep stepped in front of me. "Howdy, Bodeen. Haven't seen you around much lately either. You find someone else to hassle? Hope it's not Miss Evans here." His voice was mild, even congenial, but there was menace at the end.

"I wasn't talking to you, Baker. Why don't you just move along?" He started to brush Shep aside when Billy took hold of his outstretched arm.

"You're the one who's going to be moving along, Ed. I've warned you before; you don't make trouble for my customers." I'd never seen Billy except through the kitchen pass-through. He was a mountain of a man, making the other two men seem small.

Without another word Ed left the cafe, the screen door slamming behind him. There was a collective sigh from the other customers, and conversation started again. No one seemed surprised by this display, just glad it didn't escalate.

Billy went back to his kitchen, and Mary Lou picked up the order waiting for her. Apparently this wasn't the first time Billy had to say something to Ed. I looked around the small room. What was wrong with these people? Why did they let men like the Bodeens and Shepards rule their lives? Nothing I said or did would change a lifetime of habits.

We sat at the counter, which had become my practice. I could visit with Mary Lou when she had a spare minute between orders. I wanted to see if she knew anyone named Barnard, but instinct told me to wait until there weren't so many people to eavesdrop. I'd put the note away where I hoped it would be safe.

"Who else has Ed Bodeen been hassling?" I asked Shep.

"He owns several businesses in town, and doesn't take kindly to competition." His answer was just vague enough to warn me there was more to it than that.

"Did he try to run you out of business?" I was angry for him.

He chuckled, "He tried, but Rosie wasn't about to let him run me off. She threatened him, but she never said with what."

Each new piece of information added another layer to dig under to find out what was what around here.

Things finally started to slow down, and Mary Lou breathed a sigh of relief. "I sure am glad tomorrow's Sunday. I'm getting too old to do this six days a week."

"Oh, go on, girl," Billy called from the kitchen. "You aren't old; you're just hitting your stride." I laughed at their antics.

"Stride my foot," she hollered back. "I'm ready to fall down."

"And just what would you do if you retired?"

"Who said anything about retiring?" She sounded offended. "I may be old, but I'm not *that* old."

Billy laughed. "Like I said, just hitting your stride." This seemed to be a familiar routine with them.

"Have you heard of anyone from the past named Barnard?" I asked. There were only a few others in the cafe now.

She thought for a minute then shook her head. "Can't say that I do. How about you, Billy? You heard of anyone named Barnard?" He was always a part of our conversations even though he stayed in the kitchen.

"Nope. Never heard of anyone by that name."

"Do your parents still live around here?" If she didn't know who he was, maybe her parents would.

"Sure do. They took over my grandparents' farm when they couldn't keep up anymore." Leaning close, she confided in a stage whisper, "They put in bathrooms." We chuckled at the inside joke.

"Would you ask if they'd heard of anyone named Barnard?"

"Sure thing. What's this all about?"

"I found a note in the newel post. It was signed by someone named Barnard. It had to be meant for Rosie."

The man who tried to block the sidewalk my first trip to town stood at the register, ready to leave. He cleared his throat loudly, and Mary Lou looked at him. "Be right there, Abner." He was about the same age as Mr. S. and just as cranky.

"Make it snappy. I'm in a hurry." He tapped his fingers on the counter. My stomach churned. Was he in a hurry because he overheard our conversation? Mary Lou rolled her eyes, and went to take his money. I should have waited until everyone left before saying anything.

"Who was that?" I whispered when she came back to us.

"Abner Shepard. I thought you knew him."

My heart sank. "Shepard? As in Rosie Shepard?"

"One and the same, brother and sister. Are you all right, Sweetie? You don't look so good."

Shep put his arm around my waist. "The Shepards aren't in her cheerin' section," he said. "They'd like to run her out of town." There were still a few others in the café, and we kept our voices low. I didn't want to give them any more gossip to spread around than I already had.

"Don't you let them!" she said forcefully. Her voice carried through the small cafe. She didn't care if the others heard her. "The Shepards and old Ed Bodeen ran roughshod over this town for years. Now Young Ed has taken his daddy's place. It's about time someone stood up to them."

This is my heritage, my gene-pool? I couldn't believe my gentle, kind mother came from these people. It's no wonder she left home and never returned. "How many more Shepards are still around?" Were there more people out there who wanted to run me off?

"Walter and Abner are the last of the brothers, but there are a few nieces and nephews. Abner never married. Everyone suspected he had a stray young'un or two over the years though. 'Course he never claimed them. You've met Walter's three boys. Wilbur and Arthur have passed on to their reward, wherever that is," she whispered, her eyes downcast as though indicating something other than heaven. "Wilbur's widow left town with the kids shortly after he passed. Arthur's widow is still in town. They had a son and a daughter. Jack lives on his daddy's farm and Denise is married to none other than Young Ed. Her daddy made her marry him when your mama ran off. I don't think she's any too happy in her marriage."

"Can't say as I blame her." By now, the cafe was empty except for the four of us. "Why did she cave in to the pressure? Arranged marriages were a thing of the past for a long time." Again I felt like I'd stepped through a time warp.

She shrugged, and Billy called from the kitchen, "Girls in

that family were raised not to question the men folk. Even the wives quickly learn not to question their authority. My sister dated Charlie for a while. He's the softest of the three, and can't stand up to his old man. He asked Betty to marry him, but when old Walter started setting down some rules, she told him to forget it. It broke poor Charlie's heart, and he never married." That's the most I'd heard him say at one time.

"People think we're backwards in the South" Shep said as we left a few minutes later, "but we don't treat our women the way those men do." He shook his head. I thanked God Mom had broken away from this bunch. Now I had to decide if I wanted to stick around. The money was no incentive, but I still had so many questions. It always came down to my questions. Were they worth putting up with this bunch?

Shep reached for my hand. "Don't let them chase you away," he said quietly, guessing at my thoughts. "After you find your answers, you can make up your mind. My company can be started up again anywhere."

My heart did somersaults. Was he saying what I thought he was saying? Could it really be only a few weeks since I met this wonderful man?

CHAPTER NINE

Coming out of church, Shep introduced me to several people. I still evoked a great deal of curiosity, even among the younger generation. The fact that some of the older people had considered me Rosie's ghost was fodder for excitement. The scene with Miss Effie that first Sunday was still fresh in their minds. I couldn't tell if they were hoping for a repeat, or afraid of one.

People mingled between services, visiting and enjoying coffee and cookies. Milly hadn't come to the early service; I was hoping she'd show up for the next one. When Miss Effie arrived, she greeted me with a hug. Some people seemed a little disappointed there wasn't a repeat of the previous Sunday. After that, everyone headed off for lunch or whatever they did with the rest of their day.

Miss Effie was disappointed when Milly was a no show. Like me, she'd been hoping our meeting at her house would cement our relationship. "Do you know if she had to go back to help her sister?" I asked, hoping that explained her absence.

She shook her head. "I haven't heard from her. She just might be busy getting her house back in order after being gone so long. Those men of hers are a messy bunch. I don't think they ever lifted a finger to help her."

"Do her sons still live at home?" They were all grown men.

"Just Charlie, he never got married, you know," confirming what Billy had said. "But Walter wouldn't think of doing anything in the house. Of course, those other two boys are there every day working the farm with their daddy. I'm sure they made a big mess Milly had to clean up when she got home."

Maybe Miss Effie had heard of someone named Barnard, but I didn't want to ask her when others could be listening. I felt certain Abner Shepard overheard me yesterday,

76

hightailing back to Mr. S. If Barnard had anything to do with that family, I didn't want them trying to stop me from figuring out who he was.

"Could I come see you sometime, Miss Effie? You could help me learn about ..." I hesitated to call them family, "about Milly and her family." I finished lamely.

"Come over anytime," she beamed at me. "I don't get much company since the grandkids are all so grown up." She patted my hand.

When Shep pulled into the lane to the farm a short time later, my heart turned over. Something didn't feel right. I'd given Gus the guard and patrol order when we left for church. He was pacing along the property line, his hackles raised. Every inch of him vibrated with energy. Before Shep stopped his truck, I had the door open, jumping to the ground. "Gus, come here boy!" I patted my leg. His posture was pure military as he marched up to me, his eyes surveying his territory.

I ran my hands over his coat looking for any wounds. He appeared okay, but he hadn't come off guard duty even though we were there. "Someone was here." I looked up at Shep. "I *know* it. Too bad Gus can't talk." We checked all the windows and doors. Everything was locked tight thanks to Gus. Whoever was here hadn't been able to do their mischief. Gus slowly relaxed, but was aware of every car and truck that drove past. If only there was some way he could let us know which of those trucks had tried to get past him while we were gone.

My enjoyment of the day had disappeared behind a cloud of anger. It was useless to call the sheriff's office; I couldn't prove anything had happened. If I called every time I suspected someone had been here, I would soon have a reputation like the little boy who cried wolf. No one would believe me even if something terrible happened. I was just going to have to suck it up for now. Someday, whoever was doing this would screw up, and they'd get caught in the act.

First thing the next morning I decided to go to the gym. A workout would do me good, a shower would be even better.

Sponge baths just weren't the same as a steaming hot shower. Gus could patrol again and Shep's crew would be working in the yard. I didn't think anyone would try to get in the house with witnesses around even if they were foolish enough to try again.

It was fun driving the Model T around town, but on the open road it was much slower than the rest of the traffic. And it didn't have air conditioning. It was only the end of May and temperatures weren't too bad yet. When the humidity and the temperature were nearly the same later in the summer, I was going to be wishing I had my Wrangler. I wasn't sure if the Model T even had a heater for the winter. I was still hoping Mom, Dad and the twins would bring my Wrangler this summer.

Getting out of the car at the gym, I pulled my bag from the back seat. Turning around, I nearly ran into a young woman standing in my way. "Oh, excuse me! I didn't see you. I'm sorry." She glared at me for a moment but didn't move. She was about my age, a little taller, with long blond hair. If it weren't for the sneer on her face, she might be pretty.

"Do you know who I am?" she demanded.

"No, how would I?" Was she nuts?

"Shep hasn't mentioned me?"

"No, why would he?"

"Because I'm his girlfriend." With each statement she became a little more belligerent.

"Oh." My stomach sank a little. I didn't know what else to say.

"'Oh,' is right. I suggest you butt out of our lives."

That got my dander up. I don't like people telling me what to do in that tone of voice. "When was the last time you saw him?"

"We've been dating ever since I moved here." She avoided my question, supporting my suspicion she was lying.

"Okay. When was the last time you saw him?"

Her eyes shifted away from me for just a fraction of a second before looking back, but she couldn't quite meet my eyes. "Over the weekend," she hedged.

"Oh? When?"

"Ah...Saturday ah...night."

"Really. What time?" I was backing her into a corner. Shep had been with me Saturday evening, and again all day Sunday.

"Don't take him too seriously; he's just playing up to you. He doesn't want to lose the big contract he signed with that crazy Rosie."

"You must not think too highly of him if you can accuse him of something so unethical."

She shuffled her feet uncomfortably. "Of course I think highly of him. He's my boyfriend. We're in love." She added the last as an afterthought.

"What did you say your name is?"

"Deidre Smith."

"I'll be sure to tell him you said hi. Now if you'll excuse me, I need to go inside." I brushed past her before she could say anything else.

"Don't tell him you saw me," she called. "He'll be mad at me."

"Not my problem." I kept walking.

She was lying about most of what she'd said. Shep might have dated her at some point, but he's been spending his evenings with me lately. I didn't want to believe he'd spend time with me just to keep the contract.

For the next two hours I worked off my aggravation trying not to dwell on what she'd said. By the time I left, I'd convinced myself she'd been lying about everything. If Shep was in love with her as she claimed, he couldn't kiss me the way he did. Running my fingers over my lips, I could feel the warm pressure of his lips there. That didn't mean I wasn't going to ask him about her.

Gus was still patrolling when I got home, but he looked relaxed, unconcerned. Shep was working with his crew, and he knew Shep was a friend.

In a few days, they would start working inside. It'd be an adjustment for Gus as well as me. The first rooms would be the kitchen, mud room and bedroom at the top of the kitchen stairs. Dust would be everywhere. I wouldn't be able to fix even the simple meals I'd mastered on the wood stove.

For the next few months everything would be a mess. But according to Rosie's will, I couldn't move out while the work was being done. *Thanks a lot, Rosie.* I wished I knew why she'd insisted I stay in the house.

Shep had taken his shirt off again; sweat glistened on his broad back. I rubbed my stomach to calm the funny little flutter there. He did more to my equilibrium than any man I'd ever known. As I drove around the house to the barn, he waved but didn't stop working. Deidre's words sounded again in my mind causing doubts to creep back in. How much could, or should, I believe? I'll ask him tonight, and then forget about it, I told myself.

I spent the remainder of the day in the attic. The valuable antiques stashed away in old trunks themselves antiques, was amazing. I could open my own antique store, and not have to replenish my stock for several years. That small area set up as a living space, and kept relatively clean was still a puzzle. Who had used it and when? Who had kept it and the rest of the house clean?

Deidre's words kept intruding on my thoughts as I worked. Had Shep dropped her when he started seeing me? Why would he do that? I didn't want to believe he was so desperate to keep my contract. She had sown seeds of doubt in my mind, and I hated that. But that had been her purpose of confronting me.

Going through more pictures, I found a few of Rosie as a teenager. It was eerie how much we looked alike. The similarity was so striking I would have thought it was me, if the setting had been more modern. I set aside each one to examine later. I hadn't said anything to Mom about the resemblance, or that people had thought I was Rosie's ghost. It was time to fill her in.

I called her as soon as I knew she'd be home. "Did you ever see any pictures of Rosie as a young girl?"

"I'm sure I did, but I don't recall anything specific. Why?"

"I look enough like her that we could be twins, and she knew it. Maybe that's why she left everything to me."

"Does this mean you're coming home?" she asked hopefully.

I laughed, "Sorry, I still have a lot of questions. How did she know so much about me?"

She sighed heavily, and was silent for several heart beats. "Does that young man have anything to do with why you're staying?" Her voice was hopeful again. She's ready for grandchildren.

"You never can tell about these things." Thoughts of Deidre nagged at me.

After another of her patented sighs, I told her what people had thought when I first came here. "That sounds like something she'd do," she admitted. "If she could coerce people into doing what she wanted, she would use any means available. Since she knew how much you looked like her, she wouldn't hesitate to use that fact. You have to admit it's original. I don't know how she knew so much about you. I never sent pictures to anyone."

"Shep said she talked about me all the time."

"She's gone, Honey. I don't know how you're going to find the answers you want. Do you like living there?" Worry tinged her voice. She doesn't want me to move here permanently.

"It's different. I'm very much the outsider here. There are probably a few people who still aren't sure about the ghost thing. The older people stare at me like they're afraid my head is suddenly going to start spinning around, and the young people are hoping it will. How cool will that be?" We were both laughing when we hung up a few minutes later.

I wasn't sure if Shep would be by for dinner although that had been his habit almost since I moved in. Doubts kept creeping back. "Darn you, Deidre." Before I could dwell on those thoughts his truck turned into the lane. My stomach did flip flops. How would he react when I asked him about her?

Gus greeted him with a friendly wag of his tail, unaware of my misgivings. The fact that Shep had food, and always included something for Gus could have something to do with his warm welcome. Dogs are good judges of character, I reminded myself. If Gus doesn't think there's anything wrong, why should I?

The small wicker table on the wide front porch had become our dinner table, and I went to get plates, glasses and silverware. Evenings were perfect this time of year. The Midwest weather had a few advantages over Phoenix where it was already too hot to eat outside. I'm not sure what I'll think of winter though. I'd never been in snow for days on end.

"I ran into a friend of yours at the gym today." I kept my tone light and casual.

"Who?" He didn't sound concerned. He was concentrating on his food.

"Deidre Smith."

That got his attention. His head snapped up, his body ridged. Gus growled at the sudden change. "She's *not* a friend of mine. Did she try anythin'? Did she hurt you? You need to stay away from her." He would have taken hold of me, but Gus was standing guard, growling a warning.

"She said she's your girlfriend. Who is she?"

He paced the length of the porch, too agitated to remain sitting down. "She was *never* my girlfriend! Believe me." He ran his long fingers through his hair. "My mama always told us if we couldn't say somethin' nice about a person, don't say anythin' at all. The nicest thing I can say about Deidre Smith is she's crazy." He sat on the railing, his foot swinging like a pendulum. "I took her out three times. After that I didn't want anythin' to do with her. She'd be at my house when I came home from work. Or show up at a job site." He started pacing again. The more worked up he became, the deeper his drawl. I couldn't take my eyes off him.

"After she broke into my house for the third time, I called the police. A lot of good that did," he grumbled. "They weren't too concerned, said it was a lover's quarrel, and they couldn't do anythin'. The little 'gifts' she left behind couldn't be traced back to her."

"They didn't do anything?" I don't know why it surprised me after my own experience with that freckle faced deputy.

"They talked to her. She gave them some song and dance. Said I was stalkin' her. She's a cute little thing, and she played that up." He finally sat down again, his dark blue eyes boring into mine. "Please don't believe anythin' she says."

I swallowed my guilty conscience. "She was very convincing, but I couldn't believe you were that devious. I knew she was lying when she said you were with her on Saturday. Is there any connection between her and Mr. S.?" A crazy woman in cahoots with a bunch of power hungry old men was a scary combination.

He shook his head. "I don't think so. I never saw her with them. She came here to find her father. She told that story to everyone who'd listen. I thought we might have somethin' in common since we were both lookin' for family. After three dates she told everyone we were gettin' married, so I tried to put a stop to it."

"Did she find her father? Did she know who he was?"

He shrugged. "She wouldn't say who he was, just that he was a big deal, and he was waitin' for the right time to introduce her as his daughter. I don't know if anythin' she said was true."

For a long time after Shep left, I prowled the dark house. I couldn't quite settle for the night. Where did Deidre fit in this mess? Was she just a psycho fixated on Shep? I couldn't see any connection to Mr. S. or his family. Mary Lou said everyone suspected Abner had fathered an illegitimate child or two. Was he Deidre's father? In her mind he might qualify as someone important.

I finally gave up, and went to bed only to be awakened a few hours later. Gus was barking, pacing between the doorway and my bed. The spotlight I'd set up outside was on! Someone was in the yard.

Before I made it downstairs, a big truck engine roared to life. Dust from the lane filled the air when I opened the door.

Gus was out like a shot; stopping anywhere he caught the scent of the trespassers. My spotlight had done its job scaring off the intruder.

We had a hard time settling down again. The sky was just showing pink through the lacy curtains when I finally drifted off. The next thing I knew, another truck rumbled into the lane startling me out of a sound sleep. How dare they try again! Racing to the window, I collapsed against the sill at the sight of Shep's truck. It was morning.

I was slow getting started. My mind wasn't functioning on all cylinders. Pastor Jim surprised me with a visit an hour later. By his solemn expression I knew this wasn't a friendly visit. "I wanted to let you know why Miss Milly wasn't in church Sunday," he started, causing my heart to drop to my toes. Please, let Milly be okay, I sent a small prayer upward. I hadn't had a chance to get to know her. Mr. S. really wouldn't hurt her because she saw me, would he? I didn't know the answer to that.

"Milly's sister has been sick," Pastor Jim continued quickly, seeing my distress. "It looked like she was getting better but...I'm afraid she passed away unexpectedly two days ago. I understand you didn't know her, but I thought you would like to know."

"Of course. Thank you for telling me." My heart went out to Milly. He left a few minutes later. The funeral would be the following day in Buena Vista where she'd lived. He seemed to think it would be all right for me to attend. Milly would appreciate it. I was pretty sure Mr. S. wouldn't feel the same, though.

I was able to catch Mom before she left for work. "I'm sorry to hear that. Aunt Betsy was a nice lady. She had two boys, but I don't know where they are now. If Mom was taking care of her, I assume they didn't live close by. If you go to the funeral, tell her I'm sorry for her loss, and I'm praying for her." So typical of Mom, I thought. She had a prayer for everyone. I'm sure she'd even said one or two for Mr. S. over the years.

The boxes of pictures I'd brought down the day before were waiting for me in the parlor. Each box was a mishmash of many different years. Whoever packed them didn't have a system. Or was there? Rosie had an agenda for everything she did. Was this all some sort of puzzle I was supposed to solve?

With that thought in mind, I started sorting pictures again. Most of the people in them were strangers to me. Only a few had names and dates on the back. Maybe Mom could identify some of the people. That might shed some light on what Rosie had in mind. There was one similar to the picture Miss Effie had shown me. They looked so young and carefree. What had happened to change Rosie into a mean, vindictive harridan? Before I left here, I intended to find out.

CHAPTER TEN

I parked a block away from the funeral home. The Model T was a very distinctive vehicle. I didn't want to draw attention to myself. I was here to support Milly, not cause a scene. If I could sneak in without Mr. S. or his sons seeing me, maybe I could stay just long enough to see her, and give her Mom's message. I thought it would mean a lot to her.

I enjoyed driving the old car, but I needed to figure out a way to get my Jeep here. If I was still here when it starts to snow, I'd need a car with a heater and four wheel drive. I'd asked Mom if they'd come, and I was hoping. What could Mr. S. do to her now? She's forty-seven; he's eighty, or close to it. He couldn't physically hurt her, and Dad would be here to support her.

A lot of people were milling around outside the funeral home, and it was full inside. Apparently Betsy was a well-loved lady. It was good cover for me. I could get lost in the crowd. I ducked behind a large potted plant when Milly entered the room with Mr. S. The three stooges, as I'd begun to think of them, followed behind. The four men were uncomfortable in their suits and ties, none too happy about being there. At least they were there for Milly, but I thought it'd be better to leave them home if they were going to act so miserable.

Milly ignored them. Two men in their fifties hugged her, only nodding at Mr. S. Maybe these were Betsy's sons. They looked much more pleasant than Milly's sons even though it was obvious they were sad about losing their mother. When the service was ready to start, I waited until the family had gone in, and then sat in the last row.

After the last prayer, I slipped out of the chapel heading for the restroom. From there I could see the people as they filed out. Mr. S. and sons left immediately, but Milly stayed around with the two men I'd seen earlier. A few minutes later, she was momentarily alone. She saw me before I got to her, and her face lit up.

"Thank you for coming. It means a lot." She gave me a hug.

"I wanted you to know I was thinking of you. Mom sends her love." This brought more tears, but there wasn't time to take the conversation further. Mr. S. was pacing on the steps outside. It wouldn't be much longer before he came in looking for her. "Will you come see me?" I squeezed her hand. "I have so many questions."

She glanced at the door, her thoughts the same as mine. But something shifted in her manner, she stood up straighter. "Of course I'll come see you. Give me a few days. I want to hear all about your brothers. We've all missed so much." Sadness weighed her down for a moment. "But not anymore. When things settle down here, I'll come see you." Her voice was strong and determined.

I moved back down the hall, waiting for my chance to slip away. I wanted to get the Model T off the street before someone recognized it, and told Mr. S. I was there. A scene at a funeral wasn't something I looked forward to.

~~~

When I got home, Gus was in an uproar again. Someone had been there, I was certain of it. I don't know how anyone could get past him without Shep's men seeing them. They always brought their own lunch and ate under a tree. I didn't ask if they'd seen anyone around. That sounded a little paranoid. Instead I walked around the yard, looking to see if anything had been disturbed.

There were foot prints at the edge of the field too small to belong to a man. My guess was they belonged to Deidre Smith. She was persistent if nothing else. Well, Gus chased her away before she got to the house, I told myself. No telling what she'd do if she got that far.

Trying to put Deidre and her antics out of my mind, I went inside. There was still plenty of daylight left to sort through more boxes and pictures. When Gus started barking at the front door a short time later, I could do little more than sigh. Before I could get off the floor, the pounding on the door sent Gus into a frenzy, growling and ready to attack if they managed to get inside. This wasn't a friendly visitor.

I could see Mr. S. through the leaded glass window in the door, his hand raised to pound again when he saw me. "Open this damn door, Missy, or I'll break it down." His angry threat left no doubt to his mood.

Shep had been here when I got home, but his truck was gone now. His men were staring at the house watching the unfolding scene. Gus will protect me, and he's an old man, I rationalized. How much can he do?

Taking hold of Gus's collar, I opened the door just wide enough to speak through. "What..."

"You let me in!" he interrupted. "I'm not having the hired help listening to what I have to say."

"I have nothing to say to you. My dog is trained to stop intruders who are threatening me."

"I don't give a damn about your dog. You need to go back to Arizona, and leave my family alone. There's nothing for you here."

"Except this farm," I countered. "Rosie left it to me, not you. I'm doing what she wanted me to do."

"I don't give a damn what you think Rosie wanted. You're messing with stuff you don't know anything about."

"What stuff? What's here that you don't want me to find?" A low growl continued to come from Gus, warning Mr. S. not to force his way inside.

A look flashed across the old man's face, but was gone so quick I wasn't sure what I'd seen. Something I said hit a nerve. His hands were shaking, and a tic had developed in one eye. "Go back to Arizona," he repeated. "Leave us alone." He turned, storming down the steps to his truck.

I leaned against the locked door, not sure my legs would support me. When someone knocked on the door, I screamed. "Parker! What's wrong?" Shep called through the closed door.

As soon as I unlocked the door he pulled me to him, resting his chin on top of my head. "He must have been waitin' for me to leave. Mike called me when he started yellin'." His heart was racing under my ear, and his muscles twitched in response to the adrenalin in his system.

"I'm fine. Now." I whispered the last word. I didn't want him to let me go. I could stay right where I was for the next year, maybe longer. I finally straightened away from him, looking into his handsome face. "There's something here they're afraid I'm going to find."

I looked around the front room, my gaze settling on the newel post knob. Were there more hiding places? If so, Mr. S. probably knew about them since he grew up in this house. *Were there more notes hidden somewhere?* "I have to find out what's here." I said this more to myself than Shep.

"You have to be careful," he emphasized. "The guys said he was ready to break the door down. No tellin' what he'd do if he'd gotten in."

"Gus won't let anyone hurt me. He was trained to take a bullet, so to speak, for his master."

"He can't stop a bullet if he doesn't see it comin'. These people all have guns, and know how to use 'em. I don't want one of them mistakin' you for a deer." His words were chilling. Walter Shepard wanted me gone. That was a certainty; but would he go so far as to kill me to accomplish that? No matter how much either of us wants to deny it, I'm still his granddaughter. What was he hiding? That's what it boiled down to. But where was I supposed to look?

Going back to the box of pictures, I picked up another stack. Most were of Rosie and her brothers or a group of girls. There was even one of her entire family. It was the only picture I'd seen of her mother who died when Rosie was very young.

The similarity between Rosie and myself no longer shocked me, but one picture had me gasping for breath. It could be me and Shep in period clothing. But it wasn't. Rosie was probably fifteen or sixteen, the man in his early twenties. This is why she'd taken such a liking to Shep. He's the spitting image of this man. Is this Barnard? Could he be Shep's great grandfather? She looked so happy in the picture. What happened to change that?

There had to be more clues somewhere, something Rosie wanted me to find. These pictures couldn't be the only reason she left her estate to me. There had to be something in the house to explain her reasons, something Mr. S. didn't want me to know. But where was it? I looked around the parlor and dining room. There were so many places to hide things. It'd take a year or more to find anything hidden in this huge house. Is that why she wanted me to stay a full year?

I was tired of sitting on the floor; I needed some exercise. My back and legs ached. Shep wouldn't be through working for another hour. I'd bought steaks and baking potatoes earlier. He was going to continue my cooking instructions on the wood stove tonight. A warm feeling seeped through me.

I made sure the house was locked tight and Shep knew where I was going when Gus and I started across the back yard. There was a nice berm around the fields that made a good running track. At home I was used to running 5 miles a day, and wanted to get back in the habit. I enjoyed going to the gym, but I still wanted to run. A treadmill didn't quite cut it.

Turning on my iPod for accompaniment, we started off. The young man who rented the farm from Rosie was working the far section today. We'd met several times to say hi, but I didn't really know him.

Shep and his men were gone when Gus and I got back to the house. Sweat ran down my face, my shirt and shorts were soaked. The humidity was inching higher each day, making the temperature less comfortable. A shower would be great right now, but I'd have to make do with my usual sponge bath.

Before we reached the back steps, Gus started growling, his fur standing up. *Now what?* He hadn't shown any signs of distress while we were running. Someone had managed to get on the porch while we were gone, someone he didn't know. Cautiously, I went up the steps, keeping watch for someone to jump out at me. A dead rat was on the mat at the door, its head cocked at an impossible angle. "Oh, gross." This was the third time someone had left me little surprises, always at the back of the house, always when Gus was with me. "What am I supposed to do with that?" No one was around to get rid of it for me.

I rolled the mat up with the dead animal inside, and dumped the whole thing in the trash can by the barn. I couldn't picture Walter or Abner Shepard or one of the 'three stooges,' doing this. Even Ed Bodeen, who had taken a dislike to me, didn't seem the type to leave a dead animal on my door step. This was petty, childish. At least the broken flower pot and beheaded doll had seemed childish. A dead rat was stepping it up a notch.

The only other person who came to mind was Deidre Smith. I'd seen her in town several times since that day outside the gym. She'd sent glaring looks at me, but never spoke after that first time. Was this something she'd do?

"Yeah," Shep looked embarrassed when I told him about finding the dead rat. "I had a little surprise at my door, too. I was hopin' she'd leave you alone."

"Okay, one more person who wants me gone." I sighed.

Before I could turn away from him, he gathered me in his arms, kissing the top of my head. "There's one person who really wants you to stay." His blue eyes were serious as he slowly lowered his head, his lips softly brushing mine. "I don't want her to scare you away." His breath was warm on my face.

"Okay." The word came out on a breathy sigh. We were in the kitchen, the steaks sizzling on the wood stove, potatoes buried in the hot coals in the oven. We stayed that way for several long moments until the steaks needed attention. While Shep took care of them I went to get the picture.

"I have something that might help with the hunt for your grandfather's birth place." I handed him the picture.

Confusion drew his dark brows together. "Who...How?" Taking a longer look, his eyes grew large, excitement lighting up his face. "This could be us!" he said softly. "Where did you find it?"

"At the bottom of a box of pictures. This is the only one of Rosie with this man. It's kind of spooky, isn't it?" Seeing your face on a person from a different generation is mind boggling.

He nodded. "I wonder if this is my great granddad." He spoke quietly.

"There are more boxes of pictures down here and in the attic. That note had to have been for Rosie." Why had her father objected to her marrying Barnard? I wondered. How was I ever going to find the answers to all these questions? Milly was my only hope. From what I've learned about Rosie, she would defy her father, and run off with Barnard if she was in love with him.

Shep stayed late, helping me go through more boxes, bringing more down from the attic. But we didn't find any other pictures of the man I was now calling Barnard. It was disappointing, but we felt like we'd made a major discovery.

"We need to keep this picture hidden along with the note," I said as he was getting ready to leave. "I don't want to lose either of them. This could be what Mr. S. doesn't want me to find."

"No one in town thought I looked familiar when I moved here," he said. "If Barnard had lived here, why didn't anyone recognize me? They sure knew you looked like Miss Rosie."

"He and Rosie didn't get married. Maybe something happened to him a long time ago. Memories fade when the person is no longer around. They probably didn't remember him." It was the best explanation either of us could come up with. We lingered at the door, unwilling to say good night. Finally, Gus nudged Shep's leg, whimpering. He was ready for bed, and wanted Shep to leave.

~~~

For the next two days, I scoured the boxes we'd brought down from the attic with no results. I found more pictures of Rosie, even some of me, but none of Barnard. After taking the note and picture to a copy shop in Buena Vista, I opened a safe deposit box at a local bank. I wasn't taking any chances of losing the originals.

Frustrated with the whole situation, I didn't know where to look next. There were still boxes and trunks to go through, and the entire barn was untouched territory. I hadn't even ventured into the basement or root cellar, afraid of the bugs, and whatever else might be lurking in the dark, dank places. Was there even something left to find? Lost in thought, I wasn't aware of the commotion in my own yard until I was stopped by the sheriff's car in the lane.

"Miss Evans, you need to put your dog away before we have to shoot him." Deputy Freckle-face growled at me through the open window.

"Don't you dare shoot him! What's going on here?" I could see Gus had cornered two men in uniform. He was barking furiously, not the least bit intimidated by the guns they held.

"Lock up that dog," he growled again.

Calling to Gus, I stepped out of the Model T. He reluctantly came to me, wanting to guard the deputies. "Okay, I've got Gus. Now tell me what's going on here. If you weren't on my property, Gus wouldn't have gone after your men."

"This is a crime scene." He seemed pleased with that fact. "You need to stay back."

My mouth dropped open, and a smug smile curved his thin lips. "What do you mean a crime scene?" I finally managed to ask. "What happened?"

"A murder!" He was so excited; I thought he might wet his pants. He was actually doing a jig.

Murder?! This is small town America. I didn't think murders happened here.

"Where have you been?"

His question brought me back to the present. "Buena Vista." My mind was still reeling with the possibility of a murder here on the farm.

"What time did you leave?"

"Seven. Am I a suspect?"

"It's your property. What do you think?" He gave me a

mean little smile. He was really enjoying playing the bad cop. I wondered where the good cop was. "Why did you leave so early? The mall doesn't open until ten."

"I didn't go to the mall."

"Where did you go then?" I guess in his life experience women didn't go anywhere except the mall.

"To the gym." I didn't tell him where else I'd been. It was none of his business.

"What for? I thought you ran here at the farm." He seemed confused.

I frowned. "Who told you that?"

"Mr. Shepard."

"And just how would he know what I do?"

"He's your grandfather."

"What's that got to do with the price of tea in China?"

"Huh?"

How dumb is this kid? I wondered. "He has nothing to do with me. Don't believe anything he says about what I do." The fact that Mr. S. knew what I did on a daily basis was disconcerting. It meant he was watching me.

The deputy didn't seem to know what to say about that, so he went back to his script. "Where were you last night about midnight?" These questions were getting annoying, but I had to answer them.

"I was here. Where else would I be?" I wanted to add "in this one horse town," but kept that thought to myself.

"Were you alone?"

"No, Gus was with me."

"I need to talk to him. How do I get in touch with him?" He acted like he had caught me in a major sin.

"He's right here." I patted Gus's head. I almost laughed at the look on the young deputy's face, but this was a serious matter.

"I'll ask you again, were you alone?"

"Of course I was alone. I live here by myself."

"Can you prove that?"

"No, I can't prove I was alone. By definition being alone

means no one was with me to prove I was alone. What part of that concept don't you get?" I couldn't keep the sarcasm out of my voice.

His face turned red, but he pressed on. "I'm going to have to take your dog in."

"You're arresting my dog?!" This kid was getting more ridiculous by the minute.

"Yeah, I mean no! But I have to take him in for tests."

"What kind of tests? What does he have to do with a murder?"

"The 'vic' was killed by a vicious animal." *'Vic?' Was this an episode of "Law and Order"?* "We've had reports that your dog is vicious."

"Who reported that?"

"Mr. Shepard?" He made it sound like he was asking me.

"Gus is only 'vicious,'" I made little air quotes, "when I'm being threatened. Does that tell you something about Mr. Shepard's actions towards me?" I didn't wait for him to figure out an answer. "I'll bring Gus to the sheriff's office, along with his papers proving he's had all his shots. Just tell me when to be there."

The sheriff was at the crime scene for several hours. Before he left I saw the Coroner's van pull away from the field behind the house. Shivers went up my spine. I didn't know who had been killed, and the young deputy wasn't giving out any information. I thought about calling Mr. Meyers, but I wasn't sure what kind of help he'd be. He isn't a criminal lawyer. The fact that he's also the Shepards' lawyer had me holding back. I didn't know whose side he'd be on.

I took Gus to the sheriff's office for any tests they wanted to do. Sheriff Donovan is probably in his late fifties, his light brown hair just turning gray at the temples. At least he looked like he had more experience than his deputy. I hoped he actually did. "Gus doesn't have rabies, and he didn't attack anyone." I sat across from the sheriff with Gus at my feet. He was relaxed, and didn't look like he could kill someone.

"We have to check him out. There have been reports of trouble out at Miss Rosie's place, and you've had a run-in with the victim."

"What? Who is the victim?"

"I can't release that information until we locate the next of kin." It wasn't the answer I was hoping for.

The only "run-in" I'd had was with Mr. S. Was he the victim? My stomach churned. Milly had had enough grief recently, I didn't want any more for her. "Is it Mr. S.?" I whispered. When the sheriff looked confused, I clarified. "Mr. Shepard."

"No. Why would you think that?"

I breathed a sigh of relief. "Because he's the only one I've had a run-in with."

He considered his options for a moment, and then said, "You were seen arguing with a young woman. I believe it was over young Shep Baker? And she's been seen at your place."

"Deidre Smith? She's dead?" My head swirled. Who would do such a thing? "I only talked to her once. What does this have to do with my dog?"

"Preliminary examination at the site looked like she was attacked by a vicious animal. Your dog qualifies."

"Gus isn't vicious. As I explained to...your deputy, Gus will attack only if I'm being threatened."

"He attacked my men, had them cornered."

"Because he was protecting my property!" I exclaimed. "That's his job. I've had trouble since I moved there. I even had your deputy out once. Check with him," I added when he looked doubtful. "He wasn't very interested in taking the report, or following up on it. I had to do something to protect myself." He seemed surprised, but he didn't comment. Maybe the kid would get into trouble over his lack of help. The thought cheered me slightly.

Sheriff Donovan let Gus go home with me. I'd seen enough forensic shows on television to know the Medical Examiner could take an impression of the bites, and compare them to Gus's teeth. He did warn me not to leave the county, with or without Gus.

Shep was at the farm pacing the length of the porch when I

arrived. They hadn't been working here today while they waited for inspectors to come. "What's going on?" Crime scene tape still flapped in the field even though the crime techs were gone.

I pulled out a bag of tortilla chips. It was past lunch, and I was getting tired of cheese and crackers. Nachos and salsa sounded great. It was fast, and I convinced myself the salsa was vegetables, so it was nutritious. While we waited for the cheese to melt in the wood stove, I explained what had happened. Pouring the closest thing I had to salsa over the top, we sat down to our improvised lunch. It was a little early for a glass of wine, but after the morning I'd had, I figured "It was five o'clock somewhere," like the country western song said.

"Deidre is dead?" His face lost all color. "What happened? When?" I told him what little the sheriff had told me. "She was a little on the crazy side, but she didn't deserve to die," he said quietly.

"No, she didn't, but whoever did this wants me blamed for it. If I get arrested, I'll lose the house. I don't want to believe Mr. S. or his brother would do something like this just to get their hands on Rosie's money though."

"Money's a strong motivator," Shep said, repeating my boss's words.

"The sheriff said they had to find her next of kin. I don't think he knows her father lives here. Maybe you should tell him."

With a resigned sigh, he nodded. "He'll probably be around to question me. I'm not sure how much help it will be. I don't know who he is."

"Maybe he's the one who killed her," I suggested. "If he really is a big deal here, he might not want it known he had an illegitimate daughter."

"That's pretty cynical thinkin'. Would someone do that to their own daughter?" He frowned at me.

I gave a grim laugh. "Welcome to big city thinking. People aren't always nice to their children."

~~~

The murder was the talk of the town. And all that talk swirled around me. I wasn't just the ghost of Rosie Shepard come back to haunt them, now I was possibly a murderer. Just walking down the street was a challenge. People stepped off the sidewalk to avoid crossing my path. I guess they figured a homicidal maniac would do just about anything.

Most people wanted to avoid me, but not Ed Bodeen. As he's done before, he stopped in the middle of the sidewalk, blocking my way. "It's about time you go back where you came from, little lady," he growled at me. "You've caused enough trouble for our little town. Your mama wanted nothing to do with us. She shoulda kept you out west where you belong." The venom in his eyes was staggering. What had I done to him?

"Keep walking, Bodeen, she's not going anywhere." I don't know where Sheriff Donovan came from, but I was grateful for his presence.

"That pretty young thing is dead 'cuz of her," Bodeen argued. "She should be locked up."

"I thought you wanted her to leave town. Which is it, locked up or run out of town?"

Ed Bodeen's face got red; his hands fisted at his sides. "Doesn't matter which. Just so she's gone."

"I can't help but wonder why you care so much, Ed. What was Miss Smith to you? Why do you want Miss Evans gone so badly?"

"She was nothing to me. I...I didn't even know that girl!"

"Hmmm." A thoughtful look filled the sheriff's eyes but he said nothing else.

Ed Bodeen pushed his way between us without another word, stomping down the sidewalk.

"You've made a powerful enemy there, Miss Evans." He eyed me with a speculative gleam. "Can't help but wonder why."

"I didn't do anything to him!" I protested.

He raised his broad shoulders. "Doesn't matter. He's still an enemy. You be careful now, Miss." He ambled off without another word.

What am I supposed to make of that? Does he think I had something to do with Deidre's death? Or is he on my side? The sheriff was definitely an enigma.

CHAPTER ELEVEN

Not wanting another run-in with Ed Bodeen, I went into town as little as possible. I wanted to show someone the picture of Rosie and the man, but I didn't know who. Milly still hadn't come to see me. Was she busy after her sister's death, or was it something else? Since the murder I felt certain Mr. S. would try hard to keep her away from me. I still believed she had little say in what happened in her own home or what she did.

While sorting through things in the house, I knocked on walls, moved picture frames, and pulled knobs looking for another hiding place. There had to be something here to give me a clue who the man was, and what happened to him. She'd waited for *me* to do the remodeling. The only explanation I came up with was she hid something she didn't want anyone else to find? But where?

I was back in the attic going through more boxes and trunks. Eventually I would need to have the antiques appraised. Retro was in style; there was a demand for old clothes in good condition. These were in pristine condition.

A small steamer trunk sat in a dark corner of the attic. With the help of the lantern, I could see a shiny new padlock in the old fashioned hasp. There hadn't been padlocks on the other trunks. My heart skipped a beat. This had to be what I've been looking for! She couldn't just tell Mr. Meyers where I should look for this? She had to make it a game? I hope she's laughing now.

The key ring Mr. Meyers had given me that first day held a small key. I hadn't found anything it fit. Until now. I ran downstairs for my keys, and back up the long staircase. Taking a calming breath, I inserted the small key into the lock, saying a silent prayer it would open. "Yes!" I did a fist pump when the lock popped open. With another steadying breath, I lifted the heavy lid.

In the dim light from the lantern, I could see a few more pictures and dozens of small books that looked like diaries or journals. "Oh boy," I breathed. "This is it." A single sheet of paper was lying on top. With shaking hands I picked it up. The wavy writing was hard to read in the faint light.

Downstairs again, I took the note to the porch, sitting down on my favorite wicker rocker. "Okay, stop stalling," I told myself. "This is what you've been looking for." The note was from Rosie.

Hello Parker,

You don't know me, but I know all about you. You are my legacy. I hope you didn't find this note too early in your search for the truth. You need to get to know Shep, to come to love him and this house as much as I do, and to meet your nice relatives. Yes, there are a few of them. Don't let the rest scare you off.

I know I'm dying, but no one else knows, and that's the way I'm going to keep it. Those blood suckers would descend on me like a pack of jackals if they knew. They want everything I have because they think they have the right. But after what they took away from me, what they've done, they don't have any rights. They get nothing.

If you decide not to stay, not to look, you aren't the person I thought you were. Someone else will reap what's mine. I could have told you this up front. I took a chance, but I had to make sure about you. If you're reading this, I know I chose wisely. Everything that was mine is now yours. Look closely at everything before you throw any of it away. Some things aren't what they seem on first inspection.

I could just tell you what I want you to do, what I want you to find, but where is the fun in that? Consider this a treasure hunt. I know how much you enjoy a challenge.

Your mother was very much like me when I was young. She stood up to that tyrant of a father when he tried to force her into a loveless marriage, twice. I tried, but in my day women didn't have the same choices she had.

When she left here, I tried to watch over her. I was too late to stop what happened to your father. You need to find out who thought they would benefit from your father's death. When I saw you for the first time, I knew you were the one to right the old wrongs. You grew up strong and stubborn. Good for you!

Beware of that miserable Meyers. He isn't all he pretends to be. Don't believe half of what he says. I've left a few surprises for him, too. I wish I could be there to see all their faces when the truth comes out, but then you wouldn't be here.

Shep is a part of this; learn to rely on him while still standing on your own.

Good luck, Parker. I'll be watching over you from the other side. Forever.

Your great-aunt Rosie

I wasn't aware I was crying until a tear ran down my face, plopping on the back of my hand. I carefully set the note aside, wiping my face. I didn't want to smear the ink on the note. I reread it, hoping to figure out exactly what 'truth' she wanted me to find. What had been taken away from her? I'd fantasized about her and Barnard being in love, but something had happened to him. Was he in an accident; or did something more sinister happen to him? What did she mean about someone benefiting from my dad's death? What did she know? "Why didn't she just tell me? Crap!" The answers had to be in the trunk.

Shep had gone home to shower, and wouldn't be back for another half hour. We hadn't altered our habits after Deidre's death. That smacked too much of guilt. We hadn't killed her, and I didn't want to give the townsfolk or the police any reason to think we had.

As though my thoughts had conjured him up, Sheriff Donovan's car pulled into the lane. "Ah, crap," I whispered again. My face was dirt streaked and sweaty, added to that, my recent tears probably left trails down my face. Thankfully my hair was covered with a bandana, so it wasn't bushed out around my head. Well, this isn't a social call, I told myself.

"Evening, Miss Evans." He touched the brim of his hat.

"Sheriff." I didn't have a hat to tip, but I nodded.

"Thought you'd like to know your dog didn't kill Miss Smith."

"Already knew that." His curt, staccato sentences were catching.

He raised an eyebrow but didn't comment. "Seems someone dumped her body in your field after she was dead, used something to make it look like an animal had mauled her."

"To frame me." It was a statement, not a question.

"Thought did cross my mind. Got any enemies?" Just the day before he'd told me Ed Bodeen was my enemy. Had he forgotten, or was he fishing for information?

"Quite a few as a matter of fact, but none I want to believe would try to frame me by murdering an innocent woman."

"You think of anyone, be sure to let me know."

"Were you able to find her next of kin?"

"Seems her mother recently passed on; found a telephone number for an aunt. She won't be coming for the body. Just wants it sent to Chicago." His tone was disapproving. Maybe the woman hadn't approved of Deidre's quest.

He didn't say if he knew about Deidre's father. Shep needed to be the one to tell him, not me.

He turned to his car as Shep pulled into the lane. Waiting for him to step out, the sheriff nodded. "Baker, nice of you to drop by. I was just on my way to talk to you." My stomach did a flip flop. He wouldn't try to blame Shep for what happened to Deidre, would he? "Where were you the other night when Miss Smith was getting herself killed?" *What a way to put it,* I thought. She didn't do it on purpose.

I was here with Miss Evans until about nine. Then I went home. I was there the rest of the night."

"Got anyone who can verify that?"

"Matter of fact I do." My head shot around, and I stared at him. Did he have someone living with him, and he forgot to tell me? "I live out on Old Mill Road in the newer part of town. New doesn't always mean better. I've been workin' on that house ever since I made the mistake of buyin' it."

The sheriff scratched his head below his large hat. "Always wondered why a contractor would buy one of those cra..." he looked at me, "sorry ma'am, poorly built houses." The sheriff apologized for almost using a word I used all too often.

The little lopsided grin I found so sexy played around Shep's mouth. "I've wondered that myself a time or two. I wanted to put down roots. I'm not much on rentin', so I bought that place. I've been regrettin' it ever since. Those houses were ready to fall down right after bein' put up. Too bad nobody made Bodeen fix them." So that's why Ed Bodeen doesn't like Shep. He doesn't like the competition, and didn't want Shep bad mouthing his work.

"So who can prove you were home?" The sheriff brought the subject back on track.

"Miz Jenkins lives next door. She's a real night owl, says she can't sleep, so she sits outside most nights 'til midnight or so. When I'm workin' on the house, she comes over to 'keep me company' she says. I think she's just lonely. Seldom see her kids or grandkids come visit her." His alibi was an elderly woman! I released the breath I hadn't been aware I was holding. "She always has a project or two she needs help with," he continued. "We sat on the porch eatin' sweet rolls she'd made. It musta been one o'clock by the time I got to bed. Give me enough of an alibi?" He cocked his head.

Sheriff Donovan waited several beats then gave a curt nod. "You folks have a nice evening." He turned to leave, but Shep's next question stopped him in his tracks.

"You find her daddy here in town?"

He frowned at Shep. "Didn't know she had family in town."

"She came here to find him, said she'd just learned who he was. Never said who though, just that he was someone important. Can't say for sure how much truth there was in it though."

The sheriff swore under his breath, and turned back to his car again without another word.

"He didn't seem too happy about that information. Guess he won't be checkin' with Miz Jenkins about my alibi tonight. He here lookin' for me?" He leaned over, giving me a lingering kiss.

My brain turned to mush, and it took several seconds to collect my scattered thoughts. "No. He told me Gus didn't kill Deidre." I told him what little the sheriff had said before he arrived.

"Can't see either of the Shepards doin' somethin' like that, but you never know what people will do for money. Maybe he'll find out who her father was."

"Maybe her father killed her if she threatened to tell people," I whispered, a shiver traveling through me. I'd never been in the middle of a murder investigation before. "What do you want to eat tonight?" I asked, changing the subject. I was getting tired of thinking in circles. "It's slim pickin's around here tonight. I haven't been to town for a few days." His drawl was catching. I could hear it in my voice more every day.

"Let's head on to A Cup-A-Joe. Today's Friday, meatloaf night, and Billy makes the best."

"I can't go looking like this. Sheriff Donovan came over before I got cleaned up."

"You look good enough to eat just the way you are." He pulled me out of the rocker, and into his arms.

"Get your hands off my granddaughter! No one's going to take a bite out of her, especially you." Mr. S. walked around the corner of the house.

Gus's sharp bark and Mr. S.'s angry voice startled us, and I gave a little yelp. Gus continued to growl a warning for Mr. S. not to come any closer.

Shep kept his arms around my waist. "Evening, Mr. Shepard. You lose something around here?"

"You need to get off my property, and stay away from my granddaughter."

"This isn't your property, and I'm *not* your granddaughter. I want you to leave. Now!"

"You're still my granddaughter, and I won't have you making a spectacle of yourself for anyone driving by to see."

"It would take more than blood to make you my grandfather. You either leave now, or I'll call the sheriff. I'm sure he hasn't gone very far since he just left. But you already know that since you were lurking around the corner. If you come here again, I'll call the sheriff immediately. That goes for your sons and brother also. None of you are welcome here."

"You're just like Rosie," he growled. "She always was a mean one!"

"I'll take that as a compliment since she stood up to the likes of you. Whatever Rosie was, her family made her that way. Now slither back into the hole you crawled out of, and stay away from me and this farm." I pulled my cell phone out of my pocket, ready to call the sheriff if he didn't leave.

He turned back the way he'd come, grumbling under his breath.

I sat down, my legs suddenly rubbery. "This just keeps getting worse."

Shep knelt down in front of me, rubbing my arms. One thing I liked about him, one of the many things, he let me fight my own battles, but stayed right there in case I needed help.

"I'm all right." Confrontation wasn't my strong suit. I'd rather life ran smoothly. When it didn't, my head spun and my heart raced out of control. But today I did pretty well. That man brought out the worst in me.

Silently congratulating myself on standing up to that miserable man, I got up. "Give me a few minutes to wash up then we can get something to eat." I splashed cold water on my face and arms in the kitchen, and raced upstairs. I couldn't go to town looking like a refugee. There were too many people ready and willing to tear me down the first chance they had. At least I'd be presentable.

Ten minutes later we were in Shep's truck, Gus sitting between us. He enjoyed going to town even if he couldn't go into the stores or cafe. "Oh, wait a minute! I need to show you something." I jumped out of the truck, and ran back to the house for the letter from Rosie.

While Shep drove, I read the letter. "What do you think she meant by someone benefiting from my dad's death? What does that have to do with any of this?"

"Miss Rosie had to know more than she was sayin' in that letter.

"Mom never believed the crash was an accident. She said Dad was a careful driver, and he wouldn't take those curves too fast. The police wouldn't listen to her. Road rage wasn't something that happened much back then.

The small parking lot beside of A Cup-A-Joe was full, and we had to park nearly a block away. We rolled the windows far enough down so Gus couldn't get out, but would still have air. At home, leaving a dog in a vehicle could mean death for the dog, especially this time of year. But it wasn't that hot here. Gus pushed his snout out of the opening, sniffing all the different scents. His sharp bark brought me around in time to see Ed Bodeen standing beside Shep's truck.

"Don't touch him if you value your fingers," I warned. "He knows you aren't a friend."

"He's as dangerous as his owner," Ed Bodeen snapped at me. "The sheriff made a big mistake by not putting that cur down after he killed that poor girl."

Shep started to say something, but I put my hand on his arm to stop him. "Gus didn't kill Deidre Smith. You can check with the sheriff. Someone wanted to frame me. I wonder who wants to get rid of me bad enough to do something like that. Can you think of anyone?" I was baiting him, but maybe if he got mad enough, he'd let something slip.

His face turned red, his hands curled into fists. Shep took a step forward, and Gus was having a fit in the truck. Bodeen seemed to think better of trying something, and backed away. "Bitch. You'd better watch yourself. Bad things have been happening since you came to town." He shoved past me, and I sagged against Shep. Several people were standing around watching the spectacle. I'd been giving the town something to talk about ever since I arrived. It didn't look like it was going to let up anytime soon.

Shep nodded to several people, touching the brim of his

Stetson, but didn't stop to visit as we made our way to A Cup-A-Joe. I didn't think any of them wanted to talk to me anyway.

"Each encounter with that man gets a little worse," I told Shep and Mary Lou a few minutes later. In the time it took us to walk to the cafe, she'd already heard what happened. "What did I do to that guy? He really hates me."

"His daddy and Walter Shepard hatched the plan that your mama would marry Young Ed and combine their farms. That would've given them more land than anyone else around here, even Rosie. That was very important to both men."

"It doesn't seem to have stopped Bodeen from makin' big on his own," Shep said. "So what's his beef with Parker? She didn't have anything to do with that."

Mary Lou shrugged, "Not many people stand up to him, and he doesn't like it when they do, especially a woman." She looked pointedly at the people sitting at the tables and booths, clearly saying they shouldn't let Bodeen walk all over them. Several people dipped their heads, pretending to concentrate on their food.

"You need to be careful out there by yourself," Billy called from the kitchen. "Bodeen can be dangerous when he's riled."

Had Bodeen killed Deidre? I kept that thought to myself. The cafe was full, no telling if someone would run to Ed with anything I said.

"Gus will protect me," I said. Bodeen probably already knew about the spotlight since someone had tripped it once. I didn't think he'd try something out front. Was that why Deidre's body had been left in the field behind the house? There were no lights back there.

~~~

By the time we headed back to the farm, light was fading fast. I still wanted to go through the steamer trunk with the journals. That's where Rosie left her letter to me so I figured that's where I'd find some answers. Shep carried the trunk down from the attic so we could sort through the small books in comfort.

"How about we start fresh in the mornin'?" he suggested. "It's a beautiful evening. Feel like goin' for a walk?" He took my hand, pulling me to my feet, wrapping his arms around me the way he had before Mr. S. interrupted us.

"Sounds wonderful." My voice was breathless, my heart beating so loud he could hear it. Hand in hand, we walked down the lane, Gus following close by my side. Lightening bugs flickered around us, adding to my delight and enjoyment. We don't have them in Arizona.

By the time we got back to the farm it was fully dark. We snuggled on the large porch swing, talking very little. I felt like I was floating up the big staircase to bed when he left. I was definitely in over my head where he was concerned. It's hard to believe I'd known him only a few weeks.

~~~

Shep showed up bright and early the next morning, complete with breakfast from A Cup-A-Joe. "Do you eat every meal out?" I laughed. "I thought you knew how to cook."

"Only on a wood stove, Darlin'," he teased. "I have gas at my house." He spread out breakfast on the porch table. There was enough food to feed an army. "Are you planning on company? Or were you just really hungry this morning?"

"What we don't eat now, we can keep warm in the oven. That's the good thing about a wood stove. It always stays warm."

"It keeps the kitchen warm, too. *All* day. It's the warmest room in the house."

"Didn't your mama teach you the kitchen is the heart of any home? It has to be warm and welcoming."

The easy banter continued while we ate and cleared the table. "Want to get started?" He pointed at the trunk in the parlor.

I wanted to find the last journal Rosie wrote and go backwards. It would give me some answers, but in reality, what made her do the things she did started many years ago. "I guess we start at the beginning." Picking up the book I'd brought down with the letter yesterday, I checked the dates. "Looks like she even arranged these the way she wanted me to read them. It's probably the first one she wrote. The woman was definitely manipulative."

The words were faded and difficult to read in spots, but even when she first learned to print she had good penmanship. Her demanding father probably wouldn't have it any other way. The stories of her life on the farm were humorous; it didn't take much imagination to picture the way it had been back then. With a more encouraging parent, she might have become an author.

What wasn't humorous was her description of her father. No one questioned his decisions. *"Papa wouldn't let me go swimming with my brothers today."* she wrote one day when she was around eight. *"They get to do fun things, but I have to stay here with mama. He said girls have to take care of the house. Yuk!"* The entry for the next day was painful to read. *"I sneaked out of the house today, and went down to the mill pond. The boys do it all the time. Papa caught me. He whooped me good. I just wanted to have fun, too. Next time I'll be more careful."* Even at eight she was willful and learning to be sneaky. I felt so sorry for the little girl she'd been I wanted to cry.

Another entry just made me mad. *"Effie brought over her new kitten. It was so cute, no bigger than a handful of dandelion fluff. I wish I had a pet, but papa says animals don't belong in the house. Besides we have enough animals on the farm. I can't play with those. Papa makes me stay in the house and cook and clean. Mama's been sick again. I have to take care of her. I don't mind, really. Mama's nice to me, and I love her. I just wish she would get well. Papa says that's because I'm selfish, I'm just thinking of myself. But that's not true. I don't think Papa loves her or me. I'm not any better than those slaves before the Civil War. Papa treats me like the slave owners treated them. If I do something wrong or something he doesn't like, he whoops me. Maybe I should run away like the slaves did.*

"That man was a monster!" I didn't realize I'd spoken loud enough for Shep to hear while he worked a few feet away in the yard until he looked up questioningly. "Rosie's father," I clarified. "He beat her, and used her as a slave. That's what she called herself, a slave." Shep had been reading the journals, but had given up, preferring to work in the flower beds.

After several hours, I stretched, rubbing my tired eyes. "I can't believe she wrote so many journals! It was probably the only way she had to let her feelings out. It's going to take weeks, maybe months, to read all of them." I sounded discouraged. I wanted answers now, not weeks down the road.

"Let's do something this afternoon," I suggested. As bad as I wanted answers, I didn't want to stay cooped up any more than Rosie had at eight. The weather was beautiful; the humidity hadn't started in earnest yet. "We can't stay in the house all weekend."

We left Gus to guard and patrol when we left. I wasn't taking chances with the journals. If someone came near the house, Gus would chase them off. I didn't trust Mr. S. or Ed Bodeen.

Ted, the young man who farmed Rosie's land, was working in the fields. I could hear the roar of his tractor. Farming was hard work, not nine to five, five days a week. His wife, Julia, had been the one to help Rosie around the house and garden. Maybe after all the work was done, she could help me. If I decide to stay here, I qualified. If Mr. Meyers knew about the arrangement Rosie had with them, he never said anything to me. I don't know if he thought I would leave if I had to take care of this huge house all by myself. I still couldn't decide whose side he was on.

CHAPTER TWELVE

Sunday I was hoping Milly would be at church. It had been almost two weeks since I'd seen her at her sister's funeral. I wasn't privileged to the town gossip grapevine, so I wasn't sure if she was still in Buena Vista. Would Mr. S. keep her from going to church if he thought I'd be there?

The journals gave me insight into his upbringing. He felt it was his right to dictate to all those around him, especially women. Someone raised by a tyrant usually becomes one himself. Mr. S. certainly fit the mold.

"Good morning, Miss Evans, Shep," Pastor Jim greeted us. "I was sorry to hear about the trouble out at your place earlier this week." He took my hand. "It's a terrible thing."

"Yes, it is. Please, call me Parker. Have you seen Milly today? Or this week?" Not many people had arrived yet.

Before he could answer, Miss Effie joined us giving me a hug. "I'm so glad you're here. Milly will be glad to see you. I know she was planning on coming today. Everyone heard about the trouble out at your place this week. It's just terrible." She was like a small bird, fluttering her hands in the air, talking rapidly.

I was tired of being the talk of the town, but murder is a big thing in a small town.

Gratefully, Milly arrived a few minutes later. She looked tired. My heart went out to her. If Mr. S. treated her similar to the way Rosie had been treated, I could only wonder why she'd put up with it all these years. People in a small town wouldn't condone abuse, would they?

She was preoccupied until she saw me. Her smile lit up her face. "Parker, I'm so sorry about what happened at the farm. I didn't know that poor girl, but it's a shame. Do they know who did it?" She appeared so fragile when she gave me a hug. She was a tiny woman, and it seemed like she'd lost weight since I'd last seen her.

Pastor Jim ushered us into his study, so we could visit without the prying eyes of the others as they began to enter the small vestibule. "Are you okay, Grandma? You look tired."

Her smile was sad. "It's been hard. Betsy and I were close. We didn't have any other family. Now she's gone." Tears sparkled in her faded blue eyes.

When the organ began playing we went into the sanctuary. Shep was waiting just inside for us. Milly was distracted, not paying attention to the message. She kept patting my hand, watching Shep closely.

After the last hymn, we filed out with the others. She whispered to me, "Does he treat you well? Don't let him hurt you."

I was so surprised I couldn't immediately answer. "Shep would never hurt me." I finally managed. "Grandma, he's a good man."

"You haven't known him long. Take your time. Rosie was very fond of him, but I'm not sure how good a judge she was."

"I have so many questions about Rosie and everything. Can you come to the house?"

"Not today, dear. They're waiting for me to make dinner."

"Can't someone else do it? You need to rest."

She gave a little laugh. "No one else can boil water let alone make a full meal. I guess I should have taught those boys how to cook. But that's woman's work." Her tone was derisive.

"Will Mr. S. let you come over?" She'd scoffed at the idea when I'd asked her before. Today she didn't.

"He won't stop me, dear." I wasn't sure why she was so certain, but I didn't question her. She seemed in a hurry to go home. Maybe she did have to cook a large meal right away. If her sons and their families came over for Sunday dinner, someone should help her.

~~~

Monday morning I decided it was time to go to the gym again. I needed a good work out and a hot shower. I could stand cold sponge baths for just so long. I also needed to copy the letter from Rosie, and put the original in the safe deposit box.

I was feeling good and loose from the work out, and squeaky clean when I turned into the lane at the house. Exercise always improved my mood. That mood evaporated quickly. Two vehicles were parked in front of the house. I recognized Milly's car. The other was unmistakably Mr. S.'s truck. I immediately saw red. How dare he! He was just getting out; Milly was standing on the porch with Shep. I could hear Gus barking. Shep had wisely kept him inside.

Mr. S. was so intent on Milly he didn't even realize I was there when I quietly got out of the Model T. "What the hell are you doing here, woman?" he yelled at her. "You said you were going to Buena Vista."

Her chin rose, her shoulders thrown back defiantly. "I lied." I almost laughed out loud.

"I told you to stay away from her."

"And I told you next time you came on my property I was calling the sheriff." Startled, he whirled around to face me. "He's on his way. I can and I will have you arrested for trespassing." I kept his truck between us. He was so angry he was shaking, and I wasn't sure what he'd do if he got his hands on me.

"This is my family's farm. You can't stop me from coming here."

"Yes I can. It's mine now. As you well know, Rosie left it to me."

"Not for a year, it's not yours!"

"You will *never* get your hands on this farm," I said, a mean little smile curving my lips. "But you can take comfort in the fact it's still in the family. After all, we are blood related as you reminded me the other night. Now unless you want to be arrested, I suggest you leave."

He turned back to Milly. "Get in the car. We're going home."

"I'm going to stay and get to know my granddaughter. I've

114

missed too much of her life already. I'm not going to miss the rest of it"

Turning red in the face, he threw himself into the truck, slamming the door. "Then don't bother coming home," he growled at her through the open window. "Stay with your precious granddaughter!" Gravel spun under his tires as he sped down the drive.

When he was gone, I rushed up the steps and hugged her. "Oh, Grandma, I'm so sorry. I didn't mean for this to happen."

"It's about time I stood up to him. He wasn't always like that, you know. The older he gets the more he's like his daddy. That man was as mean as a snake."

Gus had settled down inside since Mr. S. left. Now he was whining to get to me. When Shep opened the door, Gus immediately sniffed Milly's feet, looking up at me for a sign. I patted his head. "Friend, Gus, friend." His tail wagged as he waited for her to pat him.

Shep put down the heavy wrench he'd been holding as a weapon. Mr. S had been insanely angry. "Are you all right?" He rubbed my arm; a concerned frown wrinkled his brow. "Maybe you should call the sheriff. Let him know he doesn't need to come now."

"Oh, I didn't call him." I gave them a sheepish smile. "I was bluffing. I'm not sure Sheriff Donovan would even send someone out for trespassing."

Milly laughed, "Well, your bluff worked. I know Walter wouldn't take kindly to being arrested by one of Bill Donovan's young deputies."

Shep went back to work on my plumbing while Milly and I settled in the front parlor with the last of the cold lemonade. The ice was almost gone in the ice box. Buena Vista was just far enough away that all I'd have is a puddle of water instead of ice if I bought it there. An ice chest would help with my transport problems.

"What do you think she meant? What am I supposed to find?" I showed Milly the copy of the letter Rosie left me. I didn't mention the journals.

She reread the letter, shaking her head. "Rosie always was

a puzzle. At school she was like all the other girls, laughing, giggling, and playing until one of her brothers came near. Then she became quiet, withdrawn. She was like two different people. They didn't want her to have fun. Her mother was sick a lot, and she had to stay home to take care of her. She tried to keep up with the school work, but her father just gave her more housework to do. She said once that if she had enough time on her hands for school, she could do more work around the house. After her mother passed away, it was very hard on her. She was so young when that happened.

"Did she ever have a boyfriend?"

Milly laughed. "Oh, heavens no! Elmore Shepard would have skinned any boy alive just for looking at his little girl. To the best of my recollection, he wanted her to marry someone, but I never heard what happened with that or who it was." She was quiet for a minute. "I guess that's where Walter got the idea to marry Laura off to that odious Young Ed Bodeen. Walter and Old Ed had been friends for years. They always wanted more of everything, didn't matter what. Nothing was ever enough for either of them."

"Did you ever know anyone around here named Barnard?" Mary Lou's parents hadn't remembered anyone by that name.

She thought for several minutes, and then shook her head. "I don't think so. Why? Who's that?"

"Abner didn't tell Mr. S. that I was asking about someone by that name?"

"We don't get along; he wouldn't say anything around me. He's as mean as his father ever thought of being."

I showed her the copy of the note I'd found in the newel post. "A secret assignation? Running away to get married?" She shook her head. "This could only have been meant for Rosie. She was the only female in the house after her mother died. But I don't know of any Barnard."

"Miss Effie said when Rosie was about fifteen, she changed, became mean and demanding. The rest of the family was almost afraid of her. Do you know why?"

"She was mean for so long I'd forgotten all about that. I

don't remember when it started." She thought for a minute. "When we were in high school, Elmore sent Rosie to a finishing school for a year. He said she needed to learn 'deportment,' whatever that is. She was never quite right after that."

"I think maybe she had a baby during that time. Maybe that's what they're hiding." That would explain the room in the attic. "I think she was kept here," I said excitedly. Had I finally found one answer? "I need to show you something in the attic." Rosie being sent away to "finishing school" for a year struck me as funny. I was willing to bet she'd been here all along. I told her about the picture of Rosie with a man who looked enough like Shep to be his brother. "Shep's grandfather was adopted. I think he was Rosie and Barnard's baby." I was reaching; I couldn't come up with any other explanation for the room, the picture, and Rosie telling me to 'trust Shep, he's a part of this.'

She stared at the room-like enclosure. "What is this?"

I shrugged. "I found it just like this; like someone lived up here. Rosie kept it like this." I opened several of the drawers to show her the clothes still in them.

With an indrawn breath, she picked up a blouse that was folded neatly in one drawer. "Effie gave this to Rosie for her birthday one year. She had to hide it from her father because he thought it was frivolous to have birthday parties. Why is it here?"

I could only shake my head. More questions with no answers, I sighed. Would I ever find the answers, or were they lost in time?

"What do you think Rosie meant about my dad? Who here would benefit from his death?"

"There's no telling what she meant." She shook her head. "Walter was still hoping Laura would marry Young Ed when she came back. I tried to tell him, but he was never big on listening to anyone else, especially me."

I hesitated for a moment. Did Walter have something to do with Dad's death? Would he do such a thing just so Mom would marry Ed Bodeen? How do I pose that question to

Milly? Did Deidre's murder fit in with any of this?

Hours later, a horn sounded at the end of the lane, and Gus ran to the front door, barking like the hounds of hell were outside. Charlie was standing beside his truck. Every few seconds he honked the horn.

Shep came in from the back of the house where he had been working. "What's goin' on?" He was holding the heavy wrench again.

"It's Charlie. He isn't on my property."

We went out on the porch, and Charlie stopped honking. "Are you coming home, Ma? Pa said you've had your little fit. It's time for you to come home." He sounded so pitiful, like a little boy who just lost his puppy. "We're hungry, Ma."

"I know, Charlie. You tell your Pa that before I come home he's going to have to do a whole lot of changing. I'm sorry you got caught in the middle of this."

Even from this distance we could see the color drain from his face and he gulped. "I really have to say *that* to Pa? He ain't going to like it."

"I know. And again, I'm sorry," Milly repeated. "You just tell him. Don't go getting too close when you say it."

Reluctantly, he got back in his truck and drove away. "Charlie is sweet and gentle, like your mother," she said quietly, "but without the back bone and stubbornness that kept her fighting. He just lets his Pa walk all over him. I wish Betty hadn't backed out of the wedding. She would have been good for him. He's never tried to find someone else."

I wasn't sure whether Mom or Charlie was older. It wasn't too late for him to make the break from his father, and find someone who could make him happy.

Inside, Milly picked up her purse. "It's getting late and you two young people are going to want to go somewhere to eat."

"You can't go back to him! He'll never let you leave again." Fear colored my words.

"Oh, I'm not going home, dear. My sister's boys have been after me to stay with Betsy since she lost her husband about eight years ago. They knew what Walter was like, and hoped I could get away from him. I just never had the backbone to do anything like that before. After Betsy passed, they said they wouldn't sell the house in case I ever needed a place to stay. They care more about me than two of my own." Her voice was so sad; I wanted to cry for her.

"You don't have to go to Buena Vista. You can stay here with me."

She appeared to consider that, but finally shook her head. "That would make things worse for you. Walter would try even harder to make you leave."

"He doesn't know me very well," I muttered under my breath

~~~

First thing the next morning Mr. Meyers paid me a visit. We'd had very little contact since those first few days. He put money in an account for my "allowance," and I gave him any bills I had from Buena Vista or Bentonville. The stores in town sent him any bills I ran up there. I could get used to this. I suppose he'd heard about Milly and Mr. S.'s little dispute on my front lawn since he was their lawyer as well. Was he here looking for Milly?

"Hello." I stepped outside instead of inviting him in. Instinct told me it wasn't a good idea to let him see the journals. "It's such a lovely day. How about joining me for a glass of lemonade here on the porch? What can I do for you today?" I asked when he declined my offer. He seemed more uncomfortable than usual.

"I thought I should let you know Walter and Abner Shepard are contesting Rosie's will."

This didn't come as a surprise, just that it had taken them this long to do it. "On what grounds?" I raised one eyebrow and stared at him.

"Incompetency."

I laughed. "And you agree with them?"

He shuffled his feet. "Well..."

"You haven't advised them against it?"

119

"What do you mean?" he asked indignantly. "I have nothing to do with it."

"You didn't draw up the lawsuit?" He looked down at his shoes and didn't answer. "It sounds like a conflict of interest to me."

He blanched a little, but tried to put on an innocent face. "I don't know what you mean, Miss Evans." He couldn't quite meet my eyes when he said it.

"You know precisely what I mean, but I'll spell it out for you. You were Rosie's attorney. By extension, you're now my attorney. You are also Walter Shepard's attorney. I assume you're Abner Shepard's attorney as well. That makes this a conflict of interest if you continue representing them and me. I might not be a licensed paralegal here, but I'm still aware of the law. You can't represent both parties in a lawsuit."

He didn't have a ready answer so I continued. "You know Rosie wasn't incompetent when she made her will, a little eccentric but not incompetent. I'm assuming you didn't tell them about it at the time it was drawn up, or they would have tried to stop her then. I suggest you continue to keep your own counsel, and not pass information to them, or I will have you before the Ethics Board in a heartbeat."

He drew himself up to his full height, and looked down his thin nose at me. "Is that a threat, Miss Evans?"

"Nope, a promise. If you give out confidential information on a client, that is a breach of ethics. You can be censored and maybe even disbarred. You're not a stupid man, so don't do something stupid." I let the silence stretch out.

He finally sighed and seemed to crumple in on himself. "What exactly do you expect me to do? The Shepards have been my clients for many years and my father's before that."

"In that case, I'll take my business elsewhere, and you can continue to represent the Shepards."

"No, you can't do that!"

"Why not? Was there a provision in the will that I couldn't change attorneys?" Was he afraid of losing the hefty retainer he received from Rosie's estate, or was there some other reason he didn't want me to move my business?

"Ah...well, no. My father and I handled Rosie's business since before her father passed away. It would be very difficult for someone else to step in at this juncture."

In other words it is all about the money. "Then I suggest you talk the Shepard brothers out of going forward with this. You know as well as I do they don't have a leg to stand on. Rosie was NOT incompetent."

"How do you know? You didn't even know her." He found a little backbone for just a moment.

"That's right I didn't. But you did. If she was incompetent, why did you allow her to draw up that will? Why did you let me come here? I've been living here for a month now. If she'd been incompetent, you should have done something before this. Did you suggest they contest the will?"

"Of course not! That would be unethical!"

"You mean like representing both parties in a lawsuit?" I had him and he knew it. He either convinced them to drop this, or he'd lose me as a client and risk going before the Ethics Board. I'm not sure what he received from the Shepard brothers or how big their estates were, but he probably didn't want to lose that either. He was going to have to figure out a way to satisfy both of us, and stay out of trouble himself.

"I'll do my best," he finally said, turning to leave. He looked like a beaten man. The Shepards couldn't be his only clients, maybe his biggest, but not his only.

That's his problem. That's what happens when you try to play both ends against the middle. Did he also represent Ed Bodeen? My stomach churned nervously. Walter and Abner Shepard might be nasty old men and possibly dangerous, but Ed Bodeen was definitely dangerous. I knew that in every fiber of my being.

After Mr. Meyers left, I paced around the house, unable to settle, playing the "what if" game. What if he did represent Ed Bodeen? What exactly would that mean to me? What if Walter and Abner Shepard continued to contest Rosie's will? What if Mr. Meyers tried to represent both sides? What if? What if? What if? I could go on forever. The journals had to hold all, or most of the answers. Reading through them was taking a lot longer than I wanted.

What if they made me move out while the courts decided if Rosie was competent when the will was drawn up? I would automatically lose the farm. They'd win without going to court. They could go through the house without anyone censoring what they took, they'd destroy the journals. The sheriff had Shep come out, and add padlocks on the house after Rosie passed on. Was that to keep Walter and Abner out? Did he suspect they'd empty the house of anything valuable before I got here?

My jumbled thoughts were getting me nowhere. I had to get out of the house for a while. First I had to protect the journals.

The ones I'd already read, I loaded into my gym bag. I'd take them to the safe deposit box in Buena Vista. The others I took to the root cellar. I couldn't be certain a fire wouldn't reach the root cellar since I'd never seen one before, but it seemed safer than leaving them in the parlor or attic.

I told Shep where I was going, and left Gus to guard the house. They were working in the basement now, bringing in water lines and whatever else was necessary for indoor plumbing. Running water was not too far off. Full bathrooms and electricity would take a little longer.

Summer was in full swing, and the humidity was here in earnest. Even with the windows down, I was hot and sweaty when I arrived at the bank. A shower at the gym wasn't going to do much good since I still had to drive back to the farm in the Model T. I missed my Jeep.

I'd called Mom last night after Milly left. She was relieved Milly had finally left Mr. S. She knew he'd blame me, and was concerned about what he might do. Dad was of the mind that I should give this up and come home, but he knew I wouldn't. "Do you think she'll come visit us?" Mom wanted to know. "Will you ask her for me?"

"Maybe the four of you can come here," I suggested instead. "You can drive my Jeep and fly home. I really need something to drive besides the Model T." Mom wasn't keen on that idea. She didn't want to see Mr. S. I hadn't asked her about Ed Bodeen yet. Stirring up that pot of worms didn't seem like a wise move. "Just think about it. Grandma would love to see you and the twins. She was so excited when I told her about them. It would be easier to convince her to go back with you if you're here."

Grandma had promised to come see me in a few days. I didn't know where her sister lived or her last name, so I had no way of reaching her while I was in Buena Vista. I didn't know if she was upset, or relieved over the show down with her husband. She needed some time alone to figure out what her next move should be. They'd been married close to sixty years. How much of that time had she been unable to make any decisions of her own? Could she even function without him telling her what to do? That happened to many women married to manipulative, abusive men.

~~~

I went into Whitehaven to buy groceries and ice before going back to the farm. After a month in town, people were beginning to accept me. At least they didn't expect me to float away, or walk through solid walls. Unable to keep more than a day or so worth of perishables meant I was in town often. Some people were even friendly. Unfortunately that didn't include Abner Shepard.

"Still causing trouble, I see." He stopped in the middle of the aisle in the grocery store. "Poor Walt's beside himself since you convinced Milly to walk out on him and the boys."

"I doubt Mr. S. is concerned about anything beyond his own comforts. As for 'the boys' I think they're old enough to take care of themselves. I don't see what business this is of yours anyway. Now if you'll excuse me, I need to finish shopping." I tried to walk around him, but he blocked my way.

"He's my brother, that's what makes it my business," he snarled. "We never had any trouble here until you came to town. Now we have our first murder in over fifty years. Too bad you ain't a real ghost. We could just have one of them exorcisms and be rid of you."

His outrageous statement defused my temper. I smiled at him. "Whatever." Sarcasm dripped from the single word.

He wanted to keep baiting me, but Jackson Carter, the store owner, walked up behind him. "How you doing, Abner?" He clapped the older man on the shoulder. "You finding everything you need?" He nodded at me, looking pointedly down the aisle. I'm not sure how much Mr. Carter could do if Abner continued harassing me. Abner was probably five years older than the store owner, but the younger man was a little stoop-shouldered and no bigger than a minute. Abner Shepard was at least three inches taller, and outweighed him by fifty pounds.

I didn't need to be hit over the head to get the message. I was out of the store within five minutes, heading for the farm. Hopefully Abner wouldn't try to follow me to continue his tirade.

Pulling up to the lane, a pickup was parked alongside the road. Charlie was sitting on the lowered tailgate his feet kicking at the air. "What are you doing here, Charlie?" I stopped beside him.

"I'm not on your property," he said quickly, his tone a little defensive.

"I know, but what are you doing out here?" I pointed to the road.

"I'm looking for Ma. She needs to come home. I miss her and Pa is really mad. He says it's all your fault Ma left us, Miss Evans."

"Do you think you could call me Parker?" I asked as I got out of the car, sitting down beside him. He nodded eagerly. "It's not my fault," I continued. This time he nodded miserably.

"Is Ma here? I really want her to come home." He sounded so pathetic I felt sorry for him.

"She's not here. Really," I added when he looked skeptical. "She's in Buena Vista at her sister's house."

"Why? Aunt Betsy's gone." He was confused.

"She just needs some time to think about things. Your father isn't a very nice man. He's really mean to your mom."

"I tried to tell Pa not to be like that, but he just whopped me upside the head, and told me to shut up."

"Why do you stay there? You don't need to take his abuse any more than she does."

"I don't have any place to go. Betty didn't want to marry me because Pa was too mean. If she'd married me, I'd have my own place like Wilbur and Hank."

He was at least twenty years older than me, but he seemed years younger. "Why don't you go see your mom? I'll bet she'll be so happy to see you she'll make you supper."

His face lit up. "You think so?" He sounded so hopeful I couldn't help but laugh.

"Come on up to the house. We'll call her. Do you know you're aunt's phone number?"

His eyes got big and round. "Pa said you'd call the sheriff if any of us came on the farm property again."

I patted his shoulder. "I invited you, Charlie, and I didn't know you were so nice when I said that. You can come visit me anytime you want. I just don't want your father, brothers or uncle here. *They* aren't very nice."

He nodded his head in understanding, and hopped down from the tailgate, eager to go to the house now. "Uncle Abner is meaner than Pa," he whispered, looking around to make sure no one else was listening. He was like a little boy. Maybe when Betty wouldn't marry him, he simply stopped growing up. Mr. S. certainly treated him like he was five years old. "I think you're nice, too. Pa says you're bad, this is his land, and you're trying to take it away from him. He said you don't have any right to it." I wanted to argue, but he got in his truck cutting off anything I could say. I got back in the Model T and Charlie followed me up to the house.

Gus gave a sharp bark, and settled down with a low growl when he saw a stranger on the porch. Charlie stopped short, his eyes bugging out, his breathing suddenly ragged. "Is he going to kill me? Pa and Uncle Abner said your dog is a killer. He killed Miss Smith."

"Gus did *not* kill Deidre!" My voice was sharp, too sharp, and Charlie took a step back when Gus growled again. "Friend, Gus, friend." I touched Charlie's arm. "Friend." Gus sat down, his tail wagging a greeting. I turned to Charlie. "Deidre was killed somewhere else." I explained what the sheriff had told me. "Gus didn't kill her," I reemphasized. "Do you think your father or uncle would do something like that?"

He shook his head emphatically. "No! Pa might be mean sometimes, but he'd never kill anybody. He just wants what's his." He didn't include Abner in his answer.

"This was Rosie's farm, and she left it to me. That means it's mine now." I wanted to make him understand his father was wrong, but a lifetime of being told what to do and think was hard to overcome. "Shall we call your mom now?"

Milly was glad to hear from him and as I suspected, she invited him to come see her. Sometime Charlie might have to choose between his father and mother. I hoped he'd make the right choice. When he left a few minutes later he was so happy he almost skipped down the steps. Shep came up behind me with his usual silent cat-like grace. I wasn't aware he was there until I felt his warm breath on my hair. "Was that Charlie?" His arms encircled my waist, and I leaned back against him. "He didn't try anything, did he?"

"No, I invited him up to the house. He was parked at the end of the lane when I came home. He's as gentle as a kitten. I feel sorry for him, living with that mean old goat."

"What'd he want?"

I turned in his arms, sliding mine around his neck. "His mom. He's not happy being stuck at the house alone with his pa. Milly described her father-in-law as 'mean as a snake.' I think his sons are more like him than anyone wants to admit. How's work coming?" I didn't want to talk about the Shepards anymore.

"The bathroom will be finished before long. I know you'll miss using that old outhouse," he teased. "But you'll just have to make do."

I laughed. "Oh, yes. I'm going to miss it so much I think

I'll tear it down."

Shep shook his head. "You can't."

"What do you mean I can't?" I pulled away looking up at him.

"Remember that hysterical historical society? You can close up the outhouse, but they won't let you tear it down. It's part of the history of the farm."

"Oh, brother! Who'd think an outhouse is historical? Rosie agreed to that?"

He laughed. "Remember who you're talkin' about, Darlin'. She had a hold over them, but she knew to pick her battles."

"Oh, let's forget the outhouse. When is my bathroom going to be ready?"

"It'll be another week or so. We still have the electricity to do, but we'll start working in the mud room tomorrow." The mud room wasn't the ideal place for a bathroom in the middle of the night, but it would come in handy for anyone working outside.

"Shower and everything?" Excitement rang in my voice. Who would believe I could be this excited about a bathroom?

He nodded. "Once all the plumbing is in, the shower won't take long to install." We were still standing in the doorway where Shep found me when Charlie left. Occasionally, he nibbled along my jaw, sending shivers up my spine, turning my mind to mush.

"What did you get for dinner? Should I get the stove goin'?"

"Oh, no!" I pulled out of his arms. "I forgot about the ice." Rushing outside, I opened the car door to find a puddle of water on the floor boards. Some ice remained, but not much. I wasn't sure if the meat would still be good. "So much for dinner." I looked at Shep with dismay. "When I saw Charlie, I forgot about these things."

"Not to worry." He chuckled, picking up the bags. "The meat was sittin' on the ice so it's still cool and the veggies will be fine. You're goin to need more ice though. There's enough for cold drinks after supper." He lowered his head giving me a light kiss, barely touching my lips with his. I'd never known a man who could put so much feeling, so much emotion in a simple kiss. As his arms came around me, I gasped, arched away. "What?! What's wrong?"

"That's cold." I raised his arm, pointing at the bag of ice that had rested against my back.

"Sorry. Guess I got a little carried away. You do that to me." He leaned down for another quick kiss before heading to the kitchen.

I'm definitely a goner, I thought as I followed behind him. *But who cares?*

After dinner, we snuggled on the porch swing. The citronella candles lining the railing kept the mosquitoes away while casting a romantic glow in the darkness. He kept the swing in motion with an occasional shove of his foot.

"Have you heard anything about the murder investigation?" Thoughts of Deidre's murder were never very far away. "Do you think the sheriff will be able to figure it out?"

"He isn't going to let anyone lead him down the garden path."

"How much experience does he have with murders?" I argued. "Abner Shepard said there hadn't been a murder here for fifty years. He's probably never investigated one before."

Shep chuckled. "Sure he has. This isn't the only place he's worked."

"How do you know?"

"After Deidre's body was found, I wondered if he'd be able to find out who killed her," he admitted sheepishly. "I checked him out online. He's been sheriff here for ten years, but he worked in Des Moines before that as a homicide detective. He knows what he's doin'."

That was good news, and I began to relax. "Why did the killer put her body in the field here? That doesn't make sense unless they're trying to pin it on me. I don't want to believe Walter would kill someone just to get me out of here. But Abner is a different story. From the few encounters I've had with him, he appears a lot more unbalanced. Would he do something like that?"

Shep gave the swing another push with his toe. "Can't really say. Never had much to do with him. The only other snake in the grass is Ed Bodeen. He'd do just about anything to get what he wants. I'm just not sure what he wants."

"But I don't have anything to do with him or his businesses. I can't hurt him."

"If someone was tryin' to frame me, he'd be my first guess. He never had competition until I came along. When Miss Rosie helped me get started with the restorations, it made him madder than a hornet. He'd been tryin' to get people to let him do their work for years. The way my house is fallin' down, I wouldn't want him to do any kind of work on these historical houses. Talk about hysterical historical society." A soft chuckle rumbled in my ear resting on his chest.

Ed Bodeen was still a bully. But why would he try to bully me?

CHAPTER THIRTEEN

It felt like a week instead of just hours since Mr. Meyers came with the news about Walter and Abner Shepard's latest vendetta against me. I completely forgot to tell Shep. 'Tomorrow's another day," I told Gus as we headed up to bed. "Nothing I can do about it now." I did remember to tell him where I'd put the journals. By that time, it had been pitch black in the root cellar, and I wouldn't go down there. He'd taken the lantern to retrieve several for me.

Instead of reading them in the order she'd written them, I decided to try to find the ones she wrote after she was fifteen. That was when everything changed for her. I could only guess which journals those would be. She wrote at least two a year when she was younger, writing more as she grew up.

Settling in the big bed with the lantern on the night stand and a flashlight in hand, I picked up one of the journals. Within minutes the busy day, the wine, and the darkened room conspired against me, and my eyes were drooping. The faded words blurred and ran together. Giving up, I closed the journal, turned out the lantern, letting sleep claim me.

It felt like minutes later Gus started barking and carrying on. It took a minute to wake up enough to realize what was going on. Someone was trying to break into the house. My first instinct was to confront and fight, then common sense took over. I grabbed my cell phone off the night stand.

"Sheriff's Department, may I help you?" an impersonal female voice answered on the third ring. I wondered if I woke her up.

"Someone is trying to break into my house." My voice quivered.

"What's your name and address, ma'am?" I suppose nine-one-one operators are trained to stay composed, but she sounded more like a recording than a live person. There was no inflection in her tone.

"My name is Parker Evans and I live..." She gave an audible gasp.

"I know who you are and where you live." She interrupted me. "You're Rosie Shepard's ghost, and you're haunting her house and this whole town."

"Oh, for crying out loud! I'm *not* a ghost, and I'm not haunting anything. Someone is trying to break into my house. Send someone out here. *Now.*" I could hear them rattling the doors.

"Are you sure it's not just the wind? It's gotten pretty breezy tonight." She had gathered her wits, what little she possessed, and thought this was funny now.

"Of course I'm sure. I can hear them, and my dog is going nuts." I was surprised she couldn't hear Gus barking.

"Maybe he just has to go out, or an animal is outside, and he wants to chase it." She was almost laughing now.

Before I could say anything, there was a crash downstairs. Gus scratched wildly at the door, renewing his efforts to get out of the room. Whoever was down there would be in the house in seconds.

"Send someone out here. NOW! I'm letting my dog out of the bedroom. He's a trained guard dog." I punched the off button wishing for something more satisfying, like slamming the receiver down in her ear. I opened the bedroom door, and Gus raced down the stairs, his fierce barks letting the intruders know he was coming.

Whoever was breaking into the house hadn't gotten very far. Before I made it down, Gus had the intruder. "Son of a bitch, get off me." I didn't recognize the man's voice, but that didn't mean anything. Gus was growling like he had something in his teeth, shaking the heck out of it. I heard a thump and Gus yelped. "Gus," I screamed. I could hear the man scrambling as he climbed back out the window he'd broken. "Crap." He was getting away. It was over in a matter of seconds.

Gus was shaking his head, struggling to stand when I came through the parlor doorway. The dim light from the moon wasn't enough to show how badly he was hurt.

The freckle-faced deputy got out of his car a few minutes later. I couldn't suppress my groan. Nothing was going to be accomplished with him. "What's going on now?" He sounded bored, and none too happy to be called out in the middle of the night.

"Someone broke into my house!" He wasn't really interested in looking around. Gus was groggy from the hit on his head, but he still growled at the deputy.

His high powered flashlight helped to illuminate the room, and I lit a lantern. Broken glass littered the floor. "Doesn't look like anything was taken. He didn't get very far." He couldn't care less that someone had broken in, just that nothing was taken. With a heavy sigh, he looked at me. "I suppose you still want me to write a report."

"I want you to do your job! Someone broke into my home. Isn't that against the law around here?"

He ignored my question, moving his light across the floor. "There's blood! You're dog bit someone!"

"The burglar!"

"Doesn't matter. He's a danger to the community. I'm afraid I'm going to have to take him with me." He stuck his thumbs in his belt loops, puffing out his thin chest.

"You're bent, bound, and determined to arrest my dog." I wanted to call him an idiot, but thought he might take it as a compliment.

"He bit someone," he repeated. "I can't let a dangerous animal run loose."

I've never wanted to hit someone as badly as I did right then. This kid was the dangerous one. Fortunately for one of us Sheriff Donovan pulled up in time to prevent me from doing this kid bodily harm.

"Glad you're here, Sheriff," the young deputy greeted his boss, acting like he'd just captured America's most wanted criminal. "This dog needs to be put down. Should of done it when Miss Smith was killed. Townsfolk will rest easier when he's gone."

"Stand down, Jerry. What's going on?" the sheriff asked, with a heavy sign. This must not be the first time he'd had to rescue a citizen from his overzealous deputy. He looked at me, ignoring the young man.

"Someone broke into my house and this...this..." I couldn't think of a word to describe the deputy without being insulting, so I simply nodded in his direction. "He thinks my dog is the criminal."

Before the sheriff could say anything, Jerry spoke up in his own defense. "That dog bit someone! He'd have bitten me, but something's wrong with him. That dog is a killer."

"We've discussed this," the sheriff spoke with a resigned sigh. "He didn't kill anyone. Go back on patrol; I'll take care of things here."

"But, Sheriff."

"Go!" Sheriff Donovan pointed to the patrol car. "Sorry about that, Miss Evans. He gets a little carried away."

Ya think? I wanted to say it so bad, but kept the thought to myself. I settled for a nod.

"Did you see the person who broke in? Anything that will help find him?"

"Find someone with a dog bite. Gus managed to draw blood. That's why Jerry wants to have him put down."

"Not going to happen. Don't worry about it. Got any ideas who might have broken in, or what they were after?"

"The only people I've had trouble with are the Shepards and Ed Bodeen. They want me out of here." He must have heard the talk about Milly and Walter. I didn't want to go into it if I didn't have to.

He nodded sagely. "I'll check with the docs in town, and ER's in the area for any dog bites. Hopefully it's bad enough to require attention, otherwise it'll be hard to trace."

Another dead end, it was my turn to sigh.

He found a board in the barn to patch up the window. "Have young Baker put a new one in tomorrow. This'll keep anyone out for tonight." He gave Gus, who had been sitting obediently by my side, a pat on the head before going to his car. He'd inspected the damage in the yard, but couldn't see much in the dark. "I'll send someone out in the morning to see if they can find anything."

"Just not Jerry, please. You also might want to let your dispatcher know I'm not a ghost." I suggested before he drove off.

He frowned at me. "What's that supposed to mean?"

"She didn't want to send anyone out when I called. Said I was a ghost haunting the town."

He swore under his breath. "I'll have a talk with her and Jerry both. She's his mother." So the idiot gene runs in the family, I thought.

My spotlights don't do any good when they're smashed. Whoever it was knew about the lights, and came prepared to take them out. That idiot deputy hadn't even looked into that. I hope he gets into a pile of trouble.

After sweeping up the glass, I tried to go back to bed, but sleep eluded me. Instinct told me this was the work of one of the Shepards, but which one? Mr. S.'s oldest son, Hank, was a good suspect in my mind. Higher up the list was Abner Shepard. Evil poured out of that man. My thoughts chased each other, like a dog chasing his tail.

Another thorn in my side was Ed Bodeen. I hadn't been able to pin point a reason for him to harass me except for the fact that Mom had spurned him. He was married with children, possibly grandchildren, and had several businesses. Why was he going after me?

Finally giving up any hope of sleep, Gus and I moved to the porch as the sun came up. The damage was worse than I first thought last night. All of my spotlights were out of commission; some of Shep's work was going to have to be redone, again. There was a general mess throughout the yard. How much had been done before Gus heard them? Or had I been sleeping so soundly I hadn't heard him right away? That wasn't a comforting thought. It didn't do me any good to have Gus warn me of an intruder if I didn't hear him.

Shep pulled into the lane, coming to a stop at the first sign of damage. He took it all in, then pulled up to the porch.

"What happened?" The boarded up window was hard to miss. "Are you okay?" His voice was tight, a dark scowl pulling his eyebrows into a line over his eyes.

"I'm fine," I assured him. "Hopefully someone is suffering from a good bite on the arm or leg."

"Damn. Why didn't you call me?"

"There was nothing you could do. Whoever it was took off as soon as he got away from Gus. I just hope the bite was bad enough he needs to go to the doctor."

He pulled me into his arms, holding me tight. "I still wish you'd called me. You shouldn't be out here alone when someone is trying to break in. Tell me you called the sheriff."

"Yes, for all the good it did." I kept my arms around his waist, enjoying his warmth even though the temperature was already at the hot and sticky stage. "They sent out my favorite deputy. He wanted to take Gus in for biting the burglar. He even told the sheriff Gus needed to be put down. Thankfully the sheriff is a whole lot smarter than his deputy."

Shep shook his head. "You weren't downstairs when he broke the window, were you?"

"No, I don't know how long he was out here before Gus was able to wake me. I was so tired I might have slept through the whole thing if he hadn't been persistent." Going inside, I poured a fresh cup of coffee for both of us. I filled him in on Mr. Meyers' visit the previous day. "So much was going on I forgot all about it until after you left last night."

"Do you think the break in had anything to do with the lawsuit?"

I shrugged. "Walter and Abner want me gone, but I don't think it's just about the land or the house. There's something they don't want me to find; the same something Rosie wanted me to find. 'To right an old wrong' she said. I'm not sure how I'm supposed to do it. Why didn't she just tell me?" Frustration made my voice sharp.

"Whatever it is, it's in the house," Shep said thoughtfully. "She knew it would be found durin' the renovations, or while you were sortin' through her things. That's why she wanted you to have the work done. She called it a treasure hunt. Her journals are the key. They were hidden and locked away. That's your first find."

"Do you know if there was a portrait of her hanging in the hall?" Could the missing portrait be part of her treasure hunt?

His sexy, lopsided grin curved his mouth. "Sure was. When I saw it, I commented on the resemblance between her at that age, and the pictures she had of you. She just smiled and said I didn't know the half of it. She sure enjoyed her mysteries and intrigues."

Okay, the journals and portrait were what I needed to concentrate on. Maybe she hid something behind the portrait. But where was it? I had to concentrate on finding what Rosie left for me to find. It could save my life. Instinct told me whoever was doing this was getting desperate. Just how far they'd go to keep me from finding what Rosie hid was anybody's guess.

~~~

I called Mr. Meyers as soon as I was sure he'd be in his office. "Someone broke in here last night," I stated without any pleasantries. "If you know anything about it, you need to tell Sheriff Donovan." I hadn't meant to sound so accusatory, but that's the way it came out.

"How would I know about it? I certainly didn't have anything to do with it." He was indignant and rightly so.

I took a deep breath, letting it out slowly. "I'm sorry; I didn't mean to sound like I was accusing you. Really, I'm not. I do think some of your other clients might be behind it though."

"I...my...no one..." He sputtered, unable to form an actual statement to deny one of his clients would do such a thing.

"Were you able to convince Walter and Abner to drop the incompetency suit?" That was the reason I'd called him, not to accuse him of anything.

"Ah, well, I did have a talk with them. I told them it was my opinion they didn't have a chance of winning. Rosie wasn't incompetent when she wrote the will, or when she passed away. She was in full command of her mental facilities right up to the end."

"How did they take it?"

He cleared his throat. "Ah, not well. They don't take kindly to people opposing them."

"Don't I know it!" I said under my breath. "Did they agree to drop the suit?"

"They'll talk it over, and let me know."

"Will you represent them if they don't drop it?" He knew my position, and what I'd do.

He cleared his throat again. "I told them they'd have to use another attorney for that business. I couldn't represent both parties."

"And how did they take that?" A smile of satisfaction lifted my voice.

"Not well," he repeated, sounding resigned to losing their business.

"Do you think either of them would break into the house if they thought they couldn't get rid of me any other way?"

"Walter is a hot head," he said on a sigh. "But he will listen to the voice of reason. Eventually. Abner will act without thinking about the consequences. I just don't know if there is a voice of reason for Walter to listen to right now." His voice held a note of rebuke at the end. Needless to say, he'd heard about the argument between Walter and Milly in my front yard.

I swallowed my guilt. Mr. S. had to shoulder some of the blame himself. If he wasn't such a bully, Milly wouldn't have left. "So what you're saying is either of them could have broken into the house, but Abner is the better bet?"

"Yes, that's what I'm saying," he answered resignedly. "I don't know why they are so adamant on having you out of the house; I just know it's driving both men over the brink."

He wouldn't and probably couldn't legally, report them to the sheriff. They were his clients, so confidentiality ruled. Besides, I doubted either man would come right out, and tell him they were doing something illegal. They weren't that stupid.

"Let me know what they decide."

"I can't reveal any information to you, Miss Evans." His tone was snooty. "You're the one who threatened me with the Ethics Board for revealing information to Walter and Abner. Now you're asking me to reveal information about them." He was probably thinking 'gotcha.'

I sighed dramatically. "No, I threatened the Ethics Board because you were representing both parties in a lawsuit, and you were willing to lie about Rosie at the time she wrote her will. *That's* unethical. All I want you to tell me is whether Walter and Abner are going to continue with the lawsuit. That isn't confidential information since the suit is against me. I need to know if I have to find another attorney. Have a good day." Let him chew on that for a while. I hung up before he could say anything more.

CHAPTER FOURTEEN

Shep carried the heavy trunk containing the journals into the parlor. Is this what Walter and Abner didn't want me to find? If so, I had to figure out a way to keep them safe. There had to be something incriminating in them. Picking up a book, I thumbed through it. Rosie was twelve at the time.

Mama died today. I miss her already. She said she was going to heaven to be with Jesus and heaven is a nice place. I hope Mama's right. Jesus isn't like Papa, he's nice and kind. Jesus won't hurt Mama. That's a good thing, but I wish she could take me with her. Papa whopped me when Mama died. He said it was my fault she was dead. I didn't take good enough care of her. I'm just twelve years old. I don't know about doctoring. If he had called a doctor when Mama got sick, maybe he could have fixed her up. It's Papa's fault she's dead. If I told him that, he'd whoop me again, maybe until I died. Maybe I should let him. Then I could be with Mama and Jesus. But then who would make Papa pay? Someday he's going to be sorry for everything he's done.

Abner's just like Papa. He made fun of me when I cried because Mama died. I think they're all glad she's gone. I'm the only one who will miss her. Effie said I should run away, but I don't have anywhere to go. If I did and Papa found me, he'd kill me for sure. I know he would.

Once again, her words brought me to tears. That poor girl! It's no wonder she turned into a tyrant. If she ever got the upper hand, she'd never let go. And who could blame her. She probably looked for anything to hold over them. The remainder of that journal was more of the horrors Rosie had put up with. The only thing her father and brothers hadn't done was molest her. Not much of a testimonial of their good character.

I wasn't sure how much more I could read without wanting to do bodily harm to Walter and Abner. The thought that my own sweet mother had lived in that kind of atmosphere, yet turned out as loving as she is can only be a miracle. How much of whom we are depends on nurture, how much on nature?

Each journal I paged through was filled with more of the same. Rosie was able to paint a verbal picture that was more than vivid. Her life at school with her friends was very different from her home life. She never told anyone what was happening at home. Effie knew only part of it. When her brothers weren't around, she was like any other girl her age.

Today I played hop scotch and jump rope with Effie and Milly at recess. It was so much fun. The boys didn't go to school. They had to stay home to help Papa in the field. I thought Papa was going to make me stay home too, but he let me go. I guess they didn't need me to do anything for them today. There was food in the ice box they could eat at noon. I'll have to cook supper when I get home.

They treated Rosie like a slave, worse than a slave. At twelve she had to cook and clean for four strapping brothers and her father. This house is huge; Shep said nearly ten thousand square feet. That's a lot of house for a twelve year old to take care of by herself.

She was a good student, and she enjoyed school when her brothers weren't around. She read anything she could get her hands on to escape her life in the books. She told of having to hide them so her brothers wouldn't take them away from her, but she listed every book she read, describing them in detail. Hopefully some of them had survived the years, and were somewhere in all the boxes in the attic.

I still had a long way to go to find out what had happened when she was fifteen when she was sent to "finishing school." I'm willing to bet she was right here in the attic, and she'd had a baby. I could only hope she'd written about it in one of her journals. Which one though? I still hadn't found the portrait that should be hanging in the hall upstairs. There were a lot of places to look.

Shep said the attic would be the last place he'd install

electricity so any exploring would have to be done during the day. The lanterns didn't give off enough light by themselves, leaving deep shadows, making it hard to see in the big cavernous room. The attic ran the entire width and length of the house. The separate area where I'm certain Rosie had been kept was a part of the attic. The barn also held a great many boxes and trunks. How could one person have so much stuff? It's a question I'd been asking since my first day here.

I was still sitting on the floor in the parlor, sifting through another journal when Shep finished for the day. "You about ready to get somethin' to eat? You haven't moved since you swallowed a sandwich whole at lunch. Find anything interestin'?"

"If you mean beyond the fact those men were monsters? Then no. Listen to this, Rosie was thirteen when she wrote it.

Papa told me I didn't need to go to school anymore. I was needed here at home. I told him he couldn't stop me; I was going to finish school with my friends. I want to go to high school, maybe college. I want to be a teacher or a writer. I can't tell Papa about my journals though. He'd take them away from me. If he read what I said about him and the boys, my life would be worse than it is now.

Papa was surprised when I stood up to him. He yelled at me some more, but I didn't back down. I'm going to go to high school. He can't stop me.

Shep pulled me to my feet, wrapping me in his strong arms. "You can't change the past. Miss Rosie is gone. No one can hurt her now. You need to figure out who's trying to get you out of this house and why. And I need to keep you safe." He lowered his head, kissing me with such sweetness, my heart melted.

"Come to my place with me while I shower and change," he said when he finally lifted his head. "We'll go to A Cup-A-Joe. Bring a change of clothes; you can shower, too." He added the last when I started to decline. The humidity was inching a little higher each day along with the temperature. With no central air conditioning, I felt as wilted as a flower with no water.

141

"Okay, you got me. Let me go get some clothes." I started to turn away, but he pulled me back.

Looking at me intently, he put another spin on my words. "I hope I've got you. You know I've fallen in love with you." His kiss was just as sweet and tender as before. I was stunned, and couldn't say anything when he released me. Turning me towards the stairs, he gave me a little push. "Just think about it, Darlin'. Now go get some clothes. I'll be outside with Gus."

Is this what love feels like? I want to be with him, I don't want him to leave at night. I can't wait to see him in the morning. But it's been just over a month since we met. Rosie had trusted him, said to rely on him, but stand on my own. He was always there to back me up, but he didn't try to fight my battles, or tell me what to do. I feel certain Rosie was convinced he was her great grandson. The one picture I'd found of Rosie and the unknown man was conclusive in my mind. And in hers, I thought

~~~

His house was small, one bedroom and one bath. The living room, dining room and kitchen were all one open space. "It's not much," he came up behind me, wrapping his strong arms around me. I couldn't get enough of this. "But when I'm finished with it, it won't fall down in the first strong wind that comes along." He placed nibbling kisses along my neck.

Shivers of excitement traveled along my spine. "Was this always one room?" I asked a little breathlessly, waving my arm around the open area.

He chuckled. "No, the rooms were small, walls everywhere. A small table wouldn't even fit in the kitchen. When this little community didn't take off the way Bodeen wanted, he gave up buildin' new houses, and tried to do remodels and restorations. Miss Rosie stopped him before he ruined any of them."

"Well, Mr. Baker." I turned in his arms, looking up at him. "I think you do beautiful work. Your restoration on the farm house is going to do great things for your business." It was my turn to plant a few kisses along his jaw line. His cheeks were prickly with five o'clock shadow, and his skin was slightly salty from working in the basement heat.

After several minutes of exploration, Shep cleared his throat and stepped back. "I think one of us needs to hit the shower. You go first. I'm makin' mine a cold one," he muttered as I walked away, chuckling softly.

Abner Shepard was leaving A Cup-A-Joe as we headed down the sidewalk. Spotting us, he stopped, waiting as we approached him. "You little bitch," he snarled. "Keep putting your two cents into other people's business, and somebody's gonna get hurt." He put himself in my face, his sour breath hot.

"Take a step back." Shep put his hand on Abner's chest. Before either of us realized what he was going to do, the older man reared back, swinging at Shep. He connected with a glancing blow on Shep's shoulder instead of his chin.

Shep's quick reaction saved him from getting hurt. He threw a punch of his own, connecting with more accuracy. Abner went down on his backside, shock registering on his red face. "You bastard!" He scrambled to stand up, but a heavy hand on his shoulder stopped him.

"Stay down, Abner, and cool off." Sheriff Donovan stood in front of us.

"Stay out of this, Donovan. It's none of your damn business."

"When you start a brawl on the street, it becomes my business. Where were you this morning about two o'clock?"

"Wh..." The swift subject change confused Abner for a second. "That's none of your business either, Donovan. Now let me up." He pushed the sheriff's hand off his shoulder, and lumbered to his feet.

"Kinda hot for a long sleeved shirt isn't it?" the sheriff questioned. "You trying to hide something?"

Without answering, Abner pushed past us, taking a final swipe at me in the process, shoving me into Shep's side. "Watch it, Shepard," Sheriff Donovan warned. "You don't want to push me too far. I can arrest you for assault."

Getting into his truck, Abner ignored him. He peeled out

of his parking spot, leaving rubber on the road. "Probably should give the idiot a speeding ticket, but he'd run me over if I tried to stop him now. I'd rather get him for something bigger. You okay, Baker?"

"He's a lot slower than he thinks he is. I saw his punch coming before he even knew he was goin' to throw one."

"Do you think he's the one who broke into my house last night?" That long sleeved shirt could easily cover up a bandage.

The sheriff shrugged. "No telling. I wouldn't put it past him. He's a mean one, all right." We'd started to draw a crowd. "Move along, folks. Show's over." He tipped his hat to us, sauntering off down the walk.

"Rosie left something that would point guilt at her brothers," I whispered. "Guilt is as powerful a motivator as money."

Rosie was right about one thing. I enjoy a challenge. I'm not about to let either of them run me off before I find what she left me. My questions about Barnard were having an effect on them. Was that why they were getting more and more hostile?

CHAPTER FIFTEEN

"I can't leave you here alone tonight." We'd spent the evening on the porch swing. With the mosquitoes out in force, I was going to run out of candles soon. I didn't want to give up our nights spent in their romantic glow.

"I'll be fine. I'll leave Gus downstairs on guard. He won't let anyone in."

"And what happens if they take Gus out? You'll have no protection. I'll sleep out here. I have my sleepin' bag in the truck."

My stomach did somersaults at the thought of someone getting past Gus. Still I didn't want to be a sissy. I could take care of myself, couldn't I? "You don't need to stay here. I don't think Abner, or whoever, will try anything this soon. I'll be fine."

His jaw set stubbornly. "I'm *not* leavin' you here alone. If that idiot deputy is all the protection the sheriff's department can offer, you might as well be alone. And that isn't gonna happen. I'll put the truck around back so no one can see it from the road. I don't want to start tongues a waggin'."

In this day and age, how many people thought anything of a couple spending the night together? Even in a small town I'm sure it's not all that uncommon. Still I was grateful Shep was concerned. "There are five empty bedrooms upstairs. If you insist on staying here, you can take your pick. The beds are all made up with fresh linens. Or as fresh as can be expected when no one has slept in the bed for God only knows how long."

In the dark I felt more than saw him take a gulping breath. "I'm not sure that's such a good idea."

"What do you mean?" I pulled away, frowning at him in the dark. "What's not a good idea?"

"Me sleepin' upstairs." He couldn't look at me. "I'll just stay down here."

"You're not sleeping out here on the porch." I was beginning to get angry. I didn't know why he was reluctant to sleep upstairs. A few short hours ago, he'd declared his love for me. Now he didn't even want to sleep in the same house with me? "Are you afraid I'll attack you in your sleep?" I asked with a touch of anger.

He laughed sheepishly, "No, but I might have trouble keepin' my hands to myself if you're that close."

"Oh. Oh!" I finally got what he was saying. A stupid little grin spread across my face. "You don't have to stay outside. You can sleep in the parlor." Before I said anything really stupid, I stood up. "I'll get some blankets to make the floor more comfortable and a pillow." I quickly disappeared in the house. I felt like doing a jig up the stairs.

Before I made it back down, Gus started raising a ruckus. Someone he didn't like was here. My stomach churned wildly. Shep was down there. Would someone hurt him in order to get in? You bet! My feet barely touched the stair treads as I flew downstairs. Walter Shepard's truck was pulled up to the porch steps, but he hadn't gotten out of the truck. He wasn't totally stupid. He was yelling at Shep until he saw me in the doorway.

"Get out here, Missy! You've been nothing but trouble since you came here. You convince my wife to leave me, now you've got your boyfriend beating up on old men."

"He swung first," I interrupted.

Ignoring my words, he continued to rant. "I don't know why Rosie left this place to you, but you don't belong here. Go back where you came from and leave us alone."

"I don't know why she left this to me either, but there's nothing you can do about it. We both know she was of sound mind." He gave me a strange look I didn't try to interpret before going on. "Whatever her reason, I plan to figure it out. Now leave. I wasn't bluffing when I said I'd call the sheriff if you came here again. He might even have a few questions about where you were early this morning, say two o'clock." I couldn't see his arms, but it didn't look like he was wearing a long sleeved shirt.

"Maybe Grandma just got tired of living with a bully. Try talking to her instead of ordering her around. Now get off my property!" I took out my cell phone, pressing nine-one-one without taking my eyes off him.

I groaned inwardly when the same woman answered the phone. "Send Sheriff Donovan out to Rosie Shepard's place. I have a trespasser who won't leave." I didn't want to take the chance she'd send her son out again.

"Sheriff Donovan is off duty," she replied stiffly. "And he doesn't respond to trespassing calls. He has deputies for that."

"Call the sheriff anyway. And don't bother to send your son out. He's less than useless." I disconnected before she could say anything else. Mr. S. hadn't moved. He was dumb-struck that I had actually called the sheriff. Finally gathering himself, he put the truck in gear roaring off down the lane. We had to jump back to keep from getting peppered with gravel thrown up by his tires.

"That man's just crazy enough to come back later tonight," Shep said. "He's why I'm stayin'." There was a stubborn set to his jaw.

I wrapped my arms around his lean waist, resting my head on his chest. "I'm glad you were here, and I'm glad you're staying. It might be irrational, but I'm not afraid of him. Abner Shepard and Ed Bodeen do give me pause though. They could do just about anything, and not think twice about it."

He kissed the top of my head, holding me like his life depended on it. "Has Bodeen tried anything?" He pulled me away just enough to look at me.

"No, I think he's more dangerous than the Shepard brothers though."

Sheriff Donovan pulled into the lane, another car following close behind. "Trouble again, Miss Evans?" The sheriff got out of his car, joining us on the porch.

"Watch out for that dog, Sheriff! He'll take a bite out of you as soon as look at you," Deputy Thompson called from the open window of his patrol car.

"I've got this, Jerry. Go back on patrol." He heaved a long suffering sigh. To prove Gus wasn't going to hurt him, he gave the dog's head a friendly pat, roughing up his ears. We could hear the young deputy's gasp. "Leave, Jerry. I've got this."

He was pushing the sheriff to his limit. Finally, he shifted the car into reverse, knowing there'd be trouble if he didn't leave. "You be careful, Sheriff." He had to have one last word.

"If he wasn't my nephew, I'd fire his ass," he muttered. "His mother right along with him." He turned to me, taking for granted his nephew was leaving. "What happened tonight, Miss Evans? I'm spending more time here than at the office."

"Do you think you could call me Parker then? We might as well be on a first name basis." I held out my hand in a friendly gesture.

The usually taciturn sheriff grinned at me. "Parker it is." He nodded at Shep as he took my hand in his much larger one, giving it a firm shake. "What happened?" he asked again. "I didn't think Abner was dumb enough to try something after what happened in town."

"Walter Shepard took exception to his wife leaving him. He's none too happy about Shep decking his brother either. Thinks it's my fault. I've told him not to come here again, that I'd have him charged with trespassing. I've bluffed before. This time I had to call. I'm sorry I took you away from your family."

"No family here except the two idiots working for me. My wife passed on just before I moved here." He surprised himself, giving away so much personal information, and he cleared his throat. "You were right to call. Those two really have it in for you. Walter should be glad you're here. You are his granddaughter."

"Only by blood," I said. "There's no love lost between us."

He shook his head, pulling a business card out of his shirt pocket. "If you have any more trouble, call either of these numbers. You won't have to deal with Shir...er, dispatch. I don't live all that far away. I'll have a talk with Walter tomorrow. He's got to wise up sometime." He turned to Shep with a raised eyebrow. "You sticking around tonight? She's got this 'vicious' dog here, but it'd be nice to know she wasn't alone."

"I'm not goin' anywhere. I'll be right inside. No one will get past me."

A lopsided grin tilted the sheriff's mouth. He understood what Shep wasn't saying. He wasn't sleeping in my bed, but he'd be close enough to protect me if the need arose.

~~~

By Friday I still hadn't heard whether Walter and Abner had decided against pursuing the lawsuit. If they continued with the insane idea of contesting Rosie's will, I needed to make sure Meyers wasn't continuing as their attorney in that matter.

"They haven't gotten back to me yet, but I don't think they will go forward with the lawsuit." Mr. Meyers' voice was tight and stilted. He wasn't happy with me, but I really didn't care. He'd been working both ends against the middle long enough. It was time for him to get down off the fence, and choose a side.

"Tell them to stay away from me and the farm. I don't take kindly to attempted break-ins and being harassed. The sheriff knows what they've been up to."

He heaved a heavy sigh. "I'll have another talk with Walter." He sounded so put upon I almost felt sorry for him; almost.

"Talk to Abner, too. I think he's the more dangerous of the two."

"I'll do my best. Is there anything else I can do for you?"

I wanted to tell him the estate was paying him handsomely, so don't sound like I'm taking up his precious time. I kept those thoughts to myself, and just said good-bye.

To protect me from gossip, Shep left the farm before daybreak, coming back just behind his men. I had no idea how people in town would react if they thought we were sleeping together, although I was sure Walter and Abner would have plenty to say with their self-righteous indignation. Of course, *they* never did anything wrong. Ha!

It had only been two weeks since Deidre's murder. It felt more like a month or a year. So much was going on I barely had time to think. I hadn't heard if Sheriff Donovan had any clues to her killer, or if he'd found out who her father was. He'd kept his word, making it known around town that neither Gus nor I had anything to do with it. If her body had been dumped in my field to throw suspicion on me, it had been a failure. Were the people who wanted me gone evil enough to kill an innocent woman to accomplish that fact?

Sitting on the front porch with my second cup of coffee, I tried to plan my day. The mud room and kitchen were in total chaos. Water lines and electricity were ready to be installed. There were holes in the interior walls and floors, plaster dust was everywhere. Fixing anything beyond a pot of coffee was almost out of the question. Going to town to eat was time consuming. I wanted to spend that time reading the journals. I knew in my deepest inner being they held the answers I was looking for, but I couldn't concentrate with all the noise and mess.

I finally decided to explore the barn instead. I still hadn't seen much beyond where I parked the Model T. The number of boxes and trunks was daunting, even more than the attic. Maybe Rosie had put her portrait there since I hadn't found it in the house yet. I was obsessing over that portrait. She had a reason for doing everything. I just had to figure out what those reasons were. Her letter had called this a treasure hunt; I called it a scavenger hunt with no clear prize at the end.

Propping open all the doors provided a good cross breeze so it wasn't stiflingly hot. Each stall held boxes, some were labeled, some a guessing game. I could see old furniture in the hay loft, and wondered who'd put it up there and how long ago. Rosie had been a small woman, only five feet tall. From the pictures I'd seen of her she didn't weigh more than a hundred pounds on a good day. She'd lived here alone most of her adult life. Who had worked the farm all those years? How old was she when her father passed away?

I was still hoping to convince Mom and Dad to drive my

Jeep here. Mom was beginning to soften to the idea after talking to Milly. By July more work would be done, but not so much that it would still seem primitive to the twins. They'd get a real kick out of this place even if it was a mess. The mess might even add to their fun.

Dad would agree if Mom didn't put up much resistance. He'd do anything for her. Besides, they both wanted to know more about Shep. They knew my feelings for him were growing stronger. Maybe that was how I could get them to come.

I could see a lot of Dad in Shep. He had the same inner strength, and they were both totally comfortable with themselves. They didn't have to tear anyone down to build themselves up.

As my thoughts turned to Shep, I couldn't control my goofy smile. He said he'd fallen in love with me. How did I feel about that? My heart skipped a beat just thinking about him. The boys and men I'd dated all paled in comparison. The idea of moving back to Arizona and never seeing him again was painful.

As though my thoughts conjured up the reality, Shep stepped into the barn holding a bag of goodies. "Thought you might be gettin hungry since you didn't have much for breakfast."

"Where'd you get that?" There aren't any fast food restaurants nearby, and I was sure no place made deliveries this far out of town.

Before answering, he placed a lingering kiss on my lips. I almost forgot the food he was holding until my stomach growled, and Gus pushed against my leg. Shep never forgot him when he brought food. With a last tug on my lower lip, Shep stepped back, his eyes heavy with passion held in close check. "I...I..." he cleared his throat and started again, "I sent Wayne into Bentonville for supplies. Had him stop for lunch on his way back." He roughed up Gus's ears. "I didn't forget about you, buddy." Gus seemed to know what we were saying, and he danced around, waiting for his food.

"He shouldn't have people food," I scolded half-heartedly.

"The trainer would have a fit if he knew how much we were giving him."

"What he doesn't know won't hurt us." He gave me another quick kiss before taking a big bite out of his own burger.

We were silent while we ate. Until he brought the food, I hadn't realized how hungry I was. Popping the last French fry into my mouth, I sat back with a satisfied sigh. "You're a life saver. I'm going to have to figure out what to do about meals while you work on the kitchen." We'd gone to Buena Vista last week to pick out the appliances. The kitchen cabinets still had to be refinished. I was getting excited about finally having a kitchen I knew how to cook in.

"I've told my folks about you," he stated. "When it's okay for you to leave, I'd like to take you to Texas to meet them." My heart gave a little stutter step. Meeting the parents was a big step. He leaned across the box we were using as a table to give me a few lingering kisses. His lips tasted salty and a little like ketchup, but it was all good.

Before I could say anything, *Elvira* sounded from my pocket. I fished my phone out, thumbing the connect key. "Hi, Mom. How's everybody in Arizona?"

"Wrong parent," Dad laughed. "Can't a father call his favorite daughter without being confused with her mom?" he joked.

"Sorry, Dad, and I'm your only daughter. What are you doing home in the middle of the day? Is everyone okay?"

"Honey, it's Saturday. I'm home every Saturday."

"Oh, sorry again. I've lost all track of time." I'm used to timing my week around work. With Shep working six days a week, I'd lost all track of the days. I told Dad about the renovations and picking out the appliances, and avoided talking about the trouble we'd been having.

He let me ramble for a few minutes before asking, "That young man of yours working today? He there?"

"Yeah, we just finished eating lunch in the barn." I laughed at the image.

I stopped laughing at his next question, my stomach knotting up. "How about letting me talk to him?"

More like interrogate him, I thought uneasily. Dad always had a ton of questions for any of the guys I dated over the years.

I handed the phone to Shep, mouthing "Dad" to him.

"Hello, Sir," Shep said respectfully. "How are you?"

I listened to the one-sided conversation trying to act nonchalant, hoping Dad didn't ask too many personal questions. My hopes were dashed in the next instant. "No, sir. Not until I get my weddin' ring on her finger." My face burned with embarrassment. I knew exactly what Dad had asked. How many twenty-five year old virgins were left in the world?

While Shep listened to Dad's next question, he winked at me, answering without a qualm. "No Sir, haven't asked her yet. Figured I should meet her folks first, and ask you for her hand." He didn't sound perturbed by Dad's persistent embarrassing questions, while I wanted to grab the phone and throw it away. I couldn't believe Dad was doing this.

"Thought maybe you and Mrs. Evans might come for a visit this summer. That way we could all get to know each other. I'd like my folks to meet Parker, too." He was actually helping me get them here. He was pretty sneaky. I liked it. Smiling at him, I gave him a thumb's up.

Finally Dad was finished with his interrogation, and Shep gave me back my phone. I walked out of the barn before putting it to my ear. "I can't believe you did that," I whispered harshly, half mad, half not. "I'm twenty-five years old."

"And you're still my daughter," he answered mildly. "I want to make sure no one is taking advantage of you. Your mother and I love you very much."

Those were the words he always used when I got upset with him. He knew they would melt away my anger. "Okay. But you could be a little more tactful." I was pacing up and down in front of the big barn doors when Shep came up behind me. Wrapping his arms around my waist, he whispered in my ear. "Give it up, Darlin'. You'll always be his little girl." His warm breath tickled my ear, goose bumps sprinting up my arms.

"All right, I guess I'll forgive you," I told Dad when I could breathe again. I hope he didn't notice how breathless I suddenly sounded. His next words had me jumping for joy.

"You up for some company in a few weeks, Honey? I've just about got your mom convinced that her...Mr. S. won't be able to boss her around or hurt her. She really wants to see her mom." When I put my phone back in my pocket, I ran at Shep, nearly tackling him as I jumped, putting my arms around his neck and kissing him soundly. "They're coming. Thank you." He twirled me around, laughing at my excitement.

When I finally calmed down, he looked at me seriously. "You heard what I told your dad. I was serious. Be thinkin' about your answer 'cuz when they get here, I'm askin'." He kissed me again, then released me, and went back to the house to work.

I sank down on a stump beside the barn. *Oh, boy! Things were moving fast.* Well, some things. I still didn't know why Rosie had left me her estate, or what all the secrets were.

I had trouble concentrating the rest of the afternoon. The boxes held little interest after that amazing conversation. Finally giving up on the boxes, I climbed the ladder to the hay loft. Maybe something up there would capture my attention.

~~~

There was even more furniture in the hay loft than in the attic; dressers, bureaus, wardrobes, armoires, and pieces I couldn't even name. There was a veritable fortune in antiques. How had they been kept in such pristine condition stored in a drafty old barn? A fine layer of dust covered them. Even out here, everything had been dusted and polished over the years. Rosie had taken extremely good care of everything she owned. She'd obviously known the value of everything.

Before deciding what to keep and what to sell I would have to have an appraiser come out. There wasn't enough room in the house to keep all of it. Each room was already fully furnished with equally valuable antiques. I opened drawers and cabinets, examining each item. Unlike the house, the drawers here were empty. At least she hadn't kept clothes or jewelry up here.

Ready to give up and go down the ladder, I stopped beside an unusually beautiful armoire, running my hand over the smooth surface. The rich patina of the wood gleamed dully through the dust collected since Rosie passed away. This piece would be moved into the house. How had everything been put in the hay loft in the first place? It had to have taken a small army of burly men. Getting it down would take another army of movers.

Opening one door expecting to find it as empty as the rest, I sucked in my breath. Propped against the back of the cabinet my face was staring back at me as if in a mirror. I'd found Rosie's portrait! This could be me, dressed in period costume. I'd seen other pictures of her at different times in her life, and knew how much we looked alike. But this was more, much more, than mere resemblance. This was me, right now, down to the same shade of red hair, the finely arched brow, the shape of our lips and the detached ear lobes. All of these were hereditary. But how could two people, distantly related and from different eras, look like identical twins?

Any other time, I'd say the hair color was the work of the artist who painted the portrait. Or maybe the artist had seen a picture of me. But that couldn't be. I'm twenty-five; Rosie had been in her late seventies when she passed away. This portrait had been painted fifty or more years ago. I rubbed at the goose bumps moving up my arms. This was downright spooky.

I carefully carried the large portrait down the ladder and into the house. Did she move it so I wouldn't see our likeness immediately? Or was there another reason? *Will I ever find answers to all my questions? Figure out what she wanted me to find?* I'd been here more than a month, and had more questions than when I arrived.

Placing the heavy frame on the dining room table, I took stock of the big room. The table was large with three leaves in it, ten chairs placed around it. A china hutch and buffet completed the set. In houses built today these items would leave no room to walk around. Here there was still plenty of room. Pulling the table apart, I took out the leaves, setting them aside, and pushed the table back together. Now there was even more room.

My mind was racing. This room and the large front parlor were the rooms that would require the least amount of work. No plumbing was required in either one. When Shep finished with the kitchen and mud room, I was going to have him begin with the dining room and parlor next. My bedroom could wait as long as I had a bathroom I could get to. By rearranging all the furniture in the two rooms, I'd be able to move some of what was stored in the hay loft and attic. I wanted to see exactly what was here, and if something else had been hidden in the pieces.

Shep came up behind me as I was looking at the portrait again. Wrapping me in a hug from behind, he kissed my neck. "You found it." He whistled softly as he walked us closer to the table. "I knew it looked like you, but seein' you and the picture together..." his voice trailed off. "Have you found any more pictures of Miss Rosie with the man?" he asked hopefully.

I shook my head where it rested against his broad chest. "I forgot about the pictures when I discovered the journals. Why?" I turned in his arms to look up at him. "What are you thinking?"

He shrugged. "Just wondered. It can't be a coincidence that I look like him. There's got to be a blood tie like you and Miss Rosie." He was still hoping to find his grandfather's family.

"I feel like I'm scattering my energies, first I look through the pictures until I find the journals. Then I move to the barn and find the portrait. I need to pick one thing, sticking with it until I'm finished. I just don't know which is more important, the pictures, the journals, or the portrait. Where will I find the answers to this mystery?" I told him about deciding to bring the furniture in from the barn. "How long will it take to get electricity in the dining room and parlor?"

"It's gonna' to take another week to finish the kitchen, the cabinets will be the last thing we do there. Then we'll get the bathroom fixtures in the mud room."

I sighed. I knew I was being impatient; he couldn't do everything at once. Still it felt like this was taking forever. "I guess the furniture can wait. There's no sense moving it in here, only to move it out again when you start working in the dining room."

"How about taking tonight and tomorrow off?" he suggested. "Come back to my place for a shower. We'll go get somethin' to eat and watch TV. How long's it been since you watched television?" Like most men, he couldn't live without his TV. "We can go for a drive after church and relax."

"I want to get things done here," I argued. "If Dad can convince Mom to come, I have to have room for them."

He laughed, "This house is big enough for two families. You have plenty of room, just not like they're used to. Maybe your grandma would like to have lunch with us. Afterward, I'll go through the pictures while you read more of Miss Rosie's journals."

Seeing Milly again was the clincher. I'd call her and ask her to come with us for lunch.

~~~

"You and your young man come here for lunch," Milly invited. "I'll enjoy cooking for someone besides myself." She'd decided not to come to church in Whitehaven for a while. She didn't want to encounter Walter. "Has he been giving you problems, Grandma? If he does, you can get a restraining order against him."

"Oh, goodness, Child. I'm not going to do something like that!" she exclaimed. "Can you imagine the talk around town? I really don't think he'd do me harm. He just yells a lot, and I don't want to subject the church to that. There's a very nice church here. I've gone there before with Betsy."

"Have you seen Charlie again?" I wasn't sure if Mr. S. had coerced him into staying away from his mother. It was just

157

like him to do that.

"I told him not to come for a little while. His pa's carrying on something awful." My heart broke for her. Since I came here, she'd left her husband, and she was cut off from her sons. No matter how much I told myself it wasn't my fault, I still felt guilty. If Rosie hadn't left me her farm, life would have gone on as it had all these years. But longevity didn't mean it had been a happy marriage.

After a refreshing shower, we decided on going to A Cup-A-Joe to eat. Shep didn't keep a lot of food at his place. He'd eaten most of his meals out before I moved here, and since, he'd been eating with me. Saturday night the small cafe was overflowing. People were standing in line waiting for a table. There were two other restaurants in the small town, but A Cup-A-Joe was the most popular. It was good for Mary Lou and Billy, but they put in some long hours. Two other waitresses were working with Mary Lou tonight. One was about her age; the other looked to be eighteen or nineteen; probably Mary Lou and Billy's daughter.

While we waited for a place at the counter to open up, I tried to be as inconspicuous as possible. Some of the people were avoiding me as a form of self-preservation. Walter and Abner Shepard had probably bullied everyone in town at one time or another. Few people wanted to befriend me, and risk the wrath of either Shepard. Mary Lou and Billy didn't care about them, living life on their own terms; they weren't going to be bullied. Too bad more people didn't subscribe to that philosophy.

When two people stood up to leave, I took a step toward the counter. Before I could move further, Abner walked around me. "Need to wait your turn, little lady," he growled. "We were here first." I turned to see Walter and Ed Bodeen following him in the door.

"Seein' as you just came in; I don't think you were here first." Shep stepped in front of me. If there was going to be trouble, he'd be first in line.

"Wasn't talking to you, Baker." The men give a nasty

chuckle. Abner turned away, walking into a brick wall called Billy.

"Howdy, Abner." He nodded at Walter and Ed. "Your table will be ready in a few minutes. You three usually sit over in the corner, right?" He nodded to a table where three teenage boys were sitting. "Heard them saying they're going to a movie so they won't be sticking around long."

"I'm in a hurry tonight," Abner said. "We'll sit at the counter." He tried to walk around Billy, but didn't get far.

"You know the house rules. First come first served. These young folks were waiting when you walked in."

"I'm here every night," Abner tried to get in Billy's face, but he was several inches too short. "Seems that should count for something."

"Only when you get here first." No one had noticed Sheriff Donovan stand up from a booth in the back. "Wait your turn or find somewhere else to eat."

"Billy might not like losing the business me and mine bring in." Abner wasn't ready to back down. It wouldn't do his bully-boy reputation any good.

"Me and Mary Lou won't starve," Billy said calmly.

They had no choice, but to wait or leave. If looks could kill, I'd be dead as they walked out, slamming the door behind them. It was probably the first time in their long lives anyone had made them back down.

Sheriff Donovan shook his head. "Things seem to be escalating with those three. Wonder what's brought it on." He looked at me.

I raised my hands, palms out. "Don't look at me, only thing I've done is inherit what they consider theirs. I haven't the faintest idea what I did to Ed Bodeen. I didn't even know he existed until six weeks ago." People in the cafe had taken an extreme interest in our conversation. Looking pointedly at them now, I decided to give them something they needed to hear. "Maybe if people in this town had stood up to them years ago, they wouldn't have it in their heads they could get away with walking on people now."

The sheriff chuckled, and went back to his dinner without

saying anything more. Billy had already gone back to the kitchen. "Think you got your point across, Darlin'?" Shep whispered with a barely concealed chuckle.

"I doubt it." I looked over my shoulder at the crowded room. Everyone was intently interested in their food. The entire episode had taken only a matter of minutes, but time had stretched out, feeling like hours had elapsed since we walked in.

"Hi there, Honey." Mary Lou put a cup of coffee in front of each of us. "Don't let those baboons upset you. Every now and then Billy has to come out to settle one of them down."

"How come they don't intimidate him like they do everyone else?"

She gave one of her boisterous laughs. "We never had anything they wanted bad enough to try pushing us around. Besides, Billy's a lot bigger than them. He always was. He played tackle with Young Ed in high school. No one was able to take him down. He's not about to let Ed try now. Abner and Walter are just mean old men."

"How come Ed hangs around with them? They're both old enough to be his father."

"Old Ed always hung around with the four Shepard brothers. Young Ed followed his daddy everywhere, so he was always with the five of them. By the time Old Ed, Wilbur and Arthur passed on Young Ed was part of the group. I guess they feel they have to stick together." Picking up an order, she hustled off.

I wanted to ask the sheriff about Deidre's murder, but this wasn't the place. There were too many ears eavesdropping on everything I said. I don't know why they found me so fascinating. It was finally accepted I'm not Rosie's ghost. Maybe they just enjoy the fact Walter, Abner and Ed's attention was now focused on someone else.

After the confrontation in the cafe, Shep insisted on staying the night again. "There's no tellin' what those men will try after bein' bested by the sheriff and Billy. They can't get back at Sheriff Donovan, and they know better than to mess with Billy. You're the least likely to be able to physically stand up to them."

I could see the logic, so I didn't argue. "You don't need to sleep on the floor. I can trust you to stay in your own room." I couldn't help but smile at the thought.

"Darlin' I told your dad I wouldn't sleep with you until you were my wife, and I meant it. It isn't that I don't want you, 'cuz I do." He leaned into me, touching his forehead to mine. "I appreciate you trustin' me. I just don't want to put my will power to the test."

My heart melted completely. How could I not love this man? I'd never met anyone more honorable.

I had no more than turned out the lantern and climbed into the high bed when Gus started barking and raising a fuss. Before I could get out of bed again, I could hear loud pounding on the door and someone yelling.

"It's Walter Shepard," Shep spoke softly when I came down the stairs. By now I could understand a few of the words coming through the heavy door.

"Baker, get...my granddaughter, you...Parker..."

I opened the door before he could say anything further. "That's enough! It's nearly midnight. Are you drunk?"

He brushed past me, coming at Shep with his fists raised. I had no doubt Shep could take care of himself against an eighty something year old man, but it wasn't necessary. Gus planted himself between the two men, a fierce growl emanating from his thick chest. Mr. S. stopped, the angry color draining from his face. "Call him off," he squeaked. "He'll kill me."

"Sit, Gus, stay." He obeyed immediately, but remained alert. If Walter made any move towards either Shep or me, Gus would take him down.

"What's the meaning of this midnight house call? You aren't supposed to be on my property, remember?"

Walter ignored my questions, glaring at Shep. "You've got a lot of nerve, sleeping with my granddaughter where anyone could see. You're both a disgrace." His anger was barely controlled, but he knew better than to push his luck with Gus standing just inches from him.

"Mr. Shepard, I'm not sleepin' with Parker." Shep started to explain, but I cut him off.

"I don't owe you an explanation, and my actions are none of your business. You disowned me years ago, so you have no right now to tell me what to do. Go home!"

He started to argue further, but I wasn't in any mood to listen. "Go home or go to jail. Your choice." My voice was deadly calm. Maybe because of that, he took me seriously. Without another word, he left.

Once in his truck, and safe from Gus, he shouted out the window. "You disgrace this family just like she did." He gunned the truck to life, gravel spraying out beneath his tires. That's probably the only way the man knew how to drive.

When he was gone, I sagged against the door jamb, my hands shaking, my legs rubbery. "What did he mean? Was he talking about Mom? How does he think she disgraced the family? He has no right to tell me what to do."

Shep wrapped me in his strong arms, rubbing his big hands up and down my back. "I don't know what or who he meant, Darlin'. Sometimes I think he's slippin' in his mind, confusin' the past and present. As much as he doesn't want to claim you, he can't help it. He's still your grandpa. It's just something inside he can't deny."

I was past the stage of arguing. I just wanted to go to bed, and forget this mess for a few hours. Sleep didn't come easily though. I paced my bedroom, trying to calm down, trying to figure out what to do about Walter. He didn't want me here; at least he wanted me out of the house. What was hidden here that he and his brother didn't want me to find? I finally fell into an uneasy sleep only to be awakened a few short hours later by the aroma of coffee floating up the stairs.

I was still feeling groggy when we went to church. Visiting Milly would be the bright spot in my day. Pulling into the parking lot beside the church, my heart sank. Walter Shepard's truck was parked right up front.

I tried to ignore him and walk past, but he had other intentions. "You have some nerve going to church after what the two of you were up to last night," he sneered. He felt safe since Gus wasn't with us. "Where's Milly? Why didn't she come today?" He stepped out of his truck, blocking the sidewalk. If he didn't know where she was, I wasn't going to tell him.

"Church is for all sinners, Mr. Shepard. Would you like to come in with us?" Shep asked. I choked on the laugh bubbling up in my throat. Shep had stepped slightly to his left keeping himself between me and the older man.

Walter's face turned an angry red. It's a wonder he hasn't stroked out since I came here. His blood pressure had to be through the roof. "I'm not talking to you, Baker. And I'm not going to church. I want to know where Milly is this morning. She always goes to church, why isn't she here?"

"Maybe she knew you'd be looking for her so she decided not to come today." He was a little more pathetic every time I saw him. He is really just a sad old man through no one's fault but his own.

"It's time to stop this nonsense. She needs to come home. You tell her I said so." His gravelly voice shook slightly.

"Maybe if you tried talking nice to her instead of issuing orders, it'd help. Or maybe it's too late. Good-bye, Mr. Shepard." We walked around his truck, and went inside the church. I breathed a sigh of relief when he didn't follow us.

CHAPTER SIXTEEN

Milly prepared a wonderful lunch, or dinner as the big noon meal is called in farm country. Country fried chicken, mashed potatoes and gravy, scalloped corn and baking powder biscuits. If I ate like this every day, I'd have to work out twice as hard at the gym. I groaned, and pushed back from the table after eating more than my share. "No wonder Mom's such a great cook. She learned all of your tricks in the kitchen."

She blushed at the compliment. She probably wasn't used to having people say nice things to her. "Have you talked to her lately?" she asked, "I keep hoping she'll come see us."

"Dad thinks he's got her convinced. Wouldn't you like to go back with them? I know Mom would love to have you with her, even for a little while. The twins can show you all their sports trophies."

Remembering what Mr. S. had said the day before, I asked, "Does he think Mom disgraced the family because she married my birth father? I remember he was a nice man."

Milly shook her head. "He had it in his head she should marry Young Ed. It was an insult when his only daughter wouldn't obey his orders." She shook her head again. "It wasn't like we were living in the eighteen hundreds. Girls pick their own husbands now. I never could figure out what he was thinking."

"He said you should come home, Grandma, but he's not going to change if you do." I didn't want her going back into an abusive situation.

"Oh, I probably will someday, just not right now." She patted my hand. "Don't worry yourself about it. Everything will work itself out."

I didn't want to leave her alone, but I couldn't make her come with me either. She had to make her own decisions just like everyone else.

Gus was glad to see us when we pulled into the lane. He paced back and forth between us and the road, sniffing at the ground. The big meal I'd just eaten threatened to make a return appearance when my stomach lurched. Someone had been here while we were gone.

"He's trying to show us something." Shep pointed to a small mound of meat at the end of the lane. "Keep him here; I'll see what it is." Using a rag he'd taken out of the back of his truck, he examining it before bringing it back to me.

"Someone threw him some raw meat. Good thing he didn't eat it." He held up several capsules he found stuck in the meat. "He'd either be unconscious or dead if he had."

Once again, I had to call the sheriff. This was getting old. I by-passed his dispatcher as he'd suggested. "I'll have the capsules analyzed by the state lab," he told us. "I don't know what it will prove beyond someone was trying to poison your dog."

"You know who did it," I stated heatedly. "It had to be Abner or Walter Shepard or Ed Bodeen."

The sheriff nodded in agreement. "But I can't prove it. They knew you wouldn't be home?" He raised one eyebrow questioningly.

"It wouldn't be hard to figure out," Shep answered. "She always leaves Gus to patrol when she's not here. Good thing he won't take food from strangers."

When the sheriff left, I stomped into the house. As soon as there was electricity in the house, I was getting a security system installed. "Whatever Rosie wanted me to find has to be pretty important, something incriminating. They know I haven't found it yet, or they wouldn't keep trying to get in." I looked around. "Is it in the journals or somewhere else?" My gaze fell on the portrait I'd hung on the wall in the parlor. I was always drawn back to that. Reaching up to lift it down, Shep reached over me, easily lifting the heavy frame off the wall.

He laid it down on the dining table face down. I'd already examined the back, but felt the same disappointment and frustration at finding nothing. The back had been sealed long ago. I let out a frustrated sigh. "Nothing." I flopped down in a side chair.

"Don't give up so fast." He leaned over, examining the back carefully. The backing was uneven instead of lying flat; a small slit along the edge hadn't been completely resealed. He ran his hands over it. "There's somethin' in here." Rosie wanted me to find this, but she didn't want it to be obvious there was something hidden here in case someone else started looking.

I wanted to rip the backing off, but Shep slowly, methodically lifted the edges. When he finally took the backing off, we stared at a stack of papers more than an inch thick. The frame was thick with a space between the portrait and outer edge. It was filled with papers that had nothing to do with the portrait. I recognized Rosie's shaky handwriting on the top sheet. "Another letter," I said on an exhaled breath. With shaking hands I picked it up.

My dearest Parker,

I hope you haven't found this too soon. Please don't give up if you discover this first. You need to find out the truth of what they did to me. It's been nearly seventy years, but they still need to be punished.

I kept a watch over you through the years. You'll find the pictures I had taken of you, and the reports of how you were doing. Please don't be mad at me. I had to make sure they didn't take you away, too.

When your mother remarried, I rejoiced. I knew she was safe. He wouldn't keep trying to get her after that. But I had to make sure you were safe from the others. I never knew if they realized you were born in my image, but I couldn't take the chance.

If you are able to prove what I believe to be true, Shep is also a part of me. He is God's retribution on them. They don't even see the likeness, the exact likeness. More the fools them. I didn't know he existed until two years ago. Now I'm more certain than ever they stole my love, my life. They need to pay.

I didn't want to tell you all this straight out. You need to

166

search for the answers. What you work for, means more in the end. Keep searching but remain alert. There are some evil people around you.
You both have always been in my heart.
Love,
Aunt Rosie

Shep stared at me. The horror on his face had to mirror what was on mine. How could Rosie do this to us? Why would she set us up like this? She told me to learn to trust Shep, to love him. But if we're really blood related, why would she do such a thing?

"Is she sayin what I think she's sayin? Are we related?" His voice was a horrified whisper filled with the same agony I was feeling. "I'm in love with you."

She wanted me to find the truth of her past, what her brothers did to her. She'd planned all this before she knew Shep existed. Once she met him, she planned for us to meet. She wanted us to fall in love. Would she do that if we were closely related?

"Rosie thought you were related to her, but how?" We were silent, trying to put our thoughts in some kind of order. When we first saw the picture of Rosie with the man who looked like Shep, we'd guessed, almost joked about being distant cousins; but how distant?

By unspoken agreement we avoided each other for the next week until we could figure this out. How do I find out if it's possible for us to have a life together? Who could I ask? In a town as small as Whitehaven there weren't any genetic specialists. There were few doctors, and only an emergency clinic instead of a hospital.

I spent my time trying to fit the pieces together while Shep continued working on the house. We still weren't certain Shep's grandfather was Rosie and Barnard's baby. If so, Rosie would be Shep's great grandmother. She was my great aunt. That would make us, what? Looking up the relationship on the internet I decided we were second cousins once removed. Was that distant enough? I needed to talk to someone else.

Shep and I ended up on Pastor Jim's doorstep at the same

time. "I needed someone to talk to," Shep said miserably. I wanted to comfort him, but I couldn't touch him or I'd be lost. Pastor Jim sat back, digesting everything we told him.

"Being second cousins once removed isn't like first cousins," he finally said. "I'm not a doctor, but it seems to me there shouldn't be a problem. It isn't against the law for you to marry."

"Thank you, God!" We whispered the prayer of gratitude together as Shep reached out to take my hand. I'm not sure I could have stayed for the rest of the year knowing we could never be together.

With that settled, I started looking again for the answers Rosie wanted me to find. I sorted through the papers hidden behind the portrait. From the time Mom moved to Arizona to the day Rosie passed away she had received reports about us. There wasn't any part of my life she didn't know about. But why did she do that? Unless she left other letters with more hints hidden somewhere, the journals were the obvious place to look. She had to have written about what her father and brothers did to her.

"Sort them by date," Shep suggested. "Her daddy supposedly sent her away for a year when she was fifteen. They did somethin' to her, somethin' awful. They didn't know she kept journals, or they would've destroyed them a long time ago. Whatever she left for you to find points a finger at them, they just don't know what it is."

Rosie wrote down her every thought, every emotion, everything that happened to her. She started keeping a journal when she was six or seven years old. A day didn't go by that she didn't write something, even at that early age. I needed to find the ones she wrote around the time she was fifteen, maybe then we could put an end to this.

Something in her letter nagged at my subconscious. I just couldn't put my finger on what. As so often happens, what I'd been trying to remember came to me in the middle of the night. Coming out of a sound sleep, I sat straight up in bed. "She knew who killed my father!" She hinted at that in both letters.

This was something else she couldn't prove, but she wanted me to know.

The remainder of the night, I slept fitfully, hazy dreams peopled with mean men, crying babies and women. When I came downstairs, it was only five-thirty. I felt like my head was full of cotton fluff, and had trouble placing one foot in front of the other. Shep was standing at the stove wearing only a pair of snug fitting jeans. His muscular chest and back were bare. Coffee was perking on the wood stove, and he was frying bacon and eggs. God bless him!

Coming up behind him, I wrapped my arms around his waist, placing light kisses on his bare back. This is how it'll be someday when we're married, I thought wistfully. Butterflies fluttered in my stomach at the thought.

"How'd you sleep, Darlin'? You still look tired."

"I finally figured out what I was missing in her letters. Someone here killed my birth father. She knew who it was. Why she didn't tell me?"

Shep shook his head. "Because she didn't have proof, she just let them think she did. If she had a baby, I'm proof he lived. Whatever her brothers did, she couldn't prove it and neither can we. Why are they tryin' so hard to keep us from findin' what she had if it wasn't proof positive?"

The journals weren't in any order, and it took most of the morning skimming through them to find one with the approximate dates we were looking for. I had to figure this out before Mom and Dad got here with the twins. I couldn't put them in danger.

Rosie said 'they' had taken something from her. I could only assume she was talking about her father and brothers. But had they committed a crime? If so, it had taken place sixty or seventy years ago. The statute of limitations was long past except for murder and kidnapping. But no one had even hinted a murder had taken place when Rosie was a young girl. Was Deidre's murder somehow related to all this? Had she found out something 'they' didn't want anyone to know? My thoughts were going in circles again.

It was hot and sticky outside, but at least there was a nice breeze. It was beginning to feel like an oven inside. Even with all the windows open, there wasn't enough of a breeze to cool off the house. Shep was working as fast as possible to get things done, but electricity couldn't get here fast enough to please me. At least I could plug in some fans.

Sitting in the swing, I picked up the journal. This was Rosie's first year in high school; she was about fourteen when she wrote this entry:

This is my first year of high school, Papa says I have to quit, I'm needed around the farm. He tried to make me quit last year but I refused. I won't let him make me quit now. The only thing I do is cook and clean. It's harvest time, and he's hired some men to help out this year. All the farm hands join the family for meals, so I will be cooking for ten or twelve men. Why do I have to quit school to do that? My brothers don't have to quit, they just take time off like most of the other boys. Even some of the girls take time off to help out.

Miss Grady, my teacher, said she'd have a talk with Papa, but I don't think it will do any good. He thinks school is wasted on girls even though he knows I want to go to college. He won't even talk about that, says it's a waste of money to send a girl to college. She'll just get married, and all that money would be wasted.

I don't ever want to get married! That would mean I would have to wait on a man forever. No thank you.

At least he didn't "whoop" her that day, I told myself. It's no real surprise Abner and Walter turned out so mean and backward thinking. Milly had been right when she said their father was as mean as a snake.

The next three entries were more of the same. Rosie was waiting to see if her teacher could convince her father to let her remain in school. The fourth day, she was rewarded for her persistence.

I don't know how Miss Grady talked Papa into letting me take time off but she did. I get to stay in school. For now. I don't hold out much hope he'll change his mind about college though. For now it's enough that I get to finish high school, or at least this year.

Like the boys, I have to get up at four o'clock. Ten men need to be fed. I guess I should be grateful I don't have to work in the field like some of the girls. If they don't have any brothers, their families need the help in the fields.

I made six loaves of bread this morning. By the time everyone had eaten supper, there was only one loaf left, not enough for breakfast. Papa wasn't happy. He said I should know better. Hungry men need lots of food. I'd better make sure I don't run out tomorrow. I know what will happen if I do. Papa has his strap with him all the time. I'm not sure if he would use it in front of the farm hands, but I don't want to take the chance. I don't think any of them would stand up for me though. No one wants to lose their job.

Papa always says girls and women need to be whooped every now and then to keep them in line. I wonder if he whooped Mama before she died. Maybe she just got tired of being whooped, and decided to go to Jesus. Lucky Mama.

I was so angry I had to put the journals aside for a little while. If that man were still alive, I'd beat him myself. Mom never said anything about Walter beating her or her brothers, but that doesn't mean it didn't happen. She never lifted a hand to me or the twins. Dad either. All he needed to do was give us 'that look' and we obeyed immediately. I smiled at the thought. I really miss them.

I knew without a doubt I wouldn't leave before the year was over. No way was I going to let either Shepard brother get one cent or one inch of ground belonging to Rosie. Her brothers had enjoyed it when their father whooped her. Had Walter beaten Milly? It wasn't something I could ask. She'd deny it even if it was true. Most women did; it was simply too embarrassing to admit they were the victims of abuse.

I'd been sitting on the swing for two hours and needed to get the circulation going again. Gus and I wandered through the garden marveling at all the flowers. There was a riot of color everywhere. I wasn't sure if Rosie had done the work herself, or if she paid someone to take care of the garden. It was hard to imagine an eighty year old woman doing this physical work, but she grew up on a farm so I suppose it wasn't unusual. Since I'd been here, I'd enjoyed tending them myself. In the heat of the day everything was beginning to droop. Until the water lines were in, watering was done by hand. I walked around back to the well for the watering can.

Ted was working, the green tractor sitting at the edge of the field. The corn was getting taller every day. I hoped he'd give me a couple of fresh picked ears when it was ripe.

A flash of light at the far side of the field caught my eye, but it was gone just as quick. Was someone there? Chills traveled up my arms even though the temperature was in the nineties. For several long minutes I watched, trying to see someone, but the stalks of corn were the only things moving. Had it been my imagination? Feeling spooked, I went back to the house. It was supposed to rain tonight. I'd let nature water the flowers.

Although I was safe inside, I couldn't rid myself of the feeling of being watched. I briefly thought about going to see if someone was really out there. Then common sense took over. That wasn't such a good idea. What if someone *was* out there? What would I do then? It had probably been Ted watching to see what I was doing, I rationalized. Or maybe I'd just imagined seeing something. Trying to dismiss the feeling, I picked up another journal.

CHAPTER SEVENTEEN

The uneasy sensation persisted, and my attention was divided between the journal and the view out the parlor window. I decided not to sit on the porch despite the growing heat in the house. After rereading the same entry several times, the words finally registered. "This is it! It's got to be." I wanted to shout and dance a jig. I turned back several pages to see what I'd missed.

Papa hired two more farm hands this morning. That means twelve hungry men, and they'll all be expecting a big meal come noon. I'll be glad when harvest is over, and I can go back to school. Some of the girls are glad when they get to take time off to help out during harvest, but I'd rather be in school. Papa keeps saying school is a waste of time since I'll be getting married soon.

I won't be fifteen for another four months! I'm not going to get married now or ever. I know he's plotting with Mr. Bodeen, but I'm not going to marry his horrible son.

"Huh?" How could this be? Ed Bodeen was just a few years older than Mom. He hadn't even been born yet. Then the light bulb went on in my muddled mind. Rosie wasn't talking about the Ed Bodeen I knew; she was talking about his father. He had been the same age as the Shepard brothers. What was it with these men? Why were they trying to join their families? This all revolved around money.

I focused on the journal again.

The men came tramping in like hungry hogs at the trough. Some didn't even bother to wash up or wipe the mud off their boots like they'd never been taught manners.

The two men Papa hired this morning are different though. William and Barnard said please when asking for a dish to be passed. They even thanked me for the meal before heading back to the fields, and told me how good it was. They didn't eat like they hadn't seen food in a year either. My brothers could take lessons from them. Even Papa could learn a thing or two.

I was cooking from the time I got up until just minutes before falling into bed. In a few hours it will start all over again. Two more weeks before harvest is finished. The only good thing I can say about harvest is Papa is too busy and too tired to take much notice of me as long as I keep food on the table.

I need to sleep now. Three o'clock will be here in a few short hours.

So Barnard worked for Rosie's father. But what happened to him? How had they fallen in love so quickly if he worked for her father just during the harvest? Two weeks wasn't very long. But it hadn't taken long for Shep and me to fall in love, I reminded myself.

After supper tonight, Barnard offered to help me clean up the dishes. They were through in the field for the day. The other men took off for their own beds. Morning came early for them, too. Papa didn't let anyone sleep in.

I've never met a man willing to help out with women's work. Papa had gone to bed so I let him help me. If Papa knew I was talking to a man, he would whoop me good. He didn't let me talk to the farm hands.

Barnard had been in the war. He said he had trouble sleeping since then, and liked to keep himself busy. After the war he went home to Indiana where he was going to get married, but his fiancé had married someone else while he was gone. She didn't even have the decency to write and tell him. She was just gone when he got home. My heart broke for him.

After that, he wandered around the country, working where he could. Someday he wanted to go to college, maybe be a teacher. I told him that's what I wanted to be; or maybe a writer. I told him about my journals. He's the only one I've ever told about them. He showed me a small book he kept in his pocket to write down his thoughts. He didn't get to write every day, especially while he was fighting in the war.

The time passed quickly while I was talking with Barnard. I was surprised when the big grandfather clock in the hall chimed ten. I should have been in bed an hour ago. If Papa knew I was still up, he'd whoop me.

I was riveted by the unfolding story. I wanted to skip ahead to find out what happened, yet at the same time, I wanted to see it unfold.

This morning Barnard was the first one in from the barn. He'd helped out with milking the cows and putting out fresh hay. He offered to help me get the food on the table but I had to decline. If Papa saw him, he'd be sent packing right away, and I would be whooped. The only time the farm hands could talk to me was to ask for food or something to drink. I'd have to explain to Barnard tonight. I didn't want him to be fired or worse, and I didn't want to be whooped anymore. He's the most considerate man I've ever met.

When the men came in for the noon meal, Barnard followed the example of the others and didn't speak to me. He nodded slightly in my direction, and gave me a little wink. My heart tripped over itself in my chest. He likes me, and knows I'll get in trouble if Papa sees him talking to me. Maybe one of the men who worked for Papa before told him. Papa's been watching me today. I hope no one saw Barnard helping me last night.

Young Ed Bodeen joined the other men for supper. Another mouth to feed. He kept telling me how good the food was, how pretty I looked tonight. I wanted to throw up. I guess Papa put him up to it. He's as mean as my brothers. He was just pretending to be nice. I was so embarrassed. Barnard kept his head down, and didn't look at me at all. When he finished eating, he hurried outside with the other men. He probably thinks I'm just like his fiancé.

Young Ed asked if I'd like to go for a walk after I cleaned up but I told him no. I had other work to do. I'll probably get whooped for turning him down but I don't care. I'm not walking out with that horrible man.

The apple doesn't fall far from the tree, I thought. The Ed Bodeen I know is just as horrible as the one Rosie knew. I'm not sure what all he's capable of, but I certainly don't trust him.

Shep came in, looking dirty and tired. He sank down on the floor beside my chair. "Why aren't you outside?" He rubbed my bare leg. "It's a little cooler out there than in here."

I didn't want to tell him I felt like I was being watched. I was probably imagining it anyway. "I was out there for a while. I just decided to come inside. You look really tired." I ran my fingers though his soft, thick hair that was almost gray now with plaster dust. "I think you could do with a shower. I'll bet you're hungry too."

"Boy, howdy, I'll say. Where are we eatin' tonight?"

"Right here. I'm going to cook." It was a daring statement. As long as the ice had held up in the ice box, the steaks should still be good. There were fresh vegetables in the root cellar. I'd even learned how to make biscuits in the wood stove. "Go home and shower. I'll have things going when you get back."

"What about you? Don't you want a shower?" He was reluctant to leave me alone.

"I'll be fine. It's been hot, but remember where I'm from. I'm used to 115 degree temps this time of year. I'll wash up in the sink and start supper. The cool water will feel good." I leaned down, kissing him. "Go on, get a shower. I'll have supper going when you get back."

"You're sure? There hasn't been any trouble today."

I nodded quickly. "I'm sure. Go." I gave him a gentle shove towards the door. He was a lot hotter and dirtier than me. He also needed to be able to relax for a few minutes without worrying about me. "When you get back I'll tell you about the journal entries I read today. I've found Barnard."

He stopped at the door, an expectant expression on his handsome face. "Really? So he was here."

"When you come back I'll tell you all about it." I gave him another quick kiss as he hurried out the door.

As soon as he was out of sight, I shut and locked the door. The eerie feeling was back. Either my imagination was working overtime, or someone was really watching me. Now

176

that I'd found Barnard, I wasn't going to let anything derail me. Something definitely happened between them.

I brought clean clothes downstairs and closed the curtains. I wasn't going to invite a Peeping Tom to watch me. Work in the kitchen was progressing nicely. It wouldn't be long before I had running water. Until a hot water heater was installed, it would still be cold water. One step at a time, I reminded myself. Eating in the kitchen wasn't possible though. Hurrying through my sponge bath, I quickly dressed again. I wanted to get the steaks and vegetables on before Shep came back to show him I'm not completely helpless.

The door to the root cellar was just down the back steps. Gus followed me out sniffing the air, not overly concerned about anything. Unlocking the padlock, I pulled the heavy door open, moving cautiously down the three steps. I had my flashlight with me so I could find the vegetables in the dark. We were no sooner off the last step when the door slammed shut behind us. "Hey!" I could hear the padlock being slipped through the hasp and securely latched.

Gus was going nuts, barking, pawing at the door to get at the intruder. I kept shouting and pounding on the heavy wood, but it didn't do any good. Gus and I were locked in, and the house door was open. Whoever did this had access to everything in the house, including the journals.

"Let me out. Help. Somebody help me." Ted worked in the fields late into the day. I hoped he was still out there, and could hear me, or at least hear Gus barking.

"God, please, don't let them get the journals. They're my only hope of figuring this out. If that's what you want me to do, please stop them." After my heartfelt prayer, I began pounding on the door again, making enough of a ruckus to attract attention.

Within minutes, I heard running footsteps. "Help. We're locked in. Help us." I pounded on the door until my fists hurt.

"Hey, what are you doing here? Get out of there." I thought it was Ted, but couldn't be sure. There was the sound of a scuffle, a few grunts and groans. Then a thump like someone hitting the ground, the sound of more running, this time away from the house. Then everything was quiet.

"Is anyone there?" I pounded on the door. "Are you okay?" I didn't know who landed on the ground, and who ran away. Hopefully, my would-be rescuer was all right.

"Miss Evans, are you all right? Where's the key? I'll get you out of there." Ted had heard me shouting.

"Thank you, God." I bowed my head for just a second. "The extra key is on a hook just inside the mud room." Within minutes Ted had the door unlocked helping me climb the three steps to freedom. I wanted to kiss him, I was so grateful.

"What happened? Who was that?"

"I was hoping you could tell me. Didn't you see his face?"

He shook his head. "He had a ski mask pulled down over his face."

"Oh, crap!"

"He was carrying this when he shoved past me." Ted held the journal I'd been reading earlier. "He dropped it when we struggled."

I took the small book, hugging it to my chest. "He didn't take anything else?" He shook his head, his straw colored hair falling into his face.

I sagged against the house, the adrenalin rush left me feeling weak now that it was over. Shep's truck pulled around the back of the house before I could gather myself. "Are you all right?" He looked between Ted and me.

"Someone locked Miss Evans in the root cellar." Ted explained. "They tried to take something out of the house."

I held up the journal.

"Who?" Ted and I both shook our heads. "I didn't even see him."

"He had on a ski mask," Ted offered at the same time. "Maybe you should call the sheriff."

This was getting to be a bad habit. It was only a matter of minutes before his car pulled into the lane. If I let Gus go, he'd be able to follow the scent. He might even be able to find the person in town. But what would that prove? No jury would convict on the scent trail a dog followed.

"What happened now?" Sheriff Donovan's resigned tone set me on edge. He was probably getting tired of coming here every couple of days, but this wasn't my fault. Listening patiently, he shook his head when we fell silent. "Neither one of you can identify the man." It was a statement, not a question. "He was after that book?" He pointed to the journal I was still hugging to my chest.

"He dropped it," Ted confirmed.

"So any fingerprints he might have left are gone now." I groaned. I hadn't even thought of fingerprints. I was just glad to have the journal. "I'll have a team come out and dust the doors and anywhere he might have touched."

"Won't do any good, Sheriff," Ted stopped him from calling for a crime scene team. "I'm pretty sure he was wearing gloves."

"Okay, give me the best description you can. If you saw he had on gloves, you saw something."

"I...ah..I felt the gloves more than saw them. He dropped the book when I grabbed him as he ran out of the house. I felt the rough leather from a work glove when he took a swing at me." He gingerly touched his jaw. "I wasn't expecting him to hit me," he defended himself.

"You did fine, son. What can you tell me about him, young, old?" Ted shook his head and shrugged. "How big was he? Taller than you, shorter?"

Ted brightened. "He was taller than me, thicker, big shoulders. I think he had a beer belly. He couldn't have been real old." Again he gingerly touched his jaw. "He had a pretty good punch."

That description could fit any number of men in town, but I didn't point that out. He'd come to my rescue, and kept the journal from disappearing.

The entire time we talked, I kept my hand on Gus's collar. Finally I interrupted the sheriff. "Gus can follow his scent to where he went."

Sheriff Donovan nodded and I released Gus. "Track, Gus, track." He took off across the yard and through the field. At one point he stopped where I'd seen the flash earlier in the day.

The grass was trampled down like someone had been sitting there for a long time. He couldn't take us much further though. Behind a stand of trees and bushes, out of sight of the house, tire tracks showed where a vehicle had been parked, the dirt showed skid marks from spinning tires when he sped out; another dead end. *Crap.*

Back at the house, I thanked Ted for getting me out of the root cellar so fast, and stopping the thief from getting away with the journal. "What's so important about that book?" Sheriff Donovan wanted to know once Ted left.

"It was Rosie's journal when she was fourteen. She was a prolific writer," I said. "I think they'll answer a few of my questions. Maybe tell us why people are so intent on getting me out of this house."

"Did this guy know you had the journals?"

I shrugged. "I'm not sure. Rosie was holding something over a few people in town. She left something for me to find. I don't know if she had evidence of a crime or just family secrets, but there's definitely something she wanted me to find." I held up the journal. "I've been reading this one today. I left it on the table. I guess it was the first thing he saw and grabbed it. Ted got here so fast he didn't have any time to go through things."

"I'll have a deputy drive by a few times tonight." There was little else he could do. "You might think about putting those journals some place safe instead of leaving them around here."

"I shouldn't have left you alone," Shep paced across the kitchen after the sheriff left. "I should have been here for you."

"This wasn't your fault." I wrapped my arms around his narrow waist. "He was waiting for a chance to get in the house. I shouldn't have taken Gus into the root cellar with me. If he'd been outside, the guy wouldn't have been able to get close. I wasn't thinking."

We fixed supper while I told Shep about Barnard. "Rosie was definitely fascinated by him, at least in the entries I read.

180

Her father was ready to marry her off to Ed Bodeen." Shep frowned, confused like I'd been. "There must have been Ed Bodeens in this town from the beginning of time. She was supposed to marry this Ed Bodeen's father. If she had, this Ed would be my second cousin." I shivered at the thought.

"The sheriff's right about putting the journals someplace safe. Now that someone is aware they exist, he won't stop trying to get them. How did he know what to look for when he came in the house?"

"I was reading on the front porch this morning. Maybe he saw the opportunity to get in, and grabbed what I'd been reading; hoping it was what he was looking for. He wasn't in the house long enough to read any of the entries."

"I wish Miss Rosie hadn't said you had to stay in the house while you figured this out. It's not safe anymore. Someone is gettin' desperate and dangerous. She wouldn't want you to be hurt or killed trying to figure this out."

"I'd lose everything, and the Shepard brothers would get it all. I don't care about the farm and house for myself, but I'll be darned if they're going to get it after all they put her through."

The open trunk was sitting in the parlor when the thief grabbed the journal. He had to have seen the others. I knew in my soul, he and anyone working with him would be back for them. "It's too late to take them to the bank in Buena Vista," I said. "Where can we put them so they'll be safe?"

"They'll be safe tonight. We'll put them somewhere else tomorrow. They'll be watching from now on. Whatever we do, we have to make them think the journals are no longer in the house." He was silent for a moment. "If we take the trunk to my place, they'll think we've moved them there. We can tell the sheriff. Maybe they'll keep an eye on things. If we're lucky, they might even catch someone."

CHAPTER EIGHTEEN

The next morning, we loaded the steamer trunk into his truck. The journals were back in the attic for now. We filled the trunk with any useless thing Shep could find in the basement, so it looked heavy when we carried it outside. If someone did steal the trunk, they wouldn't get anything valuable.

When we got back to the farm, I called the sheriff on his private line. No way was I going through the dispatcher. She would probably listen in on our conversation, and tell her idiot son. It would be all over town in a heartbeat.

"We took the trunk to Shep's house," I told him. "If someone was watching us, they'll think the journals are there."

"Is that a good idea?" he asked, playing devil's advocate. "If someone really is after them, what's to stop them from breaking in there? Or destroying his house? What do you think he'll do when he finds out the journals aren't there?"

My stomach lurched. "I guess I hadn't thought that far ahead. I keep hoping the journals will give me the answers, and it will all be over."

"You're smarter than that!" He sounded exasperated. "If a crime was committed back when Rosie was a teenager, there's not much anyone can do about it now. If it was a murder or kidnapping, I'd need more than a journal to prove it. You know that."

"I know," I sighed in frustration. "But maybe the thief doesn't. There's something in this house someone or more than one someone doesn't want me to find. People have been trying to get me to leave ever since I arrived. They're getting more hostile every day."

"You don't think it's just about the money and land?"

"That's part of it, but Rosie left me two letters telling me to find the truth of what they did to her."

"What is that supposed to mean? What did they do to her and who are they?"

"If she'd told me what they did to her, she wouldn't need me to find the truth about it." More than a little exasperation made my reply sharper than I intended. "And 'they' are her father and brothers. Maybe she just wanted it, whatever *it* is, made public; she wanted justice, however belated."

"Who else knows about these letters and journals?"

"Only Shep. I showed Milly the first letter. I hadn't found the second one yet. I didn't say anything to her about the journals though."

"Would she have told Walter about the letter?"

"No, she hasn't talked to him. She left him, at least for now. She couldn't take his bullying any longer." I don't know if he paid much attention to the town gossip mill.

"I suppose he blames you for that?"

"Of course. It's easier to blame someone else for all your troubles than looking at yourself, and taking the blame. He doesn't see anything wrong with being a bully since he was raised by one."

"I'll talk with the chief," he said with a resigned sigh. "We'll try to keep an eye on Baker's place, but you need to be careful. If someone really wants those journals, for whatever reason, they aren't going to stop until they have them."

After we hung up, I took the journal I'd been reading the day before into the parlor. I still had a long way to go. Rosie and Barnard had just met. Hopefully, this one will clear up this whole mess.

At breakfast this morning, I managed to get a note to Barnard telling him Ed Bodeen means nothing to me, that I hate the odious man. I can only hope Barnard believes me. I've only known him two days, but I don't want him to think poorly of me. I didn't want to say too much in case someone else found the note later.

When the men came in for dinner, Barnard barely glanced at me and my heart sank. I don't know how much more I can do to make him understand.

Papa was in a hurry to get back to the fields, rushing the men through the meal and out of the house as soon as they finished eating. Barnard waited his turn to leave, not crowding like the others did. As he walked out, he winked at me!

I floated around the kitchen, cleaning up the mess. I don't care that all I get done in a day is cook and clean up afterward only to cook again. Under Barnard's plate I found the note he left for me. He said he enjoyed talking to me, and would like to help me clean up again if it won't get me in trouble with Papa. He said he'd be careful.

I never understood Effie when she got all giggly over the boys at school. Now I feel like laughing all the time. I can hardly wait for supper time.

Papa brought Ed in for supper again tonight. I can scarcely stand to look at the man. The more I rebuff him, the harder he tries to get my attention. On top of everything else about the man, he's thick headed. When Papa left the table, he grabbed my arm so tight I'll have a bruise, and gave me a shake. "You'd better start being nice to Ed," he growled at me. Then he stormed out the door. All the men saw what he did, but no one said anything. They all knew it would only make things worse for me if they did.

There was another note under Barnard's plate when I was cleaning up. If I can get away for even a few minutes before I go to bed, he'll be out by the barn. Papa kept a close eye on me all evening though. I didn't dare try to see Barnard. Maybe tomorrow.

He really was a nice man. It wasn't hard to understand why Rosie fell for him. After the horrible treatment she received at the hands of her father and brothers, Barnard was like a breath of fresh air.

I set the journal aside, rubbing my tired eyes. The faded writing made it difficult to read in the dim light. Looking around I realized storm clouds were building off in the distance. Monsoon season had begun at home, with dust storms and dry thunderstorms. There'd been rain storms since I came here, but the clouds billowing off in the distance were bigger and darker than I'd seen before. Tornadoes weren't unheard of in Iowa. My stomach rolled. I'd never been in a tornado, but I'd seen the aftermath on the news. It wasn't something I wanted to experience.

If a tornado hit the house, what would happen to everything? How many tornadoes had this old house withstood? I didn't want to take chances the journals would be destroyed by natural causes after going to the trouble of hiding them.

Where could I put them so they'd be safe from a tornado or a thief? I looked around the room, but didn't know what I was looking for.

All the rooms were sealed off with heavy plastic over the doorways to keep plaster dust from spreading throughout the house while they worked in the kitchen and mud room. That wouldn't give any protection from a tornado though. I sat down, trying to remember what I'd heard on the television about what to do during a tornado. Unable to sit still, I got back up. The electricity in the air filled my body, making me over-energized.

I hadn't been to the gym for almost a week. I needed to work some of this energy off. Was it safe to drive that far if a tornado was coming? *Crap, I don't know!* Was there even a tornado warning system close enough we'd hear it at the farm? I'd never thought about that before.

"What's the matter with you?" I asked myself, my voice loud in the silent room. "You've never been indecisive before. Decide what you want to do and do it." Spending so much time alone, and in nearly complete silence except for the hammering, drilling, and whatever from the renovation brought out my inner nut case. I have no television, no radio, no internet, or e-mail except when I can plug my laptop in somewhere with Wi-Fi, which isn't all that often.

Gus watched as I paced across the floor, his big head cocked to one side. I had him confused, too. "Okay, boy. You stay here. I'm going to the gym. Shep's here."

Grabbing the journal I'd been reading, I raced upstairs to change into my gym clothes and grab my bag. I'd figure out a better place for the journals when I got back. If the house blew away in the meantime, I'd deal with that later. I needed to exercise!

"I'm going to the gym," I called out to Shep over the noise the sander was making. "I can't sit still any longer."

He came over, giving me a kiss, careful not to shed any sander dust on me in the process. "It's going to rain soon. Take my truck. The Model T won't be much protection in a real downpour."

"Is there going to be a tornado?" I hoped my unease didn't show itself in my question.

"Nah, just lots of rain." He handed me the keys to his truck, and went back to work.

The wind was picking up as I went outside, and the temperature had dropped some. With the humidity in the sixties, seventies, or higher and temperatures in the nineties, sweat beaded my forehead and upper lip. One hundred fifteen and forty-five percent humidity didn't sound so bad now.

Parking the big truck in one of the farthest spaces to keep from hitting someone or someone hitting it, I got out, locking the door behind me. "You and Baker shouldn't be doing what you're doing." Letting out a startled squeal, I whirled around. Ed Bodeen stood just inches away from me. Had he followed me? I hadn't paid attention on my way here.

"Just what is it you think Shep and I are doing?" I tried not to show any fear. That would feed the power he felt as he loomed over me. I looked around the parking lot, hoping there was someone who'd help me if he got out of hand.

"You're whoring with him just like your great aunt did with that farm hand."

"And how do know what she was doing? You weren't even born yet."

"My daddy told me!" he growled. "She was promised to my daddy, but then she started whoring around with that farm hand. Your mama was promised to me, too. Her daddy shoulda made her marry me. I was even willing to take her back when she come looking for help to find her dead husband.

But she just kept defying her old man. He shoulda had more backbone, and forced her marry me."

His wild looking eyes were frightening, but I had to keep him talking. Is this what Rosie wanted me to learn? Had Ed Bodeen caused the accident that killed my father? I'd managed to press the record app on my phone as soon as he started talking. This was one conversation I needed a record of. "She was still married when we came here. How could she marry you?" My heart was racing so fast I thought it might fly out of my chest.

"Her husband was dead!" he yelled, spittle flying out of his mouth.

"How can you be so sure he was dead?" Anger made his face red, and I thought he'd say just about anything, especially the truth.

"Because I made..." He caught himself before going too far. "I was right, wasn't I? He was dead. She shoulda stayed here and married me."

"Why was it so important you marry my mom? What was in it for you?"

"I just told you! Your great aunt was supposed to marry my old man. If she had, none of this woulda happened. It's all her fault."

"What wouldn't have happened?"

"Everything! Don't you listen? She was supposed to be my ma. I'd have that place now. If your ma had married me, it'd still be mine."

"What's so special about the farm? Why do you want it so badly?"

"The land! Are people in Arizona so stupid they don't know the value of land?"

So it's all about money, greed. How many people had died because of it? "You still married into the Shepard family. Wasn't that good enough?" Why did he think marrying Walter's daughter meant he'd get the farm, but marrying Arthur's daughter didn't mean the same thing?

"No!" he roared. "Your mama was supposed to marry me! She woulda got the farm."

"You don't know that. Rosie could have left it to anyone."

"You just don't understand."

He was right. I didn't understand. "Why don't you explain it to me?"

"She was supposed to be my ma." His tone sounded like he was talking to a slightly stupid child. "That farm was supposed to be mine. My daddy always told me so."

This man was totally unhinged. He lived in an alternate world that had little resemblance to reality. So far he hadn't admitted to anything illegal. I needed to get him back on track.

"You have a farm and several businesses in town. Why do you want my farm?"

"It's not yours!" he stormed at me. For a minute I thought he was going to hit me. "It's supposed to be mine."

Being told something all your life doesn't make it so, but he wasn't going to listen to me.

He drew a deep breath in an attempt to calm himself. "You need to stop whoring around with Baker." He switched subjects again. "It'll ruin your life just like it ruined hers."

"Shep and I are doing nothing wrong. Even if we were it's none of your business."

He stepped closer to me, getting right in my face. "You'll do as you're told, young lady. Now you tell Baker you can't see him anymore," he growled at me.

I refused to back up, or let him see any fear. "You have no right to tell me what to do. You're nothing to me."

He grabbed my arms, shaking me like a rag doll. "You're my daughter, and you'll do as you're told." He was screaming at me now. He'd lost all connection to reality.

"No, I'm not your daughter. I'm Laura Evans' daughter." I kept my voice calm, soft, hoping it would have a calming effect on him.

For several seconds he stared down at me, his eyes unfocused, seeing someone other than me. Then giving himself a shake, he dropped his hands, and stepped away from me. "What did you say?"

"I'm Laura Evans' daughter."

He laughed. "Well, of course you are. I'm just trying to keep you from making a big mistake. Few men want another man's leavings. That's what I always told my daughters. Now they're off to college, and will be lawyers someday. That wouldn't happen if they slept their way through every man in town."

He stared off into space again, his mind a million miles away. "I tried to tell her she should be a good girl, to go back home. But she kept pushing me, wanted people to know the truth. Well, the truth ain't all it's cracked up to be. Look where it got her."

"Who are you talking about? What truth?" Rosie kept saying I was to look for the truth. Is that the same truth he's talking about? Or is he hiding something else? Deidre came here to find her father. Could that be Ed Bodeen? Had she been pushing him to acknowledge her? Had he murdered her?

His eyes regained focus and he looked down at me, a benevolent smile on his broad face. "I just thought you should know people in these parts don't take to loose women. You need to watch what you do." Without another word, he marched off, like this had been an ordinary conversation.

I slumped against the truck fender. The entire conversation had lasted less than five minutes. Rubbing my arms, I was grateful he hadn't gotten any more physical. I could already feel the beginnings of bruises. By the time I got home I'd have five nice ones on each arm. Maybe leaving the house hadn't been such a good idea. Facing a tornado couldn't be any more nerve-wracking.

It was pouring when I left the gym two hours later. Thankfully, Shep had let me take his truck. As I predicted there were five perfect bruises on each arm. By tomorrow they'd be dark purple. I didn't want to think about Shep's reaction when he sees them. My mind was still reeling from Ed's verbal attack. Part of the time he seemed to confuse me, Mom, and Rosie. I'm not sure what the recording will prove other than the man is one sandwich shy of a picnic. I just wish he'd said something incriminating in his ranting.

CHAPTER NINETEEN

The men were still working when I got back to the farm. I let Shep know I was back, but stayed away from the kitchen to avoid questions about the bruises. That didn't need to be discussed in front of the other men. For now I just wanted to forget all about Ed Bodeen and his crazy ranting.

I pulled the journal out from under my mattress where I'd hidden it before I left. Not very original, but if Shep had to go for supplies while I was gone, I wanted it hidden. Maybe we could move the journals to the root cellar. In case of a tornado or fire, I wanted them somewhere safe. I tried to remember what I'd heard on the news about what to do in a tornado.

Settling on the hard couch in the parlor, I tried to get comfortable. I'd always considered the term "horsehair" couch to be a description of color or some such thing, not an actuality. Sitting on bricks couldn't be more uncomfortable, and short hairs pricked out of the fabric making my skin itch. Once the restorations were done, I'd get something comfortable to sit on.

Within minutes I was able to forget the couch, caught up in Rosie's story again.

The harvest is over and I fear I've lost Barnard. Papa let all the workers go. It would only make matters worse if I asked him to let Barnard stay. Papa is still intent on me marrying that odious Ed Bodeen. He's here almost every meal now that he doesn't have to work on his pa's farm. Ed agrees with whatever Papa says, even the most ridiculous things. Sometimes I think Papa says stupid things just to see if Ed will agree with him. I don't know why he wants me to marry that man. I will not agree to do so even if it means Papa will whoop me until I die. I won't marry a man I don't love.

At least I have school again. I'm working hard to make up everything I've missed. That keeps me busy when I'm not cooking and cleaning. Barnard told me some of the books he's read. I asked Miss Grady if she knew of them. She even had a few in her own library at home and said I could borrow them. She knows I will take good care of them.

When the boys miss school, they don't bother making up the work. They say you don't have to go to school to be a farmer. They would be better farmers if they knew what they were doing. Always doing things the same way isn't necessarily best. Maybe I should read some books about modern methods of farming. Papa has been doing the same thing since he was a boy.

Barnard is gone? I thought they fell in love. I turned the page, nothing. So far every entry has been dated; I knew exactly when she wrote it. There hadn't been a skipped date or page in any of the journals. The last few pages of this one were blank. I set the book down, unsure what to make of this development. There were many more to read so I knew she hadn't stop writing. I hurried up to the stairs to get another book.

Coming back down a few minutes later, Shep was waiting for me at the bottom of the stairs. "How was your work out?" He paused, frowning at me. "Did you hurt yourself?" Before I could say anything he pulled me towards the light for a better look. A dark frown drew his brows together. "Who did this? What happened?" He gently rubbed his big hands over the darkening bruises.

"Ed Bodeen cornered me in the parking lot at the gym."

"And he grabbed you hard enough to leave bruises?" Anger radiated off him even though his touch remained gentle.

"He didn't make sense most of the time, ranting that Rosie was supposed to be his ma." A shiver shook me. "The man is unhinged," I whispered.

Shep pulled me into his arms, holding me gently. "You should report it to someone even if there's nothing they can do."

I pulled my phone out of my pocket, smiling up at him. "I recorded the whole thing."

Listening to the short recording, Shep frowned. "What was

he talkin' about? Was he Deidre's father? Did he kill her to keep her quiet?"

"That's what I'm thinking, but how would we ever prove it?"

He shook his head. "He is losin' it, but how violent will he get? We need to talk to someone who knows him."

"No one is going to talk to us about him; he's one of them."

He gave me that sexy little lopsided grin. "How would you like to go to dinner in Buena Vista? We've never gone there."

The swift subject change confused me. "What? If you're hungry, I can fix something here. We don't have to drive all the way to Buena Vista."

"Wouldn't you like to take your grandma out for supper?"

I caught on to what he was suggesting. "Yes, I would." I kissed his bristly chin. "I like the way your sneaky mind works. I'll bet she can give us a few answers about Mr. Bodeen. You go shower. I'll call grandma."

He started to turn away but stopped. "I'm not leavin' you here alone. You can call her from the truck."

Grandma was thrilled with the invitation, beaming at Shep when he helped her into the high truck. But that beaming smile turned into a dark glare when she saw the bruises on my arms. "Did you do that to my granddaughter?" she stormed at Shep.

"No, Grandma! Shep didn't do this! Honest, he'd never hurt me."

"Someone gripped your arms, hard." She didn't believe me. "I've seen enough of them to know."

"It was Ed Bodeen. I'll tell you all about it; we need to ask you some questions."

Shep reached over the seat, gently touching her hand. "Miz Shepard, I'd never hurt Parker. I love her. I'd protect her with my life."

She began to relax; patting his hand still resting on hers. I wondered how many times her husband had left similar bruises on her.

192

A few minutes later we sat at a back table so the few customers couldn't eavesdrop on our conversation. She shook her head when I finished telling her what happened. "He's always been a little off in the head. There were whispers that Rosie was supposed to marry Young Ed's father. I suppose that's why Walter wanted Laura to marry him. Sort of to make up for Rosie rejecting his dad, I guess. I couldn't convince them it was a mistake. After she left here the second time, they both gave up. That's when he married, Betsy, Arthur's daughter. I always felt sorry for her."

Back at her sister's house, I played the recording for her. At Bodeen's accusation that I was 'whoring' around with Shep, she looked at us, one eyebrow raised. Shep answered her questioning look before I could. "I'm stayin' at the house, but I'm sleepin' in the parlor. I told her dad I wouldn't sleep with her until I had my weddin' ring on her finger and I meant it."

Heat filled my entire body. I couldn't believe we were discussing my sex life, or lack of one, with my grandmother. She looked at us for several long seconds then patted my hand without commenting further.

"Young Ed is one to talk about such things. There have been several young women who left town because of him."

My heart rate quickened. "Could Deidre have been his daughter? If she pushed him to claim her, would he kill her?"

Milly shook her head, "If he was her father, it wouldn't be much of a bargain for her. He wasn't a good father to the daughters he and Betsy had. They both left town as soon as they could. If Betsy knows where they are, she wouldn't tell Ed."

"Why does she stay with him?" I could ask her the same question but didn't. Why did women stay in an abusive marriage? I didn't understand that mentality.

Milly shrugged. "I don't know what it's like in the big city, but here we're kind of locked in the last century. When you get married, you stay married. Period. A few couples in town have gotten divorced, but the women didn't stay long afterward. People tend to shun them."

I didn't point out the double standard. That was a

conversation for another time. "Why does Bodeen think he'd get the farm if Mom married him? Rosie could still have left it to anyone."

Milly shook her head. "He isn't all there." She tapped her temple.

"Could he be the one tryin' to break into the house?" Shep asked, speaking up for the first time. "What would he be after?"

She shrugged. "Rosie kept most people at arm's length, but especially Ed. It surprised everyone when she took such a shine to you. Walter and Abner weren't happy about it either." She gave a small chuckle. "I took some delight in it though. Rosie just loved to defy her brothers. After Arthur and Wilbur passed on, she doubled her torment of the two left behind."

I wanted to ask if she'd made plans for herself, but it wasn't my place. I prayed she wouldn't go back to Walter. If he wasn't physically abusive, he was certainly verbally and emotionally abusive.

Gus was glad to see us when we got back to the farm. We hadn't gone running for several days, and he was getting cabin fever. We sat on the porch while Gus sniffed every bush, tree and flower in the yard. Nothing raised the slightest alarm; nothing untoward had happened while we were gone.

Since the incident with the root cellar, nothing more had happened. Whoever that had been, now knew about the journals, or at least the one. But he hadn't had time to look through it. So far, there was nothing incriminating in any of them, giving someone reason to break in.

I wondered where Barnard had gone when the harvest was done. Had he left the note for Rosie before harvest was over? Could they fall in love in two short weeks? Why had she stopped writing in the last journal four pages from the end of the book? I'd had nothing but questions with no answers since coming to Iowa. The questions and the next journal would have to wait until tomorrow. My bed beckoned. Sleep claimed me before my head hit the pillow.

First thing the next morning, Gus and I went for a run. We

were both getting bored running along the fields behind the house. It'll be nice to have all these mysteries solved, and no one out to run me over or run me off. Maybe we'd try the country road tomorrow. If I don't tick someone off in the meantime, I qualified.

The humidity was climbing higher along with the temperature. One hundred and fifteen degrees in Phoenix is like stepping into an oven. This is like stepping into a sauna. You can't get dry no matter how often you towel off.

Wayne, Mike, and Jim were aware Shep was staying here at night. We couldn't keep it totally secret. He did make it clear where he was sleeping, and he wouldn't tolerate gossip being spread around. I've never met a man so concerned with his girlfriend's reputation. Some men brag about sleeping with a woman, even if it's a lie.

I'd made arrangements with Mary Lou to have breakfast for the two of us made up each morning. Wayne picked it up on his way out to the farm. I'd offered to have her make something for them, but their wives made breakfast for them at home. I needed to go to town for more ice and to replenish what little I could fix for supper. It would have to be simple and cool. Hot food didn't hold much appeal.

Settling with a cold glass of iced tea on the front porch, I picked up the next journal. I'd been too tired last night to show Shep the journal with the blank pages. Hopefully, things would be slower tonight.

I saw Barnard today! He didn't go away after Papa let him and the other hands go. He found a job at another farm. It isn't real close, but close enough. Papa knows all the farmers for miles, so he probably knows Mr. Dunn.

Barnard came into town for supplies and came by the school yard. He was looking for me but couldn't be obvious. When I came out at lunch, he walked by, pretending he didn't see me. He dropped a note on the ground and walked away. He watched from across the street while I read it.

He wants to see me again. He says he is in love with me. I don't know what love is except for the love I felt for Mama, and that is so different from what I feel for Barnard. Papa and the boys don't love me, and I surely don't love them.

Barnard said he would be in town again on Thursday to pick up something for Mr. Dunn. He wants to meet me in the woods behind the school house at noon. Just the thought of doing this is enough to make my heart jump out of my bosom. If one of the boys caught us, they would tell Papa for sure. At least I don't have to worry about Young Ed following me. He dropped out of school after the harvest. He said he didn't need to go to school to be a farmer. I guess that's why Papa likes him so much. They think alike.

Two days before I see Barnard again. I can hardly wait. I'll hide this note with the rest in my journal.

She hid the notes from Barnard in her journals? Where? Which one? I sat back with a sigh. More questions. The date on this journal followed the previous one. So what's with the blank pages? Would I ever run out of questions?

Before I could skip to the entry when she met Barnard, Shep came running out of the house. "My house is on fire." I followed him to the truck, tucking the journal in the waistband of my shorts.

"What happened?" Shep sped down the country road, breaking all the speed limits.

"I don't know. Miz Jenkins called, and said smoke was comin' out the front window. She called the fire department."

"Sheriff Donovan warned me something like this might happen." I groaned. "We shouldn't have taken the trunk there. This is my fault."

"No, it's the fault of whoever started the fire. There has to be somethin' incriminatin' in those journals. Until we figure it out, this isn't goin' to end."

It took less than ten minutes to reach Shep's house. Fire trucks lined the street, hoses snaking across the lawn. Miz Jenkins saw us pull up, and hurried over to Shep. "I'm so sorry this happened to your house, honey. You've worked so hard fixing it up. I wish I could've stopped them."

"The house can be repaired. Did you see what happened?" He put his arm around the older woman's shoulders, offering her comfort while he waited to see how much damage was done to his house.

She shook her head. "I didn't see them, but I heard their truck. It was a big one, noisy as all get out. I was sitting on my back porch. It's been so hot in the house, you know. I heard the window break, but I couldn't get around front fast enough to see anything. I'm sorry," she said again.

"It's not your fault, Miz Jenkins. Maybe someone else on the street saw the truck." It was a slim hope. As warm as it's been most everyone stayed inside, even the retired people; but maybe one of them saw something.

A fireman came over to Shep, and they walked away a few steps. "Looks like someone lobbed a Molotov cocktail into your living room. Good thing your neighbor is alert. Lot of damage, but your house is still standing. We were able to keep the fire from spreading to the other houses."

"Did anyone see anything? Miz Jenkins said she heard a loud truck."

"Not my department. You'll need to talk to the chief." He nodded as an older man walked up.

"Sorry about your house, Baker. Got any enemies who'd want to burn you out?" He didn't sound sorry.

Shep bristled at the comment. "I could name one or two, but givin' you names wouldn't do any good." This didn't bode well for finding out who did this.

The chief drew himself up to his full height, still a few inches shorter than Shep. "Just what's that crack supposed to mean? You got a problem with my department?"

"As a matter of fact," Shep started, but Sheriff Donovan interrupted them.

"Hi, Dan, Shep." He reached out to shake hands with both men. "Couldn't help but recognize the address. Thought I'd come over to see if I could lend a helping hand."

I breathed a sigh of relief. Maybe he could help defuse the situation.

"Nothing anyone can do right now, Bill. Just getting started on the investigation. Looks like Baker's made a few enemies." He smirked as he said it.

"That so? Well, maybe I can help, after all. Seems he and Miss Evans have been having some trouble out at her farm." He nodded in my direction. "People breaking in, destroying things."

"What's that got to do with a fire here?" the chief grumbled. "Seems like they'd burn her out, not Baker."

Sheriff Donovan shook his head. "No, they want her out of the house so they get it for themselves, not burn it down." His words caused my stomach to churn.

The chief went on the defensive. "You need to watch what you're saying. It sounds like you're accusing upstanding citizens of a crime."

Sheriff Donovan gave an easy-going shrug, unperturbed by the chief's statement. "Never mentioned any names, Dan. Who do you think I was talking about?" He raised an eyebrow. When the chief failed to answer, he continued. "I've seen upstanding citizens do a lot worse than this. Miz Jenkins said the truck was loud, probably a diesel. Several upstanding citizens have those. Maybe another neighbor saw it. That'd give you somewhere to start."

"I don't need you telling me how to do my job, Donovan. This is city business, not county. Maybe in the big city they go accusing people without any evidence, but not here." He stalked off without another word.

The sheriff chuckled, "Always did like ruffling the feathers of the city big-wigs." He turned to Shep and me. "Looks like you got yourselves more trouble. Dan's been friends with Ed Bodeen since high school. This is a small town. That means he's also friends with Walter and Abner. We're all outsiders by their reckoning. I'll do anything I can to help you. Us outsiders need to stick together." He chuckled again before growing serious. "What happened to you?" He nodded at the bruises on my arms. "Or I should ask who did that? Don't think Shep here did it."

"No, he didn't. I had a little run in with Ed Bodeen." I didn't go into specifics.

"You report it?" When I shook my head, he sighed in

exasperation. "Why are you trying to take care of this by yourself?"

"Reporting things to some law enforcement officials doesn't seem to do much good. You're the only one who has taken anything I've said seriously. The chief isn't all that concerned about an arsonist in his town."

He nodded understanding. "Looks like someone just upped the ante. You two be extra careful." He headed back to his car, leaving us to watch the firemen wrap things up.

Surveying the damage after the firemen left, Shep shook his head. "I wanted to fix up the place just not quite like this. I'm glad they kept it from spreadin' to the rest of the neighborhood. These houses would go up like match sticks."

I wrapped my arms around his waist. "I'm sorry, Shep. We shouldn't have brought the trunk here."

He placed a soft kiss top of my head. "Not your fault, Darlin'. I'm just glad the journals weren't here. We've got to figure this out before someone gets hurt."

"Speaking of the journals," I laughed, pulling one out of the waist band of my shorts. "I forgot I brought this with me." He was right. I need to find the one that points a finger at someone. If things had been different for her, Rosie would have made a good novelist. I get so involved in her story; I forget what I'm looking for. I need to concentrate on the entries that will reveal some crime from the past. Whether it was punishable now isn't up to me. I need to find what Rosie called "the truth."

By the time we got back to the farm, it was late. We each took a journal, settling on the porch swing. "She hid the notes from Barnard in her journals. I haven't found them, but the last book had four blank pages." I handed him the journal I'd been reading the day before, watching as he examined the book closely. "Several pages are glued together." He took a pen knife out of his pocket and gently pried the pages apart. Inside were the notes Barnard had left for Rosie during the harvest. Looking at the precise handwriting, I was certain it would match that of the note I'd found in the newel post.

Picking up the journal I'd been reading earlier, I scanned

several entries, looking for the one where Rosie met Barnard in the woods behind the school.

During lunch today I managed to avoid the other kids, and slip away to meet Barnard. My heart was racing so hard all morning, I thought everyone could hear. He was right where he said he'd be waiting for me. He took my hands, and just looked longingly at me for several minutes without speaking. His first words tore at my heart. "I was afraid I'd never see you again. I don't want to lose you." Very gently, he kissed me; like he was afraid I would run away at his touch.

He is the most wonderful man, nothing like Papa and my brothers. Thank you, God for sending him to me.

He won't be able to come into town very often. When he can, he'll come out to the farm. He said I should go for a walk every evening to establish a pattern. If one of the boys follows me, they'll only see me walking around and get tired of following me. He'll come as often as possible, and meet me behind the barn. I don't want to lose him.

It was several days later when Barnard was there when she went for her walk after supper. Her brothers had followed her as Barnard suggested they would, but quickly got bored and left her alone. Most of their meetings were necessarily short with a few exchanged kisses. When Ed Bodeen's name came up, I stopped scanning and read the entry.

Papa says I have to marry that odious Ed Bodeen come summer. He isn't going to let me finish high school. When I told Papa I would rather be dead than marry Ed, he said that could be arranged. I don't know what Papa will get if I marry Ed.

Barnard was waiting for me tonight, and I told him what Papa said, I thought he was going to cry. He said he loves me, and wants to marry me. We're going to run away before summer. He's been saving his money, planning on asking me. I'm so happy!

The rest of that journal was more of the same. Eventually, I want to read each entry, but for now we have to find out what someone is so intent on stopping us from finding. When my eyes began to water from the strain of trying to read in the uneven light of the flashlight, it was time to call it a night. It's been a hard day for both of us, topped off by the fire. Shep is working non-stop to get the electricity and plumbing finished in the kitchen and mud room. The granite counter tops and modern appliances will be installed soon. Excitement bubbled up in me just thinking how everything will look when he's finished.

CHAPTER TWENTY

Getting a fresh start the next morning, I picked up another journal. We brought them down from the attic and will put them in the root cellar for safekeeping. If someone is watching, we need to make it look like we're putting away vegetables, not a box of books. This was getting complicated as well as dangerous.

With each journal I reminded myself to read only the entries that will tell us what happened to Barnard. They were meeting almost nightly as they planned their escape from Rosie's father. One entry caught my eye.

Tonight at supper Papa said he'd seen "Old Man Dunn" in town. He told Papa he'd hired one of the hands who worked for him during the last harvest. My heart sank. I'd been hoping Papa wouldn't find out Barnard was still around. I don't want him to suspect anything until I'm gone. But Papa just chuckled at poor Mr. Dunn. He said if he'd had boys instead of girls, he wouldn't have to hire help. Like anyone can choose to have boys or girls.

At least Papa wasn't suspicions about Barnard still being here.

I kept skimming each journal; about a month after they started meeting at night, I hit pay dirt.

It's getting too cold to meet outside. Tonight we had to go in the barn just to stay out of the wind. I don't know how long I'll be able to continue meeting him. Papa will be suspicious if I go out in a snow storm. We climbed into the hay loft, lying down on the clean hay. We talked for a long time about what we were going to do when we got married. Barnard still wants to go to school to be a teacher. Someday I'd like to be a writer.

His kisses make me feel funny inside and warm all over. When I told him that, he asked if I knew how babies are made. That made me laugh. Of course I know how babies are made.

I've lived on a farm my whole life. I've seen animals mate, and even watched some of them give birth to their young.

But Barnard said it's different with people. Married couples don't have sex just to make babies. They do it because they love each other and to show affection. He said he could hardly wait until we're married so we can make love. He wants me to have his babies. Just thinking about it, gives me goose bumps. I get all excited inside.

I wondered how much older Barnard was than Rosie. At this time, she was fifteen. Barnard had been in World War II so he was probably twenty to twenty-five. I don't know how it was more than sixty years ago, but today it's frowned on for someone that much older to date a fifteen year old. That was much too young to get married, but she needed to get away from her father and brothers. Her father was going to marry her off anyway. At least, Barnard was a nice man.

For the next two days, it rained so Rosie couldn't go out after supper. I'd read those entries later.

Papa didn't want me going out tonight because it was still muddy outside. I told him we're supposed to exercise every day. The boys don't need to exercise because they work around the farm, but he won't let me help so I need to walk or do something else. I was afraid he would say I needed to do more housework, but so far he hasn't thought of that. He probably doesn't think cleaning house is hard. I told him I would walk inside the barn, and climb the ladder to the hayloft several times to get my exercise. I almost laughed when he thought that was a good idea.

Barnard was waiting for me in the loft. He hadn't been able to come the last two nights because of the rain, but he said he just had to see me tonight. I love him so much! I can't wait until we're married. I told him I didn't want to wait until we were married to make love; I wanted to do it now. But he said it wouldn't be right. We needed to wait. I couldn't convince him. I'll try again tomorrow night.

I'd been sitting on the swing so long my back side was numb. The men would stop for lunch in another hour. As a treat, I decided to go into town and bring something back for them. I never thought I'd get tired of eating out, but I was getting close. Cooking on the wood stove is easier now, but I'll still be glad when I don't have to worry about burning down the house in the process.

"What does everyone want for lunch?" I called through the heavy plastic covering the kitchen door. "I'm going to A Cup-A-Joe and bring it back." The men had no problem eating out, even if it was brought in. With their orders in hand, I headed to the barn for the Model T. I miss my Jeep, I thought wistfully. Forty miles an hour is tops for the old car. The speed limit, even on the country roads, is fifty-five.

"Hi there, Sweetie. Back for more of Billy's cooking?" The small cafe was crowded, but there was still room at the counter for one more.

"I got tired of sitting outside twiddling my thumbs," I laughed. "It's useless trying to clean with all the work going on. I'm taking lunch back for four hungry men. Think you can help with that?"

"How's Shep holding up after the fire at his place? He was more mad than upset last night." It was too late when we left his house the night before to worry about cooking, but A Cup-A-Joe was still open.

"Thanks to Mrs. Jenkins' quick call to the fire department, there wasn't as much damage as he'd feared. He's trying to think positive. Now he can gut the entire house, and rebuild it right." We both laughed along with several people who were eavesdropping. Everyone must think those houses Ed Bodeen built need to be gutted. Or torn down and start all over again. How had they passed city inspection? How had Ed Bodeen even got his contractor's license? He didn't know the first thing about building houses that last.

"Have you convinced your mom to pay us a visit? I'd sure like to see her again."

"Dad's still working on her, but he'll wear her down. He won't let Walter bother her. Milly really wants to see her. I'm hoping she'll go back to Arizona with them, at least for a little while." Others were listening to our conversation, but I was past caring. Let them go tattle to Walter or Abner.

With my order in a thermal bag, I headed for the car. It was my bad luck to run into Abner, literally, as I stepped outside. "Big order for such a little bit of a thing," he snarled. "You spending all our money on that stud and his men out at our farm?"

Here we go again, I thought with a sigh. "Go talk to Mr. Meyers. Maybe he can convince you the money and the farm aren't yours. I'm not leaving, so you and your brother might as well accept that." I tried to step around him, but he moved in front of me again.

"You don't belong here. That house belongs to my family." He leaned over me, getting right in my face, his voice a low growl.

"Yes, it does," I agreed in the sweetest voice I could muster up. "And as much as we both regret it, I'm family. So get over it. That house and farm are mine. Now if you'll excuse me, my lunch is getting cold." This time he let me step around him.

I was shaking more from anger than fear as I drove off. Nothing short of dying was going to make me leave before the year was up. I tried to put that gruesome thought out of my mind.

While we ate in the shade of a large tree, the men told me about their families. They each had children, and were more than glad to show off their pictures. Wayne and Mike had lived in Whitehaven their entire lives. Jim was from Nebraska, but his wife's family is from Whitehaven so he had moved here about seven years ago.

It was an enjoyable break for all of us. Maybe when the house is finished, I'll throw a party and invite their families. It'd be nice to meet some people who aren't intent on driving me away.

~~~

Rosie and Barnard were meeting as often as possible. He really had loved her. If something hadn't happened to him, they would have gotten married.

We made love tonight! Barnard didn't want to at first. He said we should wait but I begged him. He explained what he would do, and said it was going to hurt at first but then I would enjoy it. When I said it hurt, he stopped and didn't want to go further. I made him. After a few minutes the hurt stopped and the enjoyment began. It was amazing.

I was sore and bleeding some when I went back to the house. Papa had already gone to bed, and the boys were somewhere. No one paid any attention to me. Barnard said I would feel better tomorrow. I hope he can come again tomorrow. I want to love him every night.

Reading the details had me blushing. Rosie was a very sensual woman. I wonder how she felt knowing I would be reading these and other entries someday. I'm not sure I could ever write about something as personal and private as making love.

It's only October 24, and the weather has turned bitterly cold. Papa won't let me go outside after supper now. Who would do the cooking if I catch cold? Thank you, Papa for caring about me. Ha! It's been two days since we made love. I hope Barnard isn't mad at me. He knows how Papa is. I told him Papa whoops me if I do something he doesn't like. I thought he would go after Papa right then. I need to be quiet about how he and the boys treat me. They would all beat on him. He wouldn't have a chance. I keep looking for him in town when I'm at school, hoping Mr. Dunn will send him for supplies.

It was another week before she saw Barnard. Did she ever think he'd been stringing her along just to get her to sleep with him? Or maybe that was a trick modern men and boys use on girls. Somehow I didn't think so. Lies and sex were as old as time.

Barnard was behind the school when I came out for lunch today. I couldn't stay inside any longer. It was cold but I didn't care. When I saw him, I didn't even feel the cold any longer. We managed to hide from sight of the schoolhouse, and sat on a couple tree stumps. He said the weather had been so bad he'd been afraid to try coming out to the farm. Mr. Dunn's place is on the other side of town. It would be a long way to walk. He is still saving his money so we can get married in the spring.

"Parker, can you come here for a minute?" Shep's voice was strained. What can be wrong now? I wondered, heading into the house.

"Charlie! Where did you come from?" I hadn't seen him since the day after Milly left Walter.

"I came in the back way so's no one would see me."

"Who would see you come here or care if you did?"

Tension filled the short hall where we stood. "Let's go out on the porch," I suggested. I gave Shep a slight nod to follow us.

But Charlie shook his head. "That's what I came to tell you. You need to be more careful. You can't sit out there all the time. They're watching you."

My stomach dropped to my toes. "Who's watching me?" I glanced at Shep. A muscle twitched in his jaw.

"Uncle Abner and Young Ed. They been watching since you came here. They know you're sleeping with Shep here."

"I'm NOT sleeping with Shep." My voice was louder than I intended, causing Gus to growl. He had picked up on the tension. I took a calming breath, patting Gus's head to let him know everything was okay. "Even if I was sleeping with Shep, whose business is it anyway? We're both over twenty-one."

"When Pa found out he said it wasn't right, but Young Ed went nuts, saying his daughter shouldn't do such a thing. Then he said how someone was supposed to be his mama, but she was whoring around, too." He dropped his voice to a whisper as though someone might be listening to our conversation. "Young Ed ain't right in the head sometimes." He tapped his temple. I rubbed the bruises on my arms as a chill passed through me. Ed's rambling diatribe remained fresh in my mind.

"I'm staying here because someone broke into the house." Shep's voice was soft, but didn't mask the anger just below the surface. "It isn't safe for her to be here alone."

"That had to be Young Ed," Charlie said on a sigh. "I

heard him talking to Uncle Abner about some book he got from the house. He dropped it when Ted chased him. They didn't see me in the other room. They don't say much around me 'cuz they know I like Parker and want her to stay." He gave me a shy smile.

"All I'm doing is reading when I'm on the porch. It must get pretty boring for them." I tried to make a joke, but no one laughed. "They can't see very much since they don't come on the property."

"They know you're reading the kind of book Young Ed dropped."

"How can they see that from the road?" My stomach was churning uneasily.

"They use binoculars." The times I saw a flash of light on the road in front of the house made sense now.

"Why are they watching me? What do they hope to find out?"

Charlie shrugged. "Uncle Abner and Pa said Rosie had something they need to find before you do. Young Ed said she had something of his, too. Pa thinks I'm slow in the head," he went on with a smug smile, "but I'm not. I know more than he thinks. If you keep your mouth shut, people forget you're there. You can learn a lot of things." He'd managed to pull one over on his pa.

So Rosie did have something on those three. They didn't want me or anyone else to find it. "Are your brothers watching me too?" I had to know how many people were watching me.

"No, Hank and Clyde pretty much do what Pa wants, but I don't think Pa knew Uncle Abner & Young Ed were watching you until today. Pa was pretty mad at Uncle Abner."

A few minutes later Charlie left the way he came, through the back door and across the field. He wanted to make sure no one saw him. His parting warning rang in my ears. "You both need to be careful. Uncle Abner and Young Ed are acting crazier all the time."

Shep pulled me into his arms, holding me close. "Have you learned anythin' from the journals today?" he asked quietly. The other men were still working in the kitchen and mud room. He trusted them, but no sense in giving out more information than necessary.

"So far there's nothing about a crime. They were going to run away and get married before her father could marry her off the following summer. She was only fifteen."

"We're goin' to wrap up here in about an hour. Stay off the porch until then." He placed a kiss on top of my head and went back to work.

We both felt pressured to get the remodeling done and finish reading the journals. If something was hidden in the house, I had to find it before Abner or Ed Bodeen did anything more. I just didn't know what I was looking for. Maybe they didn't know what Rosie had hidden either. If it was some kind of physical evidence, I could be looking in the wrong place. It'd take me longer than a year to go through everything in the house.

Gus and I went to the parlor instead of the porch. Looking out the window, I wondered where they were hiding. Did they stay there all day or just part of the time? This explained how they always turned up when I went somewhere. They just followed me. With a sigh of frustration, I picked up the journal I'd been reading before Charlie came.

Barnard is the most wonderful man I've ever met! He's kind and considerate. I know he would never whoop me or our children. I can't wait to get married. I never wanted to get married before, but Barnard isn't anything like Papa or the boys. I'm in love with him and he loves me. Papa isn't going to like it but I don't care.

Entries for the next two weeks were more of the same. She sang Barnard's praises in every entry. They met whenever the weather allowed him to walk from Mr. Dunn's farm. I'm surprised her father or brothers didn't notice the change in her. Her happiness floated off the pages of the journals. Maybe they just didn't care enough to notice.

My monthly cycle is late! (Okay, now we're getting somewhere, I thought.) *I know what that means. I have Barnard's baby inside me. I hope he isn't angry. He wanted to have more money saved before we ran away to get married. We should have waited to make love, but I wanted him so much. Please God, don't let him be angry about our baby.*

It was another two days before she could tell him.

Barnard is happy and excited about the baby! I told him I'd been afraid he would be angry and he hugged me. He said I never had to worry about that again. He knew what I meant. I was afraid he would whoop me. We're going to get married right away. He said he would leave me a note when he had everything arranged. It would take another week. I will finally be free of Papa.

~~~

Somehow Papa found out about Barnard. He was furious that I'd been sneaking around behind his back. He whooped me again. What will he do if he finds out about the baby before we can run away? He said I would ruin things with that detestable Ed Bodeen. Ed wouldn't marry me if I continued carrying on with Barnard. I'm glad of that. I will never marry him no matter what they do to me.

~~~

A sense of urgency gripped me. I was reading as fast as I could. This had to be what Rosie wanted me to find. It would have saved a lot of time and trouble if she'd just told me where to look. Maybe she wanted me to care about her and Barnard first. If someone had killed Barnard, I wanted them to pay even though it happened more than sixty years ago.

Papa said I can't go to school anymore. How will I ever find Barnard's note behind the schoolhouse if I can't go to school? One of the boys must have seen me with Barnard or that odious Ed was spying on me. (Like father, like son, I thought.) *I have to find a way to let Barnard know Papa has made me quit school.*

~~~

Barnard is gone. Papa said he left me, but I don't believe him. He wouldn't leave me and our child. He was so excited when I told him about the baby. What am I going to do? When Papa finds out I'm pregnant, he'll kill me. If Barnard is really gone, I don't know what I'll do. I want to protect my baby. Where can I go? The only family I have is Papa and the boys. They won't take care of me or my baby. I wish Barnard was here. What if Papa or the boys did something to him?

~~~

While Papa and the boys were gone to Buena Vista today, I walked over to Mr. Dunn's farm. I had to know what happened to Barnard. The day after Papa found out I was sneaking off to see him, he disappeared. Mr. Dunn said Barnard was just gone one morning. He went somewhere the night before; Mr. Dunn hasn't seen him since. He didn't take any of his belongings with him. Mr. Dunn found a coffee can in Barnard's room with money stuffed inside. That's what he had been saving for us to run away. Even the notes I'd written to him were there. I know he wouldn't leave us. He loved me and our baby.

I never told anyone about us. If others knew, they could be looking for him now. If I told the sheriff, he would go to Papa before doing anything. Papa would tell him a bunch of lies. No one will believe me.

~~~

Papa found out about the baby today. He whooped me so bad I was afraid I lost him. I think that's what he wanted. He said Barnard left because no man wants a whore or her baby. He keeps telling me Barnard ran off, but I don't believe him. Papa or the boys did something to him. I'm all alone now. I have to take care of our baby.

~~~

Papa keeps saying I've ruined everything. No one will marry me now. He means that odious Ed Bodeen won't marry me. Thank you, God. He's a horrible person. Just the thought of him touching me, makes me want to throw up.

~~~

I tried to run away, but Abner caught me. He took me to

Papa, and he whooped me again. They locked me in the attic after that, maybe they think I'll die up here. But I'm not going to die. I'm going to take care of our baby. I'll always have part of Barnard with me.

~~~

My baby is still inside me no matter how many times Papa whoops me. My baby is strong and determined to live. Papa won't let me out of the attic. The boys brought all the furniture from my room up here. At least I have my books and my journals. There are even some blank journals in my drawers. I can continue to write until Papa lets me out or I can run away. Or I die.

I don't know what they are going to do when my baby comes. Will they keep us both locked up? I have to find a way to get away from them before it's too late. I don't know what Papa is telling my friends. Isn't anyone looking for me?

~~~

I was reading the entries as fast as I could and my eyes began to burn in the fading light. Looking out the big window, I realized we were in for another storm. Would this one be a tornado? My heart shuddered. If it started raining, whoever was watching the house would leave or get wet. Maybe a tornado would pick them up, and deposit them in the next county. "Now that's what I call poetic justice." I laughed out loud.

"Care to share the joke?" Shep came into the parlor looking tired and dirty.

Laughing, I told him my silly idea.

"It'd serve 'em right." He sat down on the floor leaning against my legs. Worry lines creased his forehead; he could barely keep his eyes open. He wasn't getting a lot of sleep on the parlor floor. "How about calling it quits for the day? Let's get a shower and somethin' to eat."

"Will we be able to use the shower at your place?" I wasn't sure how much structural damage had been done in the fire.

"It's safe. All the damage was done to the living room. I can thank Miz Jenkins for that. She saved my house. Maybe even a few others because she was willin' to investigate. Not many people are willing to get involved nowadays."

"Let's get going then. I've learned a boatload of things today. I'll tell you while you drive."

CHAPTER TWENTY-ONE

Rain drops began to pepper us as we made a dash to his truck. "We might have electricity in the kitchen by this time tomorrow," he shouted as a clap of thunder crashed overhead. "Once we get the cabinets refinished and the granite counter tops installed, we'll be able to hook up the water lines."

I squealed with excitement, bouncing in the seat. Six weeks ago, I never would have thought it possible to get this excited over lights and plumbing. So much had changed since then.

Turning my thoughts back to Rosie and her baby, my excitement ebbed. This is the first chance I had to tell him about Rosie and Barnard's baby. "We know she never ran away with her baby. We need to find out what happened when she gave birth."

Shep gripped the steering wheel so hard I thought he was going to break it in half. "I'd say her pa and brothers took him away from her. She never would have given him up on her own." We agreed Rosie's baby was a boy who grew up to be Shep's grandfather. "It's no wonder she was bitter towards them all these years. If she didn't have proof of what they did, she had enough to hold over them. If they killed Barnard, I hope we can prove it. It isn't too late for justice."

This had become personal for him. "If she had something on them, we'll find it. She knew law enforcement wouldn't take her word over her father's. They were as well thought of as Walter and Abner are today. But I don't think Sheriff Donovan will look the other way to murder, even if it's them."

Making a visible effort to relax, Shep drew a deep breath, "You up for A Cup-A-Joe again or you want to try something a little different?"

I sighed. "I'd give my right arm for some piping hot and spicy enchiladas. I've been here six weeks and I'm afraid I'm going into withdrawal."

"Why didn't you say so? Did you forget I'm from Texas? I've got a little bit of cravin' for that myself. I know just the place." He winked at me, sending his sexy lopsided grin my way. "I've been tryin' to get Billy to add a few Mexican dishes to his menu, but he only does hardy downhome cooking. He's not interested in tryin' somethin' new."

Lights, a bathroom *and* Mexican food, I thought. What more could a girl ask for? I'm in hog heaven.

~~~

While I showered, Shep put a load of laundry in the washing machine. We'd pick up the clean, dry clothes before we went back to the farm. A new washer and dryer were sitting in the barn waiting to be installed in the mud room. One more step towards modernization.

During the drive, I kept watching the side mirrors for anyone following us. Traffic was light on the country road and pickups are the ride of choice in these parts. They all look alike. Any one of them could be following us.

The rain had let up as we pulled into the parking lot of a small rustic building in Bentonville. A dark blue pickup pulled in several spaces from us. When Ed Bodeen got out of the truck, I knew I'd been right about being followed.

"Heard you had some trouble at your place yesterday, Baker," He walked over, standing in front of Shep's truck. I wanted to slap the smirk off his pudgy face. He ignored me.

Shep stiffened, his hands balled into fists. "Do what you want to me, Bodeen, but you leave Parker alone. You hear me?" His voice was a low threatening growl.

The older man looked perplexed. "What's that supposed to mean?"

"Those bruises on her arms didn't get there by themselves. Come near her again and the chief won't..." I put my hand on his arm to stop him from saying more. No sense in giving the opposition ammunition against us.

Ed scratched his head, dislodging the ball cap sitting on his bald head. "I'm real sorry you got hurt." He looked at me sympathetically, "but it wasn't me who done it. I haven't seen you in three or four days."

Shep took a step towards him, until I gripped his arm. If Ed was trying to provoke him into a fight, it just might work. "Unless you have an evil twin, you were in Buena Vista two days ago." I said.

"Well, sure I was. I went to see my daughter but I didn't see you. Are you accusing me of something?"

I wanted to scream. The man is a lunatic. "Forget it." I turned away from him giving Shep a push towards the door of the restaurant. It was like trying to push a boulder up hill. Finally, he glared at the older man and walked stiffly away.

"Does he expect us to buy that act?" he asked, releasing a pent up breath. "You have that recording of the conversation. He can't deny it."

"He thinks he went to see his daughter. According to Milly he doesn't even know where his daughters are. The man is losing touch with reality."

"Shep honey, it's been so long since we've seen you, I thought you'd gone back to Texas." A middle-aged Mexican woman approached us, giving Shep a welcoming smile and a hug, cutting off our conversation.

He returned the hug with a laugh. "Just been busy and I discovered my lady likes Mexican food as much as I do." He slipped his arm around my waist, drawing me in to his side. "Juanita, this is Parker Evans; Juanita and her husband Juan own the best Mexican food restaurant this side of Texas."

I held out my hand to her, but she gathered me in for a hug. "Shep's lady gets a hug, not a hand shake." She laughed. "I've been waiting for this boy to find a good lady for himself. If I wasn't old enough to be his mama and madly in love with my Juan, I'd give you some competition." She laughed again. "Let's get you to a table. It's been so long since you had any of Juan's good cooking, you're probably starving. The first chance he gets, he will be out to see you and meet your lady." She bustled off to seat more customers.

"I take it you eat here almost as often as you do at A Cup-

A-Joe. Didn't you ever eat at home?" Red crept up his neck making me laugh.

"Guilty as charged. Makin' friends with the restaurant owners always means I've got company when I eat."

I lifted my water glass, "Here's to never having to rely on restaurant owners for company again." We clicked glasses in a toast and, in my heart, a silent vow.

A young Hispanic waitress placed a dish of warm tortilla chips on the table. "Do you want the mild salsa?" she asked me, a little grin curled her full lips

"Oh, I want the hot stuff," I assured her. Placing two dishes on the table, she gave Shep a little wink, and walked off with a swish of her hips.

"She doesn't think I can take the heat. Or is she hoping I can't?" I dipped a chip in the salsa, enjoying the biting spice on my tongue. Before she came back to take our order, I'd emptied my salsa dish and was ready for more. I really missed the hot, spicy food I grew up on in Arizona. When sizzling enchiladas and refried beans were placed in front of us, we concentrated on devouring the food instead of talking.

As we finished eating, a tall Hispanic man came out of the kitchen, approaching our table with a big smile. "I thought you'd forgotten us, but my Juanita told me you brought your lady in tonight." He turned to me, taking my hand and carrying it to his lips. "I'm glad to meet you, but my young Carlita is devastated. She felt certain Shep would never settle for someone who couldn't eat the hot like he does. Now she tells me you can outdo him on the hot sauce." He gave a chuckle. "She'll get over it when Estaban comes in tonight. She's fickle, like all teenage girls. Don't be so long bringing this beautiful lady in again." He disappeared back into the kitchen as quickly as he'd appeared, giving us no chance to speak in his whirlwind visit.

Ed was gone when we left the restaurant a short time later. The man is losing it; but is he dangerous? Rosie hadn't trusted him. That was enough for me. Did he have something to do with my father's death? After all these years, how would I find out if he'd been in Arizona at the time my father died?

~~~

As long as I stayed at the farm, I didn't have to worry about running into Abner, Walter, or Ed. They finally understood I would have them arrested for trespassing and they stayed away. But I couldn't stay at the farm all the time, nor did I want to. I wouldn't let them make me a prisoner in my own home.

In town, whether it was Whitehaven, Bentonville or Buena Vista I couldn't avoid them though, especially when one of them followed me around. It must have been Walter's turn when I went for groceries. "You're an embarrassment to this family! I'm ashamed to have people know you're my granddaughter," he growled before I could even get out of Shep's truck. He was standing so close I couldn't open the door.

"Then don't tell them. I won't mind. I don't tell people we're related." What had I done to embarrass him? "Will you please move so I can get out?" I pulled on the door handle, forcing him to step back or get bumped with the door.

"Does your mom approve of your actions?" he demanded as he stepped back. "Maybe where you come from it's acceptable for a young woman to live with a man who isn't her husband, but it isn't here."

"I'm not 'living with' Shep. Ask your brother and your buddy which one of them broke into my house one night. Or who locked me in the root cellar. Or was that you?" I raised one eyebrow in question. He seemed confused. When he didn't comment, I continued. "You should be more concerned about your own actions instead of trying to control mine. There are a few skeletons rattling around in your closet I'll bet you don't want getting out." I wouldn't make excuses for Shep staying at the farm.

"I don't know what you're talking about," he blustered. His face lost all color, giving the lie to his words. He tried to continue with his bluff. "I'm not the one sleeping around, and convincing her grandma to leave her husband of better than fifty years." He managed to put so much indignation in his voice I laughed.

"We've had this conversation before, so I won't repeat myself. I don't have anything more to say to you. I have to go shopping." I started to walk away. His next words brought me around to face him, anger flashing through me.

"You sure enjoy spending my money on all your frills. Maybe you need to take it a little easy."

"How do you know what I'm buying or how much I'm spending? And it's NOT your money. It's time I have another talk with Mr. Meyers." Without another word I marched off.

"Mr. Meyers is busy." His snooty secretary managed to look down her nose at me even though I was standing over her desk.

"I'll wait. I have all day. Just let him know I'm here and I'm very upset." She huffed, but picked up the intercom. Within minutes, she stood up. "Mr. Meyers will see you now, but he has an important appointment in fifteen minutes." She opened his door admitting me to the inner sanctum.

"Miss Evans, what can I do for you...today?" He barely avoided saying "this time." He gave a put-upon sigh.

"I thought I made myself very clear about passing information regarding my activities to your other clients. Now I find out Mr. Shepard is aware of what I've been buying and how much I've spent. He's still under the impression the money belongs to him. I've told him, now I'm telling you I will be staying here for the prescribed year. Unless you want to lose my business and the resulting fees, you'd better keep my business private. Have I made myself clear?"

"Several times. Whatever Walter knows, he found out from other sources. I've told him and Abner nothing. I've done nothing unethical." He did 'indignant' almost as well as Walter. They must practice daily.

"Who else would know anything to tell him?"

He shrugged. "There's no such thing as a secret in a small town. Anyone who saw you buying things could have passed that information to Walter and Abner. It's no secret they're upset you inherited the farm instead of them. Gossip is a favorite pastime in any small town."

I groaned. How would I ever keep anything away from Walter and Abner? Had gossip betrayed Rosie and Barnard more than sixty years ago? If that was the case, why didn't anyone remember Barnard? I turned my mind back to the lawyer. "The house originally belonged to Rosie's mother's family. Is that why she inherited the house instead of her brothers?"

"Where did you hear that?" He seemed shocked by my knowledge. He probably didn't think I would find that out.

I ignored his question. "Rosie inherited the farm when her mother passed on. Why didn't it go to her husband?"

"The house, farm and several other properties belonged to Miriam's family. Miriam and Elmore lived there, but everything remained in her family's name when she married. When she passed on, ownership went to Rosie, who she named as her primary heir."

"Did her husband and sons know that was how she had set it up?"

"My father drew up Miriam's will," he hedged, not denying or affirming anything.

"That's not what I asked. Did her husband and sons know they were getting nothing when she passed away?"

"Elmore had acquired land during his marriage, adding it to Miriam's holdings," he answered reluctantly. "Each of the boys received 100 acres of that land. Elmore was able to live in the house and continue farming the land. He received an income until he passed on."

Maybe he thought this would distract me from my original question, but he was sadly mistaken. "Answer my question. Did they know Rosie would receive everything except the 400 acres for her brothers?" I spoke slowly, emphasizing each word clearly.

He heaved a sigh. "No, Elmore wasn't aware Miriam kept everything in her name alone or that Rosie was the sole heir to the bulk of her estate."

"So your father kept her confidence and you kept Rosie's.

You just don't keep mine." Red spread up his neck. "Have you opened the envelope Rosie left in case I didn't stay for the prescribed year?"

"Of course not, you haven't left." He sounded insulted I would even ask.

"But you did tell them I have to live in the house for a year." It was a statement, not a question. "They're under the impression they'll inherit if I don't stay. Did you lead them to believe that?" His color was still high.

"At the time Rosie passed away I told them you have to stay in the house. I felt they had the right to know that much. I let them draw their own conclusions about who would inherit if you don't stay. There isn't anyone else to inherit." He'd been standing, now he sank down in his chair.

"If they weren't in the will, what right did they have to know anything in it?"

"They've been my clients and friends for years." I guess he thought that was the only excuse he needed. "That is the *only* thing I've told them about your business."

I wished I could ask him if he knew what Elmore and his sons had done to Barnard and the baby, but I couldn't trust him to keep that to himself. With this new knowledge though, some of the things in the journals made sense now.

"What would have happened if she'd married and had children?" I asked.

He gave a heavy sigh. "It would have gone to her children and grandchildren." His voice trembled, unhappy with the direction my thoughts were going.

"Those money grubbing..." The only words I could think of to describe all of the male Shepards were unladylike and very unchristian. This was why her father wanted her to marry the man of his choosing. He could control everything she had, if only through her children. If she married someone he couldn't control, he'd lose everything.

Her father must have been furious when he learned Rosie inherited everything instead of him. That's why he treated her so badly. What would have happened to everything if Rosie had died before her father? Would he have inherited it?

Somehow I didn't think so. If that had been the case, Elmore and his sons would have gladly done away with her along with Barnard and the baby. Did Mr. Meyers and/or his father know what happened to Barnard and the baby?

I turned to leave. "Thank you for your help."

"What help? Are you going to move your business?"

I turned back with a smile. "Not today." I sailed out of his office. Let him worry about what I was going to do. Back on the street, I realized I should have asked several more questions. How long had Rosie known she owned the house and farm? Did she know when her father locked her in the attic? Would she have been able to kick him out of the house and marry Barnard when she was only fifteen?

Mr. Meyers was shocked I knew the farm belonged to Miriam's family, not Elmore's. But it had been a bluff, a guess. It was the only explanation why Rosie inherited the farm instead of her brothers. If her father owned the farm, she would have received nothing. What would he do if he found out I knew about Barnard and the baby? A better question is what would Walter and Abner do? I believed they killed Barnard or had someone else do it. How much did the lawyer know about what happened back then? The journals had to hold the answers. I hurried through the grocery store to get back to my reading.

~~~

Last night the boys were arguing. They don't know I can hear part of what they say when they're in the kitchen. They were talking about Barnard and what happened to him.

I think they killed him. I have to find proof of what they did. Even if no one believes me, I need to know for sure. I have to get away before they do something to my baby, too.

~~~

I couldn't imagine being locked up and hearing people talk about the man I loved being dead. Rosie couldn't have known the house and farm were hers after her mother died. She would have done anything to protect her baby even if it meant throwing her father and brothers off the farm. Is this what Walter and Abner are trying to hide? There is no statute of limitations on murder, but I need to find proof or nothing can be done to them.

CHAPTER TWENTY-TWO

In two weeks Mom, Dad, and the twins will be here. I want all this figured out before then but I'm running out of time. I don't know what it will accomplish, I just want it done. I'll have lights in the kitchen and maybe the mud room by tonight. Even if everyone still had to use lanterns upstairs, there will be lights and a bathroom downstairs.

Milly's excitement at seeing Mom is near manic. She suggested they stay with her in Buena Vista. That might be a good option for Mom and Dad, but I'm sure the twins will want to stay here. Things haven't changed between her and Walter. It doesn't look like that situation is going to be resolved before Mom and Dad arrive.

I still need to read the investigator's reports more thoroughly. If I can prove my father's death wasn't an accident, would law enforcement in Arizona do anything after all this time? There are still more questions than answers.

"Any trouble in town this morning?" Shep lingered over the kiss as he sat down on the porch swing beside me to eat the sandwich I made him for lunch.

"I..." I cleared my throat when my voice squeaked slightly. "I ran into good old Walter. It must have been his turn to follow me. He pretended ignorance when I told him someone broke into the house, and I'd been locked in the root cellar. He's also upset about all the money I'm spending. He still thinks it's his."

"You set him straight on that point?" A crooked grin tilted his sexy mouth. For a minute, I lost my train of thought and I looked away so I could concentrate on our conversation.

"Sure did. I also went to see Mr. Meyers." I shook my head. "I sort of accused him of telling Walter what I've been buying for the house. I've never lived in a small town. Does everyone really know everybody else's business?"

He laughed, "It's a favorite pastime."

"I thought that was just rural legend, not a reality," I said with an exasperated sigh "So everyone *is* talking about us making it sound like something awful?" Shep laughed at my dismay. "What are they saying about Deidre's murder and the fire at your house? The sheriff still hasn't found out who killed her. Has he figured out who her father was?" He'd listened to the recording of Ed's ramblings, unsure what to make of it.

"People are still buzzin' about the murder. They all have a different opinion. Sheriff Donovan's not goin' to show his hand until he's good and ready. He knows a lot more than he's lettin' on. The fire is a different matter." It was his turn to sigh in frustration. "The chief isn't too concerned with findin' the person who did it. Folks in town aren't sayin' much to me." The fact that the chief wasn't really looking for the person who started the fire added insult to injury.

We were quiet for a moment, each lost in our own thoughts. Then I changed the subject. "What did Dad say when you called him today?" My stomach churned nervously. Shep called to tell Dad he was staying here at the farm. I didn't want to wait until they got here to tell them. Living in gossip central, he'd definitely get an earful from any number of people.

"His main concern was that you're safe. He wanted to know why you haven't told them what's been goin' on."

I groaned. "You told him I didn't want them to worry, right?"

He laughed. "I'm not sure he bought that excuse. You're goin' to have some explainin' to do when they get here. I made sure he knew we're in separate rooms." *That was something, at least.*

We enjoyed a few kisses before he went back to the kitchen. Alone again, I wondered if someone had been in the woods watching us. I tried to concentrate on the journal I'd been reading earlier, but couldn't keep my mind focused. With the temperature and humidity both in the nineties, my hair was a riot of ringlets, sitting heavy on my neck. I lifted the heavy mass, feeling the hot breeze.

Looking across the yard again, I wondered if someone was out there. Without any real thought, I left the shade of the porch, heading for the woods, Gus following at my heels.

He started raising a loud ruckus as we crossed the road. The bushes began moving as though someone or something was in a frenzy to get away. Gus took off like a shot; I could hear him thrashing around after whoever was out there.

"Parker, where are you? What's going on?" Shep came running from the back of the house. Anyone within a city block could hear Gus barking.

"Help, get this beast off me. Help!" Gus had captured his quarry.

"Don't go in there." Panic shook Shep's voice. He raced past me. Gus stopped barking when Shep reached him, but more yelling ensued as Shep hauled a struggling Ed Bodeen out of the woods.

"Let go of me! What do you think you're doing?" Shep had Ed's arms behind his back pushing him forward.

"You're spying on me!" I've never wanted to smack someone as bad as I did right then. I kept my hands clamped tightly on my hips.

"Can't a guy go for a walk in the woods without being accused of spying?" He sounded almost lucid but you never know.

"You just happened to be walkin' by when Parker was sittin' on the porch. Let's see what Sheriff Donovan thinks about that." Shep nodded for me to make the call.

"I ain't done nothing wrong." His manner grew more agitated.

"Why don't you just keep quiet 'til the sheriff gets here," Shep suggested. "We'll let him decide if you were doin' somethin' wrong."

It took only a matter of minutes for him to pull into the lane. Unfortunately, my least favorite deputy was right behind him. With a resigned sigh, the sheriff got out of his car, walking back to his deputy. "Get back on patrol," he growled through the open window.

"But Sheriff, you might need back up."

"Do you like your job?"

"Of course!"

"Then do it!" The sheriff turned, and stalked over to the three of us. "What're you doing, Ed? What's going on?"

"Her vicious dog attacked me. He needs to be put down."

"You don't look like you were hurt. Why were you here?" Sheriff Donovan folded his arms over his chest, his hips cocked to one side looking perfectly relaxed.

"Well, I, ah," Ed cleared his throat, giving himself time to come up with an answer. "I came to see what's going on here."

"Why? What business is it of yours?"

Ed seemed to lose focus, staring into space for several seconds. The sheriff snapped his fingers in front of Ed's face bringing him back to the present. "Well, of course it's my business. It's a father's job to keep track of his daughter."

"Your daughter doesn't live here. Parker does."

"Of course she does. That's what I'm talking about!"

"What *are* you talking about, Ed? Parker lives here. What she does isn't any of your business."

"It's my business what she does with this house. It should belong to me. I'm just making sure she doesn't destroy it."

"Rosie left the farm to Parker. She can do whatever she wants with it." He was leading Ed on to see where it would go.

"Rosie was supposed to be my ma; that farm is supposed to be mine." He sounded like a petulant little boy.

"That's ancient history. The farm belongs to Parker now."

"Well, of course it does. I just don't think she should be acting the way she is."

"How's she acting?"

"You know what she's doing, Donovan! She's living with Baker here." He shot an evil look at Shep. "I told her no daughter of mine would do something like that."

"But she's not your daughter," the sheriff reminded him. Ed was talking in circles.

"Her ma was supposed to marry me," he stormed. "Then she'd be my daughter."

"Yeah, yeah, yeah, I've heard all those stories, too. You can't have it both ways. If Rosie had married your pa, that would've made Parker's mom your cousin. You couldn't marry her and Parker couldn't be your daughter."

This confused Ed even more. He stared at the sheriff, unsure what to say. Finally, he gave himself a shake. "Well, I got me some daughters, and they don't whore around." Shep stiffened at that and Sheriff Donovan shot him a warning glance before turning back to Ed.

"Your daughters don't live here, Ed. You don't know what they're doing."

Ed gave a sly smile, puffing himself up. "I got me more daughters than you know about, Donovan, and they don't whore around."

"You got other daughters? One of them wouldn't be Deirdre Smith, would it?"

"I don't know what you're talking about," Ed blustered, his face so red I thought he might explode. "Are you going to do something about this vicious dog?"

"Nope. Stay away from Parker and the farm, and you won't have any problems with her dog. Stalking is a crime. You might want to remember that."

Ed stomped off, muttering under his breath.

Waiting until we heard the powerful engine of Ed's truck roar to life somewhere beyond the woods, he turned to us, his face serious. "You both need to be careful. He's acting more erratic all the time. There's no telling what he might think of next, or what he really believes."

"Do you think he killed Deirdre?" I couldn't stop myself from asking.

The sheriff shrugged, "Time will tell. Just remember to be careful." He headed back to his car, leaving us frustrated with his non-answer.

Before he could get in his car, I stopped him. "Can I ask you a question, Sheriff?" He looked leery, but nodded anyway. "If I found out about a crime that happened over sixty years ago, what could be done?"

"Depends on the crime, and what proof you have," he answered with an indulgent smile.

"Murder and kidnapping."

That got his attention. He stood up straight, the smile gone from his face. "What are you talking about? Who got murdered and kidnapped?"

Now my face turned red. I shrugged. "I'm not sure. I'm just asking."

His bushy brows drew together in a fierce frown. "What's going on?"

We both answered. "Nothing."

"If you know something about a murder and kidnapping, you'd better tell me. This isn't something you should be messing around with."

I sighed, "Right now, I'm still trying to put the pieces together."

"Who do you think got murdered?" When I didn't say anything, he continued. "Putting those pieces together could be dangerous if the murderer is still around." Looking at Shep, he said, "If you love her, you'll convince her to tell me what's going on in that head of hers. I don't think either of us wants her to get hurt."

I bristled, but there was no condescension in his tone so I didn't argue. Shep nodded his head toward the sheriff. He wanted me to say what we were both thinking. But all I had right now was conjecture. "If I find out anything that points to someone in particular, I'll let you know."

He shook his head, frustration written on his face. "I hope it doesn't turn out to be too late. Keep my number on speed dial." He gave Shep a stern look. "Keep close to her. Whatever she thinks she's found could be dangerous. Throw Ed into the mix, and things could blow up in your faces. Never thought Ed would be dangerous to anyone but himself, but I'm reconsidering that thought." He gave me another stern look before getting into his car.

Shep pulled me into his arms, resting his chin on top of my head. His heart pounded against my ear. "What were you doin' out here? I thought you were readin' on the porch."

"I wanted to see who was watching me." I sounded defensive.

"Please don't do that again, Darlin'. When Gus started barkin' like he'd just treed a coon, my heart about stopped beatin'."

I snuggled closer, enjoying the feeling of his arms holding me tight. "I'll try to do better." I looked up into his serious, sexy face. "I promise. I didn't think about it being dangerous." We headed back to the house. Gus sniffed the air in case someone was still out there. For the rest of the afternoon I stayed in the house reading more of the journal.

The next entry just about broke my heart.

Barnard is dead! I heard the boys arguing with Papa. I couldn't hear everything they said but I heard Abner tell Papa they buried him behind the barn. Papa got really mad. I think he hit Abner. I don't know if he's mad because the boys killed Barnard or because they buried him behind the barn. Arthur and Wilbur said he deserved what he got. Papa was screaming something, but I couldn't understand what he said, he was so mad.

I hate them all. How could they do something so evil? Mama would be ashamed to know they did something like this. She always said to believe in the good in people and I've tried. But how can I believe Papa is good when he would do something like this? Did they all have a hand in it? How am I going to protect my baby? If they get their hands on my baby, will they kill him, too?

I now had proof a murder had been committed, but no proof the Shepards did it. The journal entries weren't enough to take to a jury.

Unable to sit still after reading this, I paced around the parlor. My own grandfather had a hand in murdering someone. Even if he didn't do it himself, he was still an accessory after the fact. He should have told someone. They all should have gone to prison. At least they didn't kill Rosie's baby. Shep is living proof of that.

Even if we found Barnard's body, any evidence would be

gone after sixty years. How do I go about finding a skeleton buried that long ago? Rosie said he was buried behind the barn. Was it the same barn that stood there today?

I was still pacing when Shep came to get me. "You ready for the lightin' ceremony?" I hadn't noticed the sun slanting across the fields casting long shadows from the trees in the front yard until now.

I stared in stunned silence at the beautiful, modern kitchen. The resurfaced cupboards gleamed, the glass fronts sparkled. Granite counter tops had been installed along with the new sink. The dishwasher was in its proper place. With the flick of a switch, bright lights illuminated the darkening room.

"Wow!" I breathed the single word. Nothing else fit the occasion.

Shep draped his arm over my shoulders. "So you like it?"

"What's not to like? How did you get this all done today?" Thoughts of murder and kidnapping momentarily receded to the back of my mind.

He laughed. "I told you we'd have the lights ready by tonight. I just wasn't sure we'd have the appliances installed. Want to see your new bathroom?"

I almost jumped into his arms. "Yes, yes, yes!" I tugged on his hand, pulling him across the room. "Does it work?" I pointed to the toilet.

He laughed. "Not until tomorrow. We'll get the sewer line and water hooked up, then everything will be operational." I threw my arms around his neck, kissing him in my excitement. Who would believe all this excitement over a bathroom? "Let's celebrate! I have a great bottle of wine set aside just for this occasion." I wanted the first meal I made on the new stove to be special, but there wasn't enough food in the old ice box for something like that. We settled for simple again. After eating all the bruschetta and finishing the bottle of wine, we cuddled on the porch swing, my favorite place on the farm. "You were lost in time this afternoon. Did you learn anything new?"

"Oh, my gosh, I completely forgot!" I twisted around. "They killed Barnard! Rosie heard them talking about it. They buried him behind the barn."

"Wait a minute, Darlin'. Who killed him? How did she find out?" He sat up straight, worry clouding his handsome face.

"The four brothers, they killed him." All the fury I'd felt earlier returned, bringing my voice to a near shout.

"Not so loud, Darlin'," he whispered, pulling me off the swing, propelling me inside. "You don't know who's out there." He looked across the road where Ed had been earlier.

"I don't care," I said defiantly, following his gaze. "If someone is watching us, I hope they heard me. I'm going to make them pay for what they did to Rosie and Barnard!"

He laid his fingers against my lips as he closed the heavy door behind us. "If Walter and Abner were a part of a murder, there's no telling what they'd do to keep you quiet." He went around closing all the drapes, shutting out any prying eyes. "You need to call the sheriff. Now!" he stressed when I hesitated.

"What can I tell him? All I have is the journal of a fifteen year old pregnant girl."

There was no talking him out of it though. "All right," I finally relented. "I'll call him in the morning. If I call now, the entire town will know something's up before breakfast. The longer we can keep this quiet, the better."

Reluctantly agreeing to wait, he pulled me into his arms. "If they really murdered Barnard to get their hands on this farm, I don't want the same thing happenin' to you." A shudder passed through him before his lips covered mine in a tender kiss, robbing me of coherent thought for several minutes. When he lifted his head we were both breathing heavily, my heart pounded in my ears.

Drawing in a steadying breath, he picked up the conversation. "If they had a hand in killing Barnard, they don't want that gettin' out. They could still go to jail."

"The sheriff's going to want to see the journals," I said with a resigned sigh. "But I don't want him to keep them. They're the only way I'm going to get my questions answered.

Even Milly..." I gasped, covering my mouth with my hand. "I have to tell her about this before it gets out. I can't let her hear something like this through the grapevine." I'd been so wrapped up in my own need for answers, I hadn't thought of how this would affect others, especially Milly. "What do I do? How do I tell her and Mom that Walter might be a murderer?" Tears stung my eyes. I didn't care how this affected Walter, but I did care about Mom and Milly.

Shep hugged me close for several long moments before speaking. "We'll call the sheriff first thing in the morning; then go see your grandma. You can call your mom after we know what they have to say."

"Milly's going to hate me," I whispered. "And I don't blame her."

"She's not going to hate you, Darlin'. This isn't your fault." Calm once again, he was the rational one. "She might be able to shed some light on what happened back then, or at least put some of it into context."

CHAPTER TWENTY-THREE

It was a long night with little sleep for either of us. Every noise the old house made as it cooled throughout the night had Shep pacing and looking out the windows. I rehearsed many different ways to tell Milly and Mom about Barnard's murder, with no good outcome. Gus felt our unrest and prowled around, looking for the boogie man who wasn't there.

By five o'clock the next morning we gave up on sleep, and made our way down to the kitchen. Flipping on the light, I felt the same thrill seeing the gleaming, modern room. Finally I could fix breakfast and coffee without being afraid I'd burn the house down.

Sitting at the kitchen table with my chin in my hand, I drank my third cup of coffee. "There are eggs and bacon in our new refrigerator. Would you like me to make breakfast?"

"Why don't you give the sheriff a call? Invite him to join us."

I glanced at the clock. Six o'clock. "It's kind of early. I doubt he'll appreciate a call this early."

He chuckled. "Ask him to come for breakfast, he'll be here."

Forty-five minutes later we were sitting around the big table in the beautiful kitchen. "You've done a great job here, Shep. This place is going to do wonders for your business when you're finished." Taking our breakfast invitation at face value, at least until we finished eating, he finally laid his napkin on the table. "Have you figured out what you didn't want to tell me yesterday?" He pinned me with his sharp stare.

I choked on my last sip of coffee, and coughed until Shep pounded on my back. I thought we were being so subtle. "Um, I want to show you something." I handed him the journal I'd been reading yesterday open to the entry about the brothers killing Barnard.

He read the entry, and then several others. He finally pinned me with his hard cop stare firmly in place. I couldn't tell what he was thinking. "Who's Barnard?"

We explained what we'd learned and what we'd guessed at. "Shep looks just like Barnard," I said. "He's their great grandson. Rosie's father and brothers took her baby away from her, and put him up for adoption. First they killed Barnard." I finally fell silent.

"This isn't proof of a murder. I can't arrest anyone on the say so of this journal. All we really know is they buried him. There's no physical proof."

I stood up and stalked across the room. This is exactly what I'd been afraid would happen. No one would believe what Rosie had written. They were going to continue getting away with murder. "So you're not going to do anything," I accused. Shep's jaw muscle twitched but he remained silent.

Sheriff Donovan pushed out my chair with the toe of his boot, pointing to it. Reluctantly, I flopped down in a sulk. He leaned over, resting his elbows on his knees to look me in the eyes. "Parker, you're a smart woman. You're both emotionally wrapped up in this, not thinking straight. What would your boss do with what we have here?"

"What kind of proof do you need?" Shep sat beside me, looking as dejected as I felt.

"A body would help, but it depends on how he died. Right now you don't have any evidence an actual murder took place. Everyone thought you were Rosie's ghost when you first came here. Why didn't they recognize Shep?"

"Barnard only worked on the farm one season before he disappeared," I explained, trying to fill in more blanks. "Can't we at least try to find out where they buried him?"

"This is your farm. There's nothing stopping you from digging around. You have to be careful though. If Walter and Abner had something to do with his death, they aren't going to like you digging him up. I can't conduct an investigation without any evidence." He pointed to the journal. "No judge would accept that as evidence."

"Do you believe us?" I asked hopefully.

He was silent for several long moments, thinking it over. Then he nodded. "From the little I read here, I'd say Rosie believed they killed her boyfriend. She couldn't hear everything they said. Maybe she missed some important parts. How many more journals are there?"

I sighed heavily. "I haven't even scratched the surface. She was close to eighty when she died. She never stopped writing."

"Rosie ran roughshod over her brothers," the sheriff went on thoughtfully. "They did just about anything she told them to do. This could be what she held over them. If you continue digging around, you're going to have to be very careful."

He stopped for a moment. "When Rosie passed away, they didn't show any sadness. I figured they were relieved to be rid of a tyrant. There was a lot of grumbling when they didn't inherit the farm. I assumed, wrongly it seems, greed had been the ruling emotion. There might be a great deal more at risk here."

"Rosie ruled over them, but they were tyrants in their own families. Walter drove my mother away because she wouldn't marry Ed Bodeen. Rosie was convinced someone here had something to do with the death of my birth father. She hired a private investigator to keep tabs on me. I still have to read those reports."

He gave a heavy sigh. "For a sleepy little town, there are a lot of intrigues going on that I knew nothing about." He stood up, looking down at me. "I'm not sure how much of a conscience Ed and Abner have, so anything goes. I can't say about Walter. You need to be careful until we figure this out. In the meantime, I'll try to do some discrete checking of my own." He picked up his hat. "Thanks for breakfast." He gave Shep a nod as he left.

My emotions were in turmoil. Doing nothing certainly wasn't what I wanted. "Should I say something to Milly or wait until we know more?"

Shep took his time thinking it over. "Sheriff Donovan won't say anything, but if that deputy gets wind of an investigation, he'll blab it all over town. You need to be the one to tell her. At least show her the journal. Let her draw her own conclusions. It might answer some questions that plagued her throughout her marriage."

As much as I dreaded telling her something like this, I knew he was right. She shouldn't hear it through the gossip mill.

"Do you want me to come with you or would me bein' there make it harder on her?"

I hadn't looked at it that way. "You stay here," I said. "You still have work you want to get done. I can go alone." I managed to kill another hour cleaning my new kitchen before leaving.

~~~

Milly was waiting when I pulled up in front of her sister's house. She greeted me with a hug. How long would she want to hug me once she learned what I suspected of Walter?

"You sounded so mysterious. What's going on?" We sat down on the porch swing. There must be a swing on every porch in Iowa. "Is everything all right at the farm?"

"Did you know Rosie kept journals since she was a little girl?" I jumped right in with my explanation.

"No, what do her journals have to do with now?"

"Remember that room I found in the attic?"

She nodded. "You thought someone had been living there."

"Rosie's father kept her locked up in that room when she got pregnant."

Only mild shock registered on her lined face. "I've thought a lot about it since you showed me the room. When all the sisters-in-law began having babies she went into a depression; then she turned even more angry and hateful. I guess if I lost a baby, I might turn out that way, too."

"She didn't lose the baby, Grandma; he was taken away from her. She didn't have a say in it." I took her hand in mine, hoping to soften my words.

"Who took him? How do you know it was a boy? What

237

happened to him?" These were all the questions I'd been asking.

"I'm sure her father took him away from her. I haven't read all the journals yet, but I know she had a boy. The baby's father was a farm hand named Barnard. Rosie never said his last name in her journals. She was in love with him. They were going to run away and get married. Her father wanted her to marry Ed Bodeen Senior."

She drew in a sharp breath. "And Walter insisted Laura marry Ed Junior. Both Bodeens were a little on the crazy side. I was glad Laura wouldn't marry him. It wouldn't have been a happy marriage. What happened to this Barnard?"

This was the part I was dreading. I gulped before answering. "He was killed."

"How?" she whispered, her faced draining of all color.

I couldn't make myself say it. Instead I handed her the journal I'd brought with me. With shaking hands she opened it to the marked page. She must have read the words three times before lowering the book, bowing her head as if in prayer. "Dear God, help us," she whispered. "How could they do something like that?" She was shaking, her face white as a sheet. Afraid she'd reject my touch, I didn't reach out to her.

"I'm sorry, Grandma."

"What are you going to do? You need to tell Sheriff Donovan." She took my hand in an effort to comfort me.

"He read the journal this morning. But Rosie didn't know for sure who killed Barnard. Without real evidence, there isn't much he can do. He doesn't want ... ah, anyone to know about this but us."

"He doesn't want Walter and Abner to know," she amended. "I don't think either of them knew she kept a journal. If they find out, they'll be after them."

"They know," I said on an exhaled breath. I explained what happened when I was locked in the root cellar. "Whoever that was knows about the journals."

"They're just digging themselves in deeper, aren't they?" For a long moment she didn't say anything, and then continued. "This is going to sound like I'm sticking up for my husband but it's the truth. I can believe Elmore would do something like this. Abner is a chip off the old block. He and Ed Senior were pals from early childhood. Anything Elmore and Ed's father told them to do, they did without question. Elmore's other three boys weren't quite so compliant. The older they got, the more I saw of their father though. I just didn't know what to do about it. I can't believe Walter would help murder someone," she whispered.

"Did you know the farm belonged to their mother? Rosie inherited it when she died. It's been hers ever since."

She looked confused for a minute. "The farm never belonged to Elmore?" I shook my head. "That scoundrel! I imagine at some point people knew the farm had belonged to Miriam's family. I just assumed it was his. When he passed away, the other wives and I were surprised the farm wasn't divided between Rosie and the four boys. Now it makes sense."

She fell silent again, her thoughts lost in the past. "There were times when Rosie would come to our house demanding Walter do something. If he objected, she would lean over and whisper something. He'd always agree then. I asked him once what she'd said." She shuddered. "It was the only time I thought he was going to hit me. He said it was none of my business. It was family. I never questioned him in regard to his dealings with Rosie or his brothers again. I should have stood my ground instead of letting him set all the rules." Tears sparkled in her eyes.

The emotional morning left me drained by the time I got back to the farm. What do I do next? Should I keep digging or give up? I know her baby didn't die, but what did they tell her? Instead of going inside, I let Gus out to run. He inspected every bush, tree, and blade of grass, marking his territory. After the confrontation with Ed Bodeen, he sniffed the air for what or who shouldn't be there. Since he didn't go beyond the property line of the farm I assumed no one was hiding in the woods. Finally satisfied that all was normal and safe, Gus stopped beside me, his tail wagging when I petted him.

Almost immediately he came to attention; Walter Shepard's pickup came roaring down the lane. Either he'd forgotten my promise to call the sheriff if he came on my property again, or he was mad enough about something not to care. Gus gave one sharp bark as Walter stepped out of the truck. Smart enough not to tempt fate by coming closer, he stayed by the truck.

"What did you say to Milly this morning? What did you give her? She won't even talk to me."

"How do you know I gave her something? Did you follow me?" My voice rose along with my temper. I'd been so worried about what I had to tell her I forgot to check.

"You're just like her twisting things around until people can't even think straight. You've done whatever you could to tear this family apart."

"*I'm* tearing this family apart? What have *I* done?"

"Yes, you," he sneered. "You stole my family's farm, you convince my wife to leave me, and one of my sons would rather be with her than me. My other sons do nothing but argue with everyone. We were a peaceful family until you showed up."

"Everything was peaceful as long as everyone obeyed your orders. You don't like it when they think for themselves. Mom wouldn't marry Ed Bodeen so you disowned her. What was in it for you if she had married him?"

My question seemed to give him pause, but not for long. "Don't change the subject, damn it! What did you show her?"

"Sheriff Donovan's on his way." Shep came around the corner of the house, his trusty wrench in his hand. "You might want to leave before he gets here."

"Stay out of this, Baker. This is between me and my granddaughter."

"When it's convenient, I'm your granddaughter; otherwise you won't claim me. You can't have it both ways."

"Answer my question," he bellowed, taking a step towards me. Both Shep and Gus moved in front of me, Gus's low growl of warning stopping him again. "Why is she so upset?"

240

His tone was quieter, but no less belligerent.

The sheriff's car came to a stop beside the pickup. Gus gave a friendly woof, wagging his tail but didn't move. "Walter, it's getting to be a full time job coming out here and telling you and the others to stay off the farm and away from Parker. You need to listen up."

"This isn't any of your damn business, Donovan. I want to know what she gave Milly that upset her."

The sheriff gave me a quick glance before looking back at Walter. "Why don't we go down to the office, Walt? We can talk about it there."

"What the hell! You arresting me now, Bill?"

"You done something that I should?"

"Hell no! You been sheriff here long enough to know I don't give the law any trouble. Since she's been here, this town's had nothing but trouble."

"Now you sound like Abner and Ed," the sheriff countered. "Nothing's ever their fault. Let's have us a talk."

Walter stepped back to his truck. "Nothing to talk about. I'm through here." He opened the door, climbing inside.

"We're going to have that talk, Walter. Today or some other day, but we'll be talking soon." Walter roared off in a cloud of dust and gravel.

I slumped against the porch post. These confrontations were getting more intense with each encounter.

"I take it you had a talk with Milly this morning." Sheriff Donovan gave his head a shake. "You need to be a little more careful."

I sighed. "I didn't realize he followed me."

"He didn't," the sheriff said. "He was at A Cup-A-Joe when I got into town. His truck was out front like it's been every morning since Milly left."

I straightened up. "Then one of the others followed me. Was Ed or Abner at the cafe?"

"Didn't notice their trucks but where one is, the others usually aren't far away."

"How did he know where I went? Milly wouldn't talk to him so she didn't tell him."

The sheriff shrugged. "Was Milly able to shed any light on what happened back then?" Like us, he hoped she could fill in the holes from on the past.

I shook my head. "She didn't remember anyone disappearing back then, or anyone named Barnard."

"Files from sixty years ago are long gone, and there aren't all that many people left who would remember if someone went missing back then. He scratched his head. "I've been in town for ten years and don't recall a Dunn family. Guess I'll have to ask around some. That could stir up a whole hornet's nest. Why would Elmore and his sons kill someone just because he wanted to marry Rosie?"

"They wanted the farm. If she married someone they couldn't control, they couldn't get their hands on it. Greed is pretty powerful."

"But they had the farm. What did Rosie's choice of husband have to do with it?"

"The farm belonged to her," I explained.

He gave a low whistle. "Sounds like that marriage wasn't a match made in heaven. He was already dead when I moved here, but there are plenty of stories about all the old-timers. Never heard that one though. I figured Rosie lived here because she was the spinster sister and needed a place to live. Seems not all gossip gets passed along."

"This doesn't explain how Walter knew I went to see Milly. Maybe Abner and Ed weren't with him this morning. Or one of Walter's sons followed me. Charlie's pretty much sided with his mom. He wouldn't spy on me for his dad."

"Whoever locked you in the root cellar had the journal," Shep put in. "He wouldn't know what it was without readin' it though."

"They knew she had something on them, that's how she made them do whatever she wanted." I related the story Milly told me.

"So they know there's somethin' incriminatin' in the house; just not what," Shep said thoughtfully. "Can we trick them into revealin' what they did by lettin' them think we

242

found Rosie's 'evidence'?"

"Now you're getting into dangerous territory," the sheriff cautioned. "If they've already committed one murder, they might be desperate enough to kill again." It was a chilling thought, not one I wanted to test. I didn't want anyone else to die.

Shep stared into space for a moment then looked back at the sheriff. "Does Deidre's murder fit in with what's goin' on now?" I hadn't connected her murder to what had happened years ago.

The sheriff stiffened, his cop face dropped over his features. "Can't really say." His eyes bore into Shep.

"Can't or won't?" I asked.

"What makes you ask that?" He ignored me, focusing hard on Shep.

"Just wonderin'," he answered with a shrug. "She was in town almost a year lookin' for her father, askin' questions, and nothin' happened to her. Just seems curious to me she'd get murdered when all this starts up with Parker." His nonchalance was deceptive.

"This is an ongoing investigation. You need to stay out of it," the sheriff warned. "You got your hands full working here keeping Parker safe. Stick with that." His tone was curt, and a whole lot harsher than I'd heard from him before. I didn't know what to make of this side of our friendly, easy-going sheriff. He got in his car without another word, and drove away before either of us could say anything.

"What just happened?" I turned to Shep.

"He doesn't want interference with official business. He might be gettin' close to figurin' out what happened to Deidre. He doesn't want anyone screwin' it up."

"How does her murder have anything to do with me? She had nothing to do with this family."

"Didn't she?" He ran his hand through his dark hair causing that stray lock to fall across his forehead. My thoughts were momentarily distracted; I wanted to reach up to push it back in place. "Her mother had just passed away. For the first time she had information about her father, at least where he lived. She wanted to find him." This was all information Shep had given the sheriff at the time Deidre died. Had he found out the identity of her father? What did that have to do with Rosie or her brothers? My money was on Ed Bodeen being her father and maybe her killer.

"What if her father is someone from this family?" Shep asked, thinking out loud. "Why would they kill her? You inherited the farm. How would her murder help them?"

We'd been sidetracked by these new questions. Now I asked the ones I'd asked before. "If all three men were at the cafe this morning, how did Walter know I went to see Milly? Who was following me?"

"It had to be someone with an interest in what happened to Barnard and the baby. Who else would know about it?"

"Would Walter be dumb enough to tell his sons what they did back then?" I asked. "He has to know he can still be charged with murder." With nothing but questions glaring at us, we returned to the work needing done.

Picking up the journal I'd shown Milly, I started skimming the entries again. There were so many journals; I didn't have time to read each entry. I had to find something that would give us answers, or at least lead us in the right direction to figure out what was happening now.

With no way out of the attic, I started exploring everything stored up here. Old clothes, furniture, dishes, just about anything you could think of had once belonged to Mama's parents. I wish I had known them, but they died before I was born. I found a jewelry box today. There's so much jewelry in it I could hardly lift it. It must have belonged to my grandma. I never saw Mama wear it. She would have looked so pretty in it. I wonder why it's hidden up here. Did she know it was here?

"Or maybe she didn't want her husband to find it," I said to the empty room. She was keeping a lot of secrets from her husband. Maybe it was the only way she could keep something of her own. Elmore had been a horrible man.

Rosie took an inventory of the entire contents of the attic, describing everything; none of it had any bearing on what happened to Barnard or the baby though. The next journal was more of the same. It took her weeks to catalog everything she found. I remember seeing several pieces she described. She hadn't thrown out anything that belonged to her mother.

I continued skimming the entries, hoping to find something relevant. One jumped out at me.

I moved the old divan today. It was heavy and I didn't think I could move it. My baby is growing inside me and I can feel him moving in my stomach. He's beginning to kick. I don't want to do anything that might hurt him so I don't lift anything heavy. One of the legs on the divan got stuck on a loose board. Something was sticking out between the boards. I saw the boys move a heavy feed box once by pushing with their back against the box. It worked for me too.

I found a whole bunch of letters hidden between the rafters. Each one was addressed to me in Mama's handwriting. It made me cry. I wish she was here with me now. I know she wouldn't let Papa lock me up in the attic. She wouldn't hate me for loving Barnard. I have to be careful. If Papa finds the letters; he'll take them away from me like he took everything of hers away after she went to Jesus.

I wanted to cry for her; that man was a monster.

Mama said she wrote letters to me from the time I was born. Papa found them and took them away from her. He didn't like what she was telling me. I was seven years old in the first letter I found. She kept writing the letters but hid them from Papa. She was going to tell me where she hid them when I got older, but she passed away before she could. It's taken this long for me to discover them. I hate Papa more every day.

"You want to be the first to flush the toilet?" Startled out of the past, it took a moment to put his question in the right context.

"Are you through?" I jumped out of the chair.

"Come see for yourself." He ushered me into the mudroom. Wayne, Jim, and Mike were standing by expectantly, waiting for my reaction.

It wasn't a large bathroom, but it had all the necessary items, toilet, sink, and shower. I'd never have to use that horrible outhouse again!

"Go ahead," Jim urged with a silly grin on his face. "Give it a flush." A dividing wall and door still needed to be installed, enclosing the small room. But that wouldn't stop me from using it. I pressed the handle and water swished down the drain. We all cheered and I gave each of them a hug. No one has ever been so excited about a bathroom before. I almost suggested we have a toast, but decided the guys would think I'd lost my marbles. Shep and I would celebrate later with Mexican food and margaritas.

CHAPTER TWENTY-FOUR

Seated in the quaint little restaurant, I filled Shep in on the letters Rosie's mother had left for her. "Now I just have to figure out where she hid them." I sighed dramatically. "She didn't throw out anything belonging to her mother, so I know they're here somewhere. Will I ever figure out what happened back then?" I said for the hundredth time.

Shep gave my hand a squeeze. "Each piece adds a little more information. It's just goin' to take a lot of time."

Placing dishes of warm chips and hot sauce on the table, Callita smiled at Shep. "It's good to see you again, Shep. You don't come in like you used to." She turned to me. "Was the food too spicy for you?" She had a little smirk on her face.

"No, it's great. I didn't know I could get food that good in Iowa."

A disappointed pout curved her lips, but she remembered to smiled at the last minute. "You want your usual, Shep?" She was through talking to me.

I laughed when she left to put in our order. "You've made quite a conquest," I teased. "I guess Estaban hasn't completely captured her heart. Maybe he'll come in tonight, and heal her broken heart."

"She's playin' hard to get and keepin' him on a long leash. If he showed interest in someone else, she'd be all over him in a heartbeat." When she placed the salt-rimmed margarita glasses on our table a few minutes later, I picked up the glass. "To indoor plumbing, may it always be available." He laughed, touching his glass to mine.

With the immediate needs of a working kitchen and bathroom finished, we didn't hurry back to the farm, taking our time to wander aimlessly around Bentonville. The evening was warm, but the humidity had dropped some since the sun went down, making for a pleasant evening.

Three sheriff's cars blocked the lane to the house, and an

animal control truck was right behind them when we got home. My heart jumped into my throat. Whatever happened while we were gone, it involved Gus. I opened the door, and stepped out when Deputy Thompson noticed us. He struggled to pull his gun out of the holster. "Stay right where you are and don't move!" He pointed his gun at me, his legs braced apart ready to shoot.

"What's going on?" I stayed by the truck, keeping the heavy door between me, and that very lethal weapon in the hands of an idiot. "What happened?"

Shep slid across the seat, stepping out to stand in front of me. "Stay where you are, Baker." The young deputy tried to sound tough, but his voice squeaked emphasizing the fact that he was barely old enough to be out of high school. He was so nervous I was afraid he'd shoot Shep by accident.

"I'm not movin'," Shep said his tone mild. "My hands are right here." He rested them on the top of the door frame.

"Tell Parker to step out where I can see her."

I stepped up beside Shep, my hands in plain sight. "Only my friends call me Parker. You aren't my friend." It wasn't a good idea to antagonize him since he was holding a gun, but the kid really rubbed me the wrong way. "Why is Animal Control here?"

"I tried to tell my un...ah Sheriff Donovan that dog should be put down. He's vicious. Now he's attacked someone."

"If he attacked someone, it was a burglar," I snapped. "He's just doing his job."

"Doesn't matter, we're taking him in." He still held us at gun point, but his hands weren't shaking so much now.

"Where's the sheriff?" Shep asked, his voice still quiet, trying to defuse the situation. Before the deputy could answer, Gus started barking. Someone in the house yelled for help.

Without thinking, I took off running. Images of deputies shooting Gus overpowered rational thought. "Gus, stand down! Don't shoot him! I'm coming in."

"Stop! You can't go in there." Deputy Thompson's order barely registered.

Just inside the door, Ed Bodeen had his back pressed against the wall, his face as white as a sheet. There was a puddle at his feet, and a wet spot running down his pants leg. If things weren't so tense, I'd laugh at the image he made. "Gus, down." I spoke as calmly as I could under the circumstances, resting my hand on his head.

"Get that vicious mutt away from me! He bit me." The Animal Control guy held a long pole with a noose at the end, ready to put it around Gus's neck. I stepped between him and my dog.

"I don't see any blood, just urine. What are you doing in my house?"

"Jerry, what the hell is going on here?" The sheriff's angry bellow could be heard inside the house. "Put that damn gun away before you shoot yourself."

"He's still in guard mode," I pointed at Gus. "He won't attack unless someone makes a threatening move." I looked pointedly at Ed and the animal control guy before heading outside.

"I told you that dog is vicious. He should be put down. He bit Mr. Bodeen. Maybe now you'll listen to me." The deputy tried to sound brave and defiant.

Ignoring his deputy, the sheriff turned to Shep. "What happened?"

"Don't rightly know." Shep came around the truck door. "We just got back from Bentonville and found this." He looked around the yard at the various deputies. With all the vehicles' headlights still shining, the yard looked as bright as day. I could see a muscle twitch in his jaw with the effort to remain composed. "If Gus bit someone, they broke into the house because that's where Gus was."

"Bill, help me. This vicious dog is going to kill me if you don't shoot him." Ed called from inside the house.

"See, Uncle Bill. You got to put that dog down." Deputy Thompson reached for his gun again but stopped, taking a step back at the look the sheriff sent his way.

"I'm going to have you put down if you call me that one more time while you're on duty," the sheriff growled. The young man turned bright red, but was smart enough to keep his mouth shut. "Keep your hand off that gun before I use it on you. The rest of you, get over here. Now!" He bellowed at the other deputies and the animal control officer on the porch. They dutifully lined up, looking sheepish. They were all so young I couldn't believe they were really deputies. Not one of them was over twenty-five, and probably not much over twenty. "Your turn, Ed. Get out here."

"I can't move. This dog will kill me."

The sheriff glared at me, but I was beyond intimidation. I waited a heartbeat before calling to Gus. He came obediently, sitting down beside me. Ed followed slowly behind, keeping a safe distance from Gus. "I hope you plan on cleaning up the puddle you left on the entry floor." Several of the deputies snickered, adding to Ed's embarrassment. The sheriff's glare silenced them without a word.

"Okay, Ed. What's going on here?" Deputy Thompson started to speak, clamping his mouth shut when his uncle sent him a look that could kill.

"I just came out here to see Parker, and that damn dog attacked me. You've got to have him put down." I bristled, but kept quiet. Sheriff Donovan was a lot smarter than this bunch gave him credit for.

"Was Gus in the house when he attacked you?"

"Ah...well...ah..."

"Was the dog in the house when he attacked you?" he repeated the question with more heat. "Where'd he bite you? I don't see any blood." He looked at the wet spot on Ed's pants causing Ed's face to turn red up again. "Your pants aren't even ripped. How did he attack you?"

"He would have torn me to pieces if these guys hadn't gotten here so fast." He nodded at the row of young deputies.

"We'll get to them in a minute. Were you in the house?"

"Oh, ah, well, yeah, I guess I was. Sort of."

"Either you were or you weren't. Which is it?"

This was going so slow, I wanted to scream. Real police work doesn't move as fast and smooth as it does on television.

"Ah, I was just inside the front door," he finally admitted, his head down, talking to the ground. "I didn't even see him until he attacked me." Ed thought this was all Gus's fault. He'd done nothing wrong.

"What were you doing in Miss Evans' house? She wasn't home, so she didn't invite you in. Did you break a window?" The broken window could be seen from where we were standing, so he couldn't very well deny it. Or could he?

"Ah, that's just it, Bill. I saw the broken window, and wanted to check it out." You could almost see the light bulb going off above his head. This was his way out. "I could tell someone had broken into the house. I wanted to make sure they hadn't taken anything."

My undignified snort netted me another glare from the sheriff.

"Really. So you went into the empty house when you knew there was a guard dog on the premises. Not too smart on your part, huh, Ed?"

"Well, put that way I guess it wasn't, but my intentions were good." He stood up straight trying to sound indignant.

"Your story doesn't quite fly. If someone else had broken into the house, don't you think Gus would have gone after them the way he did you?" Ed wasn't smart enough to come up with an explanation. He stared at the sheriff with his mouth open. "Let's go to town, and finish this in my office. You have a lot of explaining to do, maybe even a few charges to answer to." Ed sputtered all the way to the sheriff's car. Once he was in the back seat, Sheriff Donovan turned to his deputies. "Get back on patrol. I'll deal with you in the morning. Be in my office at nine sharp, or collect your last paycheck." His tone left no room for argument.

When the yard was cleared of cars, and only Ed's big truck was sitting at the end of the lane, I slumped against Shep. "Is this ever going to end? Mom, Dad and the twins will be here in two days. I don't want this to blow up just before they arrive." It was nearly midnight now, and pitch black with the bright headlights from all the vehicles gone.

~~~

Drinking coffee, hoping to wake up after the late night, we each took a journal. To stop what was going on now, we needed to figure out what had happened in the past.

"Listen to this." Shep spoke into the silence, reading an entry:

That miserable Meyers came to the house today. I could see him through the small window at the front of the house. Papa treated him like royalty, taking him in to the front parlor instead of the kitchen like ordinary people. Mama told me never to trust that miserable man. He's dishonest, even for a crook. He tried to steal the farm away from Mama when she and Papa got married. I don't know what they talked about. I can't hear anything in the parlor.

I've read all of Mama's letters. She was so unhappy. I don't think she ever loved Papa, she didn't even like him. The farm belonged to her family, and it's always belonged just to her. She said she was leaving the farm and everything to me someday. When Mama passed away the farm became mine, and Papa knew it. That must have made him so mad. I don't know what he gets if he can force me to marry that horrible Ed Bodeen, but he probably figures he'll somehow be able to get control of the farm. Papa doesn't do anything without a reason.

After that miserable Meyers left, Papa brought some papers up for me to sign. When I wouldn't sign them unless I read them first, I thought he was going to whoop me again. He wouldn't even let me see them.

"That miserable little weasel! He lied to me! Elmore knew all along the farm belonged to Rosie when Miriam died. That's why he was so mean to both of them." I paced across the room. "What else did that miserable Meyers lie to me about?" I was using the name Miriam and Rosie had called Meyers Senior. They were two of a kind. Rosie didn't sign the papers, but she didn't let on she knew she was the rightful owner of the farm. As long as she was a prisoner in the attic, she was at his mercy. She had to play along.

"With gossip being king in this town, why didn't someone warn me about him?" I turned, staring hard at Shep.

He held up his hands in a placating gesture. "Don't look at me, Darlin'. I trusted that little weasel with my business. Considerin' I'm in direct competition with Ed Bodeen, I'm surprised my business ever got off the ground."

"Sorry." I released a frustrated breath. I continued pacing for a minute thinking over what he'd said. "He couldn't do anything to you or your business. Rosie twisted a few arms to get you started. I'll bet one of those arms belonged to Meyers. She had something on just about everyone. She probably had something on him, too. He couldn't do anything to you without risking his own neck. I just wish we knew what she had on everyone."

"He acts like such a mousey little guy, but it's just that, an act. He has everybody fooled."

Another thought occurred to me. "He is paying you, right? He can't withhold payment, can he? Is he paying all the bills I've racked up?

"I'm gettin' paid, and I'm sure everyone else is, too. People know he's the executor of her estate. They'd go after him if they didn't get paid."

"This is another layer we have to dig through before we can figure out what happened to Barnard and the baby." It didn't look like we were ever going to unravel this mess.

"If we could find out what she held over them, maybe we could figure this out. It has to have something to do with Barnard's death. Why didn't she tell someone? Or tell me in another letter. Meyers didn't tell Walter and Abner I was inheriting the farm until after Rosie passed away. The house was padlocked when I got here. Who put it there?" I was talking to myself, but Shep answered.

"I did. The sheriff had me come out and put them on. I thought Meyers had requested it so people couldn't get in until her will was probated, or the heir took over. Maybe not."

"You think Sheriff Donovan knows what a crook Meyers is? Would he tell us?"

"Why don't we ask him?" He pointed out the big window in the parlor. Sheriff Donovan's county car pulled to a stop in front of the porch.

"Care for a glass of iced tea, Sheriff?" I asked as he stepped out of his car.

"Sounds good, it's already been a long day after a short night." The men sat on the porch while I brought out a tray with frosty glasses and a pitcher of tea. "Thought you might like to know Ed spent the night in jail, compliments of the county. He spent most of the time yelling and complaining that he'd done nothing wrong. He's being charged with breaking and entering. There's enough evidence to make the charge stick this time."

"This time?" Shep and I spoke in unison. "You've arrested him before?" I asked. "Why didn't it stick?"

"Ed seems to think he's above the law. Having the Chief of Police as a close friend hasn't dissuaded him of that idea. This time the chief has no say in the matter. This is in my jurisdiction."

He was quiet for a minute then continued. "I put a few of my deputies on disciplinary probation. They've listened to Ed's baloney most of their lives, and they believe what he spews out as gospel. One more incident like last night and they'll all be looking for a different career path. That includes my idiot nephew. If he so much as sets foot on this farm again without my say so, I'll fire his as...ah, butt."

I wasn't sure what to say, but I was grateful for his support.

"What do you know about Mr. Meyers, Sheriff?" Shep's change of subject caught him by surprise.

"Why do you ask?" His tone was casual, but it held an edge. His cop face was firmly in place.

We sat up a little straighter, on alert by his sudden change. "Ah, we've been readin' more of Miss Rosie's journals. She mentions his father as not bein' completely honest. We thought maybe his son was followin' in Daddy's footsteps." Shep put a very diplomatic spin on our suspicions.

The sheriff heaved a heavy sigh. "What exactly is in those

journals? Start from the beginning."

"You weren't very interested before." I said. Even I could hear the petulant tone in my voice.

"You were talking about a murder that happened sixty years ago. The principals are probably long gone."

"Not if Walter and Abner are involved," I suggested.

He gave me a hard stare, but otherwise ignored my statement. "You're wandering into the here and now. What do Meyers and his old man have to do with this Barnard? I haven't had time to research a Dunn family yet."

We spent the next hour, explaining the new information we'd discovered, and our own conclusions. When we finally fell silent, the sheriff leaned back against the chair, whistling softly. "I don't have any information that will help you with what happened sixty years ago. If you come up with any proof that will hold up in front of a judge and jury, I'll be more than happy to arrest somebody, even if it's Walter and Abner. The only thing you have against Meyers is possible unethical behavior. I can't arrest him for that."

There was a hint of emphasis on his last word, and I couldn't stop myself from asking, "What are you hoping to arrest him for?"

For several long moments he stayed silent. Finally he gave a little nod as if coming to a decision. "What exactly did Deidre Smith tell you about her father?" His question came out of left field.

"That he was a big deal here," Shep answered. "She acted like she knew who he was, but she never told me his name. Having a secret gave her a thrill. She found a letter her mother left, explainin' about her father and where he was from." *There was a lot of letter writing going on here,* I thought. *Didn't people just talk to each other?* "She called herself a 'love child.' She liked to romanticize the situation."

"What does this have to do with Meyers, or what went on when Rosie was a young girl?" I asked what we were both wondering.

"It doesn't have anything to do with Rosie, at least not as far as I know. But it might have something to do with a few others in town." Our perplexed expressions told him we didn't understand, but he only asked another confusing question. "Do you know what a gentleman farmer is?" At our negative response, he laughed. "Neither did I, had to look it up. Seems it's a 'genteel' person who farms, not necessarily for a living, but as a sideline." I started to ask what that had to do with anything, but he held up his hand.

"We found that letter from her mom when we went through her apartment. She called the man a 'gentleman farmer'. Said his name was Clive Beaumont. Sounds phony to me, but Deidre must have believed it. At least for a time. When she realized no one by that name had ever lived here, she started looking for someone who fit her mother's description. Unfortunately, it was a very general description; a well-to-do older gentleman. This is a small town; there aren't that many men who lived up to the ideal in her mind. She settled on three, Abner Shepherd, Ed Bodeen and Arthur Meyers."

My mouth dropped open. I couldn't think of anything to say.

"Isn't Abner too old to fit her ideal? He's at least seventy." Shep asked.

"Her mother described him as an 'older gentleman,' just not how old."

"Did she confront all three men?" I asked. "Only one knew her mother, right?" A light bulb went on in my head. "Was her mother a prostitute?" I whispered the question.

Sheriff Donovan shook his head. "Can't say for sure, but it would explain how all three men knew her. She wasn't by the time Deidre was born. That much I've figured out. For a time, Deidre was either blackmailing them, or pressuring them to acknowledge her as their daughter. She finally settled on one, Arthur Meyers. He had the most to lose by revealing he had an illegitimate daughter."

"Did he kill her? Are you going to arrest him?" My questions tumbled out one on top of another.

He held up his hand like a traffic cop. "I'm still working

on this. I don't want to hurry, and expose my hand too soon. When I make an arrest, I want it to stick." He gave a heavy sigh. "I also have to keep this on the QT. I can't have my nephew or sister-in-law finding out what I suspect. It'd be all over town in a heartbeat." He should fire them if they didn't keep things confidential. That isn't for me to say though. "He's probably only dangerous if he feels threatened." He gave us the fish-eyed stare when he spoke the warning. "You both need to stay out of this. I don't want him to disappear if he suspects I'm on to him."

"What did Rosie have on him?" I wondered out loud. "She had to have something on him to keep him quiet about her business." The man had first class acting skills to convince everyone he was a mousey little man. Meyers wouldn't get away with all he'd done. God has a way of working all things out, even evil things done by evil humans.

Sheriff Donovan stood up to leave a few minutes later with an admonishment to stay clear of Meyers. At the bottom of the steps he turned, looking up at us. "Don't let the past overpower the present." With that he got into his car and drove off.

We were silent for several long minutes considering all he'd said. Finally Shep spoke softly, "He's right, Darlin'. I came here lookin' for somethin' from the past no one else in my family cared about. Miss Rosie had an agenda that was all about the past. She's even been controllin' you from beyond the grave. Maybe it's time we let some of this go."

"Don't you want to find out what happened to Barnard and the baby?" I wasn't ready to give up this quest Rosie had sent me on.

He thought about his answer for a minute. "They took the baby away from her, and he was adopted by a lovin' family. He's my grandpa. I can't prove it, but I know it." He tapped his chest over his heart. "How else would I look just like Barnard? The saying 'God works in mysterious way his wonders to perform' is true. Look at what all he did to bring us together." His warm smile made my heart do a little hic-up.

"So you want to give up." I stated. "Stop reading the

journals to find out what happened?"

"I just don't want it to be the only thing we think about any more. If we back off, maybe Walter and Abner will, too. They might even make a mistake that will shed some light on all this."

"There are a lot of boxes in the attic and barn to go through. Rosie had some beautiful antiques I'd love to check out." A new excitement was beginning to bubble up inside me.

CHAPTER TWENTY-FIVE

We put the journals in a secure hiding place, and locked the house before heading for the barn. Nothing could be moved into the house until the renovations were finished, but we could find out what had been stored there for years. Pieces needing to be restored were set aside. That was a project I could work on when it got too cold to be outside.

The thought brought a smile to my lips. As long as Shep was with me, it didn't matter where we lived. Looking at him, I laughed. We were both covered in a fine layer of dust. There was a smudge across his cheek, and that lock of dark hair had fallen across his forehead.

He looked up at my laugh. "What? Am I as dirty as you?" He trailed a finger down my cheek before leaning in to gently rest his lips against mine.

Gus gave off one woof the same time someone cleared his throat. We jumped apart like two guilty teenagers caught doing something they shouldn't. "Sorry." Charlie stood in the open barn door, kicking at the dusty floor. "I didn't mean to sneak up on you." His face was as red as I knew mine was. "I just wanted to come visit."

Giving him a hug, I assured him it was okay. "Would you like to see the new kitchen?" He appeared to enjoy the tour, but I'm not sure how much he was paying attention. His usual happy personality was absent today. "Aunt Rosie would like what you've done," he finally said. "She told me once the next owner would fix up the house, make it modern."

That surprised me. I didn't know he had much to do with her. "Were you close to her?"

He gave a bark of laughter at that. "Aunt Rosie didn't let anybody get close. At least until Shep came to town. She was kind of prickly. Every now and then she'd say things though."

"What kind of things?"

"I asked her once why she didn't have electricity or

bathrooms like everybody else. I always hated using the outhouse." We shuddered at the same time. "She said her Pa didn't want her Ma to have them. If the old outhouse was good enough for her Ma, it was good enough for her. It didn't make sense to me, but you didn't question Aunt Rosie. She had her own way."

We were just now beginning to understand that. Control meant everything to her because it had been taken from her early on.

"I been to see Ma today." He finally got around to what was bothering him. "I wish she'd come home. I miss her."

"Is she okay? She isn't sick, is she?" My heart pounded. She'd been so upset when I showed her the journal. Could that cause her to have a heart attack? *Please Father God, take care of her,* I sent a prayer up to heaven.

Charlie shrugged. "She said she's okay, but I know she's sad. Pa isn't the easiest person to be around, but I didn't think they'd get a divorce."

My heart sank. *I did this,* I thought. *Maybe I shouldn't have come here.*

"Pa isn't happy either," he went on. "He misses her even though he won't say so. I don't even know why Ma moved to Buena Vista. Pa won't talk about it. Uncle Abner and Young Ed are always at the house now. Maybe if they'd stay away, Ma would come home. She never did like them." I couldn't blame her, but I kept quiet.

"Your Ma just needs time to think some things over," Shep said softly. "When things work themselves out, she'll be back."

"Are you sure?" Charlie looked hopeful.

"I can't promise anything, you just have to believe things will work out for the best even though it doesn't seem like it now."

When he stood up to leave, I urged him to visit again. He hadn't been around since the day he warned us Abner and Ed were watching us. "I'd like that," he said, "but Pa doesn't want me to come here. He said everything is your fault."

When I started to object, he stopped me. "I know this is his and Uncle Abner's fault. They didn't treat Aunt Rosie right, so she didn't leave them the farm like they wanted. Ma always said you can catch more flies with honey than vinegar, but Pa's always been more vinegar than honey." He gave me another hug, and got into his truck.

I looked at the woods across the road. Was someone watching us? If so, Charlie was in for more problems when he got home. I still wasn't sure if Walter was one of those watching me. I hoped Charlie would come here, or to his mom if Walter got abusive.

"I wonder if Rosie thought of all the lives she was affecting by leaving the farm to me? Did she even care?"

~~~

Instead of sorting boxes or reading journals Monday morning, I headed for the gym. I kept a careful watch in the rear view mirror, making sure I wasn't followed. I didn't want anyone sneaking up on me again.

"See Abner, I told you she was going to the gym. I know my little girl." I had just stepped out of the truck when I heard Ed. So much for being careful, I thought. Grabbing my bag, I whirled around, swinging it out, hoping to clobber one or both of them.

"Shut up, Ed," Abner snarled. "She ain't your little girl."

"Well, she shoulda been," Ed muttered. "She wouldn't have deserted me." The man was delusional.

"Drop the bag, Missy," Abner snarled, ignoring Ed.

"And if I don't, what are you going to do?" So far he hadn't shown any weapons.

"She doesn't have that psycho dog with her; just grab it. See if she has the book."

"I said shut up, Ed. I'll handle this." Abner never took his eyes off me, not giving me a chance to take another swing at him. "Why didn't you just leave when you had the chance? You had to keep poking your nose into things that were none of your business." Ed whimpered when Abner pulled out a gun, but he didn't say anything more.

"Rosie wanted me to have the farm. Why did you keep trying to make me leave? If you had let me be, maybe I would have gone back to Arizona on my own."

"By then it would have been too late. You've been snooping around where you had no business. You would've found her things sooner or later."

"What things?"

"Don't play stupid, Missy!" he snapped. "Rosie left it all for you to find. She liked playing her little games, always threatening us if we didn't do exactly what she wanted. Well, she's gone, and I'm not dancing to her tune any longer. I'm not going to jail for something that happened sixty years ago."

"Depends on what that something is, doesn't it?" I hoped my cell phone was working as well as it had with Ed. If Abner confessed, and I lived to tell about it, maybe we'd finally know the whole story.

"You're just like her, playing so innocent while holding an ax over our heads." Ed actually looked up, checking for that ax. "Give me the evidence Rosie claimed she had, and go back to Arizona. Then life can get back to normal. Milly will go home, and Walter will stop sniveling about her leaving him."

"Sniveling?" We all jumped as Walter walked around the truck. "You don't have to spend every blooming day at my house complaining about my granddaughter. Put that gun away. You want someone to call the cops?"

For a minute I'd thought he was going to help me, now not so much. "Did you know Rosie kept journals all these years? She wrote everything down."

"How do you know? You never said anything before," Abner accused.

"Milly told me, she showed them to her." He nodded at me, but didn't take his eyes off his brother.

Great, now Abner will go after Milly too.

We'd all forgotten about Ed. Until now, that is. "How many of them damn things are there? I told you we should go back and look. I'll bet they weren't even at Baker's house." He was babbling.

"Shut up, Ed," Abner barked again.

"What's going to happen if she wrote about what happened to that man," Ed snapped. "I'm not going to jail for that."

"What the hell are you talking about?" Abner asked. "You weren't even born yet."

"Of course I was." He stated indignantly. "It was only twenty years ago."

"You killed my father!" I launched myself at Ed, but Walter grabbed my arm, holding me back.

He stepped in front of me, facing Ed, a muscle twitched in his cheek. "You killed Laura's husband? What the hell for?"

"So she'd come back here, and marry me like she was supposed to." He made it sound like, "Well, duh!"

"You see how well that worked out, don't you?"

"You shoulda forced her before she ran off the first time. Then none of this would've happened, and the farm would belong to me now."

"What the hell are you talking about now?" Abner spoke up. "The farm was never going to be yours."

"It would've been mine if Rosie had married my Pa like she was supposed to."

"What makes you think that?"

"She would've been my ma, and I'd have gotten the farm when she died."

"That isn't the way it was going to work, you idiot," Abner sneered. "Once Rosie had a kid, your pa was going to sign the farm over to us. It should have been ours, not Rosie's!" The three men had forgotten me. They wouldn't have noticed if I'd walked away. As long as my phone was recording this, I was sticking around.

"No!" Ed bellowed. "It would have been mine!"

"Shut up!" Both Abner and Walter hissed. "You want someone to call the cops?"

"I don't care. That farm should be mine. My pa told me so." They were at each other's throats. If I waited long enough, one of them would spill the beans on the others. A house divided can't stand, and these three were divided.

"Well, your pa was wrong," Abner snarled. "The farm should have belonged to our pa, but Rosie got it instead. We were going to get it back when she married your pa. He was going to sign it over to Pa when Rosie had a baby."

I gasped, slapping my hand over my mouth to keep the sound inside. Had they planned on killing Rosie after she had a baby? How did they think they could get away with that?

"I was supposed to be that baby!" Ed shouted. "He was going to keep the farm for me. He had to get rid of that farm hand before they could run off."

I gasped again. Ed Bodeen Senior killed Barnard!

"We had to clean up his mess, and she still wouldn't marry your old man," Abner snapped. I wanted to ask why they had taken her baby, but I didn't want to draw their attention back to me. Abner still held the gun, pointed at the ground now.

Before they could say more, a group of men came out of the gym heading for their cars, breaking the spell holding all of us. Abner whipped the gun into the pocket of his overalls. "We're not through here, Missy," he hissed at me before stalking off to his truck. Ed had to hurry to catch up, or be left behind.

I sagged against the side of the truck, resting my head on my hands. Walter reached out to me, but dropped his hand before touching me. "Go home and stay there."

I straightened up, facing him defiantly. "I'm not going back to Arizona until the year is up. After all you did to Rosie, there's no way I'm going to let you get your hands on what was hers."

He sighed as though dealing with a recalcitrant child. "The farm was lost to us a long time ago. Go back to the farm and stay there. You aren't safe anywhere else right now."

"Then why did you do all those things to Rosie?"

"Because that damn Meyers and his old man fed us a pack of lies for years." His harsh answer was directed more at himself than me.

"What do you mean? Rosie's instructions are in a sealed envelope to be opened only if I don't stay the full year."

He gave a harsh laugh. "You think a sealed envelope would stop Meyers? Once Rosie was gone, all bets were off as far as he was concerned. If you don't stay, the farm goes to Baker." I smiled. Sort of poetic justice, I guess.

"It doesn't matter anymore. It's done." He sounded defeated.

"Why did you take her baby away from her? Whose idea was that?"

"I said it's done. Go home." He walked away, shoulders stooped, head down. For the first time I saw him for what he was, an old man, a defeated old man.

It felt like an eternity since I left the farm. In reality it had only been an hour when I pulled into the lane. The scene in the parking lot happened in minutes instead of a lifetime. As I stepped out of the truck, Gus came up to me, whimpering softly, picking up on my mood. "That was a fast workout. Are you all right, Darlin'," Shep greeted me from the back porch, a worried frown furrowing his brow.

When my phone beeped, indicating low battery, I pulled it out of my pocket. I'd forgotten to turn it off after Walter left. I climbed the steps accepting Shep's comforting hug. "Let me plug this in so I don't lose everything." I looked pointedly at the men working in the mudroom. "Can you take a break for a few minutes?"

"I'm the boss," he joked to lighten my mood. "Let's go for a walk." He took my hand, leading me back outside. When we were well away from the house, he pulled me into his arms again, resting his chin on top of my head. "What happened? Walter and Abner again?"

"And Ed." He stiffened, starting to pull me away, but I tightened my arms around his waist. "I'm fine, physically. This time Walter was on my side. The other two were waiting for me at the gym." I related the conversation as best I could. "I hope my phone was able to pick everything up. For the first time, Walter acted like a real grandfather. He looked so defeated when he left." Mixed emotions rioted inside me. I didn't know if I could trust Walter just because of that one act, but I wanted to.

"Ed actually admitted running your father off the road and killing him?" I nodded my head sadly. After all these years I finally found out what happened to my birth father. "We need to get your phone to Sheriff Donovan. No tellin' what they'll try once they realize everything they said in front of you."

A shiver of fear passed through me. "Walter told me to stay at the farm; it was the only safe place right now. I don't know if he thinks Abner and Ed will try to harm me, or if he was just being cautious."

"Better safe than sorry." He pulled his cell phone off his belt hitting speed dial for the sheriff. In a few short sentences, Shep explained what had happened, and that I had recorded the confrontation. He listened intently, his expression growing tense. "Fine, we'll see you whenever you get here. Be careful, Sheriff."

"What happened?" I was almost afraid to hear the answer.

"Meyers took off. He must have gotten wind the sheriff was investigatin' him for Deidre's murder."

"His nephew?" I guessed.

Shep shrugged. "That'd be my guess, but there's no tellin'. When he went to question him this morning, his secretary hadn't seen him since Friday. He'd cleared his calendar after she left Friday night without telling her."

"I'll bet she's bent out of shape about that. She ran that office like it was her own little domain."

"Just more of his act, lettin' her think she ran the show. He told his wife he had to go out of town on business over the weekend. She hasn't seen him since Friday either."

"Who goes out of town on business over a weekend?"

He shrugged again. "Seems he did this about once a month for years."

I snorted. "And she didn't suspect he was fooling around? How dumb is she?" I shook my head. "About as dumb as the rest of us for believing he's this mousey little guy, afraid of his own shadow."

"Sheriff said to stay close to the house. He'll be here as soon as he can. He was on his way to search Meyers' house

266

and office, but wasn't hopeful the man was dumb enough to leave evidence behind. He didn't want to send a deputy to pick up your phone. He's feelin' a little paranoid, and doesn't trust any of them until he finds out who tipped Meyers off."

For the next few hours the men worked feverishly to get as much work done today before Mom and Dad arrived. I wandered around the house, afraid to go outside because of what Walter said, but unable to settle down with anything inside.

It was late afternoon before the sheriff was able to make it to the farm. He looked tired, and a little beaten down. "Sorry it took so long to get out this way. It hasn't been a good morning."

"How about a cup of coffee or some iced tea?" I offered. "Did you get any lunch?"

Grateful for the offer, he sat at the kitchen table while I fixed a sandwich and a tall glass of tea. "It's been a bad morning," he repeated.

"Were you able to locate Meyers?" When he didn't answer immediately, I figured he couldn't talk about an ongoing investigation. Finally he shook his head. "He's gone to ground somewhere, waiting for the heat to die down."

"How did he know you'd be looking for him?" I didn't want to ask if his nephew had tipped Meyers off.

"Seems he's been anticipating this for some time, decided it was time to disappear. We found several different identities he's been using over the years, including the one he used with Deidre's mother. It's looking good he was her father, and he panicked when she threatened to expose him."

Shep came into the kitchen just as the sheriff finished the sandwich. I picked up the plate and glass, carrying them to the sink. "Thanks for that. What about that recording?"

So the men wouldn't hear what we were talking about, thus feeding the gossip mill in town, we took my phone outside away from the house. As I suspected, the confrontation lasted no longer than ten minutes. Sheriff Donovan gave a low whistle, shaking his head when it ended. "I can't believe I didn't see all the intrigue running just below the surface in this little town. Meyers is as corrupt as his old man was. I'll contact the Arizona Highway Patrol; see how they want to handle the accident that killed your father."

"It wasn't an accident," I said hotly. "Ed deliberately ran him off the road. Dad didn't have a chance to make it out alive once his truck went over the cliff." Every time I thought about what Ed had done, I wanted to do him bodily harm.

Sheriff Donovan left a few minutes later, my cell phone in an evidence bag. I felt lost without that small piece of technology. I never went far without it even in Phoenix.

Shep and his crew worked until it got so dark they couldn't see. The washer and dryer were installed in the mud room, and they'd started with the electricity in the bedroom I was using. If there was any money left in the estate after Meyers took off, I'd make sure they got paid extra for all the time they were putting in.

I had a hard time falling asleep that night. Mom said they'd be here around noon the next day. I couldn't wait to see them. I wanted everything to be perfect, but the house was far from that. There were still large holes in the walls where Shep was installing the electrical lines, and walls for closets and bathrooms were only partially up. It was taking longer to remodel the house than building one from scratch.

CHAPTER TWENTY-SIX

Milly arrived early the next morning, as excited to see Mom as I was. "I hope she can forgive me for not standing up to Walter all those years ago." She wrung her hands nervously.

"You know she has, Grandma. She never blamed you, not even then."

For a minute she looked undecided about what she wanted to say next. Finally she drew a deep breath and plunged in. "Walter and I talked for a long time yesterday. He told me everything Abner and Ed said, things neither of us knew before. He didn't know Ed had killed your father. I hope you believe that. When I told him Laura and her husband would be here today with the twins, he actually broke down and cried." Her eyes were shiny with her own unshed tears. "I've never seen him cry before. The only emotions he ever displayed were total unconcern or anger. He's been angry for most of his life. Maybe now he can let that go, and learn to live a normal life. We talked more yesterday than we have in years. I agreed to move back home, but he has to make an effort to change. I won't go back to the way things were. I'll never let him treat me like that again."

Gus gave out a sharp bark, standing at attention when a truck drove into the lane. Shep walked to the edge of the porch ready to stop Walter from coming up the steps if he was dumb enough to get out of the truck. Milly reached out her hand, "Please let him be here. He wants to see Laura and the twins."

Of course, I thought, *grandsons*. Resentment boiled up in me. He treated me like I was scum of the earth, but he was ready to accept grandsons. I couldn't let his actions color my feelings for the twins. I love them completely. "I'm not sure Mom will be happy to see him. She's been dead to him for a long time."

"Are you going to tell your dog and your boyfriend I can get out of the truck?" Walter called up to me. His tone was mild.

"One word," I told him, "just one wrong word to Mom and you're out of here. I won't have you destroy this reunion for her and Grandma. Understood?"

He glared at me for a moment. He didn't like taking orders from me, or any woman. Finally he gave a curt nod. I put my hand on top of Gus's head; "It's okay, boy. Easy." I wouldn't go so far as to say Walter was a friend.

Shep looked at me. "You sure?"

"For now," I nodded.

Walter slowly got out of the truck, unsure whether to trust Gus. Mounting the steps and sidestepping the dog, he looked at me, really looked at me, for the first time since I came to Iowa. "You're a lot like me, girl."

"Don't be insulting!" I snapped.

Milly and Shep tensed, waiting for the pending explosion. Suddenly Walter gave a bark of laughter, stunning all of us. "You might not like it girl, but you are a lot like me."

"A much softer version," Milly added, "much nicer. Maybe you can learn something from your granddaughter," she suggested, a smile softening her words.

While we were still standing on the porch with me glaring at Walter, and him wearing a goofy grin on his face, my Jeep Wrangler turned into the lane. I let out a shriek of joy, and bounded down the steps. I'm not sure my feet even touched the ground. Before the car came to a complete stop, Mom and the twins were out wrapping me in a group hug. Dad turned the ignition off, and came around the front of the Jeep, hugging all four of us at once.

"My goodness," he laughed. "What's with these tears? You'd think you two hadn't seen each other for years instead of weeks."

"Laura." Milly slowly came down the steps. Even though they'd talked on the phone, she wasn't sure how to proceed.

"Mom!" The water works started in earnest now with both of them in tears which brought more tears to my eyes. Mom always joked that our bladders were too close to our eyes because we could cry at the smallest thing.

Before we could get ourselves under control again, Walter cleared his throat, drawing attention to himself. The happy atmosphere disappeared in an instant. "What's *he* doing here?" Mom glared accusingly at me and Milly. Until now I'd forgotten about Gus, but the low rumble in his throat brought everyone's attention to him. He didn't know what caused the sudden tension, but he wasn't going to tolerate it. Walter moved to the other side of the porch, and Shep took hold of Gus's collar.

"Wow! Is that Gus?" Justin took a step towards the porch. When Gus let out another low warning growl, I grabbed Justin's arm.

"Don't move right now." I slowly went over to Gus, patting his head. "Easy, boy. Friends." I turned to the twins. "Come here." Not sure they wanted to; they cautiously walked over to me. I took their hands. "Friends, Gus, friends." The fur on his back slowly laid down again, his tail wagging back and forth. "He's okay now, but no more tension. He takes that personally."

Looking at Mom with a nod at Walter, I said, "Listen to what he has to say. If you don't want him here then, he's gone." I gave Walter a meaningful glare before turning away. "Mom, Dad, this is Shep Baker, Shep, my folks, Laura and Ben Evans and my brothers, Justin and Jason."

Mom wasn't happy with Walter being here, but at least the tension had dissipated somewhat. I turned to the twins, "Guys, this is..." I wasn't sure how to introduce him. "Ah, Walter?" My voice rose slightly with a question mark at the end.

"Your grandpa," Walter amended. He held out his hand first to Justin then Jason. They looked confused, but were polite, and accepted the handshake. They had heard about the family feud over the years, but it hadn't been a frequent topic of conversation. If they asked about Mom's parents, the subject was mostly skimmed over, saying they lived in Iowa, and we didn't see them. "I'm glad to meet you boys," Walter added. "I hope I can get to know you while you're here."

We stayed on the front porch. I wasn't sure I wanted

Walter in the house. I didn't know what he'd say about all the changes we'd made, and the work still to be done. It felt like I was entertaining the enemy when I offered everyone cold lemonade and iced tea.

Mom kept sending dagger-filled glares at Walter, but finally she sat down with Milly on the swing both talking at the same time. They had twenty years to catch up on. Dad started asking Shep questions about all the work he was doing in the house. The twins were making friends with Gus. That left me alone with Walter. "Are you going to keep everybody outside just because I'm here?"

Was I that transparent? My face got hot with embarrassment, but I didn't back down. "I guess that depends on you. Have you really changed, or is this all for show? You've been nothing but nasty to me since I got here. I can't believe you've had a change of heart overnight." We kept our voices low, so the others wouldn't overhear.

"I didn't know Abner had a gun yesterday. It suddenly hit me I could lose my only granddaughter. I didn't want that." His voice was barely above a whisper.

"Would it matter so much? You have two more grandsons now." It still rankled that he would cry hearing about the twins.

"Of course I want to get to know them, but I've got other grandsons. I've only got one granddaughter. When Abner pulled out that gun..." He didn't say anything for a long moment. "Like I said, I didn't want to lose my only granddaughter."

"Even though she's the one who tore your family apart?" I threw his words back at him.

"Yeah, even though." He chuckled softly. In the past half hour he's probably laughed more than he had in the last fifty years. "Will you help me with your mother?" he asked growing serious again.

I shook my head. "You need to mend your own fences. It's up to her if she's willing to forgive you."

His shoulders slumped, but he didn't argue. I couldn't believe this was the same man who had spent the last eight weeks trying to get rid of me. "Why did you and Abner file suit, contesting Rosie's will? You know she wasn't incompetent."

Walter looked at me like I'd grown another head. "We didn't contest the will. Rosie was a lot of things, but she wasn't incompetent."

"Meyers said..." I stopped. We both knew what had happened. It was another of the lies Meyers used to throw us off, and pit us against each other. I shook my head. "Never mind. He'll pay for his part in all this."

Milly must have convinced Mom to give Walter a chance, because she finally stood up. "Honey, I'd like to see how you're fixing up the house. Can we go in now?" I hadn't fooled anyone, least of all Mom. "Wow, this is a big house," Jason said after exploring all the rooms upstairs. "Are you going to sell it when you come home?"

Everyone but Shep seemed to hold their breath, waiting for my answer. We both knew whatever my decision about the house and where we lived, we'd be together. "I haven't decided what I'm going to do with the house. I might stay here part of the time, and part of the time in Arizona. That way I could have the nice weather in both places, and not have to deal with the extreme seasons." No one laughed. My attempt at a joke fell flat.

Accepting my answer, Jason turned to other matters, "You said Gus likes to go for a run. Can we take him? We've been cooped up in the car for three days."

I hesitated for a minute. Whoever tried to run me off the road was still out there. I finally nodded, "Just run along the edge of the field out back."

"Can't we run on the road? There isn't much traffic."

"No!" Shep and I responded at the same time drawing everyone's attention. "Ah, the road's kind of narrow, and there's no shoulder to run on," I hastily explained. "It's safer to run around the field."

"That's boring," Justin objected.

"You heard Parker, the field or stay here." Dad's voice was mild, but as always it carried weight.

Both boys gave me a questioning look, but didn't argue further. I gave Gus the okay to follow the boys, and when the back door closed behind them, Dad turned to me. "Parker?" That eyebrow lifted in question, and I knew I was in trouble.

I didn't want to go into details right now, but I couldn't avoid it. I was silent long enough that Mom spoke. "What haven't you told us?"

Shep gave me a small nod of encouragement, and I released a long sigh. "The first time I went running on the road, I almost got hit. People aren't used to seeing runners on these narrow roads."

Color drained from Mom's face; Dad wasn't buying my explanation though. Neither was Walter, his face was dark and fierce, the way I was accustomed to seeing him. "Now give us the unedited version," Dad stated. I had no choice.

"A truck got a little too close to me, and the side mirror hit my shoulder. It knocked me into a ditch." Even that was a cleaned up version.

Mom whirled around, glaring at Walter. "Did you do that to her? Why would you do that?"

"It wasn't me, Laura. Honest. I was mad Rosie had left everything to her, but I wouldn't try to run over my own granddaughter." He turned to me. "What kind of truck was it? What did it look like?"

I shrugged. "I don't know. It happened so fast. When I landed in the ditch, he didn't stick around to see if I was hurt."

"Did you see what color it was?"

I thought about it for a minute. It happened almost six weeks ago, and I hadn't thought about it much since. I just stayed off the road for my runs. "It was one of those big pickups. It was dark color. I think the windows were tinted dark also."

"Like the truck the guy was drivin' when my house caught fire." Shep looked at me. "I didn't put it together until now."

"Just about everyone drives a pickup here. A lot of them are dark colored. There's no way to know if it was the same truck or who it belonged to." I really didn't want to have this

274

conversation now.

Walter headed for the back door when Milly stopped him. "What is it, Walter? Where are you going?"

"Going to see a man about a truck," he growled. He pushed open the door, but Dad touched his arm.

"Wait a minute. Someone tried to run over my daughter. If you know who it was, you need to call the police."

Walter snorted, "Police won't do much."

He looked like he still wanted to argue when Shep spoke up. "Sheriff Donovan won't brush it aside like the chief did, Mr. Shepherd. He knows what's been goin' on around here."

"That's more than we know." Dad gave me a dark look. There was no getting around it now. I was going to have to tell them everything whether I liked it or not.

When I finished with the abridged version, Mom's face was pale, but her glare was fierce when she looked at her father. "Is this the same Ed Bodeen you tried to force me to marry? Gee, I'm so sorry I missed all the fun he would have put me through." Sarcasm dripped from her words.

"I was wrong," Walter stated frankly. "We all were."

"I wasn't wrong," Mom said hotly. "I knew he was no good."

"I meant my pa and brothers and me. We were all wrong. I'm sorry, Laura. I hope you can forgive me someday." His words left her speechless. What could she say in the face of his apology? It was the beginning of reconciliation.

Sharp barks from Gus drew our attention. The twins chased him across the field, yelling for him to stop. "Someone's here. Someone Gus doesn't like." It could only be Abner or Ed. Pulling my new cell phone out of my pocket and hitting speed dial for the sheriff, I headed for the front of the house. He picked up immediately. By now, I could hear Ed screaming for "his daughter" to get her psycho dog away from him.

"I can't get there right now, Parker. We've located Meyers. I'll send one of my deputies." I groaned, but didn't say anything. He had his hands full; I didn't need to add more. "I'll be there just as soon as I can." He clicked off.

Dad was already on the porch, and Ed bellowed at him. "Where's my daughter?"

"Who's your daughter?" Dad's calm voice didn't work its usual magic. Ed was still visibly agitated. Gus had stopped barking, but he stayed next to the truck so Ed couldn't step out without risk of being bitten.

"Who do you think? Parker, of course."

"No, Parker's *my* daughter."

"You can't be her dad." Color drained from Ed's face. "You're dead."

"What makes you say that?" Dad held his arms out to his side. "Do I look dead?"

"I know you're dead." Ed's voice shook. "I saw your truck go over the cliff." Mom gasped, but I didn't look at her. I couldn't take my eyes off Ed. "Parker, make him go away. He's dead." His voice was pleading. "And get this psycho dog away from my truck or I'll shoot him." His mood swung between fear and anger. He picked up a gun off the seat beside him.

Before Shep or Dad could pull me behind them, Walter stepped in front of me. "Put that damn fool gun down, Ed. What's the matter with you?"

"Do you see him, Walter? He's dead." His voice had dropped to a whisper.

"Sure I see him. He's standing right here. He's not dead."

"No, Walter. I know he's dead," Ed whined. "I saw his truck go over the cliff. I didn't mean to do it. I just wanted him to leave Laura alone, so she'd come back here and marry me." The gun shook in his hand, pointing it in all directions. I wanted to tell everyone to get inside, but I was afraid to draw his attention away from Walter. As long as the two were talking, Ed wasn't shooting anyone.

The shriek of distant sirens added to Ed's desperation. I hoped they'd get here before he started shooting. "Get this damn dog away from me. Parker, you have to help me. You were supposed to be my daughter."

"Laura was never going to marry you, Ed. That was my

mistake. I shouldn't have tried to make her."

"She was supposed to marry me so I could get this farm," Ed stormed. "It was supposed to be mine." He was fixated on owning the farm, and nothing could get through to him. "I can't kill a man who's already dead, but I can kill this damn dog." Before he could lower the gun, I gave a shrill whistle. Gus turned toward me just as Ed pulled the trigger, missing my dog by a hair. "You betrayed me, too." Without realizing it, I had stepped from behind Walter. Ed lowered the gun on me, pulling the trigger a second time.

For an instant I thought I was dead. Instead, Walter dropped to the ground in front of me. He'd managed to move in time to stop Ed from shooting me. Or Ed's aim had been off. Mom and Milly dropped beside Walter to see how badly he'd been hurt.

A county patrol car roared up the lane, sirens still blaring. Two deputies jumped out. Unfortunately, one of them was Deputy Thompson, the sheriff's nephew. Nothing good could come out of this.

"What's going on here? Who's shooting?" The officious little twit walked up to us, his chest puffed up like he was someone really important. He acted like he didn't see Walter laying on the ground bleeding. "Put that gun away, Ed, before you hurt someone. Who are all these people?"

"He's already hurt someone, you moron! Call an ambulance." I'd never heard Shep talk to anyone like that.

For a long moment Deputy Thompson was so shocked by Shep's words he stood looking around trying to figure out what to say. His partner finally understood what was happening, and pressed the radio on his shoulder pad, calling for an ambulance like Shep wanted.

Grasping the severity of the situation at last, but totally missing what had really happened, Deputy Thompson glared at me. "Did your dog finally attack someone? I kept telling Unc...ah, Sheriff Donovan to have that dog put down."

I started to go after the idiot, but Jason grabbed my arm, holding me back. "Not a good idea, Sis." He turned to the deputy, "He's been shot."

"You shot your own grandpa?"

"Shut up, Jerry." The second deputy took charge. "The only one here with a gun besides us is Ed." He knelt down to see if he could help Walter until the ambulance arrived.

Jerry Thompson turned to Ed, who was still sitting in his truck, the gun in his hand out the window. "You shot your friend? Why?"

"I didn't mean to. He got in my way."

"Think you should take the gun away from him?" Shep suggested. "He might shoot you by mistake next."

"Ah, yeah, you'd better give me the gun, Ed." He reached out to take it, but Ed raised it, pointing first at Deputy Thompson then me.

"Nobody's taking my gun, especially a punk like you." With his free hand, he started the ignition, putting the truck in gear. Reversing down the lane at top speed, spewing gravel in all directions, the truck fishtailed when he hit the pavement. For a breathtaking moment, I thought he was going to lose control, and end up in the ditch. No such luck. Somehow he managed to gain control of the big vehicle; within seconds he was out of sight.

Jerry Thompson stood there useless as always, his mouth hanging open. Again it was the second deputy who took charge, calling in the fact a shooting suspect had taken off. The ambulance finally arrived, and the EMT's attended to Walter. Fortunately Ed's aim was as off base as his mind, and he only grazed Walter. They took him to the hospital in Bentonville. Milly went with him; Mom and Dad followed in my Jeep.

Several hours later we learned Ed had led deputies on a high speed chase on the narrow country roads before reaching the interstate. Just as he tried to merge onto the highway, traffic cut him off, and he ran into a bridge abutment. It might not be right thinking, but I felt it was poetic justice. After killing my birth father in a car accident, Ed died in the same manner.

"Nothing like this ever happens at home." Justin was still

hyped up when Mom and Dad got back from the hospital. "I thought small towns were supposed to be boring."

"You can thank God it isn't like this all the time at home," Dad reminded him. "I'm sure it's not like this all the time here either."

We were all silent for a minute, considering just how fortunate we were nothing more serious had happened to any of us. "Is Walter going to be okay?" I finally asked. I didn't know if the change in him would be permanent or not, but for now it was a welcome change.

Mom nodded her head, but didn't say anything for a minute. She was having as much difficulty with his sudden change as me. Walter had been the bad guy in our lives for so long it wasn't easy to forgive and forget. "He talked a lot while we waited for the ER doc to come in. I never knew my grandfather, his father. By the time Charlie and I were born, he was a sickly old man. He passed away when I was about four. I remember Mom saying once he was a hateful man, but she would never explain."

She sighed, leaning up against Dad for comfort and support. "It's always a question of whether nature or nurture is the stronger influence. For Walter and his brothers I think it was definitely nurture. Their father was so full of hate and greed he filled his sons with that as well. I can't believe I lived in this town for the first eighteen years of my life, and never knew some of the things he told me today. Or what you two learned from Rosie's journals." She looked at Shep and me.

"She left a lot of journals," I said. "I haven't read half of them, but her father was a terrible man."

Mom nodded agreement. "I don't know if the pain meds were playing with his mind, or the fact he could have died if Ed's aim had been better but he wanted to make amends. He talked more than he has in his entire life. He told how Abner and Clyde found Rosie's boyfriend's body. Did you say his name was Barnard?" I nodded and she continued. "Anyway, they found his body, and they all buried him behind the barn. They were afraid they would be accused of killing him if the sheriff knew about it."

"Did he say how he died?" Shep asked.

"No, he didn't say, just that they found him in the field where they were plowing, like they ran over him with the plow." Shep raised an eyebrow at me. "What's going on between you two?" Mom asked, seeing our silent communication.

"That's where Deidre's body was found," Shep said, shaking his head. "Her murderer tried to make it look like Gus had mauled her."

"What else did Walter say?" I didn't want to get sidetracked. Maybe he would clear up some of my questions.

"Their father wasn't happy they buried him there, but by then it was too late. When Rosie had the baby, he wouldn't let anyone upstairs with her. He said he'd birthed enough farm animals to know what to do. Afterward he told them the baby died, and he'd buried it with his 'old man'." Mom made air quotes around the last words. "They always thought their father had killed the baby, and maybe even Barnard. They didn't know for sure."

"Maybe I can shed some light on that." Sheriff Donovan stood at the back door. Gus considered him a friend, and hadn't warned us someone was there. "Mind if I come in?"

I opened the door, introducing everyone. He looked like he hadn't had much sleep in the last twenty-four hours.

"Sorry I couldn't get here when you were having all the trouble, I've had a few fires to put out today. It's too bad about the accident, but maybe it's best Ed went that way. At least he only killed himself." He sighed heavily. "And I apologize for that stupid nephew of mine. He's no longer on the force. When his fellow deputies complain about him, it's time to put an end to it. Maybe if he grows up some, he'll make a decent deputy, but for now he's gone."

He sat wearily at the table as I placed a cup of black coffee in front of him along with some homemade cookies. He smiled his thanks, taking a hefty bite. "Anyway, about Rosie's baby. She had a boy as you already know." He looked at Shep and me. "Elmore took the baby to Meyers Senior, putting him up for adoption. Elmore told Rosie and the boys the baby died, so no one would go looking for him."

"How did you find this out? Did Meyers talk when you caught him?"

"Not hardly." He gave a harsh laugh. "When we finally got him out of his hidey hole, he demanded a lawyer first thing. He still isn't talking. Fortunately for us, he was a fanatic about keeping records. There were file cabinets full of his father's records in his office. In fact, that office is just the way it was when his father was still living and working there. I doubt either man ever threw away a single piece of paper from their practice."

I looked at Mom, "Did Walter explain why he insisted you marry Ed Bodeen? Why he disowned you when you refused? Why he was so nasty to me up until yesterday? Why he and Abner didn't want me to inherit the farm?" I was still looking for answers, and my questions spilled out.

As a clinical psychologist, Dad was the one to answer. "Conditioning, Honey. When you're told something all your life, it's ingrained in your mind. His father had promised Ed Bodeen Senior his first granddaughter would marry his son since Rosie wouldn't marry him. That was your mother. He felt honor bound she marry him. When she refused, he lost face with Ed and his brothers. His father had been fixated on the farm belonging to him or his sons. His wife thwarted that idea. Rosie had dangled ownership of the farm in front of her brothers all their adult lives. Like the carrot and the donkey. When she named you as her heir, they felt betrayed. For a while after you were here, Meyers told them if you left before the year was up, the farm would go to them. It was just last week they learned the truth." He turned to Shep. "If Parker had left, the farm would go to you, not them. When Abner pulled the gun on you yesterday, Walter finally realized just what he had given up all those years ago; what he'd lose if Abner shot you. It was no longer worth it to him."

"Why *did* Abner pull the gun on me? If they didn't kill Barnard, and they didn't have anything to do with stealing the baby, what was he afraid of?"

"After Barnard died, and she was told her baby was also dead, Rosie was convinced her father and brothers had killed them," Mom said. "She always told them she had proof of 'what they did.' She wouldn't explain what that proof was or what it proved, just that they would go to jail if she made it public. Any time they went against her, she threatened them with her so called proof." She shook her head. "Their biggest mistake was listening to their greedy father."

"Meyers Senior inadvertently helped her, convincing them they would go to prison because they didn't report finding Barnard's body, and then burying him," Sheriff Donovan added. "Meyers Junior had continued the lie. Those two men manipulated everyone. When Deidre showed up looking for 'Clive Beaumont' he knew his time was running short. He started clearing out his bank accounts, even some that didn't belong to him. We found evidence he's been skimming money from several of his clients, including you, Parker. While Rosie was alive, he hadn't touched her accounts. I guess she had enough on him he was afraid to do anything. Once she passed on, all bets were off, and he started skimming from her, or you. Fortunately, he kept meticulous records. All the clients he cheated over the years will be able to get their money back, maybe even with interest. He was smart enough to invest wisely." He gave a tired chuckle.

"Do you believe Walter?" I asked Mom. "Do you think he can really change overnight?"

Her answer was so typical; I wonder why I even bothered to ask. "God can change anyone's heart in an instant, Honey. I'm willing to give him the benefit of a doubt, but I'm not so foolish as to offer him my own heart until I know this change is more than skin deep."

We might not ever find out all of the motives for what happened sixty years ago, but it was nice to know Walter didn't have a hand in murdering Barnard. If he really did have a change of heart, maybe Mom would eventually be able to forgive him. Only time would tell.

"Walter wanted to know if you had found the 'evidence'

Rosie had claimed she had against her brothers all these years?" Mom spoke into the silence.

I shook my head. "I don't think she really had anything on them. It was enough to tell them she knew what they did, and could prove it. Their guilty conscience kept them in line. It was Rosie's revenge."

Dad shook his head. "No, Honey. I think Rosie's revenge was giving the farm to you so her brothers would never get it. Once she met Shep, and realized he was most likely her great grandson, she made sure the two of you met, and had a chance to fall in love. Now her great grandson and her great niece have a chance to make something of their lives with what was hers all along. Isn't it amazing how God works to right the wrongs done by evil men?" He smiled at us.

Silence filled the room again. The twins looked at each of us expectantly, hoping the excitement would continue. After several moments, Shep cleared his throat and stood up. "This isn't exactly how I had planned on doin' this, but I can't wait any longer, so here goes." He walked over to Dad, his handsome face serious. "Sir, I'd like to ask for Parker's hand in marriage. I'm crazy in love with her."

Dad was equally serious when he looked at me, then back to Shep. "Well, Son, since you already have her heart, you might as well take her hand and the rest of her as well." A big smile spread across his face as he reached out to shake Shep's hand.

Shep walked across the room, stopping in front of me, then getting down on one knee he pulled a velvet ring box out of his pocket. "I love you. Will you marry me? This is the ring my granddad gave my grandma when he asked her to marry him. They thought it was fitting I give it to you since I'm Rosie and Barnard's great grandson and you're Rosie's great niece."

It was a magnificent old fashioned setting of white and yellow gold. The stone was probably a quarter to half carat, just right for my long slender fingers. My heart was in my throat, making it impossible to speak. All I could do was nod my head and cry. Finally I threw myself into his open arms, letting that be my answer.

EPILOGUE
Six Months Later

Sparkling white snow piled up outside the large window in the front parlor. From where I stood it was beautiful, but I was grateful I didn't have to be out in it. How do farmers or anyone who has to work outside, make a living in the winter? Just the thought of being outside brought shivers up my spine, and I hugged myself to stay warm.

The renovations on the house were finished, and I didn't have to worry about being cold. I still used the wood stove in the kitchen, and the large monster one by the staircase part of the time, more for fun than warmth. Turning away from the view outside, I marveled at the work Shep and his men have done. The house is now thoroughly modernized with electricity and bathrooms, but more than that, there is still the feel of the old farm house, warm, welcoming, and completely wonderful. I just wish Rosie could be here to see what her great grandson has done.

After all the work was done inside, Ted's wife Julia offered to help me clean. She's the one who had kept house for Rosie. She loved all the antiques, and knew what to do to keep them in top condition. The hardwood floors sparkled even in the weak sunlight, and the wood furniture had a glow as though it just came off the showroom floor. Her little girl, Sophie, came with her, and she and I had fun playing. Someday Shep and I would have our own children running up and down the stairs. The thought brought a shiver of happiness.

Next week at this time, Mom and Dad would be here with the twins along with Shep's family from Texas. When he had told them about Rosie and Barnard, his grandfather was silent for a long while. He'd never questioned who his birth parents were; it just wasn't something his generation did. Learning about them now he was grateful. I'm a little nervous about meeting his family, but they've been nothing but kind and loving to me when we spoke on the phone.

In two weeks, I'll be Mrs. Shepard Baker! My stomach filled with butterflies, and my heart seemed to swell with happiness. I never imagined this outcome when I first came to Iowa. I'd been ready to tell Mr. Meyers to forget it, and head back to Arizona. I'm so glad I was stubborn enough and curious enough to want to find out what was really behind Rosie's bequest. Think of all I would have missed.

I finally finished reading all of Rosie's journals. She didn't spare herself in any of her writings. After her baby was born, and she was told he died in childbirth, she was sad and depressed which is understandable. Finally, she turned angry and spiteful. She told of all the times she had cheated her brothers out of land or money in dealings she had with them. In the end she regretted her actions, but knew if she hadn't been strong, her father would have done even worse things to her. Her final journal entry was to me.

My Dearest Parker,

If you're reading this, I know you stayed long enough to find it and Shep. He is a wonderful man, just like his great grandpa. In every way he reminds me of Barnard, the love of my life. My prayer is health and happiness for both of you. I just hope Jesus can forgive me for all the mean things I've done over the years. If any of us could go back and live our lives over, knowing then what we know now, we would do everything different. I know I would stand up to Papa long before Barnard died. I wish I knew if Papa is the one who killed him. But there's nothing I can do about it now. Papa has to answer for his own actions just like the rest of us.

Give your dear sweet Mama a hug for me and love Shep with all your heart. I'm always with both of you.

Your loving great aunt,

Rosie

Thinking of her words now still brings on tears. She didn't have an easy life, and she hadn't made very good choices part of the time. In the end though, she knew love is what matters most.

With Mom and Dad here for two weeks, and the threats

from Ed Bodeen and Mr. Meyers removed, Shep had moved back to his house. He repaired and improved it beyond anything Ed Bodeen had ever built. It was now up for sale. Miz Jenkins was sorry to lose him as her neighbor, but we both promised to visit often. Shep was fixing up her house so it would also be better than when she bought it. When Walter and Abner realized there had never been any real "proof of what they'd done," Abner was ready to spit nails, but Walter thought it was funny. "A guilty conscience is a pretty strong driving force," he'd said. Slowly he's becoming the grandpa he should have been.

Walter showed us where they'd buried Barnard, and we had his remains moved so he was with Rosie. There had been a small handmade marker buried nearby.

Shep came up behind me, wrapping his arms around my waist. Leaning back, I rested my head against his chest. "What are you doin', Darlin'?" he asked in that soft Texas drawl I love.

"Just enjoying all your hard work. You've done a beautiful job."

"Couldn't a done it without my crew. They do good work. Now we're ready for the next big job."

"Well, don't get too involved," I laughed. "We have a honeymoon coming up." I looked at him over my shoulder, wiggling my eyebrows suggestively.

"No way could I forget that." He turned me in his arms, his kiss heating me like all the wood stoves in the world couldn't do. After a long moment he lifted his head, taking a step back. He cleared his throat before speaking. "Two more weeks." His words spoke volumes.

"Have you decided what you're goin' to do with the barn?" He changed the subject to a less suggestive one. The building itself is still in good condition, and almost as big as the house. We'd toyed with the idea of fixing it up so it was livable. Maybe someday we'll turn it into a Bed and Breakfast. It would be a lot of work, and didn't have to be done immediately, but it was definitely something to think about.

"We'll see how things go this spring," I answered. "We

still need to do something with all the furniture out there." We could furnish another house with what had been stored in the barn all these years. "I'm thinking we're going to be busy for the next few years." Shep raised his eyebrows in silent question. "I want to fill a few of these bedrooms upstairs, and not with paying guests."

Shep reached for me again, a low growl in his throat. Just before his lips claimed mine, I thought I heard him say with a groan, "Two more weeks."

ACKNOWLEDGEMENTS

I thank God for all He's given me. He has answered my prayers to be able to write my books and have them published. Without Him I can do nothing.

I also want to thank Diane Scott, Irene Morris, Gerry Beamon, Cathy Slack, and Sandy Roedl for all of their editing skills. Ladies, your help and encouragement is greatly appreciated.

OTHER BOOKS BY SUZANNE FLOYD

Revenge Served Cold

Coming Soon

A Game of Cat and Mouse

Dear Reader:

Thank you for reading my book. I hope you enjoyed reading it as much as I enjoyed writing it. If you enjoyed Rosie's Revenge, I would appreciate it if you would tell your friends and relatives and/or write a review on Amazon.

Thank you,
Suzanne Floyd

P.S. If you find any errors, please let me know at: Suzanne.sfloyd@gmail.com. Before publishing, many people have read the book, but minds can play tricks by supplying words that are missing and correcting typos.

Thanks again for reading my book.

ABOUT THE AUTHOR

Suzanne is an internationally known author. She was born in Iowa, and moved to Arizona with her family when she was nine years old. She still lives in Phoenix with her husband Paul. They have two wonderful daughters, two great sons-in-law and five of the best grandchildren around. Of course, she just a little prejudiced.

Growing up and traveling with her parents, she entertained herself by making up stories. As an adult she tried writing, but family came first. After retiring in 2008, she decided it was her time. She still enjoys making up stories, and thanks to the internet she's able to put them online for others to enjoy.

When Suzanne isn't writing, she and her husband enjoy traveling around on their 2010 Honda Goldwing trike. She's always looking for new places to write about. There's always a new mystery and a romance lurking out there to capture her attention.

Made in the USA
Middletown, DE
02 August 2018